I0712792

La Pâte à Bombe

A Novel

MICHELLE CHRISTENSEN

Sibylline
DIGITAL FIRST

AN IMPRINT OF ALL THINGS BOOK

Sibylline Press

Copyright © 2025 by Michelle Christensen

All Rights Reserved.

Published in the United States by Sibylline Digital First,
an imprint of All Things Book LLC, California.

Sibylline Press is dedicated to publishing the
brilliant work of women authors ages 50 and older.

www.sibyllinepress.com

Sibylline Digital First Edition

Ebook ISBN: 9781960573599
Print ISBN: 9798897409884
Library of Congress Control Number: 2025931638

Cover Design: Alicia Feltman
Book Production: Sang Kim and Olivia M. Hammerman

This is a work of fiction. Names, characters, places, brands, media,
and incidents are either the product of the author's imagination or
are used fictitiously. Any resemblance to similarly named places or to
persons living or deceased is unintentional

To Ronnie. I'll always make the best cookies with you.

Prologue

I squashed the cockroach on the ground underneath my clog. Its carapace cracked under my shoe.

No matter how often my father fumigated the kitchen, the damn things always returned. They were a front line of soldiers, ruthless in their assault.

It wasn't our fault. My father kept our tiny kitchen meticulous. We scrubbed and worked to keep the place clean. Even though it was a shitty catering kitchen in an old strip mall in Venice next to a rough and decrepit smoke shop.

Old Man Gus's shop had been around since the sixties. He bragged that he used to sell weed to Jim Morrison.

But that was a long time ago.

Now his shop was a worn-out husk. Who knew the last time Gus cleaned or hired a fumigator? A faint aroma of filth lurked beneath the putrid stench of marijuana. It always made me want to gag.

This is what we got for all our hard work.

It was hard not to be angry when I saw my father struggle. In a lot of ways, I felt like the practical one. I was dark to his light.

I took a paper towel, wiped the dead cockroach carcass off the ground, and threw it in the trash. I washed my hands and made my way to the worn wood worktable.

Wedding cake tiers were set out before me. I'd worked late into the night piping the delicate buttercream roses and shells. I couldn't wait to put the tiny porcelain bride and groom on the cake after I built it at the site.

I was well beyond my sixteen years when it came to being in the kitchen. Cake, as they say, was cake to me.

My father taught me well. When I was six, he'd given me small tasks to keep me busy. Peeling apples. Shaving carrots. I knew how to roast chicken and bake crème brûlée when I was twelve. Being in the kitchen with my father made me grow up quick.

Roasted chicken and veggie prep was fine, but my heart always lingered on the sweet side. Pastry was my passion. And my father taught me how to make the best. The best gâteau. The best profiteroles. The best soufflé. I could make a wedding cake faster than a couple took to say "I do" at the altar.

I loved everything about pastry. It was all I thought about.

"Come on, Fiona. Box that cake up. We're going to be late," my father said as he grabbed a tall stack of hotel pans and hefted them in his outstretched arms. I was always amazed that he could carry so many. I could barely carry two.

His tall, gangly frame always warmed my heart. His mess of short, blond, curly hair constantly needed a good brushing. It added somehow to his enthusiasm. His bright blue eyes were always laughing, betraying his positive attitude.

"Your cake turned out beautiful. Good job. The bride will be proud," he said.

I beamed inside as I grabbed a box and started packing it. I hoped Mrs. Jamison would approve.

The Jamison party had been a nightmare from the start.

Mrs. Jamison originally wanted chicken and tri-tip as the meat choice. Then she's switched to salmon and prime rib.

There was another voicemail from her on my father's phone.

My father hadn't called her back. He'd already bought the prep, and he couldn't afford for her to change her mind again.

"Fiona, tell your dad Angelo's not coming in. He's sick again," Juan said. His clean white T-shirt had tomato sauce splattered on the front. I knew he'd let the ragu for the parmesana boil over again. I hoped he hadn't burned it.

"Why can't you tell him?"

My father was getting annoyed by Angelo's continual absence. Every Saturday, he was mysteriously ill. Could it be that he'd partied too hard with his Rolling Stones cover band? He was always playing backyard parties late into the night.

My father walked back into the kitchen to grab some more hotel pans. "Call him back and tell him that if he stays home today, then stay home for good. I can easily get someone else."

Yeah, right. I knew he didn't mean it. His heart was too kind. His forgiving heart wouldn't help us.

He struggled to find someone who was dependable and stayed for very long. And why would they? We were a struggling catering company. Someone could get a job somewhere else, at a respectable kitchen, for more money.

My father always attracted the outliers, and they only stayed for a short time.

I stacked the cake boxes in my arms and left.

Our refrigerated catering truck stood outside, parked next to the door. A dirty orange extension cord stretched from the front door to the generator. Hopefully, we'd be charged up with enough juice for the day.

My father had spent all his money on the beat-up truck. It was the only thing of value that we had. When he'd lost his restaurant, he'd cobbled the remaining money for the darn thing.

He tried to make his dreams come true with my mother by opening his own restaurant. He'd barely lasted a year. Then my mother died.

Now we were just a struggling catering company.

I couldn't understand why he didn't push for something more. Why was he happy here? Why did he seem so content when we could barely afford the money for the prep we needed? I didn't get it.

He navigated party planners who stretched their dollar by negotiating a better deal. They held other catering companies over our heads. So, in the spirit of entrepreneurship, he always gave in to their lowball offers.

I wished I could motivate him somehow to want something better. But what could a sixteen-year-old do? I hated myself for being so cynical.

I walked up the truck's steps, put the cake boxes on a shelf, and studied our work. We still needed to finish the antipasti and the prep for the Caesar salad if we were going to make it to the event on time.

"Fiona. Where are you?" My father called. He popped his head in the truck. "Come here."

I stepped out of the truck, and he beamed, holding a cigarette and the crumpled food section of the *L.A. Times*. "We have to check this place out. Marci Strand says it's supposed to have the best posole. We should go tomorrow."

"I don't know, Dad. Marcopa has the best. How can you beat that?" I said.

"Well, you know, Marci Strand always knows the best."

Marci Strand was the queen. With her "best of" list in the *L.A. Times*, she could single-handedly make or break your restaurant.

She could tell you where the best taco was. Bobo's was the best taco in the city. She could tell you the best *yukjaejang*. If you wanted to be fancy, she could direct you to the most romantic restaurant in the city. She had her pulse on the spirit of food in Los Angeles.

My father was a devoted fan. We'd venture to exotic parts of Los Angeles on our days off to discover new food. *Birria tacos, shwarma, carpaccio* to start.

My father was convinced that his restaurant failed because he'd never become a chef at another restaurant where he was recognized as a top chef. He thought that if he'd made his reputation that way first, all his work would have been worth it. It was an excuse for his failure, really. I marveled at him. Somehow, he'd let the disappointment go. He'd found a way to move on.

I was going to learn from his mistakes.

I dreamed of having Marci Strand walk into my restaurant and anoint me as the best. I had it all planned out. I would work my way to the top at a star-rated restaurant. I was going to be validated by the best. Then, I would open my own place on my own terms. That was the only way to do it. That's how all these successful chefs in the food section did it. It was the surest way to success.

But that was a million miles away.

Right now we were off to another catering gig. Another setup. Another teardown. Another day of standing in the hot sun watching wedding guests eat and be merry.

"I guess we should get going. Grab some lettuce and the cooked pasta. We can make the rest at the site." He put his cigarette out and threw the newspaper into the open cab of the truck. "We can't be late. I've already ignored Mrs. Jamison. I can already tell she's going to be a nightmare."

"Dad, I love you," I said as I hugged him. I felt guilty for being so negative.

"Fiona, I love you, too. You're the light of my life. You know that, right?" he said as he kissed me on the head. My negative feelings washed away.

A wistful smile crossed his face. "You know, you're the spitting image of your mother. I knew the moment that I saw her that she was the one. I remember it like it was yesterday ... Christmas morning. She wore skis in her front yard when it was eighty degrees out. I never understood why someone would give her skis for Christmas. She lived in Yucaipa, for goodness' sake ...

His smile turned to a sad grin. "Your mother was the most beautiful woman I'd ever seen. I knew the moment I saw her that she would be my wife ..."

"Dad. Not now. Not this story again. We don't have time." He'd told the story so many times that it seemed like a distant fairy tale. It didn't seem real.

"I'm sorry, kid. I guess I miss her. You only get one in your life. And I'm thankful that she was the one. And she gave me you."

I squirmed impatiently. We didn't have time to go down the rabbit hole. "Dad. Not now. We have to go."

He shifted from his revelry, and his eyes came into focus on the moment.

"Okay. Let's go, my dear. It's going to be a great day!"

He made his way back into the kitchen for another load. I took a deep breath. My negativity came back to me in a rush. I was dreading the long day ahead.

Juan had traded his disastrous whites for a crisp black shirt and dark pants. It was our uniform.

My father insisted on black, even though it was brutal in the heat. He said it made us look like we came from the best restaurants in town. Plus, black didn't show the messy nature of our work.

A gold Japanese Lucky Cat waved to me on the kitchen shelf as I entered the tiny bathroom to change into my uniform. Its happy smile radiated at me like a cute little Buddha. My father would use anything to harness us a little luck.

I dreaded putting the uniform on. It meant that the day was officially getting started. I'd watch as Mrs. Jamison drove my father crazy. I knew she'd complain about the prime rib. My poor father was always patient with her.

It was going to be a brutal day. I hoped the buttercream wouldn't melt in the sun.

I shut the door and breathed deeply, trying to cleanse my bad feelings.

The bathroom was a mess. Mops and brooms were shoved in a corner. Boxes of various foodstuffs were bursting from the shelves. There was barely room for a human to move.

Optimism is a perfectly legitimate response to failure …

The quotation was taped to the warped mirror hanging over the tiny sink. My father had a host of positive quotations taped to the mirror—they somehow gave him the strength to carry on. *Work hard. Be positive. Make it happen.*

I gazed at myself in the cracked mirror. My wispy brown hair was a mess. I had buttercream smudged on my chin. I ran some water in the sink, slicked my hair back into a respectable ponytail, and scrubbed the buttercream off it.

I gazed at myself for another moment.

Why did I feel this way? Why was I so discontent? I should be happy. My father was. But that stupid quotation kept ringing in my mind. I couldn't let go of it. Work hard. Be positive. Make it happen … *make it happen …* It was like the words to a spell. Was it possible to work hard? Stay positive? Make it happen? All I wanted for myself was a little success. I didn't want to end up like my father. Toiling in a shitty kitchen, trying to make the rent.

When I grew up, I was going to go to Le Cordon Bleu in Paris and be the best pastry chef in L.A. at a top restaurant. Then I was going to open my own place. I wouldn't be like my father and toil in a dirty kitchen with no hope of getting out. Or getting better.

I would get out of this bug-infested kitchen, be validated, and make something of myself.

My hungry eyes stared back at me. I could almost see the flecks of green in my irises. My father said that I had my mother's eyes. I wished I remembered her. The only memory I had of her was her lavender perfume and the smell of her chocolate chip cookies.

"Come on, Fiona, we're going to be late. The truck is packed. Juan's on his way to the site. Let's get out of here."

I shrugged on a black shirt, buttoned it, and grabbed a hefty stack of linens on the shelf. We'd almost forgotten them. I juggled the stack of tablecloths as I jiggled the door open.

"Let's go, my dear."

I followed my dad as he made his way out the door and locked it behind me. I could hear the bell on the door jingle as it hit the glass. "Let's do this! It's going to be great! Your cake is going to be the star of the show."

I laughed. "No. Your chicken confit will be the showstopper. You make the best."

"Well, thank you, my dear. But Mer Le Vie is better. Mine is a pale imitation."

I jumped into the open door to the truck's cab and slammed it behind me. The cab was hot, making my shirt stick against my skin. I couldn't wait for my father to start the engine so I could turn on the air conditioning. It would be the only time I'd feel anything like a cool breeze. It was already seventy degrees outside.

"Okay, sweetie. Let's do this thing." He smiled as he plugged his keys into the steering column and turned the engine over.

It groaned and chugged. "Dear God, not today." He pressed down on the gas and gave it another go.

The truck wouldn't start.

"Crap. The fuel line is fucked again." He grabbed some electrical tape from the dashboard and darted outside. He hefted the hood of the truck and went to work. Would his jerry-rigging work one more time?

We couldn't afford to take it to a mechanic, so he would always find a way to fix it himself.

The anxious silence of the cab made me nervous. This was the last thing we needed.

I saw the *L.A. Times* food section sitting on the seat. I picked it up, and the winning chef stared back at me. His beautiful smile radiated as he held up a bowl of posole.

It must have been pretty great to be validated by Marci Strand. What did it feel like to bask in the glow of success?

What did it feel like not sitting in the cab of a broken-down truck? Going to a catering gig where the customer was already planning your demise?

"Okay. Let's start this baby up again. Cross your fingers," my father said as he slammed his door shut and started the engine again.

This time, it turned over, groaned a beat, and then came to life.

My father beamed. "The gods have shown us favor today. Maybe everything will come together after all."

I always loved his optimism. He'd taken the worst and made it somehow work. Even in the face of adversity, his attitude was contagious. I sighed, relieved, as he pulled into traffic.

"Another day, another chance at greatness, Fiona. Always remember that." He smiled.

Greatness? What did he consider greatness? I had no idea.

Yes. Another day for greatness.

Even though we were stuck, at least we had each other.

I gazed at the chef in the picture again. His smile ignited my fire. I wanted his life more than anything.

My dad's quotation stuck on the storeroom mirror whispered to me again: *Work hard. Stay positive. Make it happen.*

Could I work hard? Stay positive? Make it happen?

Could I become a validated chef and open my own place someday? Could I make it happen? I was going to try with all my heart.

Marci Strand was going to feature me in the *L.A. Times* someday. I was going to be the shining star. Yes! I was going to work hard. Stay positive. I wouldn't be stuck in some dead-end kitchen toiling away for nothing.

I was going to make it happen.

1

The line was brutal.

I worked in a flurry to keep up with the tickets spitting out of the machine. Dacquoise with pastry cream canelé and a flourish of basil reduction. Chocolate torte with Madagascar ice cream and Valrhona-infused caramel. Strawberry crumble complemented with a cardamom crème anglaise. I used my tweezers to fashion the various sprigs of flowers and accouterments to each dish. My fingers were getting numb.

The sweat trickled down the nape of my neck. Another night of pushing it to the limit.

"You're not serving the torte properly. It should be cut into a square. Your rectangle isn't balanced right with the lines of the plate, Fiona. Recut this and fix it," Angela, the head pastry chef, admonished me over my shoulder. "Reduce the amount of crème anglaise on the plate for the crumble. You're serving too much. It should just be a kiss, not a pool,"

She always seemed nervous, like she was holding on for dear life.

"Yes, chef," I said.

Here I was, twenty-seven years old and still just a cook. Always the cook. Never the chef.

I'd never followed my dreams of going to Le Cordon Bleu. I got my pastry degree at the Institute of Culinary Education in Pasadena. That was something I was proud of. I didn't have the money to fly off to France to become a pastry princess. ICE was a fine choice though, and I didn't feel bad about it.

I'd worked in many fine dining establishments, but I had yet to succeed. Was it my own fault? Each job brought another opportunity to learn something new. I was fortified with knowledge. But at the end of the day, my hopes of becoming a chef seemed so far away. An impossible dream.

It always ended here. On a hot line, shuffling plates and desserts. Someone else's menu. Someone else's vision. No one wanted to hear what I had to say about anything.

Work hard, be positive, make it happen ... My father's quotations kept ringing in my head. Sometimes it was the only thing that kept me going. Was I working hard? Was I being positive? Was I making it happen?

It was happening slower than I wanted.

So far, in my first year working at Lucien, I was another cog in the machine. When I answered the ad from a job board, it promised promotion and rewards. But I was yet to see any manifestation of those rewards. Still, I kept hoping that Julia would anoint me.

Julia Stone was a hero in the L.A. restaurant scene. She'd owned Lucien for ten years and it was a splash right from the beginning.

Lucien had two Michelin stars and a top five rating on every "best of" list in L.A. Julia had written five cookbooks, all *New York Times* bestsellers. She catered for the most exclusive events in the city. And hosted the most exclusive Grammy and Academy Awards parties in town.

She was a legend. Everything I wanted to be. And more than anything, I wanted to be her pastry chef.

Initially, there was a slim chance for me to make a mark. But I was beginning to get that sinking feeling that my imagination was getting the best of me again. I always started with grand aspirations, but each job ended in disappointment. Was I working hard enough? Was I being positive? I certainly wasn't making it happen.

A hush suddenly filled the kitchen. The cooks paused from their work. I glanced up from the torte in front of me.

It was a standoff. The cooks stood silent. The brute force of anger fell on the small galley. Something was about to blow.

My breath hitched in my throat. I'd never seen the crew so angry before. They were united in fury. All their rage trained on Chef Logan.

"Don't you dare lay down your knives! If you leave, you're all fired!" He bellowed.

Tickets spewed from the machine, the only sound coming from the line. The tickets chugged like a machine gun. No one was picking them up. They spilled over the counter like a staccato snake.

One by one, the line cooks laid down their tools and walked out of the kitchen.

"Come on, guys, let's talk about this," Sammy, the sous chef, pleaded.

The cooks brushed past, ignoring him. He turned and chased after them in a desperate last-ditch effort to make them come back.

The galley was suddenly empty. Chef Logan and Chef Angela were the only two left standing.

"What's going on? Why did everything stop?" Julia stormed into the kitchen. Her calculated eyes took everything in.

She straightened her perfectly pressed, dark denim Hedley & Bennett apron. It was her armor. She paired it with black tapered pants and designer black T-shirts, giving her a polished, chic demeanor.

She pursed her lips. For Julia, it was the glare of death.

"Logan and Angela. It's over. Both of you. Pack your things. You're gone. I've had enough."

Angela's eyes sprouted tears as her nervous, skinny frame cowered. Shock crossed her face.

"It was nice working with you." She brusquely brushed past me and pushed out the kitchen door, stifling a sob

"You can't do this!" Chef Logan's brutish frame stood taller in the kitchen. He was an intimidating man: fiery red hair, barrel chested, six feet tall, and could have easily been confused with a convict. It was hard to believe he was one of the best chefs in L.A.

"It's done. Pack your knives. It's time for you to go." Julia stared, coldly.

Logan studied her a beat, incredulous, giving her a murderous glare. Finality crossed his face as he realized his fate. "Fuck you and fuck this place! You're a fraud. All you care about is your stupid reputation. You don't care about the food. You never did."

His eyes trained on me, furious. "Watch your back, Fiona. She'll be after you next."

He passed through the kitchen and slammed through the double doors that swung back and forth.

The tickets continued to spew out of the machine on the line. They were an impossible pile now.

I panicked. Was I going to be fired next?

I frantically gathered the tickets on my station and hung them up in front of me. I grabbed a pile of plates and started laying them out before me. I studied one of the tickets, but I couldn't read it in my fog of panic.

"Fiona. What are you doing?" Julia trained her eyes on me.

My stomach plummeted to the floor. Here it was. The moment of death. I was next on the chopping block.

My body washed into a fever. I could feel the sweat evaporating on my body. I was a fiery mess.

"Fiona," she said, short and sharp. "What are you doing?"

"I have to get these desserts out. I … I…" I couldn't find the words in my scrambled brain.

"Come here," she said.

I took two steps toward her. My feet heavy with every step.

Julia studied me. Her intensity unsettled me.

She smoothed her blonde hair back into her bun, which twisted at the nape of her neck. In her late forties, she was skinny and lean, like a ballerina. A taller, blonder version of Audrey Hepburn.

I looked around at the empty kitchen. I scrambled for something to say. "What are you going to do?"

"Sammy's talking to the crew. Everyone's coming back. We'll be fine. This isn't the first time this has happened to me."

She pursed her lips. "I should have fired him sooner, but he came from that restaurant Iruna in Spain. He ran with the bulls, for God's sake."

She studied me for a long beat.

I stood there. Awkward. Was she going to fire me, too?

"Your can-do attitude is quite impressive. Why didn't you leave with the other cooks?"

"Um … it's dinner service. Things have to get done …" I stammered.

She stood there a beat. Sizing me up.

The long moment made my stomach churn. Should I have left? Should I have followed the crowd? Was she going to send me out after them?

She finally spoke. A vague smile crossed her face. "You know the catering, right?"

"Of course," I said sheepishly.

Her eyes locked on mine, drilling me. "I know you're organized. Are you comfortable telling people what to do?"

"Sure ... Of course ..."

She kept thinking. "I can guide you on the menu. I can do that."

She sized me up, thinking. Her eyes squinted as her lips pursed, coming to something. "It's Tuesday, so we have time to figure things out ..."

She was in problem-solving mode. "Yes, this could work."

She gave me a calculated smile. "I have a proposition for you." She grinned. "Think of it as an opportunity."

I stood there, confused.

She gazed at me.. It was the first time she'd noticed me. The attention made me uncomfortable. A fresh wave of sweat sprung on my neck, becoming cold.

"You know, I gave Janice Mangold and Bryce Adams the same opportunity, and look where they are today."

Janice and Bryce were both heavy hitters in the pastry game. Janice owned her own bakery in Japan Town, and Bryce was the top pastry chef at Spago. Both were considered some of the best pastry chefs in Los Angeles.

"I'm going to give you a month. Prove you have what it takes, and I'll make you Pastry Chef."

The air in my lungs pushed out of me.

"Get rolling on the catering orders first thing tomorrow morning. You'll need to call the ice sculptor by ten for the party in the atrium. It's farmers' market day tomorrow, and I'll want your menu by Friday. I want to phase into summer for the weekend. We also have the Tony Award's party to think about."

I froze. Hit upside the head.

Was this really happening?

"Thank you, Julia. I'm honored." The words tripped out of my mouth like they didn't belong to me.

She waved her hand. Almost annoyed. "We also have a shoot for *Bon Appétit* on Monday. I want to do the chocolate soufflé recipe I got in Marseilles. You'll find it in my third cook-book. Page two-ninety-six." She turned and left through the doors Logan had blasted through before I could respond.

"Get the summer menu together immediately. Don't disap-point me, Fiona," she called as the doors swung shut.

I stood frozen. Confused. What the hell had happened? *Did I have the opportunity to become head pastry chef?*

A wave of terror and elation bloomed in my brain. I was stunned. Numb.

Here it was, the moment of truth. The moment I'd always dreamed of. The first step to greatness.

Holy shit.

I couldn't believe it.

Everything she expected flooded my brain. Catering orders ... ice sculptor ... farmers' market ... Tony Awards party ... *Bon Appétit* ... summer menu by Friday ...

I stifled back a panic attack. It was all too much.

The cooks filed back into the kitchen, picking up the tick-ets from the board and returning to work. Sammy returned to the pass and started calling off orders again. The tight machine turned back to normal. The whole drama was forgotten by the push of service. Life had to go on, and dinner had to be served. Drama didn't matter.

The only thing that mattered was getting it done.

My heart surged with terror and joy. This was it. My moment. And I was going to make it happen.

* * *

"Fiona! Over here!" Kate waved to me from across the packed bar.

I smiled at familiar faces in the packed crowd as I passed. They were all a circle of friends and fans in the local band scene, and they all hung out at Marcel's.

Marcel was behind the bar, making sure everyone was taken care of. A TV hanging from the ceiling was turned on to some random sports wrap-up show.

He gave me a happy wave.

Marcel had a mysterious past that everyone speculated on. Had he been a roadie for the Descendants or had he been in jail? No one knew, and he wasn't giving up hints.

"Fiona!" Come on!" Kate beckoned.

Kate was beautiful in her own quirky way. Her shoulder-length blonde hair was pulled back from her face in a tight ponytail, accentuating her high cheekbones. I loved her short floral skirt, beat-up Doc Martens, and one of her handmade silk-screened T-shirts.

We'd been friends since we were sixteen when she'd dared me to jump off the Venice Pier in the middle of the night. She'd pulled me to shore when I remembered that I couldn't swim.

When she wasn't playing in her band, she sold handmade jewelry and silk-screened shirts at farmers' markets and flea markets. She also painted murals all over the city. She was infinitely creative.

"Chef! You finally made it!" She gave me a big hug. "I can't believe it. Do you feel like a superstar yet?"

Marcel slipped me my drink in a flourish and moved on. Grey Goose with grapefruit juice. Maybe the fruit from the juice would cancel out the poison from the alcohol.

Kate lit up as we sat down, her hands waving in a flourish. "I can see it now. *L.A. Times* food section. *New York Times.* Food Channel. You're going to be the best pastry chef in the world!" She held up her glass. "Here's to your new life!"

"Not so fast, Kate. I have to prove myself first."

" It's just a formality, and you know it!"

I raised my glass. Our glasses clinked. And I took a sip, thankful that Marcel had been generous with the Grey Goose.

Kate laughed. "It's about time you made it. I was starting to get worried about you. What was it that you always say? Always the cook. Never the chef."

"If I don't pull this thing off, I'll be a cook again."

"For someone so positive, you're really negative right now." She smiled as she took a drink.

"I'm not being negative. I'm being realistic."

"Well, I know you, and you'll do great. Just keep the faith." Her eyes trained the crowd, and she smirked, almost choking on her drink. She gave me a sly smile.

"Lucky you! Look who's here," Kate said. "Wait. Don't look. It'll be too obvious."

I turned, reflexing in confusion.

"You should go over and say hi. He was a nice guy. You looked cute together. He's a good drummer. I mean, I'm not into The Cure, but overall, they're not that bad."

My eyes trained on the familiar face in the crowd.

Eric.

His long hair was coiffed perfectly into the mane of a rock star. It was amazing to me how much time he'd spent on it. It had always annoyed me that he'd squish the ends of his hair as he'd talk. Scrunching up the curled ends and fluffing it up around his shoulders. He'd always traded product tips with me.

I had no idea what I'd seen in him. The fact that he was a drummer may have had something to do with it, though. I was always attracted to the crazy ones. Maybe it was because I didn't have time to dig deep into anyone. I wanted instant gratification. I didn't want to invest the time into anyone. It was easier to latch onto someone with flash and drama. I didn't have to do the work.

And Eric wasn't a bad guy, necessarily. When he wasn't fixing his hair, he was a bartender at The Huntley Hotel. He was a patient person when it came to dealing with impossible tourists and locals who wanted the best. He'd regale me with stories of his customers and their life stories. He'd talk to me about his dreams of going on the road with his band. He was obsessed with skate punk bands and always listened to obscure music that sounded like chaos. He may have spent a lot of time on his hair, but inside, he was a good person.

I'd found so many nice guys who, in one way or another, were amiable and kind, but it always ended the same. The kinetic first attraction would die out, and then I'd lose interest. I'd go back to thinking about my work and my dreams. No one lasted for long. I'd have two or three good dates with someone, and then real life would slip in, and the whole thing would evaporate. My attention span would wane, and I'd be back at square one.

That magic was missing. In every relationship I'd had, that one piece was missing. What was it?

My father's descriptions of my mother were an enigma to me. An impossible dream. How could I meet someone and connect on that level? In L.A., that was impossible. Everyone had their own life and their own friends. They didn't have time for magic moments. It was easier to buy into the superficial persona.

Somewhere in my heart, I still longed for it, though. A clandestine moment with someone. A cool breeze would wash across my face, and the air would evaporate into a hum. The sun would shine a little brighter. I'd be transported into another dimension where time and space didn't matter.

Honestly, I was exhausted by the whole thing. It was easier to dig deep into my work and forget about the mess of my love life.

Eric waved to me from across the bar, flipped his hair back, and gave me his most winning smile. I gave him a thin wave and turned back to Kate.

"He's a mess. I'm not even going there," I said.

"Well, he's a hot mess, but you did have fun with him."

"Yeah, only for about five minutes. Before he tried to fix my hair."

"Well, at least he was trying to help." Kate laughed.

"What does that mean?"

"Well, you could do something besides the tired ponytail. I can't remember the last time I saw you in the wild."

"Thanks. I think." I sipped my drink, trying not to think about it. How could I think about my hair when I was in the trenches? In the kitchen, no one cared how you looked.

I could hear Jake tuning his bass across the room on the tiny stage. Kate set her drink down, excited. "A manager is coming to the show on Sunday. He's supposed to have connections to Universal and Sony. He set George's band up with their deal at Brimstone Records. This could really be something," she said. "Now, tonight's set is even more important. This could be it. It could be the opportunity we've been waiting for."

Bands frequently used Marcel's stage to test their sets. It was customary to see bands working through their set to ensure it was suitable for their bigger shows.

Kate's band, Alizarin, was considered one of the best bands in the scene. She played guitar and sang. Harvey, her bassist, and Jake, her drummer, had backed her for two years. They always brought a crowd, always packing the High Hat. They'd even sold out The Echo once.

Alizarin's punk and garage rock mix, influenced by everyone from L7 to The Distillers, took you off guard. It grabbed you by the neck. Kate was a fiery frontwoman, and I loved her music.

"Wow, Kate. This time, it could be it for you."

"Well, keep your fingers crossed. Who knows, crazier things have happened. Look at what happened to you?"

I took another sip of my drink, the vodka finally taking my head over in a pleasant hum. "I really don't know about this. I was a dog at the end of a fence. I've been working so hard for it for so long, and now that the opportunity is here, what the hell am I supposed to do?"

"Just do your best. What's that thing you always say that's so annoying? Work hard, be positive, make it happen?"

"Yeah, but positive quotations aren't going to help me. I actually have to perform."

Her face melted into a reassuring smile. "Things are working out for you. Don't worry …"

"Chef Fiona!" Charlotte pushed through the crowd, tackling me with a hug.

She was beautiful, with her long auburn hair piled into a messy bun on top of her head and her fine nose adorned with a light dash of freckles. Tall and lean, she wore her usual black jeans, a black tee, and white Vans high-tops.

We'd become instant friends at ICE when we discovered our collective love of cookbooks.

She always had a glint in her eye, like she was about to do something unexpected. She was always up to some harebrained scheme to make it. She was fearless and brave. Maybe a little too fearless and brave. Right now, she struggled with her patched-together food truck.

In a lot of ways, she was like my father. Her way of life struck fear into my heart. She was fickle, and I wondered how long she'd stick with it.

Charlotte hopped up and down in excitement. "You're pastry chef for Julia Stone! This is everything you've been dreaming of."

I sighed, exasperated. "Charlotte. It's an opportunity …"

A wave of terror washed over me. "I don't know if I should be elated or terrified."

"Come on, Fiona. Be real. This is your chance. You can finally stretch your wings. Show your vision. Unleash your magic upon the world!" She lit up. "What are you going to do first?"

"I have no idea. I have to think of something quick, though. We're shifting to the summer menu by Friday."

"You should do that apple Kouign-amann thing that you make. That's phenomenal. Or you could do your Mille-feuille with roasted strawberries. Or you could do your ..."

Kate cut her off.

"Girls. Stop geeking out. I don't want to stand here while you bond about chefferly things. This could go on all night. When you both start, I can't get you to stop."

"Don't you like to eat?" Charlotte asked.

"I do. But I don't want to know how the chef makes the sauce."

"Kate! Let's go!" Harvey called from across the bar. "Soundcheck."

Jake set up the mic stand, adjusting it to Kate's height. He had a dead pall on his face. He never smiled or laughed, for that matter. And forget about carrying on a conversation with him. He was a great musician, though. And that's all that mattered.

Kate jumped up. "Keep an eye out for mistakes. This is the last practice before Sunday. I don't want to leave anything to chance."

"We got you. Don't worry," I said, patting her arm.

She danced her way over to the stage and grabbed her Les Paul. She plugged a cord into her Orange amp, adjusting a few knobs as Harvey and Jake took their positions. They were relaxed and ready. The bar crowd made their way to the front of the stage.

"Check, check," she sang into the mic. It rang out loud across the room. The sound guy gave her the thumbs up.

The lights dimmed to a dark shade of red.

"We're Alizarin," Kate growled into the mic as she struck her guitar with the first chord. It ignited the room as the kick drum mingled with the dark, heavy punch of the bass.

Kate played her guitar, carrying the high end as her husky voice growled out into a scream.

Charlotte stood beside me in the crowd, smiling as her head nodded to the music. I laughed as my head matched hers.

I loved my crazy sisters. At least I had them. They had a way of making me crazy, too.

* * *

I stood outside Lucien's back door, pulled my hair into a tight ponytail, and took a deep breath. My head tingled from the scrunchy's tension and the vague hangover I had from last night's craziness.

I needed to get my head together.

I peeked at my phone. A chain of random texts from Charlotte filled the screen: *Are you coming to yoga this morning? Shit, you're late. Where are you ...? Guess you're not coming ...*

I took a deep breath, looking at the loading door. This was it. The first day of the rest of my life.

I took a step forward and pushed the door open. It slammed behind me. It punctuated the hope and terror in my heart.

Could I actually pull this off?

I went to the dry storage room, grabbed my white chef coat hanging on the peg behind the door, and cruised past the pastry shelves. We had everything we needed for the morning, even pastry bags. Thank God. I made a mental note to order shredded coconut and feuilletine later today. At least I wouldn't have to stress over missing ingredients.

I buttoned the last button on my coat.

I loved my chef's jacket.

My name was embroidered in bright red thread on my uniform. I was a committed soldier in the brigade and was proud to be part of a team. I had to admit I also felt a little smug.

I strolled to the dining room. The atrium was stone silent. The grand ficus tree, one of the oldest in the city, stood tall in the middle of the room. Its twinkly lights sparkled in the dark. It stood, wise and waiting. White-linen-clothed tables were set up with the required crystal and silverware.

It was the setting for special and important things to come. Intimate dinners where proposals happened. Dinner parties where mergers and deals were made. Important people ate and celebrated here every night, eating the best that Julia had to offer. It was a grand room that had seen a lot of Los Angeles history.

Lucien hosted the top Academy Awards and Grammy parties in town every year. Julia knew how to make a splash. She made important food that looked good with statues and trophies. On awards night, it was nothing for the Kardashians and Mathew McConaughey to go elbow-to-elbow with Denzel Washington and Emma Stone.

It made me proud to know that my desserts would be a star of the important show.

I walked through the hall and pushed through the kitchen's double doors. I always set my intention for the day with my first step into the kitchen.

Always right foot first.

I glanced around.

The dish pit stood silent. It exploded with dirty pots, pans, and scraped dishes. It was a disorganized, stinky mess from the night before.

It was the fallout of another dishwasher quitting again.

The kitchen was quiet. The kitchen would fill with cooks in half an hour, and the pandemonium would begin.

The prep cooks, line cooks, and dishwashers all preparing for the day. The smell of bacon would waft from the ovens. Cooks would hustle as they chopped squash and onions, prepping the meat. The line cooks would set up their stations, chopping chives and cilantro as they made the vinaigrettes.

Mexican rock, nineties old-school rap, and French punk would blast through the kitchen.

The crew came from everywhere: San Juan, Puerto Rico, El Salvador, Moscow, Paris, and Berlin. The kitchen was a melting pot brought together by the familiar language of food and a mishmash of foreign languages.

They worked tight. No bullshit allowed. They cast you out if you couldn't hold your own in the kitchen.

I'd seen many come through and be rejected by the crew.

Couldn't lift a bag of flour? Couldn't chop potatoes fast enough? Spilling stuff and working like a dog? They were done with you. Some poor souls barely lasted a week.

I was lucky. The pack had yet to turn on me.

I willed my frozen body forward, went to the bakery, and turned the lights on.

The wood tables were clean and ready for prep. The sheeter, the mixer, and the Hobart stood at attention and ready for service. The beautiful paned windows had a view to the street outside. They let in the rising sun to complete the cheerful space.

And it was mine.

It was all mine.

I was going to be the captain of this ship. Or at least try to be.

All the days and years I'd stitched together, making endless chains of cake batter and Kouign-amann. The armies of tarts and tortes I'd prepared. All the decadent desserts I'd plated with the precision of a surgeon, with my tweezers and offsets. All the long hours on the line, the brutal nights of service.

It all came down to this moment.

I thought of the look on Angela's crying face as she fled the kitchen. A dark wave of dread filled my stomach. She was a brilliant chef, but fate wasn't kind to her.

How could I possibly fill her shoes?

And was it awful of me to feel this way? She'd been fired, and I was reaping the rewards of someone else's downfall.

I checked the deck oven to ensure it was set to 400 degrees. I gently poked one of the loaves of bread proofing on the rack next to it. We'd have to get everything in the oven soon.

I loved the oven. It was a relic from an old bakery in Alsace. Julia had gotten it on one of her many trips to France. I'd shoveled so many loaves of bread into its gaping mouth, thinking of its history. How many croissants had it baked? How many baguettes and galettes had it toasted to perfection? Only it knew, and it wasn't giving away any secrets.

I felt guilty. I was dancing on someone else's grave. I was the winner of a nasty situation. Was I ready for this?

"Good morning," Camilla mumbled as she buttoned her coat and tied her apron around her waist.

She had a crown of rose ombré hair and beautiful rose and vine tattoos that crawled up her arms. It was a stark contrast to the formal white chef's coat. She was almost like an anime character, not of this world.

She set her coffee on the table and grabbed a big metal bowl off the shelf, giving me a cool glare. "Congratulations. I heard the news." I could tell by the look in her eye that she wasn't pleased. "What's on the schedule … chef?"

Here it was—the moment of truth. I grabbed the prep sheet hanging on the wall and cruised through it quickly. At first glance, it seemed like random symbols scratched together on one page. The words suddenly became clear.

Camilla glared at me. She had been close friends with Angela. "What do you want me to do first?" she asked.

"Start on the custard for the cheesecakes and make and mold the Marquise au Chocolat."

Right foot first. Best foot forward.

She gave me a cynical smile. "Yes, chef."

I could see the prep cooks were arriving, sharpening their knives and setting their stations up. "Good morning, chef." Leo nodded at me and smiled.

A flicker of excitement coursed through me—a tinge of pride.

If I played my cards right, I could be the head pastry chef. The only thing I had to worry about was surviving Julia.

Surviving Julia ...

Could I do it? I had no idea.

2

"I'm so sorry, Fiona."

Rose held the oven doors open. I could see sheet trays of black torched bodies that used to be cookies. The smell was smoky and rancid. I hated the smell of burnt chocolate.

Rose was a mess.

"Take a deep breath. Chuck these in the trash and start a new batch," I sighed.

Rose was always panicking. She was eighteen and wound tight. She went to Los Angeles City College in the morning and worked as a pastry commis at night. She'd come in at two and work production. Around seven, she'd work the line, plating desserts.

Rose said she had pastry experience when she was hired. But she'd been a black hole of disaster in her two months of working here.

Everything seemed to break or burn under her watch—worst-case scenarios would always happen. She'd torch the cakes to a crisp. She'd jam the Hobart with an errant offset that got stuck in the bowl. And breaking dishes on the line? She was a master—butterfingers, at best.

She hung onto the oven door for dear life, frozen.

"It's okay, Rose. Mise the butter and the sugar and get it creaming in the Hobart. I'll get your eggs."

I headed into the walk-in and let the door slam shut behind me.

I stood there, enjoying the stone-cold silence.

It was a sanctum. The walk-in was safe and insulated. Quiet and protected. A cloud of breath escaped my lips. There was only so long someone could stand four degrees.

I closed my eyes, enjoying the peace. I needed a moment to myself. The drama of the past twelve hours was catching up with me.

The door flew open, and Sammy darted in. He had a sneaky look on his face.

I jumped, brought back to life.

He grinned as he pulled the door shut. He was ready to dish.

The walk-in was where all the juicy information was traded. Some of the most critical meetings happened in the walk-in. It was the perfect place to commiserate.

"Thank God Logan's gone! That asshole was a piece of work."

I loved Sammy. He was Julia's secret weapon. He was African American, six feet tall, and had a larger-than-life presence. He'd been Julia's sous chef for ten years.

Sammy knew all of Julia's dark secrets and had a knack for knowing what everyone was up to.

He knew when a purveyor would send the shit lettuce and how to work three stations simultaneously. He even had a spidey sense of when one of the endless chains of dishwashers would decide to quit.

I loved listening to him when he worked the line. He was always bragging about his barbecue concept that he would make a reality.

Sammy was the backbone of Lucien. He was smart enough to know that being head chef put a target on your head. So he was satisfied with conducting the operation in the background.

"Are you ready for the big leagues, girl?"

I took a deep breath. "Of course." The question made my fragile nerves even more brittle.

"You better get ready, honey. You don't know half of what's going on. This whole situation's about to get real."

I grabbed a cambro of cooked apples and pulled it forward on the shelf. I shuffled the various pastry cream and butter containers around on the shelves, looking for the almond cream.

Shuffling the shelves was like playing Jenga. The old stuff had to be in front, the new in the back, first in, first out. Organizing was a great way to hide how desperate I was for details.

Sammy shivered. "Lucien's on the firing line, and Julia's getting nervous."

He crossed his arms. I could tell he was starting to get cold. "We haven't been getting the normal media engagement. Reservations are down. The Michelin inspector will be snooping around in disguise any day now. Julia's stars are on the line. Rondo, one of the servers, thought he recognized one of the inspectors last week."

He grinned, excited. "Liam is her big move."

"Who's Liam?"

He laughed. "Oh, you don't know ..." He shook his head. An annoyed smile crossed his lips. "That's just like Julia." He paused a moment. "Liam Auclair."

My stomach dropped.

"You mean *the* Liam Auclair?"

He chuckled nervously. "Yes. The one and only.

I stood there, dumbstruck. It couldn't be.

He came from the trenches in London. He'd worked his way up under Steven Degrass at Via Del Reverie. He became a shining star at Alain Ducasse at The Dorchester. The *London Times* had ordained him the best new chef in five years.

Then he hit New York and landed at a little place called Juniper. He'd blown it up and had easily earned it two stars. He was a legend.

And now he was coming here?

Sammy shook his head. "This could be a new start for Julia. He's actually someone worth working with. Maybe this time it'll be different. I'm tired of chefs coming in trying to impress someone."

That was true. Before Logan, there was Gary Mantrel. And before Gary, there was Marcel De'Blanc. Each one came with their own ideas, reorganizing the kitchen to their own liking.

"Julia's going full-on for this one. She's giving him full control. They're both ready to shoot for that third star." He shook his head. "I have to tell you, girl, it's going to get real."

"What do you mean?"

"You know his reputation, right?"

"I've heard he's tough, but how bad could it be? We've survived worse."

"I don't know. I have a friend who worked with him in New York. He said Liam was overbearing and over the top. Always pushing too much, going too far."

Dread floated over me. "Let's not make any judgments until he gets here. It's going to be fine."

He grabbed one of the tiny caramel brownies prepped for the party off the rack and took a bite. "You're always so optimistic. I remember you said that about Logan and look what happened."

I stashed a cambro of pureed pumpkin on a side shelf. My fingers were getting numb.

Sammy shook his head. "I wish Julia would stop with this whole three-star Michelin business. She didn't even care about it before Rabin came. Now she's obsessed. I don't even recognize what she's become." He chewed on his brownie, frowning. "I hope this works out. I really do."

I leaned against one of the shelves. I was getting hypothermia. "Don't go into this with any expectations, and you'll be okay."

"You're always so fucking positive, Fiona. That's what I like about you." He smiled.

The door opened, and Lou peeked in. "Hey, boss, we need you out here."

Sammy grinned at me. "Don't mind me and my paranoid bullshit. But I'm warning you, girl. It's going to be next level."

He turned as he walked out the door. "Maybe you can fix the brownies. These are terrible."

I smiled to myself. I already had the perfect recipe. La Brama de Tee chocolate with a bite of cinnamon. It would be delicious.

He pushed through the door. Lou said something as Sammy put his arm around him and laughed. Sammy was always kind to the cooks on the line.

The door shut, and I studied the racks.

The sheet trays were packed with the desserts, ready for the Gucci party. The tiny opera cakes and raspberry lemon tarts were delicate and perfect, lined up like pretty soldiers.

I felt uneasy.

Liam Auclair.

Now I really had a gun to my head. A pit bloomed in my stomach.

Michelin's three stars were the highest award you could ever hope to receive in the restaurant business. Sure, there were other accomplishments. James Beard awards, *L.A. Times*, and *N.Y. Times* accolades. But three Michelin stars was the gold standard.

Everyone knew that chef who jumped off a bridge and killed himself because he lost a star.

This was serious business.

And L.A. didn't have a three-star restaurant.

For all of L.A.'s vast treasures of food and culture, the third star was missing.

Julia had the right business model and the earth's finest ingredients. She just needed the right person.

I'd heard Liam was meticulous. It only made sense that he'd try to grab the brass ring with Julia. And I'd be in the white-hot center of all that.

A strange twinge of giddiness washed over me. This could be the opportunity of a lifetime.

I could make a name for myself in my own right. Some of his stardust might rub off on me if I did well.

Look at Sebastian Rhuel? He was Thomas Keller's right-hand man. They were symbiotic.

I broke my gaze from the shelf. I needed to stop getting outside my head, or I'd freeze to death. I picked up my cambros of almond cream and apples, stacking some eggs on top for Rose's dough. She hadn't come in for them yet. I felt bad for her. I knew with each mistake she made, she felt terrible. I felt bad for her, too. She just needed to be patient with herself. She'd learn with time.

I kicked the door open and danced around it, swinging the eggs on my hip. The warm air from the stoves instantly brought my fingers back to life.

I glanced at my watch. It was already ten o'clock. Where had the time gone? I had the atrium to deal with, and I had to prep pastry cream and laminate the croissant dough. And that was just the beginning of the prep list for today. We still needed to start on the prep for dinner. I was behind.

And where would I muster the energy for service tonight?

I was already exhausted. I needed a quadruple espresso with the four fancy sugar cubes Julia liked so much, and I'd be good to go.

Thank God I had the day off tomorrow. I needed it. I needed to figure out my game plan.

Rose was at the Hobart, looking fearful of what was in the bowl. "Chef, is this right?"

I glanced inside the bowl. The dough was a gummy mess. Sure enough, she'd forgotten the eggs. "Throw it out. Mise the butter and sugar, and let's do it again."

She frowned, flushed and embarrassed. Like she was going to cry. "I'm sorry, Fiona. I really am."

I set the eggs on the table. "Don't be sorry, Rose. Really. Don't worry. It's okay. Just remember the eggs next time."

She unhooked the bowl from the machine and tilted it on top of the trashcan. Letting the contents of the bowl spill into the trash.

I hated seeing the wasted French butter and Callebaut chocolate. It was an expensive mistake. I didn't want to do the math.

I took a forgiving breath. The same thing had happened to me so many times before. Everyone screwed up at one time or another. It's what happened in the kitchen.

Camille brushed off her white coat as she approached. I couldn't read her. Her neutral vibe made me nervous. "The Gucci party prep is almost ready. I just have a few final touches to finish. The truck's coming in an hour. I'm hitching a ride to set up."

"Thanks, Camille. You're the best."

She growled under her breath, "Angela would have written her up."

"Well, I'm not Angela."

She scoffed, "No. You're not …"

A breath hitched in my throat at the insult. "Just get everything ready."

A wave of fear washed over me, overwhelmed. How was I going to do all of this?

Panic flashed in my heart.

It was Wednesday. The farmers' market. Shit. I almost forgot. How would I go there when I had so much to do here?

I took in the scene around me. Camille was putting the final flourishes on pastries with her pastry bag. Rose was measuring out the flour and sugar for the cookies. Was I directing the ship? Was I doing a good job so far?

"Rose, after you finish the cookies, get started on the pot au crème for service tonight. Relax, and you'll be okay."

"Yes, chef," She said.

"Chef." It was so good to hear it. My heart bloomed in my chest. I still couldn't believe it was true. Well, close to being true.

And Liam Auclair was coming to win Julia's three stars.

Sammy was right. This was about to get real.

* * *

Santa Monica Farmers' Market on the Promenade was the place to be on Wednesday and Saturday mornings.

I couldn't believe my luck. Coming here was going to be one of the perks of my job.

The best produce in the city was laid out in booths around four city blocks. The tables were piled high with the choicest produce of the season. Some of the best chefs in Los Angeles roamed the crowd, haggling over boxes of shiitake and enoki, chard and endive.

I saw Maggie Sands from Argyle inspecting avocados in the distance. Jason Sprig from Piper was waving his hands at another booth, trying to get a better deal on the broccolini.

I looked around, unsure, searching for the Fleurcine Farms booth.

Of all the farmers, Delia was known to be the best. Julia always trusted Delia to supply Lucien with the freshest produce. I couldn't wait to meet her. I'd heard so much about her.

She always had the best cherries, peaches, figs, and strawberries in the summer. She would have the best apples, pears, and grapes in the fall. Wintertime brought sweet and juicy blood oranges, persimmons, and pomegranates.

Angela always brought interesting jars of jams, marmalades, and boxes of fruit when she returned from the market. Delia was known for her obsession with jam.

I turned the corner, passing a flower vendor. The perfume of marigolds lingered.

I was at a loss. What the hell was I supposed to do? How was I supposed to know what I needed? How much? I stopped midstep, overwhelmed.

Delia's eyes locked on mine across the crowd, laser-focusing on me. She smiled. "Come here, sweetie."

I stepped towards the booth.

"Julia's new pastry chef, right?"

Her broad sunhat protected her bright eyes from the sun. Her festive garden clogs were adorned with pictures of tulips and bumblebees. They complemented her bright blue overalls.

I extended my hand. "I'm Fiona. It's nice to meet you."

She grabbed my hand with both of hers and pulled me close. "I know you're confused, but don't worry …"

I instantly felt her nurturing force. She had an energy of creation and calm. She was a mother of the earth.

"It goes like this. I show you the best of the season. You tell me what you want. I'll help you with how much you'll need. I can give you hints along the way. I've known Julia forever, and I know what she wants." She nudged me forward. "Come on, sweetie, come meet my son. He'll be happy to help you out."

She grabbed my arm and led me to Fleurcine's booth. "He just moved back home. He's going to be helping me out a lot. It's good for you to meet him." She smiled.

We approached the booth, and I saw him.

His faded blue jeans and white tee complemented his tall, suntanned frame. His work boots were scuffed from wear, and his short brown hair was bleached from the sun. He gave a customer a hearty handshake and handed the man a bag of rhubarb.

He was easily the most handsome man I'd ever seen.

The sun haloed his head as he gave the chef a friendly wave. It was almost too bright to see. My breath caught in my throat.

"There he is. There's my son. Come on." Delia grabbed my hand and pulled me forward. We approached the booth, and all the skin on my body broke out into goosebumps.

He gave me a welcoming smile as he extended his hand. "Hi, I'm Rory."

A cool breeze washed across my face. My eyes tried to adjust to the brightness of the air. I tried not to stumble over myself as I shook his calloused hand. "Hi. Fiona."

"You're going to see a lot of Rory. He has a vineyard in Santa Ynez, but he's decided to move back to my farm." Delia beamed, proud. "His Chenin Blanc was featured in *Wine Spectator*."

He grinned. He was used to his mother bragging about him. "Mom. It's not a big deal."

"Well, you should be proud." She lit up. "He brought his goats with him. He makes cheese."

He smiled at his mother's enthusiasm "I play around with it."

"That's so cool that you make cheese" I kicked myself for not sounding more intelligent. Who said "cool" without sounding like an idiot?

He shook his head, chuckling. "I like to tinker with it. The weather and the grass here are better suited for the goats. We'll see how it goes."

His eyes met mine. They were a subtle shade of cornflower blue. The crinkles around his eyes betrayed someone who laughed a lot. I tried to push down the blush forming on my cheeks. My body wasn't cooperating with me.

Delia turned as another customer approached the booth. She gave me a reassuring pat on my arm. "Julia's not a piece of cake, I can tell you that. Just keep moving forward. Don't get caught up in the little stuff and you'll do fine."

She turned to the lady, hugging her as she shoved an apple into her hands.

Rory turned to me, giving me an embarrassed grin. "She's a little overwhelming, but she has good intentions, I promise." He laughed. "That's why chefs love her. She likes to mother people."

"She seems nice. I like her already."

"Well, just know that she has your back. She's never let a chef down yet."

I met his eyes for a beat, euphoria blooming from my toes.

He gave me a friendly smile through his relaxed gaze. "So, Fiona, where would you like to start first?"

I stalled. My mouth wasn't working with my brain. "Why don't you show me? I'm a little out of my element here."

He picked up a peach, wiped it off, and sliced a small section, handing it to me.

"Try this. It's our Montmorency. I think you'll like how tart they are. They're good for baking. They'll give you a little bite to balance the sweetness. It's also a good, all-around solid peach. You can do a lot with it."

I popped it in my mouth. It was delicious. "This would be great infused and paired with Cointreau. Perhaps I could do a clafoutis or a sorbet," I said. My excitement was getting the best of me.

"I'll put some of these in your order. I'll throw in some Aprium apricots as well."

He grabbed another variety of peach off the table, cut a piece, and handed it to me. "This is the Arctic Rose. My favorite. Honestly, I'm surprised how sweet they are."

The slice melted in my mouth. My tongue came alive with the firm texture of the meat. It would make an incredible peach crumble if I paired it with a simple Madagascar vanilla ice cream.

Rory watched me with excitement lighting up his eyes. "It's good, right?"

I met his gaze as I wiped the juice off my chin. The sweet flavor of the peach brought me back to earth. Suddenly, everything became sharp and clear. I could see the definition in the colors of the different fruits and vegetables surrounding me.

I struggled for something to say. "It's amazing." It came out almost like a whisper.

He smiled and handed me the rest of the peach and a paper towel. "Consider it breakfast. I'll give you some of those, too."

"Thank you." His knowledge reassured me. A wave of relief washed over me. Maybe this wouldn't be as hard as I thought it would be.

"Come on. Follow me. I'll get your order together."

He guided me to the back of the big white loading truck. "Fleurison Farms" was emblazoned on the side. He effortlessly jumped in the back. "I'm bringing the Armking nectarines next time. You'll like them. They ripened early this year."

I watched him as he shuffled boxes in the back of the truck. His moves were graceful as he moved the boxes around, searching for the right things.

A confusing wave of giddiness washed over me as I watched him.

"I'll also give you a sampling of our stone fruit and some blackberries and persimmons. I think you'll like them. I'll send the rest along later with your delivery."

"How's everything going? Is Rory helping you out?" Delia smiled as she stood close to me. "I've got some apricot chutney and sweet cherry butter I want you to try. I just made it."

She rummaged around in a box sitting on the ground and pulled out two mason jars. She handed them to me. "Tell me what you think."

I juggled the peach and grabbed the jars. "Thank you. I can't wait to try it."

"Don't be afraid to be honest. I really appreciate the feedback." She smiled.

Rory approached with a dolly stacked with flats of fruit and berries. "Are you ready?"

"Sure," I said. "Well, at least I think I am."

"It was nice to meet you, sweetie," Delia said. "Remember, we're here to help."

"I appreciate it. Thank you."

Delia waved to a customer and turned, winking at me. "I'll see you next time. Don't worry too much. Everything is going to be okay."

I waved to her as we made our way through the crowded market.

I followed Rory as we walked through the mesh of people. He had a relaxed gait as he pulled the dolly. His calm demeanor washed over me as my steps fell into cadence with his.

"So ... why did you move here?" I asked, trying not to trip over myself.

"There's a lot of stuff happening with my mother right now, so I need to be supportive. My vineyard in Santa Ynez is at a point where it almost runs itself. The commute isn't too bad, so I can split my time between places."

We veered around an old lady with a pushcart filled with vegetables. I scrambled to get out of the way.

"I like the mix of farms and families in Moorpark, and I'm glad that my daughter will be able to grow up in the same place that I did. So everything sort of made sense."

A piece of my heart fell. He had a daughter. Surely, he had a wife. He was officially off-limits. My heart sank in disappointment.

I took the last bite of the delicious fruit and threw the pit in the trash, along with the wet paper towel. "How old is your daughter?"

He smiled proudly. "She's five. Her name is Grace." He stopped and reached for his wallet. He flipped it open and showed me her picture. She was a beautiful kindergartener. Her messy ponytail framed her broad smile, showing two missing teeth.

"She's beautiful. How's she holding up with everything?"

He smiled, amused. "So far, the goats have distracted her. She likes to chase them around and make them scream." He slipped his wallet back into his back pocket, and we continued down the sidewalk.

"She makes them scream?"

"It's hard to explain unless you've been around goats. Trust me, no animals are harmed. I promise." His laugh was friendly and warm.

My heart fell as I asked the obvious question.

"What about your wife? Is she doing well with the move?"

His face darkened a bit. It was strange to see the light change in his eyes. "I'm divorced. She lives in San Francisco. She hasn't been in my life for a while."

"I'm sorry to hear that," I said. I squirmed, hearing the lie coming out of my mouth. A part of my heart surged again. I tried to push down the excitement in my brain.

"Well, sometimes things work out for the best," he said. "I'm doing great, and we still have Grace. So I can't feel too bad," he said, changing the subject. "Where's your car?"

"I'm up here." I led him down the alley.

He slowed as we made it to my piece of shit Land Cruiser. "Let's get this stuff inside before the heat turns it to jam."

I opened the back, and he grabbed the boxes of peaches and berries off the dolly and placed them on the back seats. He put the last box in, and I shut the door. He brushed his hands off and rolled the dolly next to him.

I extended my hand, trying to pull myself together. "It was good to meet you, Rory."

He took his hand in mine. As I shook it, I felt all the calluses on his fingers again.

He chuckled. "You have something on your chin."

It was peach juice. I wiped it off with my sticky hand. "Thank you."

"I'm glad you enjoyed the Arctic Rose. It's a beautiful peach."

I smiled. "Yes, it was amazing."

The silence hung as I gazed into his eyes. They were amiable and electric.

"Good luck with Julia," he said.

"Thanks. I'm going to need it, believe me."

"Well, just let the power of the fruit speak for itself, and you'll do fine. There's a magic in its simplicity." He smiled.

I deliberated a beat. Thinking. I thought of one of my father's quotations on his mirror.

Do or Die!

"Listen. Would you like to go out sometime?"

"What do you have in mind?" He smiled.

I blanked. The only thing I could think of was Kate's show. "My friend is in a band, and she's having a show on Sunday."

His face lit up. "I'd love to come."

My sticky fingers fumbled for my phone. I opened a blank text window, handing it to him, trying to hide my shaking hands. "Here, put your number in, and we'll sort out all the details."

"What kind of band is it?

"Well. It's kind of rock. Kind of punk. It's a little hard to define."

He handed my phone back and smiled. "It's been a while since I've been to a good show. It sounds like fun."

"It will be. She's quite entertaining."

We stood there in the alley for another beat. The air evaporated into a hum. I was transported to another place and time as his gaze lingered on mine.

I'd never felt like this before. It was foreign and familiar at the same time.

He broke from the moment. "I have to get back." He extended his hand, and I took the friendly handshake.

"I'll see you Sunday." His face brightened into another friendly smile. "I look forward to it."

"I'll text you all the details," I said. I wanted to say something more, but nothing came to mind.

He turned, walking back down the alley, trailing the dolly behind. His graceful frame glided past the dumpsters and graffiti.

I couldn't believe my luck.

I slipped into the Land Cruiser, plugged my keys into the ignition, and started the engine.

Rory turned at the end of the alley and waved at me.

I waved back, and he was gone.

I smiled to myself, triumphant. I'd survived my first trip to the farmers' market, and now I was going on a date.

Excitement and elation bloomed in my chest.

Being head pastry chef definitely had some perks.

I was beginning to like this.

* * *

I swung my exhausted body over the edge of the bed. It was eight-thirty a.m. I'd gotten home at three. Kate, Charlotte, and I had come home so late that I'd flung myself into bed with my clothes still on.

We'd hung out for an impromptu performance by Ransack. They played beyond half an hour, well past midnight, and then we closed Marcel's down.

At the time, it felt good to be light and in the moment. Laugh and forget everything. Now I felt like shit.

Charlotte stirred next to me. She was still in her clothes as well. "I need Gatorade. Something like eggs and bacon. Or maybe an egg McMuffin," she groaned. "Something salty."

I hauled myself to the kitchen. Charlotte followed me and started making coffee.

Kate and I had a good space together. It was a mixed mess of old furniture and rugs from the Salvation Army and Goodwill. Billowy tapestries hung on the walls. Candles and incense littered the windowsills and end tables.

A floral mural on the brick wall behind the couch boasted warm shades of red and purple. Kate was a punk rock Georgia O'Keeffe, and she'd conjured a welcoming space with what we had.

Her silkscreen operation was set up in one corner, and an old drum kit was set up for practice in the other. It was a nice place to call home.

Luna greeted me with paws and a full-body wag, his happy rump bumped back and forth. He was an Australian calico Shepherd. His beautiful fur was splotched in grey, orange, and black. Every patch of fur on his body had a different texture. His light blue eyes were striking, almost like a husky.

My fingernails dug in his fur as I scratched his body. He instantly made me feel better. I'd been with Kate when she got him as a puppy. So, by default, he was my dog, too.

"Do you want some food, sweetie?" I asked him. His rump swayed behind him with even more force. His tail knocked against the wall, in excited anticipation. He gave me a chirpy bark.

I opened a can of food for him and put it in his bowl and slid it on the floor to his spot. He instantly went to work, forgetting about me.

I opened the fridge, took a quick look inside, and slammed it shut. The only things we had were egg whites and vegan sausage. "Poor Kate. She'll never understand the magic of eggs and butter."

Charlotte shook her head. "It's the tragedy of a lifetime." She leaned against the counter and crossed her arms, waiting for the coffee to brew. She seemed fragile.

I felt her pain. "Do you want some Advil?"

"I'll take three if you have them."

I needed some, too.

I went to the bathroom, shut the door, and peeled my sticky clothes off. I grabbed my ratty leggings and my vintage Souxie and The Banshees tee shirt and pulled them on.

I looked at myself in the mirror and smiled.

Today was the first day of the rest of my life. My menu would be the most crucial one I'd ever put together.

I scraped my messy brown hair up into a ponytail. My eyes were red and tired. I leaned down and washed my face. The cold water was invigorating. I grabbed a towel, dried off, and studied myself again.

Here I was. Making it happen. My tired eyes transformed into a fiery gaze. My lips curled into a reflexive grin. Even though my tired ponytail hung high on my head, I was still vibrant through the hangover, determined. I smiled to myself. I was ready, and I would give it everything I had.

I grabbed the Advil from the medicine cabinet and made my way to the kitchen.

Charlotte shoved a cup of coffee into my hands. "Here you go. Black with tons of sugar. Just like you like it."

"You want to hang out while I make my menu?" I asked.

"Only if there's breakfast involved after," she said, a hungry smile crossing her face.

"I have to get back in time. I'm seeing my father later," I said. "I can't wait to tell him the news."

She drained her coffee and set the cup down. "I'm going to take a shower. I have to hydrate from the outside. I'll be back."

I turned and stood in front of my bookshelf. I was proud of my collection that reached from floor to ceiling.

My books were my pride and joy. Some people cruised the Internet for their inspiration.

Not me.

I had to have cookbooks. There was something reverent about seeing the recipes on paper. Seeing the pictures. Reading their stories and directions. It was a tactile experience. All my mentors whispering to me from one place.

I was a junkie. I cruised used bookstores, swap meets, and garage sales for the best. I had everything from Dominique Ansel's *Secret Recipes* to *Bouchon Pastry*. It was a must-have bible, written by Thomas Keller and Sebastian Rhuel.

Jacqui Pfeiffer was the god of French pastry. I read *The Art of French Pastry* so much that half of the pages were dog-eared and torn. He'd opened the French Pastry School in Chicago.

One of my favorites was Brooks Headley's *Fancy Desserts*. He approached pastry in a renegade way. It made sense because in his past life, before he was a pastry chef, he played drums in a hardcore punk band.

You had to respect that.

My father had opened the door for me with the gifts of his haute pastry books. *Grand Livre de Cuisine* by Alain Ducasse. *Elements of Dessert* by Francisco Magoya. *Mastering the Fundamentals of French Pastry* by Christophe Felder. I particularly liked that one because it had exhaustive pictures detailing the painstaking steps of complicated processes.

Alice Waters and her *Chez Pannis Cafe Cookbook* were there for me as well. Her pastry recipes were simple and elegant. Julia had helped with the recipe testing for the book when she'd been in Alice's kitchen.

Alice was one of a kind. She was the first woman to win the James Beard Award for Outstanding Chef, and she'd done it with a simple salad.

How rock star was that?

I also had all of Julia's cookbooks, but my favorites were *French Holiday* and *Lucien*.

And, of course, no one approached cooking without the Grand Dame cookbook of all ... All roads stopped at Julia Child's book, *Mastering the Art of French Cooking.*

Julia Child was my hero. She plowed through Le Cordon Bleu in Paris when it wasn't proper for a woman to be in the kitchen. And she'd even been a spy with her husband in WWII. How could you not respect that? In my off time, I liked watching her old YouTube shows. I loved her quirky accent.

My favorite cookbooks were the vintage published cookbooks from church ladies and women's guilds. It was the old cookbooks that gave me the most inspiration. I collected them like some people collected vinyl.

Yellowed pages held together with cracked plastic binding, delicate from wear and tear. Pages would be missing. Had they simply been torn out and lost? Or had someone stolen the best recipes from some unsuspecting housewife?

Who knew?

I'd spend hours devouring their pages, recipes that ranged from pickled watermelon rinds to chocolate mayonnaise cake.

Church ladies always had the best cobbler and pie, so I studied those recipes like the Bible.

I discovered the best pie dough recipe. The trick was an egg and a dash of milk. The egg kept the dough together, making it elastic enough to work with.

I grabbed random books off the shelf, stacked them on my dining room table, and sat down. The trick was to take all this information and make it my own.

Where was I going to start?

The Pastry Chef's Little Black Book stared at me from the top of the stack.

I cracked it open and flipped to random pages, trying to land on something interesting. I passed recipes for pastry cream, dacquoise, and croquembouche.

My fingers stopped on a picture of a Pavlova. It was gorgeous. Luscious strawberries peeked out of layers of merengue and sherbet.

That was it.

The Pavlova was the perfect place to start.

Production would be easy. I could build the meringues in advance. I had the Arctic Rose peaches Rory gave me. They would be the showcase. I'd celebrate the simple glory of the fruit.

I'd celebrate the sweetness of the Arctic Rose.

Rory flashed in my brain.

I thought of how he'd smiled at me when I wiped the peach juice off my chin.

The Arctic Rose was his favorite, too.

I lingered on the memory.

He was an anomaly. He had his own vineyard, made his own wine, and even tinkered with making cheese.

Who was this guy? And how did he find the energy and drive to do so much and still be so laid back.

The familiar warmth and giddiness washed over me. I smiled. I couldn't wait to see him again.

I checked myself. I had more important things to think about.

I shifted in the chair. *Pierre Herme Pastries* fell on my foot. The binding landed on my second toe, and a searing pain shot up my leg.

Charlotte emerged from my room in my jeans and a pink tee I never wore anymore. I liked how she respected the boundaries of my wardrobe whenever she went shopping in there.

She picked up Elisabeth Prueitt's book, *Tartine,* and started flipping through its pages.

"What do you think of this?" She held up a picture of a beautiful tea cake.

"I need something more formal," I shrugged as I dipped into the next book on the stack.

She put the book down, straightened up, and collected herself. "You know, there's always something else you could do. You don't have to work to impress anyone. You could be your own person … I've been thinking …"

I paused a beat. "What do you mean?"

She paused, deliberating. Her voice was struggling for something to say.

She wilted, losing her nerve. "Never mind. It's nothing.

"I'm going to make a Pavlova and a peach sorbet with a hint of Riesling as the first layer. Crown it with sweet, glazed peaches. Accent it with a delicate flourish of Tahitian vanilla whipped cream."

She thought for a moment. "You could use a hint of cardamom in the peaches. It'd brighten them up."

I smiled. It was coming together. "I could plate it with fresh raspberries and maybe Chamomile blossoms to finish."

Charlotte shut a cookbook and set it on the table. "Aren't you a little worried about working with Auclair?" She pulled her phone out from her back pocket. "Have you checked out his Instagram yet?"

I rolled my eyes. "No. You know I don't hang out on Instagram like you do."

She leveled me with a look. "For real, Fiona?" She scrolled through her phone, searching.

She lit up, "OMG. He's one of those guys." She held back a laugh. "He's Che Guevara with a chef's knife!"

She smiled as her thumb kept scrolling. "I can't believe he even has the motorcycle."

I cringed. "Oh no. Not the motorcycle."

She scooted in closer, showing me the screen. "Check this out." She thumbed through his Instagram feed.

Sure enough, there was the bike. It was expensive and fast.

He leaned against it in some alley in New York. He was tough, with his tattoo-laced forearms crossed in front of his chest, in full display.

"Holy shit, he's crazy hot. Did you know he was so good-looking?"

"Shut up, Kate. That's not the point. Keep going."

There were loads of pictures of plates he had prepared. They were elegant and precise. Other pictures of him dressed in his pressed yet rumpled chef's coat at various functions.

I recognized a few of them as famous or prominent chefs and celebrities. Pictures of him around London, Paris, and rustic locales. Was that Italy, perhaps France?

Charlotte rolled through picture after picture of him posing and smiling with local chefs, all smiling at the camera in their chef whites and aprons. "Wow, he's been everywhere."

Charlotte kept on, impressed. "Look at this. He's been on Iron Chef." The phone showed a quick clip of him being judged by the panel. The camera swung from his plated dish to him being crowned the winner.

Charlotte continued scrolling.

There was a black and white picture of him holding a cigarette and a glass of wine in a group of chefs. It was a rowdy party as he raised his glass in a laugh to the camera.

He lived the dream that mere mortals think of when they think of becoming a chef.

Charlotte continued, "He has respectable followers. Respectable likes. And he likes to post."

He was striking. Refined. He had a hard, devilish smile. His eyes stared me down. I looked away. I couldn't see anymore.

I grabbed another cookbook as she put her phone away.

This was whom I had to impress?

My body broke into a cold sweat.

"He's been on Iron Chef. He's got two stars. I can't compete with that," I said, grabbing my copy of Margarita Manzke's *Baking at Republique*. "I hope I can outwit, outlast, and survive. Julia's trigger-happy habits with her chefs make me so nervous. I just want to be the one that survives. So many chefs before me have reached the top under her ..."

Charlotte shook her head, frowning.

"Forget Julia. I hope you can survive Chef Auclair. Word has it that he fired everyone at Juniper when he took over. Your menu might be a waste of time."

She put down the book she was flipping through. "Let's get some breakfast. I need pancakes and sausage. Sodium and sugar. I need carbs. And you need to think."

I pushed away from the dining room table. "Let's go." I grabbed my sweater and bag off the hook by the door. Luna followed. "You want to go with us?" I asked.

His tail wagged, excited. I grabbed his leash too. At least he was happy.

I took a deep breath. What the hell was I going to do? I was in over my head. Was my vision going to stand up to the likes of Chef Auclair?

I had no idea.

3

I pulled up in front of my childhood home. Magnolia trees lined the dusty and dirty street.

It was a nondescript stucco cracker box in Mar Vista that was exactly like every other house that surrounded it. I grew up in a neighborhood where every house looked the same.

The only things that separated the scenery from one yard to another were tattered roses and lilacs twisted in chain link fences. Kids' toys strewn in someone's yard, next to another house, where someone was tearing apart a car—pieces and parts scattered in the driveway.

My father's yard was a wonderland of succulents and agave. He'd fashioned garden gnomes and silly garden trinkets around the cactus and jade plants in his yard. When I was a kid, I would play for hours with them, fashioning battles between gnomes and terracotta squirrels—fighting battles between the forces of good and evil.

Our neighborhood stretched for miles. There were so many neighborhoods like this in Los Angeles. Sometimes, figuring out what part of the city I was in was hard.

I grabbed a greasy bag from the passenger seat and made my way inside. It was good to be home.

"Dad?" I called from the living room. He still had the same furniture that he'd had his whole life. The tattered couch and La-Z Boy chair in the corner were dusty and cracked from wear. The carpet was worn from years of use. Old school pictures of me in various stages of growth littered the mantle, along with faded pictures of my mother.

"I'm outside," he called from the backyard.

I slid the glass door open and stepped outside into his wonderland. The smell of green and earth hung heavy in the air.

"Fiona, over here!" He set down his gardening shears and gave me a bear hug

"Good afternoon, Chef Fiona!"

I laughed. "It feels weird for you to say that."

"Well, get used to it. Good things are happening for you. You deserve it," he smiled.

I handed him the greasy white paper bag. "I got extra tzatziki, just like you like it."

He pulled a foil-wrapped gyro out of the bag and held it to his nose, inhaling the beautiful smell of the meat. His eyes rolled back into his head. "They should make gyro cologne."

"You're really nutto, Dad." I laughed.

"Remember when we went to Bakaliko for the first time? I think you were eight." He smiled to himself. "You wouldn't eat the dolmades because you said they looked like slugs."

"Yes. Sadly, it was an awful mistake," I said as we sat on the garden bench. Planters of basil and mint surrounded us.

I loved his backyard. My father tended it with the love and affection he gave his front yard. He had corn, tomatoes, beans, cucumbers, and more than enough kale and romaine to keep him happy for days. Tall sunflowers drooped on the stalks from their weight.

He cared for his avocado tree and tangelo tree with all the attention one might give to a secret mistress.

"How do you feel? You have a chance to break through to the other side. You could finally make chef." He bit into the gyro, unwrapping the foil from the bite zone. He was in a state of pure happiness.

I grabbed a sprig of basil from the plant next to me and popped it in my mouth. It tasted fresh with a vague hint of licorice. "Well ... It's all happened so fast, it's hard to say."

He stopped chewing, thoughtful. "To be chef with Julia Stone is huge."

I smiled sheepishly. "It gets even bigger. I'm going to be working with Liam Auclair."

He lit up, excited. "No. You mean that guy from Juniper in New York? That's amazing, Fiona."

"Honestly, I'm kind of freaking out. I'm trying to decide if I should be worried."

He scoffed as he wiped his mouth. "There's nothing to worry about. You're brilliant, and you work hard. That's a winning combination."

"Yeah, but I'm still worried I won't be good enough."

He patted me on the back. "I'm sure you'll do fine. Don't underestimate yourself. And who knows? Maybe he'll make you famous. Working for a chef of that caliber could really do things for your career. You could be validated and open your own place. Maybe I can chop apples for you if you'll let this old man in your kitchen."

"Aw, Dad, you can chop apples for me any time." I laughed.

He chewed the gyro, thinking. "Just don't be too nice. It's a liability in the kitchen. You know how you get."

I braced, defensive. "And how' that?"

"Well, let's just say that sometimes you don't stand up for yourself." He gave me a gentle smile. "I'm just being honest."

"Thanks, Dad," I said. I was trying not to get offended.

"I went to Bordella last night with Astrid. It's that new place in Hancock Park that Marci Strand reviewed. The ossobuco was out of this world. I got Astrid to take a bite of tiramisu. She pretended she didn't like it, but I know otherwise."

He thought for a moment. "You've met Astrid, right?"

"The vegan hippy lady, right?" I laughed. "You keep telling me about her, but she seems like a figment of your imagination."

"Well, maybe we can go to vegan Thai. She'd like that. And you like Thai too. That'd be a great way to meet." He smiled.

"That'd be fun. It's been a long time since we've had a food adventure."

He stuffed the gyro wrapper into the greasy bag and wadded it into a small ball, throwing it in a trashcan next to the garden shed. "She's not your mother by any means, but she's fun. So don't get the wrong idea."

"It's okay, Dad. I just want you to be happy. I smiled.

He sighed, enervated. "I can't believe it. You're actually going to become a chef. I'm so proud of you, Fiona. I mean, I knew it'd happen for you. But to think that you have a chance. It doesn't seem real."

"It doesn't seem real to me either. It's going to be a challenge, though. Liam's tough, and Julia's fickle. She's fired so many chefs since I've been there. I just have to keep my head down and breathe. Otherwise, I'm going to be just a stupid cook on the line. That'd be soul-crushing after everything I've been through."

"Well, it's just like Babe Ruth said: *It's hard to beat someone who never gives up.*"

I laughed. "Dad, I don't think positive quotations are going to save me here."

"Well, just do your best. That's all you can do." He smiled. "And with a little luck, you'll go far."

I gazed at his lemon tree. The branches were heavy with ripe lemons. "You really have to do something with your lemons. They're going to rot if you don't do something."

"I've been meaning to pick them. I have a few ideas. Maybe you could swing by the kitchen and do some of those lemon bars. I could use them for my menu. They've always been popular with the guests."

"How's the kitchen doing?" I asked, guiltily. I hadn't been there for a while.

"It's good. I have a new guy who seems to know what he's doing. I think I'm going to promote him. He could manage it a bit more and take the stress off for me." He laughed. "I did a gig for our old friend, Mrs. Jamison. She threw an anniversary party for one of her friends. She still tried to switch out the menu at the last minute. Get something for nothing. Some people never change. You're lucky you don't have to deal with things like that anymore."

"That's true." I laughed. A wave of thankfulness washed over me.

He grabbed my hand. "Just know that I'm proud of you. And just think, maybe Marci Strand will write something about you."

The thought of it made my head spin. "Dad, let's take it one step at a time. Don't get too ahead of yourself."

He grinned. "I'm just saying, you never know."

I took in his aging face. His greying blond hair still needed a good brushing. But his laughing blue eyes still shined bright with optimism. He still had the same enthusiasm.

"I love you, Dad. Thank you for everything you've done. I couldn't have done it without you."

"Well, I gave you the tools. And see what you've done with them. Stay positive. At the end of the day, that's all your heart has to hold onto."

He gave me a generous hug. "Chef Fiona! I like the sound of that. Maybe that's what I'll call you from now on."

Chef Fiona. The sound of it was still strange. Like it was someone else. I hoped I could make it happen. "Are you still hungry?"

"I'm starving. Let's go to Benny's truck down the street. I'll buy you a cheeseburger. You need to eat."

The thought of one of Benny's burgers made me instantly hungry. "Let's go."

"It's the perfect way to celebrate. I'll even spring for the onion rings." He grabbed my hand and pulled me through the garden.

His warm hand was strong in mine. It felt good to have my father be so proud of me. It was better than anything else in the world.

* * *

"They're beautiful." Rose studied my work. The torte was like a chocolate fantasy, dense and rich. I'd flourished the plate with caramel and a tiny crown of sculpted sugar.

The mini peach Pavlovas were delicate and feminine on the plate, adorned with berries and tiny pansies. The torched top of the crème brûlée was a brilliant amber, and the raspberry coulis I'd used to decorate the plate arced in a romantic flourish.

I'm ready to face the music. I took a deep breath. "I'll put the ice creams on right before Julia sees everything."

"Don't worry, Fiona. They're amazing," she said. "Julia will love it."

"I hope so. It certainly sets the tone for everything." A twinge of nervousness came over me.

"I'm going to get some fresh air. Clear my brain before I show Julia everything," I said. "How are we doing on prepping for the Chandler event? Have you prepped the ingredients for the lemon mousse?"

"I have everything ready for you to show me. I hope I don't screw it up."

"You'll be fine, Rose. Don't worry." I turned and made my way through the kitchen.

I glanced around. The air was eerily quiet. The dish pit was empty. The front kitchen was deserted. The cooks were pushed tightly together in the prep area like a single organism.

What was going on?

The tension was thick and heavy. I approached the crowd, seeing what the fuss was all about.

My stomach dropped.

His black chef's jacket was perfectly pressed. The sleeves were rolled up to show his subtle tattoos. His long, dark, curly hair was pulled back into a messy ponytail. His face was striking: long nose, strong jaw, and piercing eyes.

Chef Liam Auclair.

He made me think of that famous black-and-white photo of Marco Pierre White. The only thing missing was the cigarette.

He stood at the head of the clean, scrubbed wood table. A beautiful, un-filleted King salmon lay horizontally in front of him. An expensive ten-inch Santoku chef knife was set out beside it, almost reverent.

A bottle of El Tesoro Reposado sat in the middle of the table. It was set for a ceremony.

And Chef Auclair was the priest.

I watched him study the crew, taking everyone in, deliberating.

His eyes landed on me.

My stomach lurched as he took me in. His fierce green eyes held mine as he momentarily regarded me through the crowd.

The power of his stare lingered as his eyes moved on.

The crew of cooks pulled in tighter around the table. The quiet buzz of industrial appliances hummed in the air.

Julia stood behind him, her head held high. A faint, proud smile crossed her lips. She was like a queen.

Chef Auclair looked around. His eyes flashed brightly as he began. "A salmon is a force. Single-minded and focused. It's one of the only fish to swim in fresh and salt water. It can smell its way back home when it spawns a thousand miles away. Through rivers, waterfalls, rapids, and damns. Dodging bears, eagles, and other fierce predators. Some salmon even change color. They grow humps and fangs. It's a fight to the finish." His hand caressed the fish. "A salmon is the most beautiful machine in the ocean."

His voice was strong. Hypnotic in its baritone. "I like to think of my kitchen like a salmon. The head holds the brain with a single-minded purpose. The body is the muscle that brutes the body upstream. The tail steers the way."

He stroked the fish lovingly. The skin glimmered like stainless steel in the light.

Then he picked up the Santoku and swung it with all his strength. The blade slammed on the table, and the cooks jumped.

The head of the fish separated from the body, and the dead eyes stared into space.

"When the team doesn't work, there is no single-minded purpose."

He took the knife, swung his arm around, and chopped off the tail with the same dramatic force. The tail landed with a bounce, separated from the body. "When a kitchen doesn't work, there's no direction."

He swung the knife with a flourish and stabbed the fish's body. Blood dribbled from the wound. A tiny rivulet spilled on the table.

"When a kitchen doesn't work, there's no muscle upstream. It's a dead organism. It's doomed."

He let go of the knife and left it in the fish. It stood tall, like a flagpole.

"I have a single-minded purpose—one goal. I want our food to be worth the journey. I want it to transform. And to do that, I need my team to work as a salmon. To fight. Change color. Grow humps and fangs if it must. And no matter what, be a tight unit."

He glared at everyone, standing tall. The crew stood on, completely rapt.

"And what is the journey, you may ask?"

He stared everyone down. "I want to win three fucking stars."

He let the words hang there for a moment. "I want your blood to drain on the table. I want nothing left. And when that's done, I want more. I want everything. In return, you can say that you built something bigger than yourself."

He sized everyone up. "Anyone who can't give me that can leave."

He paused for a moment.

I caught Sammy's eye. He was studying Liam, fear in his eyes.

I studied the crew. There was a collective energy of comaraderie being born. An alliance was being made.

Liam smiled, seemingly pleased that no one was leaving.

He grabbed the bottle of El Tesoro Reposado off the table and uncorked it.

"We're going to do great things together." He raised the bottle. "To Lucien. To our work! To our three stars! Together!" He took a deep swig from the bottle and passed it to Leo.

Leo smiled at Liam with a fire in his eyes. He took a slug from the bottle and passed it on. The cooks pushed together in their white coats, each taking a sip. It was like a collective contract between them. They were instantly loyal converts.

Chef Auclair had made them believers as they gathered around him to celebrate.

Camille joined the group. She took a sip from the bottle. She was one of the guys.

Sammy frowned and broke from the group. He skunked off toward the line.

Chef Auclair watched him go, with a calculated stare.

Julia grinned, oblivious, watching the crew. She took an awkward sip from the bottle.

This was too much. The theatrics. The show of raw male bravado. My body broke out into a cold sweat. Terror bloomed in my stomach. Was this what I was going to have to deal with?

Julia caught my eye and nodded. She was ready for me.

This was it. My moment of truth.

I grabbed the ice creams and sorbets from the lowboy freezer and adorned the plates with the frozen confections. It was time to face my fears.

"Julia said you had some desserts to present."

I turned, my stomach dropping to my feet.

Chef Auclair's tall frame faced me. His emerald eyes met mine as he extended his hand. "It's nice to meet you."

His handshake was intense, like he was deciding whether to arm wrestle me.

"It's nice to meet you too, Chef Auclair."

He smirked. "Please, call me Liam."

He studied the bakery. His eyes lit up. "Wow. What a fantastic space. I could really do something with this."

He took everything in a beat and then turned back to me, his hard gaze drilling into me. "Your tasting is a great introduction for us. I'm excited to see where we stand."

"I'm glad you both have met." Julia broke the moment, approaching from behind. "I can't wait for Chef to see your vision." Julia appraised the table. She grabbed a spoon. "What do you have for us?"

I stood tall. The game was on.

"The first is an apricot brûlée. I used Aprium apricots to dress the top and a cinnamon pastry cream to complement. I infused the raspberry coulis with Beirão, a Portuguese liqueur."

They studied it a beat before they dove their spoons in, taking a bite. I smiled to myself. I could hear the perfect crack from the caramelized sugar on top of the brûlée. I'd torched it just right.

I watched them as they slowly judged it. I couldn't read either one of them.

Julia moved onto the chocolate torte and took a bite. "I taste the hint of bourbon in the cherries. I like that you didn't overpower it. It goes well with the ice cream. Is that Earl Grey?"

"Yes."

Liam dove in and took a bite. He chewed quickly as he moved on to the Pavlova.

He took his spoon and lifted the meringue shell, inspecting the layers.

"I used Flourcine Farms Arctic Rose peaches for the filling and the sorbet," I said.

He fractured the shell with brute force and took a bite, tasting it for a quick beat. He shook his head and frowned.

The vibe in the room turned.

Julia stared at him, taking his lead. Her lips started to purse, and her eyes flashed dark.

He gored his spoon down into the trifle. It stuck out of the top, standing in the strawberries and coconut whipped cream. He left the spoon standing in the glass, not even tasting it.

He stared me down, searching for the right thing to say. "They're rather sentimental."

He thought for a beat. "I'm looking for something more, well how do I say this …? More structured. More modern. More, Kazutoshi Norita. Have you seen what they're doing in Tokyo?"

My body seized up at his rejection. "Sure."

I'd seen her work, but I was more like a distracted tourist regarding Japanese pastry. It wasn't on my radar.

He stood over me. "That's what I want. Something more interesting. Something different."

He shook his head. "We'll go with this for now, but see what else you can come up with."

I stared at him as he rounded the corner and left. Abrupt. Rejection and anger hit my gut like a wrecking ball.

Julia cast her spoon down on the table. "I need you to try harder." She adjusted her apron, lifting her chin. "I need to have confidence in your abilities. After all, we want our food to be worth the journey." She gave me a cool gaze. "Think of that salmon swimming upstream."

She turned to leave. "Don't forget. We have *Bon Appétit* Monday." She rounded the corner and left.

I stood there, betrayed, staring at the carnage.

The trifle sat there like it'd been cast out of the tribe. Liam's spoon was sticking out of the top. It was like a murder victim. Strawberry glaze oozed like blood.

I felt like the salmon on the table. No head. No tail. Stabbed in the chest.

Did I want my blood to drain on the table?

I had to go deeper. Grow humps and fangs. Was that even possible?

I should have taken a swig of that tequila. It might have prepared me better for my first round with someone in the big leagues.

I knew one thing: I had to step up. Otherwise, I'd ruin my reputation and end up back in that sweaty catering kitchen with my father. Killing cockroaches and dreaming of bigger things.

A dark wave of dread washed over me.

As much as I loved my father, there was no way I was going back there.

* * *

"Our mantra will be Ohm, Shakti, Ohm ..." Yogi Dave said. "Breathe a loving breath in and out ... Ohm is the hymn of the universe ... Shakti is the power within. I'll give you five minutes."

He stood on a platform barefoot, peaceful in his linen pants and a simple tee. Pretty prayer beads in an assortment of colors adorned his neck.

Yogi Dave's studio was tiny and packed despite how early it was. The warmth from all the bodies in the room loosened me up. The heat got the negative, toxic energy out of my body. It was an excellent reset button.

I peeked open an eye and glanced at Charlotte. She was cross-legged, and her posture was perfect. Her hands were formed in a prayer position at her chest as she repeated the mantra.

I was quiet.

I always felt silly and uncomfortable repeating the script. I couldn't settle down. My monkey brain was raging.

All I could think about was Liam, my paranoia mixed with Ohm.

Was he Julia's Shakti?

What was my Shakti?

Could I harness Shakti to figure out what the hell I was doing? It was all jumbled up in my head, along with the flashes of Japanese desserts I'd studied until two a.m.

I had to get back to Ohm. The rhythm of the universe. I tried to clear my brain.

Rory popped into my head instead.

Rory's graceful gait as he walked down the alley. His eyes were warm as he smiled. A strange twang of excitement washed over me. Why did that image float in my brain? It was hard to focus.

I went back to Ohm. Ohm. The rhythm of the universe. Yes. I just needed to find it within the mess of my mind.

"Okay, children. Bow your heads," Dave whispered. "I honor the light in you that is also in me. Namaste."

The echo of Namaste from the class reverberated through the room. Everyone quickly picked up their yoga mats to get out before the next class.

"Let's get out of here," I told Charlotte as I shoved my rolled-up mat into my bag.

We made our way down the stairs and out onto the sidewalk.

The morning was crisp and new. I breathed in the fresh air. All I needed was strong coffee, and life would be perfect.

We strolled down the sidewalk on autopilot to our usual place.

Charlotte sighed heavily. "I hope that stupid shawarma truck doesn't take my parking spot at the market again. It's my lucky space. He keeps parking there, and it's messing with my customers."

I guess she hadn't found her Shakti after all.

I gave her a reassuring pat on the back. "Why don't you go to the Pico Market? You always have a lot of luck there," I said.

"Yeah, maybe. I don't know. The competition is getting the best of me." Charlotte frowned. "It seems like there's a new truck every week trying to wiggle its way into my best spots."

We approached the coffee shop, and she grabbed the door. "Have a seat. It's my turn to buy. The usual?"

"That'd be great."

She disappeared inside, and I sat at one of the wrought-iron tables next to the shop.

The ghost of meditation lingered. I couldn't get Rory out of my brain.

I liked that he was so tall. There was something to that. I liked that he knew so much about peaches and persimmons. Wine and cheese …

… I liked his kind eyes and his friendly persona … I couldn't wait to see him again.

"Hey! Fiona! Where are you?"

I snapped back from my moment. Charlotte was standing there with my coffee. "Here you go. Just like you like it. Three shots and four packets of sugar."

"Thank you," I said. I was grateful for the caffeine as I stood up from the table. "I guess we should be going. I have to be at work by eight. And you have to get to your spot before the shawarma truck shows up. Let's get this day started."

Charlotte froze for a moment, a glint of something in her eyes. "Okay." She took a breath of confidence as she steeled up. "I want you to keep an open mind."

"What are you talking about."

She fumbled with her coffee as she shifted from one foot to the other. "You have to see it first. Seeing it will give you perspective."

"See what?" I was starting to get nervous.

She grabbed my hand and pulled me down the sidewalk. I almost tripped as we crossed the street, barely able to keep up.

She stopped abruptly in front of an abandoned storefront. We'd passed it a million times. The windows were cloudy with dirt, and a dusty "For Rent" sign hung in the window.

"What do you think?" She beamed, hopeful.

I looked at her, confused. "What do you mean?"

"About the space? It's perfect, right?"

"What the hell are you talking about?"

"This." She grabbed me by the shoulders and gave me her biggest winning Charlotte smile. "We should just open our own place. We could call it Looking Glass."

I backed up.

"Charlotte. No. What are you talking about?"

"I'm serious. I hate my truck, and you're doing something you don't like to do. It'd be perfect."

"Charlotte, I never said I didn't like what I was doing. I have a chance to make chef right now!"

"Fiona ... seriously? You're meant for better things than some crazy woman whose loyalties blow with the wind. She doesn't respect your talent."

She was like a child asking for a cookie. "At least look inside."

I shook my head and stepped back to get a better look. The space was sad among the other colorful businesses on the street. An eyesore, actually.

"It's zoned for restaurant use. It'd be great. I could do my savory stuff, and you could create your pastry magic. There's even an oven."

"How do you know this?"

"Marco told me about it. His friend manages the building. It's been on the market for a while. It'd be perfect. We could be like Mary Sue Milliken and Susan Feniger. Remember Border Grill?

I stood there, overwhelmed. There was no way in hell I was even half prepared to open my own place. I wasn't ready for this yet.

"Charlotte. I don't want to hurt your feelings or be unsupportive, but there's no way I can do this right now. I don't want to sound mean, but this is just another one of your harebrained schemes."

Charlotte's cheeks flushed. "Look. I know the pop-up was a bad idea. No one came. I know now that I didn't promote it right. And I know the food truck was a bit of a wrong turn. I got a little too carried away with the menu. You cannot have a French bistro with a five-course menu. Who can pull that off Coq au Vin, Gaston, or Cassoulet in a little truck? It's too much.

I know that now." She stood tall. "This isn't one of my hare-brained schemes. This is serious."

She had a pleading look in her eye. "This place is perfect for us. It's the perfect size. I can do the food I want, and you could have your French bakery and do your sexy desserts on the side. Like I said: it'd be perfect."

The way she kept saying "perfect" made me uneasy. "I'm not ready for something like this. It's a huge step. I have to make a name for myself first."

She leveled me with a stare. "Fiona. At a certain time, you have to come to terms with your fear and desire. I know you could do this. You have a unique vision. And we'd be doing it together. We'd have each other's back."

I was put on the spot. I wanted to run away.

"If you're so excited about it, why don't you do it on your own? I'd totally support you. I'd even be down to make your bread. You know I'm here for you."

"It's not the same. We're symbiotic. We're sisters from different mothers. I've always dreamed of doing something together with you. We know each other's language."

She was serious. She really meant it. "It'd be wrong to do it any other way. We could share the work. Share the resources. And you'd be doing something for yourself. We'd be amazing together, and you know it."

I stood there, frozen. "There's no way, Charlotte ..."

"Let's just look at it. It can't hurt anything. I know you're completely turned off about the idea, but maybe you'll change your mind."

The truth of my father's disaster rang in my head ... *Make chef first. That's the only way ...*

"No. I can't. I have to make a name for myself first. I have to establish myself as a chef before I even consider anything like this." I took a cleansing breath. My Shakti was gone for the day.

Charlotte flashed me a pleading smile. "At least look at it. Give me that much."

It was too early in the morning for this.

"Okay. For you. But I'm still going to say no. Let's get that straight. I love you, but I'm not going to do it."

Charlotte jumped up and down. "It's meant to be, and you know it."

I watched as she dialed the number on the sign, excitedly pacing back and forth. I took a sip of my coffee. I needed caffeine.

And maybe a different mantra. Ohm wasn't going to cut it.

4

Service was turning into a shit show.

Tickets hung over the station and were multiplying as my stack of clean plates shrank by the second.

I gazed through the pass to the atrium. The tranquil room was filled with customers enjoying their food under the grand, illuminated tree. It made me jealous.

Rose and I were trying to stay out of the weeds. Prepped ingredients were separated into nine-pans on top of the lowboy. Squeeze bottles with various sauces, crumbles, and edible flowers littered the tight station.

Rose may have been a disaster in the kitchen, but she had a gift for plating. Her hands were graceful as she swirled caramels, chocolate, and reductions on plates. She finished them off with delicate flowers, sugar, and chocolate accouterments. She dove into every ticket and delivered the results to the pass. Her only problem was looking down. She was a mess if the service got too intense.

Sammy was expediting, calling out complete orders, and wiping the plates. The plates were whisked away on the pass by frantic servers. It was the front line of the battle.

I pulled another swath of tickets and hung them out. We were in the second wave. The first wave of covers was a walk in the park compared to this.

I gazed over my shoulder at the line.

Tickets were rolling in even faster over there. The staff worked like a pit crew in their sweaty chef's coats, frantically grilling meat. Finishing sauces. Arranging and plating.

Liam was in the middle of it.

He was an intense maestro in the small space—a general orchestrating a war like a conductor driving a symphony.

He dodged between the cooks. Tasting sauces, checking the garde station, his spoons at the ready. He adjusted each plate accordingly, checking every element.

He made me nervous.

I'd scoured the internet for pictures of Chef Natsoku Shoji, trying to figure her out. I had been up all night, researching recipes and stacks of books full of ideas, trying to think of ways to tilt them.

I'd spent all day in the kitchen, reinventing everything. The challenge had been to use all the elements I'd prepared for my other menu. I didn't want anything going to waste.

The new dessert plating was precise, almost mathematical.

The meringues were beautiful. They were paired with the Montmorency cherries, almond pastry cream, and a refined arrangement of candied rose blossoms and violas.

I'd made tiny, delicate peach tarts from the disaster of the apricot ones. I arranged the thinly sliced peaches around the tops of the tarts in tight, fanned-out circles, like a blooming lotus flower. I'd also ground macadamias and made a thin crust. It was beautiful.

I'd thrown the chocolate torte out and made a tiny chocolate opera cake. It was delicate and beautiful. Dainty.

It was breathtaking.

Rose and I constructed everything with our tweezers, spoons, and offsets. We were adrenalized and amped from the stress. We just had to get through the next two hours.

"What are you doing!?" a voice boomed from the line. I turned. Leo was frozen, cowering. Terror shined in his eyes as Liam towered over him.

"The sauce has too much butter. Think next time."

Everyone on the brigade shrunk back and put their heads down. They were trying to look even more busy. I could tell Leo was trying not to lose it.

Liam caught my eye from across the kitchen. His eyes focused on me.

My brain flatlined.

Oh God.

He pushed his way between Rose and me and studied the dish that Rose was plating.

"What the hell is this?" He sighed, annoyed. "Stand back." He tipped the plate, and the contents fell into the trash.

I stood there, dumbstruck.

Rose looked at him, horrified, as he shoved the dirty plate in her hands. "Take this to dish."

He grabbed another plate along with a squirt bottle and offset. In a flourish, he redecorated the plate for the peach tart. He inspected the flowers on the station. He tossed them over his shoulder and adjusted a cannel of pastry cream so it balanced precariously on the edge of the crust. Then he slammed it on the station.

"That's how I want it done, Fiona. Pull yourself together."

He went back to the line and the business of a crushing service.

A wave of embarrassment coursed through me. How could I have made such a disastrous mistake?

Rose returned from the pit, terror in her eyes. I patted her on the arm. "Don't worry. Let's keep rolling."

Rose took a deep breath and dove back into the madness. She hung tickets from the machine over the station and grabbed one. "Oh no. A ten-top. And someone is vegan, gluten-free, with a nut allergy," she said.

I rolled my eyes. "I got it."

I had sympathy for people with allergies. I loved tinkering with what I had to make things safe for them, but I could smell the fakers from a mile away. Those people who made it their mission to make cooks' lives hell. Vegetarian. Vegan. Lactose intolerant. Allergic to meat and eggs.

It was always the triple threats that sent things back. Complained. Made life difficult. How many people had an allergy to everything except water?

I took a deep breath and thought of what I had on hand. I had the whipped coconut cream from the trifle I'd retooled into a mousse. I had the raspberry sauce. And the apricot Riesling sorbet was all of the above.

I was sure they weren't allergic to alcohol.

I grabbed one of the crystal glass ice cream bowls from the freezer and fashioned the sorbet into three quenelles in the bowl. It was like a blossom. I flourished the top with raspberry sauce and the opera cake's sugar accouterment. I grabbed my tweezers and adorned it with the posies from the tart and placed it on the pass.

My eye caught Sammy's from across the room. He gave me a long, dreadful gaze. He shook his head at me, overwhelmed. I blanched. Sammy was never out of his element. He was usually the coolest one in the room.

"Fiona! Help!" Rose pleaded. "I'm out of the cherry reduction and tarts."

My head flashed to the business at hand. I patted her on the back, reassuringly. "I'll grab some more. Whatever you do, don't freak out. Just focus on one ticket at a time."

She nodded and went back to work.

"I'll be back." I made my way into the walk-in. It shut behind me, and the familiar cold and silence felt good.

Liam had called me out. Another moment. Another embarrassment. Was the humiliation ever going to end?

Stress made my stomach ache as the rumbling of a headache blossomed at the back of my skull. I groaned. I didn't have time to stand here and second-guess myself. I had to roll. I grabbed a nine-pan of raspberries and a fresh squeeze bottle of cherry reduction.

The door swung open, and Liam stood there, imposing. He squeezed his way in and shut the door. We stood there, tight.

I studied his pulled-back, curly hair and green eyes as he stood over me in his rumpled chef's coat. His eyes were on fire from adrenaline. The cockiness from his confidence radiated off him.

Kate was right.

I diverted my gaze to the bridge of his nose. I couldn't look him in the eye. The aura was too weird.

"Look. We've gotten off on the wrong foot, but I don't take shit on the line. It's the eye of the battle. I can't have you acting like a girl."

Offense flashed in my brain. *Like a girl …?*

He saw the confusion on my face, and his face melted into a slight smile. "Look. My friend, James Frye, is opening his new place, Dominique, tomorrow night. He came up with me at Juniper. He was my sous. Come with me. You'll find some inspiration. You need it."

Did I need inspiration? "But I studied Natsoku Shoji like you asked. I changed my menu."

"Fiona. You need to learn my vocabulary. You need to understand my vision."

The nine-pans were getting slippery in my hands from condensation. I was sure Rose was freaking out and in the weeds.

"I'd love to come. It'd be enlightening."

He gave me a slick smile. The stress blooming in my stomach turned into something else. I was having trouble keeping up.

"Good. Get back to the line. The big wave is coming." The door slammed behind him, and I stood there, reeling.

I needed inspiration?

Hot tears sprouted from the back of my eyes. Was I acting like a girl?

The door opened again. Rose gaped at me, desperate. "Chef. Come quick. I can't figure out what Chef Auclair did. I forgot what the swirls looked like. I don't know what to do."

I grabbed another squirt bottle of raspberry reduction as she held the door for me. I shook off the moment as I made it back to the line.

Tickets were spilling all over the workspace. It was getting out of control. I quickly picked them up and hung them above the station. "Come on, Rose. We can do this." I handed her a ticket and a plate.

I gazed at the pit behind me.

Liam was commanding the show. He was striking as he put the final touches on a rack of lamb. His larger-than-life presence took up the air in the kitchen. It was impossible not to notice his elegant movements. His laser focus.

He caught my eye. Our eyes locked for a moment.

The chorus of the kitchen floated away for a long second. A slight grin passed his lips.

My head froze at the connection.

"Chef, are you okay?" Rose asked.

I snapped back into the moment.

"I don't think I can do this." She was pale beneath the sheen of sweat on her face.

"Rose. Let's go. I've got your back." I grabbed a ticket. It was the peach tart. I pushed my sleeves up, grabbed a plate, and pushed everything out of my mind.

It was time to work. It was time to be in that brain space where nothing else mattered except the opera cake. The next scoop of sorbet. The next masterpiece.

It was the only thing that would get this Chef Auclair mess out of my brain.

It was too much.

* * *

I'd forgotten about the shoot.

I should have remembered. I'd scheduled Camille and Rose to come in later in the morning. I'd even left a prep list for Rose to complete.

The service last night had left a fog on my brain. Even yoga hadn't saved me.

I walked into the bakery, and everything was rearranged.

There was a small crew of three people. The cameraman, the director, and the producer. Lights were set up around the woodwork table. They'd moved it to the middle of the room, in front of the French oven, so Julia and I could be in the best light.

The KitchenAid, various bowls, utensils, and two induction burners were ready for battle.

"Fiona, you're late. Tell me you're ready to do this." Julia's limited-edition Hedley & Bennett was bursting with color with bright summer flowers. She knew it'd pop on camera.

I smiled, confident. Right foot first. "Of course! Everything is ready to go. I just have to grab the prep and set it up."

She gave me a skeptical glare. "Do it fast. And put some blush on. You're a bit pale."

Los Angeles was the home of movie stars, but I wasn't like most women in L.A. I wasn't a fan of being in front of the camera.

I was trying not to panic.

"I know you have that party for the Director's Guild to prep for, so we'll try to make it quick." She rolled her eyes, annoyed. "If these amateurs can figure out what the hell they're doing, it won't take too long." She watched the cameraman set up his camera. She pursed her lips. "I swear, *Bon Appétit* always sends these fools who know nothing."

She turned and directed the cameraman to set his camera up closer to the table. She'd done this so many times that she knew the perfect setups.

I headed to the walk-in and grabbed my stuff. Rose's prep was stacked on the shelf. Eggs were already separated into containers of whites and yolks.

I took a pint of raspberries off the shelf and slipped a chilled mixing bowl under my arm. I stood there for a moment to catch my breath.

I could do this.

It was only a stupid video, for God's sake. But it was *Bon Appétit*. And I was going to be assisting Julia on camera.

Ellie Rand had starred as Julia's pastry chef in episodes like this one, and now she had her own Internet empire. How hard could it be?

I didn't have any blush to touch up my face, but maybe the cold from the walk-in would give me some color.

I kicked the walk-in door open, juggling everything, and went through the growing crowd of curious cooks, trying to figure out what was happening.

I checked the oven temperature. It was already preheating at three-hundred and seventy-five degrees.

The director approached me. "We'll be ready in five minutes."

I could do this ... I could do this ... It was a mantra in my head.

Julia approached the table, her eyes burning intensely as she studied everything on the table, judgmental. "We're doing the soufflé recipe I got in Marseille, right?"

"Yes. Dramatic. Easy to make. It'll be great." I tried to stand tall as I poured the ingredients into the separate bowls and discarded the containers under the table. I'd take them to dish later.

Julia studied the table. She pointed to a bowl. "Ecuadorian sixty percent, right?" Her hard gaze made me shudder.

"Of course. Just like your recipe."

"You should have already been melting it. We don't have time once we're on camera to wait."

I took a deep breath. "I'll do it now." I placed the bowl of chocolate on the bain-marie, set it up on the induction burner, and turned the water on to boil. I wished it would melt faster.

"We're ready!" she announced. She was annoyed. Put off by everyone's ignorance.

Blood rushed through my ears.

The director nodded as he focused the camera on his tripod and pointed it at us.

Liam rounded the corner. He leaned up against the wall, off to the side. He balanced his tiny espresso cup and saucer in his hands.

He smirked at me, amused.

The assistant snapped the clacker, and Julia's face triggered into a bright smile. In a flash, Julia turned into another woman.

Her eyes were kind. Motherly. Her voice tuned an octave higher and rang out in a friendly tone, like someone visiting your house on a Sunday afternoon. "Today, we're going to be making chocolate soufflé from a secret recipe I discovered back in my days in Marseille." Her face flickered with a warm smile. "This is still one of the best recipes I've ever made." She smiled at me, nurturing and kind, in full performance mode. "I have Fiona, my head pastry chef in training, to demonstrate as I guide you through this delicious and delicate dessert."

She motioned to the chocolate melting on the bain-marie.

"The first thing you'll do is melt your chocolate and whip your sugar and yolks." She peered at the camera like she was telling a secret. "Now, a thing before we start. Always use good chocolate. If you use quality chocolate, you'll get beautiful results." She stared off into the camera, remembering. "In Marseille, I was fortunate enough to have La Madison du Chocolate as my source. I remember walking through the cobbled streets as a poor student. I would sacrifice my grocery money to buy it." She shook her head. Smiling, wistful.

I poured the yolks and sugar into a mixing bowl and turned the mixer to the highest speed.

"Next, you will make a beautiful roux using butter and flour." She motioned to me.

I placed a pot with flour and butter on the burner. Were my hands shaking? It was hard to say because my eyes were blurry.

Liam's silhouette was in my peripheral.

I tried not to think of his eyes on me as I stirred the roux.

Julia was bright and animated as she spoke. "Be sure you smell a nutty aroma from the toasted flour as you stir it."

She touched my arm in a friendly way. She was seriously crossing my signals.

She grabbed the spatula, faintly frowning at my hands, and smiled at the camera as she stirred for a moment. "Don't burn it. Just stir it until it slightly thickens into a paste." She smiled, remembering. "When I was a mere cook at Vonnas, I made the roux with fine French butter from the local cows. They roamed the countryside and ate the best grass. French butter is always the best."

As quickly as she took it, she shoved the spatula back into my hands and moved to the next task.

"While you're waiting ..." Julia grabbed some butter and rubbed some into the ramekins. "Be generous with that sumptuous butter; rub it to the top of your ramekins."

Julia wiped her hands off on a towel and grabbed a bowl of sugar. "Now, with the sugar, be sure to coat your ramekins all the way around. Every time I sprinkle sugar, it brings me back to my days in Paris in winter. There's nothing like seeing the Eiffel Tower in the snow." She held the ramekin to the camera.

I glanced up, and Liam caught my gaze. His lips registered a judgmental smile. He was enjoying this.

Julia continued, her eyes flickering the energy of Yoda. "When sprinkling the sugar, think of the batter crawling delicately up the walls, using the sugar like a ladder to come to life. Like guiding a shy child out of their shell!" She turned to me. "What do we do next, Fiona?"

Now I understood what the phrase "deer in the headlights" meant. I was living it in real time as I grabbed the other mixing bowl and hooked it to the KitchenAid.

"Next is the meringue. Put the egg whites into a chilled bowl and turn the mixer on. When the eggs are frothy, slowly add your sugar," I said as my voice echoed in my ears while I sprinkled sugar into the mixing bowl.

Julia butted in. "Now, meringue is like a different kind of animal. Vibrant. Fragile. You must treat it delicately, or it will be under-whipped. Ignore it for a minute, and it's stiff and unusable." She waved her hands around like she was conjuring a spell.

The director watched the viewfinder on the camera, a pleased smile on his face.

I quickly folded the roux and the whipped egg yolks together and folded them into the chocolate for the next step.

I could get through this if I just looked busy.

I could still feel Liam's eyes burning on me. I glanced over at him. He was holding back a laugh.

"Not too fast, Fiona! Tell them what you're doing."

"Mix the chocolate with the roux and whipped egg yolks," I croaked.

She grabbed the bowl and spatula from me and showed the mixture to the camera as she stirred it, taking it into an emulsion. "Simply beautiful," she tisked.

The meringue was ready to go. I shut the mixer off and unhooked the bowl. It was beautiful. Fluffy and light. Julia grabbed it from me.

"And speaking of beautiful, look at this meringue!" She lifted the whip attachment from the bowl. A perfect flourish of meringue saluted from the top.

A ghost of a frown crossed her face. "Thank you, Fiona." She grabbed the bowl with the chocolate. "Now, always mix in your meringue in thirds into the batter; otherwise, you'll overwhelm your batter, and it will wilt. Fold, don't mix, your beautiful meringue into the chocolate." She stared at the camera, making eye contact with all the home chefs. "If you stir it, you'll deflate all the air pockets." With slow, dramatic movements, her elbows extended for maximum effect for the camera as she folded the meringue in with the chocolate mixture.

She held the bowl up to the camera. "See how beautiful that is? It's perfect. Now you're ready to scoop your batter into your ramekins. Fiona, show them how it's done."

I grabbed the bowl and a yellow scoop and quickly scooped the batter.

Had Ellie Rand felt this way?

Julia set the ramekins on a half sheet and adjusted them. They were perfectly spaced on the tray. "Next, take your creation and bake them at three-seventy-five. Once you put them in, never open the oven. Trust them to grow up on their own!"

"Cut!" the director said.

I exhaled. I could breathe again. Thank God we were done.

Julia's demeanor changed from kind to exasperated as she rounded the table. "Let's do the close-ups. Your angle was all wrong."

Julia turned to me. "Get the table prepped again. Your hands were shaking like crazy. Figure it out."

She walked towards the director, annoyed. She started bossing him around as he set up for the next shot.

I caught his eye. He looked stressed and beleaguered.

She turned around, drilling me. "And what were you thinking? Your meringue was too stiff. Don't whip it so long next time. It was grainy. I wanted to yell cut. We almost couldn't use it."

I blushed. That was an amateur mistake. It was inexcusable.

I glanced at Liam. His smile whispered condescending mockery.

I wished it was over. Being in the spotlight wasn't something that I was liking very much. I didn't like it at all.

* * *

I pulled up to the valet in front of Dominique. I tried to find parking, but everything in the neighborhood was permit parking only.

Parking was always a problem in L.A., and I was always paying parking tickets. Old offenses littered the top of my dashboard.

The valet took one look at me and frowned as I got out and handed him the keys. He wasn't impressed by the Land Cruiser. I held my head high as he gave me a ticket, refusing to let him car-shame me.

I took a deep breath. I felt like an imposter in the black dress and dusty black heels I'd found in the back of my closet. For some ungodly reason, Charlotte had given them to me for Christmas last year. She'd wanted a proper girls' night out, but we'd never actually made it happen.

I'd cleaned the dust off the shoes and suddenly I was like Cinderella when I'd slipped them on.

Dominique was beautiful and understated. Distressed wood and glass came together with white tablecloths and votive candles to create an inviting, romantic place. Small and intimate.

It was expensive and important.

The energy in the room was thick with attractive people—the who's who of cheferdom in L.A. I saw Jose Wrangle from Amour mingling with Jane Macron from Pino. The room was hot with all these talents in one room.

Food bloggers and photographers were carousing and archiving the evening for their blogs and Instagram feeds.

Sammy waved to me from across the room. "Girl, look at you!" Sammy sized me up, smiling. "You look amazing. Did you just get here?" His eyes darted across the room. "I just saw Dane from Icon. He has the biceps of a longshoreman."

I stifled back a laugh.

Sammy was always ogling the delivery guys and vendors. He even shamelessly flirted with the health inspector. I was pretty sure Sammy was the reason we always got a perfect score. "James's a lucky man." He waved his hands around like he was hot. "His girlfriend is that actress in that series. Shit, what's the name of it?"

She was standing across the room. Her honey-blonde hair was blown out, and her eyelashes were long and perfect. She was tall and tiny in a burgundy designer number, hanging out with a crowd of gorgeous men and women who were recognizable as A-list.

"I don't have time to watch TV, Sammy."

I glanced around the important room, overwhelmed. "What's James like?"

"I don't know. I haven't seen him yet," Sammy said as his eyes cruised the crowd.

I'd done my research on James. After graduating from the CIA, he'd made his bones in various high-class establishments.

He'd traveled around Italy and Portugal before landing at Barrique in Spain.

Then he made the pilgrimage to Juniper and then Chase in New York. And now he was here. Staking out L.A.

From the crowd, it was evident that the scene had adopted him immediately. He was an instant rock star.

"Look over there," Sammy said. "It's Marci Strand"

I turned to see what Sammy was talking about.

Sure enough. I couldn't believe it.

It was Marci Strand.

Her stylish, horn-rimmed glasses accentuated her perfectly coiffed bob. Even though she was dressed in a conservative dark pantsuit, the raucous energy of the room was trained on her. She held the energy of the room in her palm.

Was I really in the same room as my hero? What would my father be thinking now?

I watched her as she disappeared into a crowd of chefs. I couldn't believe my luck. I was finally in the same room as Marci Strand. *The* Marci Strand.

This was crazy. Terror coursed through me. I was in an important room with important people. The heavy hitters of the restaurant scene.

My eyes cruised the room for a server. I needed a drink.

"What do you think of Liam so far?" Sammy drilled me with his stare.

I repressed a shudder, thinking of the disaster of service and his smug judgment from the *Bon Appétit* shoot. "I'm trying to keep an open mind."

He shook his head, concerned. "He's destroying everything Julia stands for. I can't believe she's buying into his narrative. I'm really worried."

I grabbed a glass of Chardonnay from a passing tray, "Maybe it'll be fine once things settle down."

"I don't know. Julia's under Liam's spell. It makes me really nervous."

"Sammy. Relax. I know everything is difficult now but give it time. It'll be okay."

"I don't know, Fiona. This isn't like before."

"Sammy, you always say that, and it always works out," I said, and I sipped my wine.

I took a deep breath, pushing the negative thoughts out of my mind. I had to keep up a cheerful face. Dwelling on the fact that I could be sacked at any moment was not very comforting. I pushed it out of my mind.

Sammy spotted a server with a tray of small plates surfing the room. "I guess I better try this guy's food." He shook his head and flourished his hands. "Maybe it'll be a transcendental experience."

He waved to me as he made his way through the crowd.

"Fiona?" Someone touched my arm. I turned.

It was Rory.

Rory!?

He was handsome in a simple dark blazer, blue shirt, and jeans. His shirt highlighted his striking blue eyes. His short hair was loose and relaxed.

My startled smile lingered with his for a moment. "You're beautiful tonight. I almost didn't recognize you."

A blush blossomed from the bottom of my toes. "What are you doing here?"

"My mother grows all James's produce. I'm one of his wine suppliers." He nodded to my glass. "How do you like the Chardonnay?"

I took another sip. It was sweet. Dry. Delicious. "It's amazing."

"I'm supplying James with a few of my varieties. It will be nice to be featured on his wine list."

I struggled for something to say. That familiar giddiness washed over me again.

"You were right about the Arctic Rose. The Pavlova I made with them was so delicious ... So sweet and ..." I couldn't think of the right word under his stare.

"That's good to hear. I'll save some for you the next time you're at the market." He grinned. His eyes sparkled despite the dimness of the room.

A distracted blogger getting the perfect Instagram shot shoved into him. He bumped into me.

He was so close that my nose caught a hint of how good he smelled—a clean aftershave that flirted with my nose. My heart fluttered.

He smiled at me. It was the same smile he'd given me at the market. The crinkles around his eyes betrayed his happy nature. "Are we still on for tomorrow night?"

"Of course. I can't wait," I said.

"Neither can I." The din of the room quieted around me. He was the only thing of clarity. We held the moment for a beat. My heart skipped a beat as I gazed into his eyes.

"Rory!" Liam grabbed him from behind by the shoulders and gave him a bro hug. "I tried your new Pinot. It's out of this world. Give me a call, and we can discuss updating Lucien's wine list. It needs a lot of help." Liam smiled at me. "And you already know Fiona."

Liam wore a leather motorcycle jacket and dark pants. His long hair was slicked back away from his face, making his features sharp. It complemented his long nose and green eyes.

I couldn't help but compare them.

Rory was relaxed.

Liam was hyped and dangerous.

Yin and Yang.

"When are you dropping the Chenin Blanc?"

"We're still on track. I'll let you know when I'm happy with it. I'll send it to you first."

I was getting a weird buzz in my head. I took a sip of my wine, trying to refocus. I watched their faces as they spoke. Liam was animated. His arms were waving in the air, punctuating what he said. Rory stood back, nodding along.

"Fiona …?" Liam scrutinized me. I broke from my trance. "What do you think?"

I came back to earth. "I'm sorry. What did you say?"

Liam laughed. "I was telling you how Rory has one of the best wineries on the West Coast. You have to try his Shiraz. It'll be the best you've ever had."

"You'll like the vintage from 2018. I'll send you some. I'm pretty happy with it. It's crisp and a little fruitier. It's much better than the 2017.

Liam nudged me. My stomach tightened.

"I hope you don't mind, but I need to show Fiona something."

Liam shook Rory's hand. I could see that he was doing that same dominance thing he did with me. Rory went with it, not minding.

It made me like him even more.

Rory smiled at me. "It was good to see you, Fiona. I'll see you tomorrow night. I'll bring you some of those peaches."

I blushed again. Tomorrow couldn't come fast enough.

He disappeared into the crowd as Liam pulled me forward. It was hard to keep up in my shoes. "You're different as a civilian," Liam called over his shoulder. "Very nice."

"Thank you." I ditched my empty wine glass on a table and grabbed a fresh one from a roaming tray.

The taste of Rory's Chardonnay fortified me. The flavor of apples and grapes soothed my palate. It gave me strength somehow as we made it through the crowd to the kitchen.

My breath caught in my throat as I took in James's kitchen.

There were no words.

The kitchen was glorious.

The shiny stoves gleamed. The brick oven crackled, hot and bright, with the aroma of oak and cherry wood. Stainless steel refrigerators and freezers stood at attention. I could only imagine what was inside.

It was the kitchen of a winner.

Chef James Frye put down his saucepan and finished garnishing another small plate for the party.

He was tall, blond, and lean. He looked like he played lacrosse between running a restaurant and canoodling with his skinny, famous girlfriend.

"Fiona, I'd like you to meet James."

He sized me up and gave me a knowing smile. "You're the one," he chuckled with indifference.

An awkward wave of embarrassment washed over me. "Nice to meet you."

He continued working, ignoring me.

Liam glanced around. "Where are your desserts?"

James pointed to the expediting station. "They're on the counter in the back. We haven't started serving them yet."

"I'm going to show Fiona how it's done."

Confusion zipped up my spine. What was that supposed to mean?

He grabbed some plates from the counter and balanced them in his arms. "Come with me."

I followed him to an empty table. He pulled out a chair for me, set the plates down, and grabbed two clean forks from the middle of the table. He handed one to me. "Now this, this is what I'm talking about."

I studied each plate. They were vibrant and elegant. Effortless. Lines of reductions and chocolate sauces swirled around unique desserts that were practiced and modern.

"Now this is how it could be." He smiled, taking a forkful of the first dessert.

It was a short, square glass filled with layers of silky mousse, brandied caramel, and whipped crème fraiche.

I took a bite. I could taste the hint of tarragon with lavender. Or was that chervil? The flavors were challenging. I didn't know what to think.

Was this considered a dessert?

"I want you to start thinking outside the box. Like James. He's always thinking of new things."

"James did this?" I was surprised.

"He comes up with everything. He doesn't need a pastry chef."

Was he trying to tell me something?

He dug his fork into the next dessert. "Try this one."

I pushed my fork into the next dessert. It was a cherry and rose deconstructed panna cotta dressed in a flourish of burnt sugar, raspberry reduction, and a flag of candied peach. It was effortless and elegant on the plate.

"This is an example of how far we can go." He took another bite of the panna cotta, smiling, almost blissful. "I need you to challenge yourself. To explore. I want you to keep someone on the edge of their chair. Right now, your desserts play too much on the nostalgic side." A fierce light glinted in his eyes.

"I'm not here to make someone feel good. I want to make people wake up. To question. Make them uncomfortable." He put his fork down. "Sentimentality won't make it with me."

The silence hung heavily between us briefly as I held his gaze.

"You know I'm not an amateur, right?"

His face flashed in surprise. He stood strong. "You could be better." He dove into the next dessert. "Try this." He held a fork at me.

I didn't take it.

I left it hanging, overwhelmed. I was done. I stood up to leave. "I'll think about this. I'll come up with something else."

His smile melted into a serious frown, and his eyes turned cold. "Fiona. Be a good sport. This is a good opportunity for you. I can do things for you if you go with the flow of change."

"Chef Auclair!" Candice Jacobson broke our moment as she came over and kissed him on the cheek.

She was tall and lithe, with a thousand-watt personality. Her dark hair was pulled into an elegant pile on her head, complementing her delicate features. Her perfect makeup accentuated how stunning she was.

She was otherworldly.

Her blog on international fine dining was one of the top five food blogs in the world. Somehow, she'd managed to stay in the white-hot center of what was happening. She was a heavy influencer who made and broke restaurants with a single sentence.

I was a bit starstruck.

"I want to talk to you about Lucien. I hear you're saving a dumpster fire!" She shouldered her way in front of me.

Liam turned to her, ignoring me. We were done.

I stepped back into the crowd. What the hell had just happened? His whole demeanor was so offensive.

I checked myself. I was playing a dangerous game. If I wanted to do something important, I'd have to clear my mind and open myself up to new things. I'd have to follow Liam's lead. But how was I going to do that?

Was Marci Strand still here? I could go up and ask her the secret to winning. The secret to being a top chef. Would she give away any secrets?

Or maybe Rory was still here. We could talk about peaches. That'd make me feel better. My eyes cruised the thick crowd of important people, searching for him.

He was gone. The crowd was lit up into a higher gear of celebration. The chemistry of food and arrogance mingled in the air in a toxic mix.

I grabbed my keys out of my bag, along with my valet ticket. I wanted to go home and take my shoes off. They were pinching my little toes.

The ball was over. My carriage was waiting for me outside. I couldn't wait to slip behind the wheel of the Land Cruiser and escape from this place. I'd had enough for one night.

Liam had made me feel small. Stupid. Confused—just a trainwreck cook with sentimental pastry.

A nobody.

5

The only thing that'd gotten me through the day was my thoughts of tonight.

My first date with Rory.

I hoped I wasn't too punk rock. I wore my skinny black jeans, a fitted Wolf Alice tee, and a thin floral scarf tied around my neck. The feminine scarf balanced out my beat-up Doc Martens.

Wolf Alice was my favorite band. Ellie Rowsell's quiet ferocity moved me.

I shook my hair out, so my long bob grazed my jawbone and smudged my smoky eye slightly more. It'd been a while since I'd worn makeup. I was an alien to myself as I peered at my reflection.

This was it. Would Rory like me? Or would he run?

We'd definitely find out.

I smiled to myself, a bit proud. I'd had the audacity to ask Rory out. I'd taken the aggressive role. I'd overcome my stupid insecurities and been brave.

It was scary to face the unknown. But here I was ... *Do or die ...*

I grabbed my jacket and opened my bedroom door.

The room was in full pre-show chaos mode. The boys were taking apart the drum kit and gathering all their equipment.

Kate ran over to me. "How do I look? I don't look too crazy, right?"

She wore skin-tight pink jeans and a tee-shirt emblazoned with "BANG" across her chest. Her hair was pulled into a tight ponytail, spilling down her shoulders. Her red lipstick was crafted perfectly on her lips.

"You look amazing," I said.

"Should I wear the heels, or do you think tennis shoes will be okay?"

"You won't do very well with pumps in the pit. I think you should go with the slip-ons."

"You're right." She searched around for her black Vans.

"Fiona?" Rory's head peeked through the open door.

My heart stopped.

He was handsome in a dark leather coat, faded jeans, and a black T-shirt. He was carrying a fancy paper bag.

Harvey growled as he bulled past him with the bass drum. Rory danced to get out of the way.

I rolled my eyes. "I'm sorry. I'm still trying to figure out if he speaks."

Luna greeted Rory and started his familiar butt wag. Rory bent down and scratched his ears and smiled at me. "It's good to see you."

We stood there for an awkward moment. It was thrilling and terrifying all at once.

Kate broke the silence. "Who's this!?" She extended her hand, excited. I was a little betrayed by her enthusiasm.

He shook her hand. "Rory, nice to meet you."

"I'm Kate. I'm Fiona's best friend." She leaned in and gave him an air kiss on the cheek. She pulled back, giving me her naughtiest grin. I was going to kill her later.

I elbowed her. "When's soundcheck?" I wanted her out of there before she could embarrass me anymore.

"It's in half an hour. I'm late. We gotta roll." Kate slung her guitar bag over her shoulder as Harvey hefted her amp in his arms and carried it downstairs.

"Come see me backstage. The booker said that we sold out. It's gonna get crazy." She adjusted her guitar on her shoulder. "I hope that manager guy shows up. It could change everything. Keep your fingers crossed."

She winked at Rory, flirting. "It was so nice to meet you. Have fun kiddos." She blew me a kiss as she walked out.

Now I really was going to kill her.

I shut the door behind her and locked it, leaning against it. It was finally quiet.

"Finally. Thank God they're gone."

Luna turned three circles and lay down on his bed.

Rory glanced around. "I love your place. It's not what I expected."

"It's Kate's doing. She's the consummate artist. I'm not here enough to decorate."

He set his paper bag on the counter and pulled out some jam and a tall, slender bottle of wine. Its sides were sweaty from the trip.

"My mom wanted me to give this to you. It's the spicy tomato chutney." He smiled. "Do you have a bottle opener?"

"Here, let me grab one for you." I slid beside him in the kitchen, pulled the junk drawer open, and fished the opener out.

I reached around him and grabbed two wine glasses from the cupboard. They were elegant as he poured a small amount of wine into the glass.

"I hope you like Riesling. I'm trying to decide if this one is ready."

My eyes met his, and he held my gaze. The intimacy of our closeness felt daring.

I took my glass as he took his. He swirled it around, smelling it. "I tried to capture the hints of apple and apricot." He grinned, tempting me. "Try it."

I held the glass to my nose. It smelled incredible. The best orchard fruits mingling in the same glass.

I took a sip.

Even though it was a bit warm from the trip, it still tasted amazing. Refreshing. It was the perfect balance of acidic and sweet.

"What do you think?"

"It's perfect," I marveled. "It's better than the Chardonnay."

"I wanted to capture the taste of summer. The smell of the apricots as you walk through the orchard in early August. It's such a specific smell ..."

"Well, congratulations. You pulled it off," I said as I took another sip.

He thought for a moment. "That's what's so satisfying about making wine: catching the essence of a place and time. The perfect moment of a ripe apricot. The perfect moment of ripened grapes that are ready to pick. That's my challenge. To capture the beauty of the bounty that I'm so lucky to be surrounded with. Nature has been so gracious to me."

He took another sip of his wine, laughing. "I bet you think I sound like a nut. I think I get a little too excited sometimes ..."

I smiled at him. "I completely understand. I try to celebrate the taste of a specific type of chocolate. Highlight the flavors of fruit at their peak of perfection ... It's so satisfying when things come together ... It's something that you can't explain ..."

"Exactly." He smiled in understanding.

I took another sip of wine. A part of my brain searched for the sketch of the moment he was trying to convey. A ghost of summer orchards and warm sunshine. The snapshot of a specific place and time.

I sensed it.

I took his hand and guided him to the window. "Come with me."

"Where are we going?" He smiled, intrigued.

I opened the tall paned window by the kitchen and handed him my glass. "Trust me." I crawled through the tall window and grabbed both glasses from his hands.

He followed through the window and took a deep breath as he stood. I handed him back his glass.

The night was breathtaking. The air was cool and still. The lights of the buildings around us were bright.

"This is amazing." He turned around, taking in the view.

Kate and I had a makeshift deck on the roof of the unit next door. Tall buildings hugged the space around. Random office lights illuminated the night. The sounds of the street echoed from below.

"I like to sit here after work. It's a good place to think." I stood on the edge of the roof, finding the best part of the view. The city lights were putting on a show just for us.

He stood next to me. I could tell he was impressed. "I can see why."

We both took another sip as our eyes connected.

I caught his smile in the dim light. "You're beautiful," he said, quietly, almost imperceptibly.

The silence went to my head as my body drifted closer to him. A force I couldn't understand took over me.

I balanced my wine glass as he pulled me in. I lifted my chin and he kissed me. My head tilted up as he moved in close.

His kiss was crisp and sweet. Gentle. Like the Riesling. His chemistry mingled somehow with the apples and apricots.

He finished the kiss with a gentle flourish and smiled.

The view, the wine, and the kiss were going to my head. I was giddy with the sounds of the city. That familiar pocket of losing space and time overcame me.

My phone buzzed in my pocket.

The amazing moment was broken.

Damn, my stupid phone. "Hold on."

I broke from his embrace and pulled it out of my pocket. *Help! Bring the pumps. I think I've changed my mind*, Kate texted.

"I guess we should go," I said. "Kate's in the middle of a wardrobe emergency."

"Let's go then. Whatever you need to do, I'm here for you."

I juggled my glass as I pulled him back through the window. "Watch your step." I felt the friction of his skin as he followed behind. I loved the warmth of his hand.

The connection made me happy as I uprighted myself back in the kitchen.

We stood a beat, facing each other. It was foreign to be so lit up from the inside.

"Let me grab Kate's shoes, and we'll be off," I said.

I wandered into her room and found the shoes thrown on her bed. I scooped them up. My eye caught my reflection in her mirror.

My cheeks were rosy and flushed. My eyes were bright. I hadn't seen myself like this in such a long time.

My vibe hadn't scared him off. He was open. He was genuine. He was kind.

Where was the night going to take us?

* * *

The Uber pulled up to the sidewalk on an anonymous city street. Rory looked at me, confused. "Where are we going?" he asked as we stepped out.

"Follow me." I grabbed his hand and pulled him down the dark street, past a chain link fence.

The Smell was a small venue in the middle of downtown. The entrance was in a dark alley. It'd be easy to miss if you drove past. The only hint of its existence was the crowd waiting for the show.

I nodded to a friend of Kate's as we made our way through the bodies. I paid the guy at the front door, and we headed inside.

It was a typical punk venue. Arty graffiti covered the walls, and a dark room with a stage hung in the back. People were already gathering by the stage in anticipation of the show.

It was weird to see the drum kit, usually a fixture in my living room, set up onstage, with techs micing it up. Kate's guitar and Harvey's bass were on stands in front of their amps. Ready to go.

Kate was bent down, trying to figure out what cords went with what. She was deep in her own world.

"I'm going to give Kate her shoes. I'll be right back," I said.

"I'll get us something to drink. What would you like?" he asked.

"Surprise me," I smiled.

I made my way to the stage. Kate smiled, seeing me. "You made it!" She made her way down the steps on the side of the stage. I slipped her the shoes.

She pushed the bag back into my hands. "Thanks. I think I'm going to stick with the tennis shoes."

"Oh my God, Kate. You're driving me crazy," I said. I slipped her shoes back into my bag.

"Wow, Fiona. I'm impressed by your friend. He's so delicious. It's been a while since you've been on a date."

"Delicious?" I balked, eyebrows raised.

"Well, I was trying to be like you and Charlotte. I was trying to use a food word."

She smiled. She had a devilish glint in her eye.

"Kate?" An older man wearing an expensive motorcycle jacket came up from behind us. He was like so many older men in Los Angeles. There was an anonymous age behind his slight tan and good life. He extended his hand. "I'm George. You're busy. I just wanted to let you know I'm looking forward to your show."

Kate smiled a ten-thousand-watt smile at him and shoved her hand past me to shake his hand. "I'm glad you came."

"I brought a few of my colleagues. We're all excited to see you," he said. "I'll leave you to your conversation. I just wanted to say hi." He nodded and disappeared back into the crowd.

"Holy shit. It's him." She growled.

"The manager?" I asked.

"Now I'm nervous." Her smile was gone. Terror flashed across her face.

"Just get your game face on. Forget about it. You've survived way worse," I said. "You look great. You sound great. It's going to work out."

She glanced over her shoulder back to the stage. "Maybe I should wear the pumps."

"Stop with the shoes. You have more important things to think about." I gave her a reassuring squeeze. "Just go kill it like you always do."

"Okay. Try to keep your eye on him. Let me know how he reacts."

"I'll try. Just go."

She took a deep breath. "I got this." The fear in her eyes made me think otherwise as she returned to the stage.

I turned and saw Rory through the crowd. He smiled at me.

He handed me a beer in a plastic cup. "I hope this is okay. It looked like the safest bet."

"This is perfect," I said as I took a sip.

Rory studied the crowd. He raised his voice for emphasis. "You have quite a life, Fiona."

"What do you mean?"

"All of this. Your job. Your friends. You're living the dream."

My eyes met his. The sounds of the people around us melted away for a beat.

Someone bumped into me, almost knocking me off my feet, breaking the moment. I grabbed onto Rory's arm, steadying myself.

"Are you okay?" He laughed.

"I'm fine. Do you mind going up front?" I yelled over the noise of the crowd. "I'm warning you. It might get a little crazy up there."

His eyes cruised the room. "I'm game for anything. Show me the way."

I led him through the tight crowd, pressing against the front of the stage. My body squeezed into his as we were jostled through the crush.

Usually, I was a little nervous about being in front. People stage-dived and pushed forward like sardines. A crazy mosh pit would ignite in the center that was friendly but a little fierce. I'd been swallowed into them a time or two and barely survived.

I glanced at Rory, sizing him up. He stood strong in the center of the crowd. I knew I'd be protected.

This would be fun.

Kate prowled onto the stage and grabbed her guitar. The boys followed, taking their positions.

The crowd pushed forward and started cheering like crazy.

She leaned down and propped her foot aggressively on the monitor. She was barefoot. She'd ditched her shoes altogether.

"Are you ready!?" she yelled into the mic, staring everyone down. The crowd screamed, waving their arms in the air.

She stared them down with a cocky grin. "We're Alizarin!"

An airplane roar sliced the air. Kate's guitar ignited the room.

The band blew up in a bass frenzy, the first riff taking off. The crowd exploded. People elbowed and raised their fists.

Kate screamed and sang as she attacked her guitar. Harvey conjured a groovy bass riff as Jake hit the drums to a heavy and deep beat.

Rory smiled at me. He was just as excited.

The mosh pit was on fire. People were desperately squirming onto the stage and diving into the crowd. Rory grabbed an errant leg, and I ducked as someone flew into our faces. We laughed together. He held an arm around me, protecting me from the crush.

My beer flew out of my hands as the crowd shoved us even tighter. I loved being pushed into him.

My head instinctively nodded to the music. Kate's ferocious energy was taking me over. It made me empowered. Bold like her. Brave. Like I could take on anything. The adrenaline coursed through my body.

I looked over at Rory.

His head was into it, too. It took me by surprise.

We both gave ourselves into the crazy moment, laughing, as the mosh pit lit up behind us. Music was a secret handshake, and he had passed the test.

It made me like him even more.

* * *

The night air was charged as we filed out into the cool evening. Rory was flushed and sweaty from the show.

Street vendors on the side of the walkway were roasting bacon-wrapped hot dogs. The heavy, savory smell was hypnotizing.

I stopped and pushed the button on the lamp post for the walk sign. "What did you think?" I held my breath, expectantly.

"I think my heart is going to explode. That's the most intense show I've ever been to." He grinned. "Your friend is quite a character."

I rolled my eyes. "That's an understatement." The light turned green, and we crossed the street.

"Where are you taking me?" he asked.

I guided him by the hand down the sidewalk. "Somewhere special."

Our feet settled on a rhythm together, our pace matching. The rhythm of his steps grounded me. Peaceful calm washed over me.

"How do you like living downtown?" he asked.

"Despite taking my life into my own hands when I walk down the street at night, I love it. There are lots of good places to eat, and the mix of cultures makes things interesting."

"I can see what you mean."

I turned the corner and stopped at a tiny restaurant with a red awning. The sweet smell of coconut milk and curry filled the air.

"Here we are."

We walked in, and I led him to a front table on the candle-lit patio where we could people-watch. He pulled out a chair for me, and we sat down. It was quiet and romantic, just as I'd hoped. It was the best table in the house.

"Do you like Thai food?"

"It's okay. It's been a while since I've had it." He smiled.

"You'll love this. It's the best Thai in L.A."

Thai food was my favorite. The sweet and spicy flavors took me to a special place.

"Fiona!" Apsara, the owner, called over. She was always friendly and sweet. She set down a sweaty carafe of water and two glasses on the table.

She glanced at Rory. I tried to ignore her knowing smile. "How are you?"

"Very good. It's been quiet tonight. Do you want the usual?

"Of course. And I'd like to add another order of shrimp and fresh summer rolls."

She nodded and disappeared into the dark.

I studied Rory. The adrenaline had settled, and we were just together. Sitting in a peaceful moment. I couldn't tell if my endorphin rush was from the show or being around him.

"You must come here a lot." He smiled.

"I like to come here with my friends. It's one of our places."

"What's it like hanging out with rock stars?"

I laughed. "It's not that glamorous. Trust me. That old cliché of being broke and a musician is pretty much true. She's always trying to piece the rent together."

Aspera set two Singha beers and glasses on the table and disappeared.

I returned my gaze to Rory. "My other friend Charlotte runs a food truck." I shook my head. "She's trying to get me to open a restaurant with her."

"Wow, that's impressive," he said as he poured my beer into a glass and filled his own.

"She's crazy. She's always getting grand ideas. She's tried pop-ups, booths at farmers' markets, everything. Her current great idea was to buy a food truck. She thought she could fit a French twelve-course tasting menu onto four wheels. She's a bit ambitious."

He studied me a moment, thinking. "Isn't it what every chef dreams? The grueling work and long hours, all for the glory of owning your own place?"

"I want to someday, but I have the opportunity to become chef at Lucien. I have to make a name for myself with Julia first. It's the only way."

He smiled. "So, how did this all begin? Where does this obsession that you have come from?"

"It was a dark and stormy night …" I laughed.

He joined in my laughter. "No, I mean, I'm so curious. It's inspiring that you're so committed to the dream."

I thought for a moment. "My dad has a lot to do with it. Food has been the glue that has kept us together. He owns a catering company in Venice. It was the backdrop to my childhood. I grew up in the kitchen.

I paused a beat. "My mother died when I was four, so in hindsight, I think the work was the only thing that kept him together. I can't imagine going through what he did. It must have been tough …"

"How did your mother die?" he asked before he took a sip of beer.

"Random act of violence. She was run over by a drunk driver while she was walking down the block to the grocery store. Completely senseless. Something that didn't have to happen …"

I paused, getting my thoughts together. "It's scary how life changes on a dime. One minute everything is fine, and the next …" I trailed off.

Rory gave me an understanding smile. "I know exactly what you mean. One minute, you think you have everything together, and then everything changes. You realize that nothing is safe. It's all an illusion. You can't take anything for granted."

I felt appreciative that he could understand. "Sorry to get so dark. I didn't mean to go down that rabbit hole."

"No. It's okay. I asked. And I'm interested. I want to know more about you."

"Well … I'm not really that deep … Work is the most important thing to me. It's my whole life. I wake up. Go to work. Come home. Sleep. Wash, rinse, repeat. And I'm really happy with my life. As much as I'm a freaked-out mess with this Julia and Liam situation, it's the opportunity I've been dreaming of."

I searched for the right thing to say. "If I'm lucky, I might be able to pull this thing off."

I thought for a moment. "My father has this phrase, 'Work hard … stay positive… make it happen …' I'm just trying to live by that code."

"That's a pretty good code to live by." He smiled. "If your heart is in tune with the universe … If you know what you want … that code sort of falls into place. It's a good way of thinking about it."

"Well, I'm trying. It's a work in progress." I smiled.

"How's it working out for you? Is Liam as complicated as they say?"

I studied him for a moment and then sighed.

"It's been a little rough. We don't really see eye to eye," I said. "I thought when Julia promoted me that I'd finally be able to bring my vision to life. So far, Liam's rejected my whole approach."

Rory laughed. "Be good to yourself. He's notorious for being impossible."

"There's a difference between being entertained by tall tales and actually living it."

"Maybe there's a way to meet him halfway. Celebrate your vision and, at the same time, reflect what he wants."

"I don't even know … Liam wants weird things … I'm down for exploring, but he's trying to twist the conventions of dessert … It seems like it's for no other reason than to be different …"

I thought of the strange dessert that James had made. "Liam's on another plane than me altogether. Who puts chervil in pastry cream anyway? That's just strange."

"Is Julia being supportive?" he asked before he took another sip of beer.

"Yes …? No …? I'm trying to figure that out. I think she's waiting for Liam's acceptance before she supports me," I said.

Rory gazed at me. "At the end of the day, food is about the language. It's about the beauty of sweetness. The surprise of tartness. The stability of savory."

A flirtatious grin crossed his face. "Sometimes, it's about the simplicity of a peach."

The familiar blush rose as I gathered my thoughts.

"Anyway, I'm just trying to figure out what language Liam speaks. It's certainly not mine."

"Well, you just started. Give yourself time. There has to be a way of giving them what they want and preserving what you want to say. Think of it as a sonnet. They're giving you the structure. You just have to paint the colors within the boundaries."

His gaze relaxed me. The light of the volitive candle on the table accentuated how handsome he was.

"That's a beautiful way of seeing it. I wasn't thinking about it like that."

His smile deepened as he leaned forward. "Trust yourself. Trust your voice. At the end of the day, you have your heart. Don't lose it."

He touched my hand, tracing my fingers with his thumb. There was confidence in his vulnerability. A gentle peace.

"Here you are, Fiona. I included the extras. They're on the house." Apsara broke the moment. She set the curries and rice down with the pork satay and fried shrimp rolls. She winked at me as she left.

I picked up one of the shrimp rolls, dipped it, and held it up to him. "Try this."

He took it from me and took a bite, not breaking our gaze. He dipped it again and held it to me. "I hope you don't mind double-dipping."

My lips touched his fingers as I took a bite.

It was the best shrimp roll I'd ever had. The shrimp burst in my mouth, mingling with the salty, deep-fried crust and tangy sauce.

"What do we have here?" He directed his gaze from me to the feast in front of us.

"This is Kor Moo Yang. It's Thai-style barbecue." I pointed to a plate. "This is the Panang curry. It has braised beef, pepper, and coconut milk. It's very spicy. And of course, satay. Pork satay is the best."

He dug into the jasmine rice with his chopsticks, spooned the curry on top, and took a bite of the Koa Moo Yangtook.

"This is incredible. There are so many different flavors. The way the spicy mingles with the sweet—the basil and cilantro highlight all the flavors. And you can really taste the coconut milk and ginger, too. It's amazing."

I took a bite of my red curry, watching him eat. The spiciness of the curry brought tears to my eyes. It was an exercise of pleasure and pain with every bite.

"Are you okay?" he asked.

"I've never been better," I said as I took another bite.

6

harlotte was late.

 I stood by the entrance of the vacant space, pacing to keep warm. It was a cold, grey L.A. morning. L.A. gloom.

Days like this always pushed on my soul and made me sad. Days like this made me depressed.

But this morning, my heart was singing. I was alive.

The way Rory had kissed me on the doorstep had transported me. I'd had crushes and mild attraction toward people before, but this was different.

This was a hard-wired, intense, full-bodied experience. I was anchored and elated.

Present.

I glanced at myself in the reflection of the dusty glass. My ratty yoga clothes made me a bit embarrassed. I tried to hide the hole in the knee, but it was bigger than I could conceal. I really needed to get some new pants. At least my Talking Heads T-shirt was impenetrable. I'd had the darn thing for ten years, and it still held strong.

I took a deep breath. What the hell was I even doing here?

It was like that Talking Heads song ... "What is that beautiful house ...? What is that beautiful wife ...?" Was that how it went? The perfect lyric to follow would be, "What is that beautiful restaurant...?" or, "How did I get here?" was more like it ...

My eyes rested on the warped "For Rent" sign. Why had I taken Charlotte up on this stupid endeavor?

Owning my own place? It was crazy.

"Sorry. Traffic sucked." Charlotte hugged me. Her eyes were bright with excitement. "Larry's coming in a minute."

I gave her a hard stare. "Seriously, I don't want you to get excited. For the record, I'm not on board with this crazy idea. I don't even know why I'm here."

"I guarantee you'll change your mind when you see it."

"Good morning, girls!" Larry strode down the sidewalk. He had a long wool overcoat that hadn't been washed in years. He could be mistaken to be homeless if it wasn't for his perfectly crafted, pomaded hair and sharp shoes. He shook our hands, warm and firm.

"Let's take a look, ladies." He unlocked the door, and we walked in.

"Look around. Tell me what you think," Charlotte said.

I stepped forward. The stale air hung heavy in the shadows. The wood floors were rough and charming. Under the dust, white walls had a lot of potential. There were tables and chairs stacked in a corner.

I went to the kitchen and held my breath as I walked in.

A generous beat-up wood table covered a nice series of low-boy refrigerators. An old and punished six-burner stove was pulled away from the wall. An old Blodgett oven stood against the wall. It was tired and ready for retirement. I wondered if it even worked.

Charlotte linked her arm through mine. "What do you think?" she asked. "Larry says we can use everything. He bought all the equipment from the last tenants. I guess they needed money, and he felt bad for them."

I took a deep breath. My stomach mixed with my brain in a strange, terrible mix of fear and panic.

"Charlotte. First off. You're crazy. Second, where the hell would I even get the money? I have no idea how much it would cost, and I know nothing about how to make a business plan, let alone run a business. This is out of my wheelhouse."

"We could get a loan. You could borrow money from your dad. I'd even put my ego aside and go to my parents'. We could make it happen."

I glanced around the kitchen. The stove, the refrigerators, and worktables. The oven.

Deep in my heart, a ghost of longing crept up inside of me.

Rory's words whispered to me. Wasn't this what it was all about? The hard work, the taking shit from others, the long hours.

What was it for?

A metallic taste sprung in my mouth.

Charlotte wandered around the kitchen, opening doors and inspecting the dry storage area. She was mentally moving in.

She turned and squared up with me. Serious.

"Something like this doesn't come along every day. You either take it or look back on it and kick yourself for the rest of your life. I don't want to be one of those old ladies who cry over lost chances. I want to be the one who seized the day."

I let the silence take over a beat. I didn't want to disappoint her.

"Look, Fiona, I know you have doubts. Trust me. We'll get the money somehow. I'll show you how to do a business plan. That's easy. Building the menu will be easy, too. The hard part is just saying yes."

I studied the space.

This is how I broke my arm with Kate when I was seventeen. She'd dared me to ride my skateboard down the steps at the Santa Monica Courthouse. I broke my dominant arm and couldn't help my dad for six weeks. It'd been a terrible, itchy experience.

This wasn't an arm.

An arm could heal. It had healed.

This was different.

This was an ego crusher if we failed. It would be a mark on my soul forever if it didn't work out.

A force in my brain, bigger than I could understand, was blocking me, holding me back. "There's just no way."

Charlotte deflated. All her manic energy disappeared. Anger flashed in her eyes. "You'll regret it. I know you will." She turned and walked out of the kitchen.

I felt terrible. Why had I even come here?

I rubbed my arm. The one that had been broken. Was this a mistake? In the grand scheme of the universe, was something like this even possible?

Maybe someday. But not today. I had things to accomplish first. I had to make chef first. I had to make a name for myself.

This place reinforced just how far I had left to go.

* * *

Camille met me outside by the loading door as I drove up. She opened my car door for me, aggressively swinging it open.

"Chef is fucking crazy."

"What's going on?" I asked, dreading the answer.

"Come see for yourself."

I stepped out of the car as she waved me forward, angrily.

She burst through the back door, charging through the back hall. It was hard to keep up as she pushed through the swinging kitchen doors.

I crossed the threshold to the kitchen. I realized that I forgot to lead right foot first. And I didn't have my chef's coat on. I felt vulnerable.

"Look at this!" She led me to the pastry walk-in and opened the door.

On the floor was something huge, wrapped, and raw—thick plastic wound around something that obviously, at one point, had been alive. The sweaty white skin stuck to the plastic.

Was that a pig?

And it got worse.

All our pastry ingredients were shoved onto one side of the refrigerator. Random and sloppy.

New cambros of prepped vegetables and sauces filled the spacious side of the refrigerator. Our once organized ingredients of pastry creams, cake batter, eggs, and French butter were thrown on the small shelves, without any respect for order.

I could smell the earthy tones of herbs and dead flesh. "Take care of this. I'll get to the bottom of it."

I needed to find Sammy. Quick.

I opened the savory walk-in. Leo looked up, surprised, as I poked my head in.

"Where's Sammy?"

"He doesn't work here anymore." He seemed indifferent as he sorted the potatoes.

"What?"

"Sammy doesn't work here anymore," he repeated.

What the hell?

I was slapped in the face.

Sammy gone? What the hell was Leo even talking about?

I charged back through the doors in a panic. Down the hall to the office.

Sammy couldn't be gone.

Sammy was my life raft. He was always there for me. He always had my back.

I made it to the office just as Sammy opened the back door. "Sammy? Wait!"

He turned, tool bag in hand and tears in his eyes.

"Why are you leaving?"

He winced, barely holding it together. "I don't fit the new vision. I guess I'm too old school for them."

I held his gaze, shocked. "This isn't right. This can't be! You've been here for forever."

"It is what it is." He juggled his armful of stuff, hugging me. We stood there a silent beat. He squared his eyes with mine.

"It was good working with you. I'm going to miss you."

"I'm going to miss you, too," I said.

He gave me a final hug and then pushed the door open to leave. "I'd watch your back, girl. It's not safe here."

The door closed behind him.

I stood there in the silence for a beat. What the hell just happened?

I rounded the corner to the office. Julia was on her phone, pacing in a circle, waving her arms around. She paused when she saw me. "Let me call you back."

She took a deep breath and squared herself up. "Liam wanted to make some changes. To rearrange some things." She held her head high, controlled. "I know you and Sammy were friends, and yes, he's been a help over the years, but Liam thought he was holding on too tight to the old ways. It was time for him to go."

After ten years with you, he's just gone ...? rang in my head. I didn't have the balls to say it. I was trying to process the heaviness of the betrayal. I was speechless.

Julia peered at me, guiltily. "Fiona. Sometimes, striving for the best means letting go of what you care about. I know it's hard, but Liam will get us the three stars we deserve. It's going to be better than it's ever been. Trust him. He knows what he's doing."

I stood there, frozen. What was wrong with me? Why didn't I have the courage to say anything?

My mind flashed to my disaster in the walk-in.

"But ..." tumbled out of my mouth. I didn't have anything else to follow it.

Her phone rang. "Excuse me." She took the call, escaping the exchange. She paused mid-sentence.

"And Fiona. Get the recipes together for the cookbook. I need to review them by the end of the week."

I frowned. "Cookbook ...?"

She rolled her eyes. "Haven't you been listening? The photo shoot for my new cookbook. Bake some stuff from the master pastry bible. I'll choose what's best for the photos."

She turned her back, dismissing me.

I rounded the corner and pushed out the back door. I had to get some fresh air. I had to process everything.

The heavy metal door slammed behind me. I stood there in silence.

I thought of the stupid pig in the walk-in.

It was like that part in *The Godfather* when the mobster finds the horse's head in his bed.

Tears sprung in my eyes. I tried to control the adrenalized stew that was running through my brain.

This situation was spinning out of control. I was losing all ballast. The twinge of full-on losing it was taking over.

I took a deep breath, pushing it back.

I had to get my shit together quickly. I needed to stop acting like a girl. If someone saw me, I'd be disrespected by the whole crew.

I couldn't cry here. I had to breathe it in.

I took a deep breath and pinched the bridge of my nose to stave off the tears.

I could do this. I could stand up to this jerk. I pulled my shoulders back, head held high as I walked through the back door.

I grabbed my chef's coat from the hook and quickly buttoned it.

Right foot first, Goddamnit.

Liam unloaded boxes of kale and radicchio off a dolly, inspecting each specimen like a scientist. He sorted random bunches of romaine, making sure they were perfect.

"Ah, just the person I want to see. I have some cookbooks I want to go over with you." He smiled like nothing was wrong.

I braced myself. As intimidating as he was, I had to stand up to him. "Why is my stuff shoved to the side? I need that space. It's for pastry." The words fell out of my mouth too fast and tepid. Where was my ferocity when I needed it? I kicked myself for my cowardice.

"I need the space to fit the new prep. We're going to have more variety, so I need it." He passed a box of radicchio to a prep cook. "Come on. I have the books waiting for you in the bakery."

I swallowed my rage as I followed him back to my kitchen.

A colossal stack of cookbooks was waiting for me on the worktable.

Camille was piping chocolate into tiny mousse cups for the party at MOCA. She glared at Liam, set her pastry bag down, and left.

I didn't blame her. I wished I could leave, too.

He peered around the kitchen. "I do love this space. It's the best part of the kitchen. It inspires me." He thought for a moment. "I keep thinking I could really do something here ... I'm trying to figure it out ..."

I steeled myself up, trying to find an ounce of bravery. "What about Sammy? He's been here forever. How could you just let him go?"

He stopped studying the kitchen and gave me a calm smile. "We can't have someone holding on to the past. It's not conducive to the team. I don't think Sammy understood the salmon metaphor."

He motioned to the books. "Take a look at these. Maybe you can get some ideas."

He flipped one of them open. I instantly recognized it as Francisco Migoya's book, *The Elements of Dessert*.

He opened it to a picture of a tiny cake covered with a strange mirror glaze. The shaved chocolate towers were ominous. It defied the rules of gravity. "This is where I want you to start. I want to top this."

He opened another book. "I want something more inspired than this." It was Alain Ducasse's *Grand Livre de Cuisine*.

Andrea had cribbed from it too many times to count. A picture of beautiful berry layers was held up by delicate, thin, filo dough. Another example of refined artistry. Alain was a grandmaster. My heart ached whenever I flipped through one of his books.

More inspired than this?

Where would I even begin?

"Take this, too." He handed me a dog-eared book worn from wear. Some of the pages were warped from being in the kitchen.

"These are flavor profiles. I want you to study chapters three, ten, and fifteen pertaining to different sweet profiles. I think you'll find it educational. No more relying on cinnamon, cardamom, and vanilla. I want something more interesting."

"Thanks. I think." I took the book. A cloud of dread and fear assaulted my brain.

My eye caught a glimpse of the tattooed siren on his arm.

Her dark eyes were staring me down. A phoenix rising from the flames.

I suddenly noticed how close he was to me. I stepped back, overwhelmed.

He scrutinized me. "Honestly, if I see another dessert that tugs at my heartstrings, I'm going to kill you."

"Perhaps I could fashion a tiny chocolate volcano. Infused with lavender foam with flames on a plate for you. Now, that would be stunning. A real showstopper." My mouth said it before I could stop myself.

He lit up. "See? That's how I want you to think!"

He dropped the last book on the table and opened it. It was Thomas Keller's tome, *French Laundry*. "I know I'm expecting a lot, so I'm going to help you. Give you a freebie, so to speak. For the Bel Air event on Thursday ... I want you to make the Verjus sorbet with poached peaches and strawberry sorbet shortcakes with sweetened crème fraiche sauce. That's the foundation. I want you to take it further. Find something more interesting. Prep everything, and we'll go over it at the site."

"I don't think you understand. I can do a lot more than ..."

He cut me off. His steely, overpowering expression I knew so well returned.

"Just do it, Fiona. The biscuits should be cut with a one-inch ring. We'll go from there."

I kicked myself for not standing up to him.

He turned to leave. "I'll have my pig out of your walk-in in a minute. They just delivered it, and I had nowhere else to put it." He was matter of fact as he disappeared. Like it was no big deal.

I stood there a beat. I'd been railroaded.

And my walk-in was fucked.

Sammy was gone.

And now I had to conjure God knows what and do better than the masters.

I was numb with rage and terror. I turned and stomped back to the walk-in.

Camille was putting all our stuff back in order. The shelves were compacted with product. Everything was turned, labels out, and organized with tight precision.

She shook her head. "I don't know about all of this. This situation can't be good."

I kicked the pig. My foot met the carcass with a cold, dull thud. I cringed at the smell. It was disgusting.

Camille shoved the last cambro of egg yolks on the bottom shelf. "Angela would have stood up to him," she said as she brushed past me and left.

I stood there alone as the door closed behind me. My walk-in was turning into a morgue. Wasn't this a health code violation?

* * *

"*... In Marseille, I was fortunate enough to have La Madison Du Chocolate as my source for the best chocolate. I remember walking through the cobbled streets when I was a poor student. I would sacrifice my grocery money to buy it ...*"

Julia's voice rang out from my iPad sitting on the table. It was the *Bon Appétit* production in full display. I was pale and nervous. It wasn't one of my finest moments, that was for sure.

"She seems like a nutcase," Kate said as she threaded some beads onto a chain. "I can see why you're so stressed out."

An old beat-up toolbox stood open with various threads and tools. Bowls were set around the table with assorted beads and pendants. Kate peered through cat-eyed reading glasses as she used a long, rounded needle to string beads on a chain.

"Nutcase isn't the right word. She's more like a monster."

"Well, good for you for hanging in there. I'm impressed, Kate."

Grand Livre de Cuisine, The Elements of Dessert, and *French Laundry* sat in front of me, along with the flavor profile books. I closed *The Flavor Bible* and set it down. My eyes were glazing from the scientific approach to flavors. It was mind-numbing.

Kate gave me a quizzical gaze. "He still hasn't called you? It's been three days."

Luna was farting under the table. His tail was rhythmically thumping the floor.

"I guess I had it all wrong," I said.

"Could it be that something's going on with him? Did you ever consider that?"

I picked up my phone and cruised Instagram. It was the usual food photos, selfies, and cat pictures. I reflexively hearted the pictures that looked halfway decent.

"I spooked him. I should have been more conservative. He just seemed so open and nice." I took a sip of my drink. "I can't believe I let myself be vulnerable. I forgot that there were certain rules to this whole thing. I don't know why he didn't text me back," I said.

"Seriously, Fiona. Just let him go."

My eyes rested on Liam's latest post. There was a picture of him and James at the opening of Dominique. They were locked in a bro-hug. "Who Will Be First?" headlined above the image.

I clicked on the link to the *L.A. Times* story. Liam's face smiled back at me. His energetic grin made me uneasy. I flipped to the next story.

"Listen to this. This is what Alicen Chase had to say. "Liam Auclair and James Frye are like cowboys, strutting into town, ready to win their Michelin stars. They played London. They rocked New York. And now it's time to take on L.A." I shook my head. "This is what I have to deal with. A new sheriff in town."

"That's a little cheesy. What kind of blogger writes that stuff?"

"I don't even know ..." My thumb scrolled back up and studied the picture of Liam. I couldn't help but linger on it.

There was something about Liam's smile. He was larger than life in the photo, like a superstar. It made me uneasy.

I handed my phone to her. "See what I mean? Look at that ego."

She grabbed it, studying the picture.

"How do you go to work without your brain turning into scrambled eggs every day? I can only imagine him in real life. He must be hot in his chef coat."

"Yes, Kate. He's hot in his chef coat. He stands over a smoldering stove all day."

She shook her head. "That came out wrong. What I'm trying to say is that he's gorgeous."

She put her glasses on her head and smiled at me, excited. "Imagine this. You could have a torrid affair with him. Ride on his motorcycle." She smirked, naughtily. "He's new in town. You could show him the sites. Show him your favorite taco ..."

I rolled my eyes, taking my phone back. "You and your big imagination. You really need to stop."

"I'm just saying. He might be kind of fun. Obviously, he's not someone you'd take home to meet your father, but who cares? It'd be a great way for you to purge Rory out of your life for good. I mean, look at him. You know sex would be crazy awesome with him. How could it not be?"

"Are you forgetting that he's my boss? That's a whole bag of mess in and of itself."

"Your consenting adults. It doesn't matter. Do you think that stops people? Why do you hear so many stories of chefs working in the kitchen and getting married? You can't be in a space that close together and not have fireworks. It's going to happen. It's the way it is."

I shook my head, annoyed. "Why are we even having this conversation? He's a monster. He hates my desserts, and he's so rude." I shook my head. "He left a dead pig in my walk-in and took over the best space. He has no regard for anything. He even fired Julia's right-hand man, Sammy."

My gaze shifted to the open pages of *French Laundry*. A beautiful picture of a deconstructed strawberry shortcake stared back at me. I took a deep breath, overwhelmed.

"I'm so confused by him. Or me. I don't know ... I'm supposed to be humble and take criticism ... I know I have to learn things ... but he's so offensive that he's gorked my brain."

Kate studied me a moment. "It's a growth thing. How you face adversity says everything about your character."

"I know, I know. But I'm so confused. I should be grateful for the opportunity. I just wish he didn't push my buttons."

"It's like those old movies I watched with my mother. Katharine Hepburn says, 'Oh, he's such a jerk. I'll never even consider him,' and then thirty minutes later, they're kissing in the foyer."

"Now you sound like a stupid romance novel. And what the hell is a foyer anyway?"

Kate grinned, slid her glasses back on, and continued with her beads. "I'm just saying ..."

I turned my phone off and set it on the table. "I'm going to be in the moment. Take it as it comes. Be in the present."

She rolled her eyes. "You and Charlotte and your New Age crap. You should align your chakras and open an ashram instead of a restaurant."

My heart stopped. "Oh no. What did she say to you?"

"She said that you saw the place. You're gun-shy. She's sort of annoyed by you right now."

"Well, she's putting me on the spot. I hate when she does that."

"You two are hilarious. I love watching you go back and forth. It's beyond entertaining."

"I'm glad you find it amusing. I feel bad for letting her down," I said.

"Her food truck is not working out like she thought it would. I could see why she'd want a place to call her own," Kate said.

"The problem is, she has such a short attention span. She's only had her truck for two years. She's still building it. Maybe if she thought out of the box, she'd do better ..."

I paused, scrambling for the right thing to say.

"And now I see her doing what she always does. She's jumping ship. And this time, she wants me to be her life raft."

Kate set her string of beads down and studied me a beat. "There are two ways you can look at it: you can see someone fleeing a situation, or you could see someone realizing that something doesn't work. Sometimes, people keep going down the wrong path because it's safe. Familiar. They're afraid to change course because of what could happen. I applaud Charlotte. She's unhappy and trying to solve the problem. She's not letting life just happen to her. She's the master of her own destiny."

I thought for a moment. "Owning your own restaurant in L.A.? Come on. The success rate is like a negative five percent. Most places close after the first year. It's the ultimate gamble. And I don't know if I have the stamina to handle that. It takes so much. Tenacity. Talent. Confidence. Charlotte's fearless. Me? Not so much."

"I think you're a little hard on yourself. Something about jumping into a situation you're terrified of can help you see what you're made of."

I took a deep breath. "You don't know what you're talking about. You're fearless, too."

She laughed. "Are you kidding? Don't you think I freak out before a show? I can't tell you how many times I've barfed in the bathroom before I went on. But it doesn't matter. Fear is just fucking fear. It's just a feeling."

She put the last bead on her string and grabbed a clasp to finish the necklace. "You may feel afraid. Terrified. But you don't bite into that. If you look past it and dig deeper, something happens. You find yourself. You learn a little more about the boundaries of your car. Facing fear strengthens your resolve. Every time is a little easier."

"I guess. But opening a restaurant isn't like playing the Echo. If I fail, I'll be taking other people down with me who have to pay their rent. Buy groceries. And on top of that, who knows what else could happen? I saw my father do that. It terrifies me to think of it."

"Fiona. Don't overthink it. There's a certain point where thinking becomes the enemy."

"It sounds like you're taking her side in this."

"No. I just don't want to see you missing an opportunity because you were too chickenshit to make the leap. That's worse than failure. It's death."

She took her glasses off, pinching her nose. She sat there a beat, deliberating. I'd seen it before. I knew what was coming.

"I can't pay all of the rent this month ... Can you help me out? I have the commission coming from the mural job in Venice ... but they haven't paid me yet ..."

I smiled. "Of course. You know I'm always there for you."

She sighed, relieved. "Thank you, Fiona. I don't know what I'd do without you."

"It's nothing, really. It's just the way things go sometimes. Don't worry about it."

I sat there for a moment. Luna smelled worse by the minute. "We have to do something about Luna's food. He smells terrible."

"You're right. I got him this food that has kale in it. I thought it'd be good for him, but I don't think it's worth the stench."

I reached down and scratched behind his ears.

He licked my arm, his tail thumping harder on the floor.

Dogs were lucky. They didn't have to think about dating, jobs, or crazy friends. All they had to do was sleep, play fetch, and give out love to accepting humans. They didn't have to worry about getting rejected, burned, or face failure.

In my next life, I wanted to come back as a dog. Being a human was too complicated.

7

The air was hot, with a slight breeze from the sea. An endless line of palm trees swayed in a canopy. The green grass stretched out to the horizon like a golf course. A thin line of ocean edged the distance.

A mansion the size of the Beverly Center towered over everything.

So ... this was how billionaires lived.

Large round tables were set up on the lawn, the tablecloths billowing in the breeze. Servers in black shirts and long white aprons set the tables with the requisite glasses, silver, and linen for the evening.

A psychotic party planner ran around, bossing everyone in sight. She waved her hands in the air, making last-minute changes to the stage and dance floor placement.

Julia watched everything like a hawk. She was elegant and in charge with her simple dark Hedley & Bennett, paired with a white chiffon blouse and pearls.

Some poor photographer was following her. I turned and fled in the opposite direction before I could be pulled in by the madness.

Our kitchen was set up in the gazebo. A large stove, a small oven, and a generous workspace were provided for us for the evening.

The party was a political benefit for a potential presidential candidate. Two hundred of the most influential tech giant billionaires, political heavy-hitters, and who's who of Hollywood were coming.

It was going to be a beautiful evening of beautiful people.

The desserts had been easy to prep for. I'd prepared poached peaches to complement the strawberries. It took five of our biggest rondos to cook the peaches in the delicate honey and poaching liquid. The honey had mingled with the moist meat, giving them an even sweeter taste.

I'd used Verjus to complement the peaches. Verjus was a vinegar of unripe grapes. It had been popular in the Middle Ages. "Green juice," they'd called it.

The taste was a revelation.

My peaches were worthy of knights, kings, and queens, like Merlin had teleported to me a magic elixir.

I'd paired it with a reduction of rosemary and star anise. The result tasted complex. Interesting. It was bold. I hoped it wasn't confusing.

Using Rory's peaches made me sad in a way. What did I do wrong? Why did I drive him away? Could I text him again?

No. I'd look like a stalker.

I pushed the whole thing out of my mind.

I had more important things to think about.

The biscuits for the shortcake were baked and ready to be toasted off right before serving in the small oven. I'd made a basil and marjoram-infused Madagascar vanilla ice cream that I hoped would please Liam.

I'd made it challenging. Thought worthy.

I'd made it the way he wanted.

Rory's magical strawberries were prepped with superfine sugar and honey. Their taste was sweet and clean.

Was I pleased with the result? I was still trying to work it out.

I just wished I could be pleased with the whole Rory situation. My heart still hurt. Or maybe it was my ego.

I sighed.

It was time to let it go. He was obviously a misstep. Wednesday at the farmers' market was certainly going to be strange. I felt weird about it. Would it be embarrassing or just awkward?

"Fiona." I turned. Julia touched me on the sleeve. "I want you to meet Jesse. He's my photographer for the new book I'm working on."

Jesse extended his bored hand. He was unimpressed by Julia's antics.

She turned to him. "Why don't you go get some pictures of the tables? I want something elegant. Maybe you can do some shots with that bokeh effect or whatever you call it." She waved him off and turned to me. "Where are we with your plates? I want them to be perfect. Evie said Elon Musk is supposed to be here."

"I'm going over them with Liam in a minute. Don't worry. He gave the recipes to me. It'll be fine."

She relaxed a bit.

"You're lucky to be working with him, you know. He's a genius. This is the opportunity of a lifetime for you. I remember when I worked with Chef Romer. It was back in the days when chefs threw things. He was impossible, but he taught me how to think on my feet. And duck, for that matter ..."

She glanced into the distance. "Damn them. They forgot the Cabernet glasses. And here he is, taking pictures. Excuse me." She stormed off towards the tables. Everyone scrambled to attention.

"Fiona! Over here!"

Liam waved to me from the gazebo.

The white structure was like the helm of a ship. He was the capitan of this high-class production.

Billionaires required Michelin star chefs. And Liam fit the bill.

The gazebo accentuated his height somehow. It emphasized his larger-than-life presence.

I pushed forward, watching him as I approached the gazebo. He was striking in his white chef's coat. I averted my eyes. Damn Kate for messing with my mind.

He glanced up at me from his sauté pans as I stood on the grass in front of the gazebo.

The gazebo looked like a stage. Was this stage fright? Or just dread.

"Grab some plates and your prep. Let's go over what you got."

He flipped another pan. Mirepoix went airborne and landed with a sizzle. I always loved watching when the cooks did that. It was defying gravity.

My stomach twisted. Would he like my menu? Would he approve? Or would he chuck it in the trash?

I walked up the gazebo stairs. Shoulders straight and head held high. He wouldn't humiliate me this time.

Here it was. The moment of truth.

Do or die ...

I grabbed two plates off the stacked china for the evening. I pulled out the hotel pans with the prep and set them on the counter before him.

"Let's see what you got." He lifted the lid off the peaches and reached in, grabbing one. He popped it in his mouth, thinking for a minute.

"Next time, pull back on the Verjus."

I kicked myself, disappointed. How had I gotten it wrong again?

He lifted the lid off the hotel pan, grabbed a spoon, and took a bite of the marjoram and basil ice cream. "It's a bit overpowered with basil. I don't know how I feel about the pairing. It's sort of pedestrian. We'll adjust the serving size so it's not noticeable." He smirked. "Maybe they'll be so drunk by the time dessert rolls around they won't notice."

I couldn't even think of a response.

He spread all my components out and grabbed some tools. "Let me show you how I want this to look." He started working on the plate. An electric silence filled the air.

He shook his head as he worked. "One of the things I've noticed about you is your compulsion to make something complex. A cream. A custard. A pudding or a cheesecake. It's a crutch."

"Isn't that what dessert is?"

"I want you to look one step deeper. Don't think of the dessert on its own. Think of the whole dish. Think of it as a roller coaster. Different flavors. Different components that tie into the whole. What do you think Thomas Keller has done here?"

"He's made a strawberry shortcake?"

Was there something more here that I was missing?

"A good chef will know how to transform something simple. Like your peach, for example." He fashioned the plate, thinking. "The point is to twist the food into what you want. Dominate it."

I watched his hands work. His fingers were precise. His moves were graceful and quick, with the concentration of a surgeon, as he made a quenelle with basil and marjoram ice cream. He set it delicately on the plate with the components of the shortcake.

His plating was beautiful. Clean. Elegant. Precise. There was a certain austerity in his work. It looked otherworldly.

He tilted the plate, stepped back, and handed me a fork. "Try it now."

I took a bite. What the hell did he do? The flavor burst in my mouth. His fingers had cast a spell on my work.

I was speechless.

He set his offset down. "That's what I want."

Rose broke the moment. "Sorry, I'm late. My class got out late."

Liam returned to his work. "Let's prep the plates and get them racked up. We're running behind."

Rose darted past him to get her apron.

I stood there. Studying the plate, looking at Liam.

How the hell did he make my components taste even better than I had made them?

I glanced at him. His confidence and bravado commanded the air. He was a paladin.

Could I do the same thing? Could I make my work stand up to his?

Or would the guests be too drunk to notice?

* * *

The canopy of palm trees stood close and tall above me. I watched from a distance in the dark, enjoying a glass of champagne I'd clipped off a server's tray.

Some famous pop star was gyrating on the stage in the distance as people danced on the dance floor.

I hated contemporary pop. I couldn't hook into it, but the crowd seemed to eat it up.

The night had gone off without a hitch, but I could sense the heavy tension in the air. The tension you could only get by having this much ego in one place. What was it like trying to be the most important person in the room?

"Fiona," Liam whispered behind me. He was dark in the majesty of the trees.

His white coat was unbuttoned at the top. His ponytail was perfect, with whisps of hair around his face. Perfect whisps that betrayed an evening of working on the line. He leaned against a palm tree and pulled a cigarette from the pack in his pocket. He extended it to me. "Do you mind?"

I nodded.

He was intimidating in the dark as he lit up and took a drag.

"You could have pulled back on the crème fraiche. The ice cream didn't balance on the plate properly. And what the fuck did you do with the strawberries? You didn't listen to me ..."

He flicked an ash into the air.

I deflated a bit. How could this be so complicated? It was just dessert.

He saw the look on my face. He softened a bit, motioning to the party. His lips curved into a thoughtful smile.

"L.A. is crazy. Everyone's a movie star here." He laughed. "It really is the land of beautiful people. I thought New York was, but now I'm not so sure ..." He gave me a small smile.

I shrugged. "I guess I don't notice. I've just grown up with it. It's not a big deal."

He gazed at the crowd in the distance, thoughtful. "I'm still trying to figure L.A. out. There's no center. New York was easy. London was easy. This is a whole different enchilada. Speaking of which ... do you know where I can find one?

My laugh mingled with his in the dark. The warmth of it took me off guard. His antagonistic energy diffused.

"I'm still getting a feel for it here. I've been digging. Visiting different neighborhoods. Different landmarks. It's hard because finding one focal point of energy is impossible. It's like having a compass that never turns north," he said.

"The point is you can get noodles in Korea Town for breakfast and then go to the beach for sushi in the afternoon. It's a patchwork. It's not like finding north. You just have to let go and let it take you. Embrace it all," I said.

I watched him. I could tell he didn't get it.

He thought for a moment. "And the other thing. Everyone's obsessed with parking here. In one way or another, all my conversations lead back to parking availability. How hard is it to park a fucking car? It's crazy."

"You're lucky you have a motorcycle. You can park anywhere. You're free from tyranny."

"That's true."

A silence fell between us.

"Do you want to get out of here?" He asked. "Show me something. I'd like to try something new. Maybe you could show me your favorite place. You didn't drive here, did you?"

"No, I came with the guys in the truck." I smiled, trying not to laugh. "I was afraid I wasn't going to find parking."

He smirked, shaking his head. "Let's go. Leo and the guys can pack up. We can sneak out the back way."

I froze in place.

Confusion washed over me. I stalled for a beat.

He turned. "Are you coming?" His silhouette was strong in the dark.

Was this what I thought it was? No, it couldn't be.

"Come on, Fiona, let's go," he beckoned.

I kicked myself for being so dramatic. It was nothing. I was just going to show him around.

I took one step forward, right foot first, and followed him back to the house.

His motorcycle was parked between the white party vans. The celebration echoed in the distance.

"Let me grab my stuff." I opened the Lucien truck's door, crawled into the cab, and grabbed my backpack.

I paused as I shrugged my chef's coat off, shoved it into my bag, and pulled my jacket on.

My breath caught in my throat. Was I doing something wrong? I mean, I was just going to show him some place that I liked. That was all.

I zipped up my backpack and slammed the door of the cab shut.

I shoved my fear down as I approached the bike. Liam handed the extra helmet to me. "Put it on."

"Were you expecting me?"

"Ha. Leo came with me." He swung onto the bike.

"What would you like to try?" I asked, trying to be cool. My powers of calm were failing me.

I was terrified of the bike. The slick machine was an overwhelming monster. How the hell was I going to ride that without falling off the back?

He smiled at me. "L.A. is famous for its tacos. Show me your favorite."

I stared at the bike in terror.

He chuckled and as he regarded me and the bike. "Don't tell me you're scared. It's just a bike."

"Are you kidding? I do this all the time."

A breath hitched in my throat as I swung right foot first onto the bike.

"Let's go." The bike lurched forward, powerfully, as he started the engine. It rumbled to life underneath me. The monster roared to life. I put my arms around his waist as he pulled forward.

I tried to block our closeness out of my brain. It was just too weird.

I squeezed my eyes shut, not looking down as he picked up speed. Looking down would trigger my panic.

Just be cool ... just be cool ... repeated in my head like a mantra.

It wasn't working.

My heart rate accelerated with the speed of the bike as we drove down Sunset. Past the threshold of Beverly Hills and into West Hollywood. The lights zipped past in a blur.

Sunset Boulevard was lit up. The sidewalks were crowded with clubbers and musicians mingling in front of the Rainbow and the Whiskey.

My brain was scrambled by Liam's closeness and the motorcycle's engine.

Here he was. Some hotshot superstar chef. And I was riding on the back of his bike. I rolled my eyes to myself. Was I living the cliché?

I didn't want to think about it right now. I just wanted to survive.

* * *

I was trying not to have a panic attack.

We had to be going at least seventy miles per hour on the 110. I could see the pavement below me going way too fast as the wind pressed against my body. The only thing keeping me on the bike was my death grip around Liam's body. I was a terrified cat—all eyeballs and claws.

Any moment could be the moment of my death.

Liam pulled off the freeway, and I loosened my embrace. We drove down the dark city street, past the ragtag assortment of garages, suit shops, and cafes. He parked his bike in front of Grand Central Market and swung into a tight spot between two cars.

I was impressed. He was free from parking tyranny.

The sparse crowd in the market mingled around booths for sushi, pizza, and falafel as the market settled down for the night.

Liam pulled his helmet off and unhitched the strap under my chin. He helped me pull mine off. "You've never been on a motorcycle before, have you?"

"Was it that obvious?"

He laughed. "You were holding onto me like you were about to die. I could barely breathe."

"I think maybe you were going a little too fast." The adrenaline coursing through me made me jittery.

He smiled at me, expectant. "Show me what we came here for."

I glanced around. The taco stand I loved so much was still open. "Let's go."

I put the helmet under my arm and led him through the market. His presence next to me was wired, and his energy exploded from his body like a thousand-watt bulb. I was beginning to think he couldn't help it. "Where are we going?"

I motioned to a table. "Sit down over there. That seems like a good spot."

His green eyes were electric in the hue of fluorescent lights. His intensity was unsettling.

I handed him the helmet in my hands. "I'll be back."

I turned and made my way to my favorite taco stand: Bobbo's.

The little booth's menu consisted of only five things: corn and flour tortillas, salsa, beans, and pork.

I loved watching the cooks prepare the huge hunks of meat on the wood-cutting boards. Slow braised rumps of roast pig fell apart to the touch. They'd figured out how to let the fat melt into the meat to create a juicy and flavorful taco that was the best in the city. You could easily eat it without any condiments.

It was that good.

I ordered a batch of tacos and two beers and watched as the cook shredded the meat with a large scraper and a knife. He was quick with his hands.

It gave me a moment to think. The adrenaline was melting me into a relaxed state. Like I'd taken Yogi Dave's power class.

I glanced over my shoulder. Liam didn't see me staring at him. He was busy taking everything in. His rumpled ponytail from the helmet. The dark leather coat zipped up. It accentuated his broad shoulders.

He was dangerous.

Why did I always associate the word dangerous with him? Perhaps I needed a thesaurus.

He turned and met my gaze.

His green eyes were hyper-bright. His intensity pulled me in from across the room. I looked away, embarrassed.

"Lady. Your tacos." I turned around, and the man behind the counter held out my tacos, some salsa containers, and my two Pacificos.

"Thanks."

I made my way to the table and sat down.

"Get ready for greatness. These are my favorite." I smiled, proudly.

"It's going to take a lot to impress me. I'm warning you." He picked up the first one and took a bite.

His intensity melted into pleasure as he took another bite of his taco.

"They're excellent, right?" I smiled, proud and expectant.

"They're okay." He finished off the tacos and eyed mine. "Are you going to eat those?"

I smiled. "Go for it."

He slid my paper taco boat in front of him, poured the verde salsa over the beautiful meat, and devoured it.

"It's true. New York tacos are for shit, but I've had better."

I gazed at him, disappointed. How could I not take his reaction personally?

"Family meal is truly the best. Just wait for Leo to make carnitas. You're in for a treat. Some of the best tacos I'd ever had were at family meals. The cooks can take almost anything, put it between a corn shell with some jalapeños, and make it magical."

He peered at me, doubtful. I tried to think of something else to say. I hated rejection.

"Do you miss New York?

He thought for a moment. "Yes. No. It's complicated."

He finished the last taco. He grabbed a handful of paper napkins from the receptacle, wiped off his hands, and sipped his beer.

"I'm a fish out of water but like a sponge at the same time. Like I said, I'm still trying to figure it out."

I thought for a moment.

"Doesn't your success help you out? Don't you get a secret pass into the real scene? You can see the lay of the land better than anyone."

He focused on me. "Listen. This star chef thing? It's all bullshit. It's just a means to an end. Don't buy into it." He took a sip of his beer. "I'm just some guy from a small town outside Las Vegas. Your typical one-stoplight town. I was lucky to get the fuck out."

His honesty was disarming.

"I thought you were French somehow, Auclair being your last name and all."

He laughed. "I made it up."

"What do you mean?"

"My last name. I made it up. It's actually Smith." He swigged his beer. "'Liam Auclair' has a nicer ring to it than 'Smith.' It sounds more in charge."

I studied him, shocked.

"Listen, Fiona. Image is everything. Perception is king. If you don't want to be disrespected, you have to create the proper narrative."

I wasn't sure what to think.

"How did you get from Liam Smith, living in a one-stoplight town, to winning Iron Chef and earning two Michelin stars?"

He peeled the label off his beer with his nimble fingers.

"It's kind of boring. My mother loved Giada de Laurentiis. Rachael Ray practically raised me. But my favorite on the Food Channel was Mario Batali. The way he'd talk his way through regional Italian cuisine got to me. The deal was sealed when I saw *Hell's Kitchen* and Gordon Ramsay. I knew his kitchen was the only place for me."

I laughed. "What could possibly make you think getting screamed at was a good life choice?"

"It was something more. The intensity of the kitchen. The energy between the chefs on the line during rush. Something as simple as a plate being dressed. The military precision spoke to me."

He took a sip of his beer. "As soon as I graduated high school, I could have gone to CIA or Le Cordon Bleu or even made my bones in Vegas. But it didn't seem right. I was obsessed with Marco Pierre White. I'd read his book *Devil in the Kitchen* too many times. He'd worked his way up through fine dining in London, so that's what I decided to do. I moved to London and I started as a dishwasher at Le Gavroche. The rest, as they say, is history."

I laughed to myself. Marco Pierre White was his spirit animal. If you were going to copy someone, he certainly was worthy of the prize. But I was impressed. Something about making it from the dish-pit was noble. More impressive.

"What was it like working for Jamison Davies? Was he the monster that they always say he is?"

"La Vie was tough. I'm not going to lie. Jamison was intimidating. But his take-no-bullshit attitude made me a believer. I learned all the important things from him. It's true about the loyalty his chefs have. I'd fucking die for him."

He took another sip of his beer. Our gazes met over the table. I could see the auburn flecks in his eyes. I couldn't look away.

The air had shifted. I finally felt comfortable around him. His harsh demeanor had evaporated. He finally was a human being and not some larger-than-life persona.

"This Michelin business. Why do you even care? It's just an award."

He almost choked. "You've got to be kidding me. You don't get it?"

He leaned forward, almost offended. "It's not just any other award. It's the one and only award that means anything to me." He paused, thoughtful. "I've got two stars. I have exceptional cuisine worth a special journey. But I want to be known for food that's elevated to an art form. That's the definition of three stars."

He smiled at me. "You know, there's nothing like winning the prize … You'll eventually understand …" He let his gaze linger on mine. His intensity drew me in. "What other reason is there for doing all of it?"

"Why don't you open your own restaurant? Surely, your three stars would mean so much more if it was your own place."

"Are you kidding? Why would I want the responsibility of running a restaurant when I could focus on the prize? I'll have my own place when I finally win."

His answer spoke a certain truth to me.

He leaned forward. "I like your energy, Fiona. There's something about you. I can't put my finger on it." His lips curled into a vulnerable smile.

All the air and noise sucked up into silence around me.

Where was this going?

Liam grabbed the garbage from the table. "Let's go."

I grabbed our garbage and my unfinished beer off the table, threw it away, and followed him through the market. The last of the booths were shut down. The crowd was sparse, thinning out for the night as we made it back to his bike.

"Let me take you home." He grabbed the helmet from my hands and fitted it over my head, his eyes meeting mine. "Where do you live?"

I paused. What was I getting myself into?

"Not far. I'll guide you."

I swung behind him on the back of the bike, and we pulled into the night. I was thankful we didn't have to go down another freeway. The thought of going supersonic made me shudder.

I squeezed his left side, and he turned the corner at the intersection. The friction of his body felt awkward again as I pressed his right side, guiding him to turn onto my street.

What was I doing here? What was I playing with?

I squeezed him with both arms, motioning him to stop in front of my apartment.

Anticipation bloomed in my chest. How was this going to play out?

I got off the back of the bike and took my helmet off. He turned off the engine and swung off the bike, facing me. "I had you all wrong."

"What do you mean?"

"Normally, pastry chefs are wound a little tight. They're a little OCD. But you're different."

"Thanks. I think."

He gave me a sly grin. "I had fun with you. When can we do this again?"

I laughed. "How about tomorrow? After you eviscerate my menu."

He frowned as his shoulders squared up. "Fiona. You've gotta stop taking this shit personally. I'll end up destroying you."

"Is it really that bad?"

He grabbed my helmet out of my hands and strapped it to the bike's back seat. "I don't fuck around in the kitchen."

He got back on the bike and put his helmet on, staring at me a beat, deliberating. "This is war. I have a vision. I don't have time to coddle people."

The silence suddenly got awkward.

The moment was done. Familiar unease returned. My body was braced for an attack.

He paused a moment for emphasis. "Don't fight change. Don't hold onto your preconceived notions. Trust me."

He turned on the engine and revved it. "Think about the Tony Awards menu. Give me something good. Show me that you understand what I mean," he said over the roar of the engine.

He hefted the bike forward and pulled into the night. His taillights disappeared down the street.

I exhaled a nervous breath.

What the hell was I doing?

Whatever it was, I was in over my head.

8

Fog and drizzle hung in the air as I parked in an alley behind the dumpster. My wipers dragged on the windshield, picking up the light rain drops. The sound was grating.

What the hell had happened with Liam last night?

And what about Rory?

The thought of his kiss on the rooftop. His body mashing against mine in the pit at the show. The lingering kiss on my doorstep.

It felt like a million years ago. The rejection still stung. Would he be nice? Would he act like it never happened?

I stepped out of the car and locked the door. The rain sprinkled my face, bringing me into the present.

I approached the busy market and rounded the corner. I walked past the flower vendor that smelled like gardenias and lilacs, past the booth with olives and vinegar. The lady selling avocados was in her usual place.

Fleurcine's booth stood in the distance.

Rory was helping Ben Chang, the chef from Alabaster. I'd heard good things about Ben's place. His dim sum was supposed to be out of this world.

Rory had a graceful confidence. He exuded a quiet, Zen-like presence as he helped Ben load his cart with Bok choy.

My heart was beating too fast. I should leave. Maybe I could come back later.

"Fiona!"

I turned. It was Delia, holding a coffee in each hand.

She wore her straw sun hat, flowered clogs, and pink overalls even in the rain. She was a garden queen. "Good morning!" She extended one of the coffees to me. "Would you like one?"

I was caught. "I'm sorry. I'm over-caffeinated."

"Rory said that you two had a date." She nudged me with her elbow, smiling. "How'd it go?"

"It was fun. He's great."

She sipped one of the coffees. "It's not often that he goes out with people, you know, with Grace and all ..." She gave me a conspiratorial smile. "When are you going out again?"

"I don't know, he didn't call me back."

She shook her head, disappointed. "That sounds about right." She gave me a consoling smile. "Don't take it personally. He's just busy, that's all."

"I understand."

She brightened. "What are we standing here for? Let's go get your stuff."

As we approached the booth, my mouth flashed with dryness to match behind my eyeballs. Delia was leading me to the slaughter. I could barely think.

"Rory! Look who I found wandering in the crowd." Delia boomed.

Rory smiled at me as our eyes met. A ray of sunlight that broke through the clouds illuminated his tall frame. He was otherworldly in the bright light.

I shifted uncomfortably. I couldn't read him.

Delia set the coffees on the table and picked up two Mason jars. "I've been working on some plums in honey syrup, and I've been playing with the ratio of honey. I want you to tell me what you think." The flowered labels were cute, scrawled with her old-fashioned handwriting. "I want you to be honest. I mean it." She grabbed a bag to put the jars in. "Rory, tell her about the festival."

Rory glanced at a lady testing the nectarines at the next table. She was squeezing them a little too hard—enough to bruise them. "Mom, I think that lady needs some help."

Delia glanced at the lady and frowned. "Does she ever."

She broke from our conversation and flew to the other side of the table. She reached into the woman's hand and grabbed the nectarine like she was saving its life.

We stood there for a moment. Awkward. I didn't know what to say. A piece of my heart sank, thinking about what I'd lost. Or what could have been.

"About last week. I'm sorry I didn't call or text you back. It was unforgivable of me."

"That's okay. I get it."

"No, you don't. I just have a lot of things going on right now in my life. It's been a bit overwhelming. I hope you'll forgive me."

"It's okay. I've been busy too," I said.

"I don't want you to get the wrong idea. I enjoyed spending time with you. I had a lot of fun." He smiled.

A piece of my heart melted. That familiar giddiness washed over me again. "I thought I scared you off."

"It takes a lot to scare me off."

He gave me a warm smile. "Come to our summer festival. We're going to have berry picking. I have a food truck coming to make bread and pizza. I've also got some wines that I'm introducing. It's going to be fun."

Excitement sprung in my heart. "I'd love to come to the farm. It'd be nice."

"Excellent." He turned to his clipboard. "So, how can I help you today, chef?" He beamed. "Dates are coming into season, so you'll want to utilize them this week. We're also going to give you more Chelan cherries and greengage plums. They're peaking right now."

He sliced a date in half and gave it to me. "Try this."

I popped it in my mouth. The sweetness of the fruit melted in my mouth.

"What would you do with that?" He asked. A warm glint in his eye.

"This is so good. I could do a ginger date pudding or maybe a truffle."

He grinned, pleased. "If you like that, then try this." He held out a slice of plum to me. "This is the greengage plum. There's a tang behind the sweetness that I think you'll appreciate. The meat is pretty firm, too, so it's easy to work with."

I put the slice in my mouth and tasted it. It was easily the best plum I'd ever had. The tart skin held together a burst of soft sweetness that I'd never tasted before.

He grinned at me with a slight curve in his smile that made my toes tingle. "What about it? What amazing thing could you make with that?"

I savored it. "I could do a Kouign-amann tart with these. Maybe a passionfruit pastry cream to complement ..."

He smiled at me, taking me in. "That sounds amazing."

He grabbed a cherry and sliced it in half. "This is my favorite. This is the best season we've had for the Chelans. Easily one of the best cherries you'll ever have. I think I will use them for my Merlot this season." He handed the slice to me.

I tasted it as a cool breeze washed across my face.

The lusciousness of the bite was out of this world. The subtext of sweet assaulted my brain. It was something beautiful to eat. "Wow. You're right."

"Tell me what you'd make with that. I'm curious." His gaze lingered with mine as I thought.

"This deserves something special. Like a flourless chocolate soufflé with Guanaja ... Or a tiny tres leches cake ..."

"I'd certainly like to try that." He smiled. My heart filled with warmth and a familiar peace.

We stood there in the busy chaos of the market. I wanted him to show me more. I didn't want the moment to end. "How about your berries?"

"The blackberries are the best. They're bursting with juiciness right now. I can only imagine what you'd do with them." He handed me one. "It's a celebration of summer. It doesn't get any better." He smiled.

I tasted the berry. Savoring its sweetness. He wasn't wrong. The hints of summer burst in my mouth. My mind wandered as I held his gaze, wondering what I'd make out of them."

"What do you think you could make out of that?"

I was coming up short. He left me speechless. A hum in the air hypnotized me.

"Hey, mister. I need to get some Swiss chard. How do I weigh this out? Or do you do it?" An old lady with a pushcart full of kale stood, expectant.

Rory broke from the moment. "Here, let me get my mother to help you."

He caught Delia's eye.

Delia smiled in recognition. "Madeline! I was expecting you. How's George?" She put her arm around the lady and ushered her toward the vegetables on the other side of the booth.

He turned and met my gaze. His smile was genuine and sweet.

I hated to end it. "I have to go."

"I know. There's so much more I'd like to show you." He glanced at his clipboard, thinking. "Give me a minute."

He turned to the piles of boxes behind him, selecting random ones and putting them on the dolly. His familiar body in his T-shirt and jeans made me think of our bodies close together as he kissed me on the rooftop.

"I'll see you Sunday, right?" Delia snapped me back from my moment. She took my hands in hers. "Don't forget to try the plums." She patted me on the back and went to another customer.

Rory pulled his cart forward. "Are you ready?"

No. I wasn't. I wanted to stay longer. "Let's go."

We walked through the market. The crowd was picking up with the morning rush.

He was relaxed as he walked. "What kind of wine do you like?"

I thought for a moment. "I like Riesling the best."

He gave me a knowing smile. "You're open-minded. Resilient. A Riesling has less sugar, so it has the longest age-ability of any wine. You have lasting power. I like that."

"Thank you." A tiny beam of pride washed over me. "Why do you say that?"

"Your favorite wine defines your personality. It says something about who you are."

"What's your favorite?" I asked.

"I'm still trying to figure it out."

We made it to my car. I opened the back, and he started loading the boxes in.

I was sorry the moment was over.

He loaded the last box, closed the doors, and stood tall before me.

His familiar warmth washed over me. "I can't wait to see you Sunday. It's going to be fun."

We faced each other. I had this overwhelming urge to kiss him, but I held back. Was that appropriate? I mean, it had been a week since we'd kissed last. And was there some kind of rule for that?

He leaned forward and kissed me on the cheek. I could smell his familiar smell. The familiar giddiness returned.

"Goodbye, Fiona. I'll see you Sunday." He turned and walked down the alley.

I admired him from afar as he reached the end of the rough alley.

He turned and waved to me before disappearing around the corner. He was gone. But his energy lingered.

I opened my car door and slipped in. I sat in silence for a moment and took a deep breath. I thought of the fruit he'd given me.

Maybe I'd make him a pie. I'd take it to the festival. I smiled to myself. Yes. That's exactly what I'd do.

I turned the windshield wipers on and glided into traffic.

I couldn't wait for Sunday.

* * *

This time, I was going to get it right.

Rose piped chocolate into ice water, making delicate chocolate branches for the mousse. Camille was finishing the tiny Kirsch tortes. She poured a delicate matte cherry glaze over them, smoothing the tops with an offset.

I'd pored over so many books, including *French Pastries and Desserts* by Lenotre, *Patisserie Maison* by Richard Bertinet, and *Pierre Herme Pastries,* to name a few. I'd worked late into the night coming up with the menu.

I was going to dominate the food this time. I was going to show my muse who was boss.

Liam wouldn't catch me off guard. Not again.

I dug deeper into making the Zabaglione. It was a simple mousse with sweet Madeira wine. It'd complement the delicious blackberries that Rory had given me.

I glanced at my pot. My cooked sugar was ready on the induction burner. I knew just by looking at it that it was at a softball stage.

I turned on the Hobart at high speed to mix the egg yolks.

Pâte à bombe time.

I loved a pâte à bombe. It was my favorite thing to make.

It's the dark sister of meringue, which is delicate yellow. Pale and bright.

Pâte à bombe is the color of the Manipura chakra. The Manipura is the get-it-done chakra. The chakra of strength. Manifestation. Power.

Meringue is fragile and ephemeral.

A pâte à bombe is immortal. Whip egg yolks forever, and they wouldn't break. I streamed the hot sugar, cooked to 240 degrees, into the bowl.

Pâte à bombe has superpowers. It's sumptuous to the palate yet indestructible.

Unbreakable and lasting. I wanted to be like that.

I wasn't a delicate merengue.

I was substance. I was strength. I was a bomb.

I watched the yolks and sugar come together in a gorgeous yellow concoction. It was magic.

I poured Madeira into the bowl and let the Hobart go. It'd whip until it cooled and was ready to dress up with the Callebaut twenty eight percent. The white chocolate would complement the berries. It was going to be beautiful.

"And here's the space I was talking about." Liam rounded the corner into the bakery. Julia and an architect followed behind with a clipboard and a tape measure.

Liam gave me a thin smile. His high-energy attractiveness caught me off guard.

I was outmatched.

Rose and Camille dug deeper into their tasks, trying to be invisible.

The architect walked around, studying the room. He jotted some notes down on his clipboard.

"With the window situated where it is, we can get a lot of engagement from the outside," Liam said. He ignored my presence. "This is the heart of the kitchen. The soul. I want you to capture this somehow. I want the rest of the kitchen to embody the energy of this space."

Julia turned, studying the space like she'd never seen it before. She met Liam's eye. "I think you're absolutely right. When I imagined this space, I wanted it to reflect the bakery I'd spent time in when I traveled through Auvergne. The chef was known throughout France for his croquembouche."

The architect took his tape measure out and measured the space around the oven. "I don't know about the oven. It might have to go," he said.

My hackles went up.

"What do you mean remove the oven? It's only the most important thing here. Why would you do that?" I asked.

Julia frowned at me, her lips pressed together.

She turned to the architect. "Yes, well, we'll discuss that later. Let's go to the prep area. Liam has some ideas about that space as well."

Liam turned to me, calling after them. "I'll catch up with you. I'll be there in a minute," he said as they left.

He gave me a high-wattage smile. The warmth of it took me off guard. "How can you win three stars if the kitchen is from 2015."

"But what about the oven?" I asked. This was making me uneasy.

"It's just a concept. Everything is liquid right now. We're in the idea phase. You have nothing to worry about. It's going to be fantastic. Trust me."

He glanced at Rose working on the chocolate branches. "How is it coming with the Tony Awards menu? It's on Tuesday, you know."

"We're testing the menu right now. I'm confident it'll be ready today, and we can start production."

He took in Rose and Camille's work in progress. Studying the plates on my table with incomplete sauces swirled on them.

"Torte ...? Mousse ...?" He frowned, thinking. "I don't know, Fiona. This honestly looks like a shit show."

A defensive wave overtook me. "What do you mean? You haven't even seen everything put together."

"Your pieces aren't homogenous. They look random. Like you plucked everything out of the air without thinking."

I simmered, fuming. My old anger was back with a vengeance.

He frowned. "Your plates need to tell a story. I don't see any story here. I don't see anything but a bunch of dessert."

I stood frozen. Speechless.

He grabbed a tasting spoon off the table and tasted the torte. He frowned, thinking. His eyes recalibrated. "I got it."

I gave him a quizzical look.

"Come with me tonight. After service. I'll arrange it with Jordan, and we can have a late dinner."

"Jordan?"

He smiled at me like I was an idiot. "You know, Jordan Kamou."

My breath caught in my throat.

"Vestrano? You can't be serious."

Vestrano had two Michelin stars. It was one of the best restaurants in L.A. Everything about Vestrano was about mystery. Even the Eric Owen Moss constructed building conveyed the whispering of another world.

I'd never felt worthy enough to go.

And now Liam wanted to take me? On a whim?

Vestrano was an event. Something to treasure. Not some after-work afterthought.

Liam thought for a moment. "On second thought, I'll book a formal table for the evening next week. That way, you can experience the full grand production. It'll be worth it. Then, you'll understand what I'm trying to do." He smiled. "Think of it as a field trip."

A field trip?

"You know, a field trip. Like in elementary school, you'd go to the aquarium to see the sharks. It's just like that."

"I'd love to. It'd be enlightening."

His eyes locked on mine. His intense gaze pulled me in a beat. It made my stomach twist.

"It's too late to do anything about this menu. We'll serve it. But honestly, I thought you were better than this. It's extremely disappointing. I hope you pull it together."

He let it hang in the air as he left.

I stood there. My familiar disappointment returned.

I'd read the books. I'd studied the profiles. What did Liam want from me?

Camille smirked. Was she laughing at me?

She grabbed the tray of tortes and slid them on a rack. "I'd watch your back chef." She grabbed another tray of tortes and set it on the table to garnish with the glaze.

Rose gave me a sympathetic look and turned back to her chocolate stems.

I'd just been stabbed in the heart. Just like he'd done to my Bavarian strawberry cream the time before. Like that stupid fish.

And now he was talking about sharks ...?

I didn't feel like a bomb.

I was a deflated meringue.

* * *

"As Lama Surya Das once said, 'With every breath, the old moment is lost. A new moment arrives…'"

I peeked through my closed eyes, impatient. Yogi Dave was pacing in the front of the room, holding his hands in prayer, deep in thought as he spoke.

Yogi Dave was always so chill. What kind of girl did he find attractive anyway? A woman with linen robes and long hair flowing in the wind? A mistress of tranquility. Someone to align his Anahata with?

I couldn't wait for class to be over. I was itchy. Uncomfortable. My brain was on overdrive. How could I focus on Savasana when I had the Tony Awards to think about?

"Exhale …" Yogi Dave continued. "Let go of the person we used to be … Inhale and breathe … Welcome the person we are becoming …"

Welcome the person I was becoming …? Who was I becoming? It certainly wasn't one of the best pastry chefs in Los Angeles. I was becoming more like a mess.

Maybe Liam was right. Perhaps I couldn't understand what he was trying to say. Maybe I was going to crash and burn.

"Let us lay a moment and let the silence align us for our beautiful day …" Yogi Dave said in his soothing voice.

I peeked from my closed eyes again and peered around the room. How could my whole yoga class be so calm? So centered? How could they all be so Zen?

Was I the only person whose life was falling apart here? I felt like I was back on Liam's motorcycle, going eighty down the 110.

I squeezed my eyes shut again. Maybe dinner at Vestrano would be a game-changer. Jordan Kamou was a maestro, after all. Maybe his mysterious menu would whisper something to me. Maybe the experience would awaken my inner third eye for dessert. Maybe I'd see the light.

I tried to focus on my breathing.

Fiona. You can't take this shit personally. I'll end up destroying you if you do.

I tried to push him out of my brain. There was no way I was going there.

I tried to think of something happy. Why was I meditating on this toxic mess when I could think about something better? Someone like Rory?

Rory ...

His kind blue eyes ... The fun I'd had with him on our date ... His kiss on my cheek at the farmers' market ...

Yes. That was peace. That was tranquility.

Why was I languishing in toxicity when there were much happier things to think about?

I couldn't wait to see Rory at the festival. To see him in his natural habitat. Would we eat peaches all day? Or maybe he'd show me how he made cheese. He could show me his new Chardonnay or Riesling.

The thought of him made me warm inside.

He'd said I was open-minded ... Resilient ... He'd said I had lasting power ...

A pang of excitement washed over me. Peace overcame the stress.

Why the hell was I obsessing about Liam when I could easily think of Rory?

"Savasana is coming to an end. Walk through today open to the light. Open to new possibilities. Keep reminding yourself that you are the universe. Namaste." Yogi Dave whispered. The low frequency of his voice gave his message weight.

I opened my eyes and sat up as the room stirred around me.

Charlotte was already rolling her yoga mat up. Determination was in her eyes.

I rolled my mat up and followed her out of the yoga studio. The crush of sweaty classmates carried me out of the door. Champagne light greeted me as I walked outside.

Yogi Dave was right. It was going to be a beautiful day.

"OMG ... Look ..." Charlotte lit up and nodded for me to turn.

A man ran past, pushing a double stroller down the street. A shiny sheen of sweat glistened on his perfectly shaped, muscular upper body. The only thing he had on was a pair of red running shorts. His muscles flexed as he ran. Two toddlers smiled as they ate their granola bars.

Charlotte grinned. "That's gonna be what my baby daddy looks like someday."

I laughed. "I can see it now. You'll meet him at a gym. You'll get buff together, and he'll ask for your hand in marriage."

Charlotte smiled devilishly. "It'll be just like one of those Hallmark movies where he proposes under a tree with twinkly lights. And suddenly, from like ten generations back, your whole family shows up out of nowhere and starts clapping and crying. It'll be great."

She nudged me forward. "Let's get some coffee," she said. "We need to talk."

I squeezed the yoga mat strap on my shoulder tighter in my hands and followed her down the street.

This wasn't going to be good. "Charlotte, listen ... about the space ..."

She turned on the sidewalk midstep to face me. "You've had time to think about it? When are you going to change your mind?"

"Charlotte. I told you I wasn't going to do it. Please just let it go."

She sighed, frustrated. "Fiona. This is our shot. It's not going to happen again. You need to make the right choice."

My yoga mat was a million pounds on my back. "Look, this isn't like deciding what movie we'll see or where we will eat. This is a life choice. It's forever if we fail. I'm not ready for that."

Charlotte pursed her lips. I could tell her anger was building. "Yes, it is a life choice. But ask yourself—what if we win? What if we succeed? What if we actually take a chance and make it happen?"

"I have to make my name with Julia first. I have to succeed with Chef Auclair. There's no way I could go off on my own at this point without some sort of pedigree. I need that affirmation. It's career suicide now if I leave," I said.

"Fiona. You don't need someone else to say that you are great. You think because someone's important they have to vouch for you. Why do you think you have to be approved by others to be good enough?

She squared me with a stern gaze. "You don't need someone else to say that you're great. You are great, Fiona. You're one of the best pastry chefs I've ever seen. You're talented. You are gifted, and yes, you can do this."

Her eyes gazed at me, pleading. It made me even more uncomfortable.

She held her breath in anticipation.

The weight of the moment made me pause.

The thought of the whole thing: My own place ... My own voice ... My own rules ...

"No. I can't, Charlotte. I'm sorry."

Charlotte frowned, deflated. Her eyes shone with tears.

She took a disappointed breath. "You're a coward. And deep down, you know you are too."

She turned and walked down the sidewalk.

"Charlotte. Wait ..."

She didn't turn back as she disappeared around a corner.

She'd punched me in the gut.

I swung my yoga bag onto my other shoulder, letting the heavy moment sit there.

Was I a coward? Was I making a mistake? Was Charlotte right?

$$9$$

"No ..." Liam frowned as he tried the demo plates on the lowboy. He sighed, exasperated. "Vestrano can't come soon enough. You really need help. I don't know what to do with you."

He cast his spoon on the table. "Romance is dead. Innovation is king."

Romance is dead!?

I deflated. Another failure.

I went to the dark server's pit, watching the action in the atrium from afar.

The Tony Awards party was just getting started. Actresses in beautiful designer gowns. Directors and producers in tailored tuxedos mingled the room with moguls. And other people who were too important to identify. Would Denzel Washington and Leonardo Di Caprio show up? The evening looked promising.

Chinese lanterns and sparkly lights glowed from the wise old Ficus tree growing in the middle of the atrium. Dim candles lit the tables, giving the room a romantic and intimate glow.

Linen tablecloths, votives, and grand floral arrangements made it beyond elegant. The plates and various glasses were set precisely on each banquet table.

It was going to be a powerful night.

One of the servers cruised past. I grabbed a Prosecco off the tray. It tasted cold, sweet, and refreshing.

I'd worked so hard on the menu to make it just right. How could he not be happy? How could romance be dead?

I'd been so proud of the menu. Now, it was an embarrassment. A failure. I was so sure this was the menu that he'd approve of.

The Joconde was beautiful with its raspberry layers. The tiny square was nestled on top of a flourish of lemon curd and reduction. The swirls were vibrant and eye-pleasing on the plate. Along with the dark cherries, mini dianthus, and borage blossoms, it was a showstopper. I was pleased with how symmetrical it had turned out.

The flourless chocolate cake was a bit more dramatic. I'd used a diamond silicone mold for the cake and dressed it in white chocolate, saffron gelato, and a delicate fan of thinly sliced brandied peaches. I'd taken the saffron and made a simple crème anglaise with flecks of red in it. Shaved seventy percent Valrhona and tiny candied rose blossoms that kissed the plate.

The last dessert was the summer squash tart.

I'd taken the seeds from the squash, toasted and ground them down, and used the flour for the pâte sucrée. I'd used a Garam marsala to spice the squash and to complement the butterscotch ice cream.

The whipped crème fraiche was sweetened and simple. It served almost like a palate cleanser for the richness of the tart. Whisky caramel dressed the plate, and Orange Nasturtium and ruby Sweet William blossoms to create the final finish. It was gorgeous.

An overwhelming fog of disappointment washed over me. Should I be ashamed of what I had to offer to such an important event? What was I missing?

Maybe Vestrano could show me the way. Chef Kamou was mentored by Sebastian Rhuel, after all. Perhaps he'd have the answers I was searching for.

I took another sip of the Prosecco, enjoying its crispness. My eyes cruised the room, searching for someone famous.

"Beautiful, isn't it?" Julia crept up behind me, holding a glass of Chardonnay. She didn't have her apron on. She was wearing a simple black turtleneck and tailored pants. She was elegant.

"I love these evenings the most." She watched the elegant crowd. "My first real chef job in Marseille, I would always sneak a peek at the patrons eating my food. It was the first time my food had been grand. Important. It made me proud. Powerful."

She took a sip of her Chardonnay. "It's quite something to feed someone. There's something to be said for having the power to convey that which has no words. Just a sensory experience. And if you're good at it, you can change the world. There's power in the perfect bite or a perfect meal. Once you have that feeling of accomplishment from making something, you can never go back."

She took another sip. "Maggie Hughes understood that. Jonathan Agnew understood. I'm proud that I could impart that passion in them, and they could go on and become so successful." She smiled, pleased. "Maggie's place in Sonoma is giving Single Thread a run for its money, you know," she mused. A proud smile crossed her lips. "What do you think about Liam?" she asked.

I froze. How could I even begin to articulate everything? Even after his disappointed reaction to my menu for the evening. "He's been challenging. But I've been learning so much from him. I'm lucky for the opportunity."

"Yes. You are." She smiled. "His vision for Lucien is the most inspired yet. With everything he has planned, we will change the face of Los Angeles dining. We're going to conquer Michelin. I'll get my three stars and finally be able to rest. I'll finally be able to call my empire a complete work."

I looked at all the beautiful people mingling in the atrium. Laughing. Eating. Drinking. Having sensory experiences that set the mood.

I was suddenly overwhelmed. The idea of having power over them was too much.

"We need to start thinking about *The Taste*. We're the top show on the main cooking stage, opening night. I don't want Tartine to outshine us again like they did last year," she said, studying at me intensely. "I want you to demo something dramatic. Elegant yet elementary enough for an amateur."

My heart dropped to the floor.

The Taste?

It was the most significant food festival in Los Angeles. All the top chefs, critics, bloggers, and foodies assembled in one place to celebrate the best of Los Angeles food culture. And I'd be at the white-hot center. It'd be my time to shine.

Jonathan Agnew had demoed there. Maggie Hughes had become an instant star after her demonstration.

A punch of thrilling terror flashed in my stomach. "Wow, Julia. I don't even know what to say."

She frowned, annoyed. "Don't say anything. Just deliver. You and Liam are going to unveil the new Lucien. It may be the most important night of the year for us. If you pass this test, good things could happen for you."

A flicker of hope coursed through my body. Could this be it? Could this prove that I could be chef? Was I that close?

Her eyes recalibrated across the room. "That dirty bastard. How dare he? That's not part of the rules." She fumed.

"What are you talking about?" I turned, trying to see where she was focused.

"The tall man in the dark suit. He's hidden in the crowd. He's eating one of the lobster canapes."

I looked at the throng. It could have been anyone.

She set her glass down angrily on a passing tray. "It's Maxwell Davis. He's one of the Michelin inspectors." She thought a beat. I could see a whiff of panic on her face.

"Who's on the line? Who's plating? Where's Liam?"

She turned to me. "Get your desserts ready. I want them spot on. I need you to plate like your life depends on it." She turned and whisked through the servers' pit and into the kitchen.

My eyes cruised the party. A wave of panic hit me. Was my summer squash tart sweet enough? Was the flourless chocolate cake rich enough? Would the whisky caramel complement the complex flavor of the Valhrona? Would the Joconde's raspberry layers come together with the tartness of the berries and lemon curd ...?

My mind flexed into overdrive.

Did my desserts have the power to convey the ultimate sensory experience? Enough power to win three Michelin stars?

Did I have the power to wield taste like a paladin? Did I have the power to change someone's perception with one bite?

One of my father's silly quotations floated in my mind: *Optimism is a perfectly legitimate response to failure ...*

My gaze rested on the old Ficus, watching over the important guests.

Its wisdom whispered to me from across the room. It gave me a hint of inspiration.

I just had to reflect on the tone of the moment. The elegance of the surroundings. The romance of this time and place.

Romance is dead ... Liam's words disturbed me.

Could I be optimistic in my moment of failure? Was this a failure? Or merely a simple setback.

Maybe I still had a chance.

Who cared if Cate Blanchett enjoyed the tart? Maybe Maxwell would take one bite of my Joconde and be transported to another dimension.

I turned back toward the kitchen.

I could see Liam directing the kitchen brigade with tight precision. He was a titan, fierce in his white coat as he led the charge.

Famous people eating my desserts ... Michelin snooping around ...

And now there was *The Taste* to think about ...

All I wanted was to get it right.

* * *

I pulled into Rory's driveway. The parking lot was full. I was lucky to get the last spot.

Kids and parents carried boxes and baskets as they made their way to the farm. I could hear music in the background through my open window.

I tried to push last night's failure out of my head. It was just too much. The Michelin inspector had disappeared into the throng of revelers. Was he a figment of Julia's imagination? Was she that paranoid?

I got out of the car, opened the back door, and let Luna out. He stopped dead in his tracks and sniffed the air. He was like an astronaut on another planet. I glanced around as I grabbed his leash. "Now Luna. I want you to behave. Be a good boy. I'm trying to make a good impression," I said as I scratched his body. He gave me a hearty bark. Could dogs understand human language?

An orchard of peach and cherry trees stood tall in the distance as far as I could see. Fields of every type of green and vegetable carpeted the horizon. Newly planted grapes were staked and perfectly lined up on acres of tilled soil. The parallel lines of the rows were an optical illusion in the distance. Goats and miniature pigs were penned behind a white fence, nuzzling the fresh hay on the ground. Kids were mingling and playing in a petting zoo.

Luna pulled the leash, ready to make new friends.

I approached the main area where all the activity was happening. The farm was in full celebration mode.

Two people with acoustic guitars played a Baroque duet together under a small tent. A food truck was parked under a big tree. Unconventional glass-paned windows were pulled up to showcase a wood fire oven and various gourmet pizzas.

Long wood tables were laid out in front of the main barn. People were sitting and enjoying wine, pizza, and pint containers of fruits in the shade.

I looked out to the fields. People mingled and picked fruits and vegetables.

"Fiona! Over here!" Delia waved to me as she stood at a table, weighing the fruits and vegetables for a long line of people paying for their bounty. "I'm so glad you came!"

I rounded the table, and she hugged me. "This is my favorite day of the year."

She grabbed a box from a ten-year-old and placed it on the scale. "That'll be eleven dollars," she said, smiling. A tired mother juggled a diaper bag with a baby on her hip. She reached into her purse, looking for her wallet.

"Give me a ten, and you're good, sweetie." Delia smiled.

The woman floundered in her wallet, pulled out a wrinkled bill, and handed it to Delia. "Thank you so much!"

Delia motioned to one of her workers to take her place. "Let's go inside."

"Delia, your place … It's beautiful."

She smiled, proudly. "It's a work in progress." She petted Luna with a generous scratch behind the ears. He instantly wagged his tail in excitement.

"Rory's working the wine bar." She gave me a wink. "He'll be happy to see you."

Curiosity took over me as we walked toward a rustic barn. Posies were planted in wine barrels. It even had water dishes for four-legged friends. I looped Luna's leash on a pole and followed Delia inside.

People mingled in the wine bar. Shelves of Resiling, Chenin Blanc, and Shiraz stood tall with endless jams, salsas, and canned vegetables. Somehow, everything Rory and Delia grew was crafted into something special.

A tall woman touched Delia's arm. "Ma'am. Do you have that pear butter you had last season?"

Delia lit up to the tall woman. "Do I ever. Let me show you." She turned to me. "Give me a minute." She stepped behind the counter and back into the kitchen.

Rory was at the wine bar. His hands punctuated the air as he explained something to a stuffy man in his sixties. The man swirled the wine in the glass as he tasted it. He smiled, pleased, and took another sip. You could see Rory's quiet passion from across the room.

I stood back. I wanted to see him from afar—to capture him in a natural moment. He was handsome in his usual T-shirt-and-jeans uniform. His tan skin. The light behind his eyes as he talked to the customer.

I took a deep breath and stepped forward through the crowd. His eyes lit up as they met mine. "I'm so glad you came."

He reached under the counter, grabbed a chilled glass, and poured me a generous drink of wine. "If you like Riesling, you'll really like this."

I met his eyes as I took a sip. It was light, cold, and delicious. It was more acidic and citrusy than a Riesling. I liked it.

"That's my Pinot Gris. Sometimes Pinot gets a bad reputation, but this one is fantastic. The fruit and citrus are well balanced. 2017 was a good year."

I took another sip.

He was right. It was an outstanding year, indeed.

"Give me a minute, and I'll finish up."

He went to the back, and a young girl with a friendly face came out, tied an apron on, and stepped in his place.

"Let's go." Rory grabbed my hand and pulled me out of the door.

The music from the guitars filled the air outside. The yeasty aroma of the pizza from the truck smelled delicious.

A little girl was playing with Luna. He growled, frisky, and his rump bumped to and fro as they pulled a chew toy. It was a fair match.

I instantly knew it was Grace.

She had Rory's blue eyes and brown hair. She was sporting a pair of purple overalls, just like Delia's, and lime green Crocs.

Rory smiled, amused by his daughter. "Grace, be careful. You're always too friendly."

She let Luna have the toy and hugged Rory around the waist, smiling up at him.

You could see their bond. It was deep and sweet. "We should open the pen and see if he'll be friends with the goats."

"I don't think that's going to happen, honey. He'll just make the goats scream. We don't want to scare people."

He bent down to scratch Luna's back. I smiled. It couldn't get any better than a man liking a dog.

"What's his name?" Grace asked.

"This is Luna. He's my roommate's dog, but sometimes he's mine, too. What's your name?"

"Grace." She fell to her knees and let Luna lick her face. His tail went into overdrive. He'd made a best friend.

Rory laughed and glanced at me from the love fest. His blue eyes caught the sun and turned vibrant. "What would you like to see first?" He asked. "We can see the strawberry fields, or I could show you the orchards."

"Surprise me." I smiled.

He grabbed my hand and led the way. I tried to keep up as he pulled me towards the vast vineyard.

Grace bounded with Luna in the distance, playing with a stick. They were having the time of their lives.

I took in the scene around me. The trellises were spidered and green with the new grapes he had planted. The perfect rows went on forever. The air was dense with the smell of earth and sunshine. The breeze from the ocean gave me goosebumps.

The landscape took my breath away.

"Rory ... This is amazing ..."

"I just finished planting this. It was quite a project. I'm feeling pretty good about it, though." He smiled to himself. I could see the pride in his eyes.

I was intrigued by the new growth around me. "How long will it take for the grapes to grow?"

"About three years. This is a huge experiment. There are a lot of factors in play. The sun, the soil, the air, to start. This region is completely different from Santa Ynez, so trying something new is exciting."

We glanced ahead. Grace and Luna were continuing their tug-of-war match with his leash. "She won't stop. She'd do this all day if I let her."

"I'm sure Luna wouldn't mind," I said.

"Grace, go check on Grandma," he called. "Make sure she doesn't need any help. Maybe she can get you a piece of pizza."

"Is it okay if Luna has a piece?" His tongue was hanging out of his mouth, lopsided and pink. He was a city dog, after all.

"Sure, he can," I said.

Grace grabbed his leash. "I'll make sure there's no pepper-oni. You don't want stinky dog farts later."

I laughed. I liked this girl.

Rory pointed his finger at the house. "Grace. Go."

She tugged Luna and bounded to the house.

He turned to face me. His eyes met mine. My smile mingled with his.

"It's good to see you. I'm glad you came."

We stood there for a moment, bookended by the rows of grapes. The scent of the plants, mingled with the breeze, made me dizzy looking at him.

"Let's go see the strawberries first. I want to show you every-thing," he said as he grabbed my hand again. It was so good in his as we approached the field. Adults and children dotted the horizon, harvesting the berries.

The earthy smell of the soil mingled with the sweet, fragrant smell of the fruit. Bees buzzed and dodged here and there, pollinating the plants. The strawberries were like jewels peeking from the leaves.

I followed him as he walked down the narrow row. He bent down and picked a strawberry.

"Here you go. Try this." He pulled a cloth from his hand, wiped off the berry, and handed it to me. "This is a variation on a Mara de Bois. My mother crossed it with an Allstar. That's where the extra sweetness comes from."

I popped it in my mouth. It tasted even better than the little pint baskets he'd given me at the farmers' market. It was warm from the sun and extra juicy.

He jumped over a couple of rows, expertly navigating the plants. I tried to follow but ended up tripping over my own feet. I recovered quickly, trying not to look like an idiot.

He took a turn down another row and stopped. He picked another strawberry, wiped it off, and handed it to me. "Get ready. This is going to be your secret weapon."

I took a bite.

My body tingled.

It was the best strawberry I'd ever tasted. It was beyond description. "How the hell did you do that?" I wiped the juice off my chin and finished it off. "I don't even know what to say."

"It's a cross between an Ozark Beauty and a Chandler. My mother and I have been tinkering with this one for a couple of years. They didn't do as well in Santa Ynez as they have here."

I met his eyes, and my heart skipped as my foot caught on a plant, and I stumbled again. He grabbed my hand. "Are you okay?" He laughed.

"Never mind me. I'm trying to find my sea legs." A surge of a smile blossomed from within as his eyes met mine.

"Let's go see the orchard. I want to show you the apricots. They're turning out to be something special."

I took everything in as we strolled towards the orchard. The land was so beautiful. So peaceful. It was a living extension of Rory's energy.

"The orchard was the first thing my mother grew when she moved here with my father. They built Fleurcine from this small little orchard. It all started here."

The extraordinary smell was heavy and fragrant as I walked under the canopy of peach trees. I followed Rory closely as he walked between the rows of trees.

"Have you ever tried a Bonita?" He stopped and picked a peach from a tree. "These are almost ready to harvest." He handed it to me, daring me with a smile.

The deep red blush and yellow color mingled on the skin. I took a bite. The flavor was tart, and the texture was firm. Not ready, but I could taste the flavors of what was to come.

"I can tell these are going to be delicious."

"I'm very excited about them. I know you'll make something great."

He took the peach from me and tossed it into an errant bushel under the tree. He stepped closer to me. He made my heart surge. Something about being here made my creative juices come alive. I was more connected with the cycle of life.

And to think Rory had the power to do all of this.

We stood alone under the peach trees. The sound was dense from the canopy of leaves.

"Let me show you the best view. I'm sure you'll like it." He grabbed my hand. I tried to keep up as he pulled me along through the orchard.

He rounded around the perimeter of the trees, and I saw the farm up high at a different angle.

It was epic.

The vineyards. The fields. The Orchard.

"Pretty amazing, right?"

"That's an understatement," I said. "This is beyond anything I expected."

He smiled, proudly. "I'm blessed to be able to live my life like this. I'm lucky."

The moment took my breath away. Rory and his mother created magic. And this truly was a magical place.

* * *

We made our way to a small shed half-buried in the ground. He let go of my hand and swung open the doors open. A wave of dense, cool, putrid air wafted out.

"I want you to keep an open mind. I'm not a serial killer, I promise."

I laughed. "Should I feel stupid for falling for your trap?"

"Maybe? Maybe not. You're going to have to trust your instincts." He laughed. "Come on."

I followed. The steep wooden stairs disappeared into the darkness.

He pulled a chain from the ceiling, and a hanging lightbulb lit up. My eyes adjusted to the dim light, then cruised the room. It was a good-sized room with brick walls and a dirt floor.

Wood shelves were lined with different-sized wheels of cheese. A beat-up table stood in the corner. Mysterious machines stood in the dark.

"I've been tinkering with different kinds of goat cheese." He grabbed a wheel of cheese from one of the shelves and set it down on the table, grabbing a cheese board and a knife.

My eyes finally adjusted. "How many secret corners does your farm have?"

"This was my fort with my friends when I was growing up. We used to kick the shit out of each other with homemade swords. We used apples as grenades. And I hate to admit it, but a little D and D was played here. He laughed.

I liked the way he sounded. His laugh was genuine. Strong and full of joy.

"I moved all of this from Santa Inez. The temperature of this space is perfect for what I'm trying to do, so I'm pretty confident about it." He smiled. "I have a friend in Brooklyn who ages his cheese in an old abandoned subway tunnel on his property. This is the same environment, so I'm pretty sure it'll work."

He beckoned me to his side. "Come here." He held the purple round up to my nose. "Smell this."

I leaned in.

The smell was beyond rank. It was pungent and ripe. I was surprised how my nose hooked onto the smell and wouldn't let go.

"This is a washed rind cheese. I've been washing it with a Merlot to give it a fruitier tone. The wine keeps mold from forming. It also promotes bacteria growth, giving it its savory but fruity flavor."

He pulled a peach out of his pocket and sliced a wedge. Then, cut a piece of the cheese. He handed both to me. "Try it."

It was soft. Not too pasty or rank, like I was expecting. It was excellent. I swallowed. "It's complex. Tangy."

He smiled. Proud. "Now, taste the peach."

I popped the wedge of peach into my mouth. It tasted even sweeter and refreshing. The peach paired perfectly with the cheese.

He poured a mysterious rose-colored wine into a glass on the table and handed it to me.

"Now, for the finish." He smiled.

I took a sip of the wine. The taste was perfection. "I'm speechless. I have no words." I took another sip of the wine. "You're a magician."

"No. I just like to try new things."

We lingered there for a beat, taking in the energy.

He pulled me close and guided my chin up to his lips.

He gave me a gentle kiss. I pushed even closer to him as his arms wrapped around me, and he kissed me deeper. His lips gently searched mine, finding a connection.

This was heaven.

"Dad! Where are you?" Grace yelled from the door above. We quickly broke apart, putting a good amount of distance between us.

She bounded down the stairs and tugged Luna's leash in her hand, and he peeked his head in the door. He pulled back, not wanting to go down.

"Something's wrong with Grandma."

"What do you mean?"

"She fainted. Come quick."

Rory took the stairs up two at a time, and I followed.

The sunlight assaulted my face as I walked out of the cave. It made me hot and sweaty. The perfect moment was gone.

I tried to follow Rory as he walked to the house. He was too fast, and I couldn't keep up. Grace led the way, Luna trailing after.

Delia was sitting on the porch. One of the farmhands was next to her, giving her a moist towel and some water. She looked embarrassed as we approached. "Don't worry. I'm fine. I'm fine."

"Tell me what happened." Rory was in concern overdrive. He felt her forehead with his hand.

She brushed him away. "Don't make a fuss. It's okay."

"You pushed yourself too far. I told you to be careful."

"I just got a little sunstroke. I'm okay now. Let's forget it." She chuckled, trying to laugh it off.

"No. This is serious, Mom."

She gave him a stern glare. It was deadly. "It happened. I'm fine. Let's drop it."

"You're seeing the doctor. I mean it." He stared her down a beat. He meant business. I could sense the balance of power shift between them.

She averted her gaze. "Fine. Whatever you want."

Rory took a deep breath. I could tell he was trying to calm down.

Delia grabbed my hand as she stood up. "I'm sorry for the little mishap. Please don't let this ruin your time here."

She turned and made her way back to the house, ignoring Rory. She stood straighter in her overalls, with her hat held high. I could tell she was trying to get her dignity back.

Grace caught up and grabbed her hand. They were cute together with their matching overalls.

I glanced at Rory. He was shaken and pale.

"Are you okay?" I asked.

He brushed it off. "I'll be fine."

We stood there a beat. I didn't know what to do. The magic spell that had woven between us was broken.

The musicians were packing up, and I could see the food truck in the distance, closing its windows and getting ready to leave. The crowd had thinned as well. The party was over.

"I should go. If I go now, I won't hit traffic." I studied my dirty shoes. I was never going to wash them or wear them ever again. They were my souvenirs from one of the most perfect days of my life.

Luna's tail drooped, sadly. He knew it was time to leave, too. I grabbed his dirty leash.

"Let me walk you to your car." He took my hand, gentle and firm. Our fingers interlaced as we walked to the parking lot.

My car was the last one left.

"Listen. I'm going up to Santa Ynez in a few days. Why don't you come with me? I could pick you up. It'd be a great way to hang out."

My whole body beamed. "I'd love to. Consider me there."

We made it to my Land Cruiser, and I unlocked the back door. Luna jumped in and circled three times before he plopped down in the seat. He laid his head on his front feet and heaved a heavy sigh as I shut the door.

Rory laughed. "I think Grace broke your dog."

"This was good for him. He got to see how a real dog lives."

I suddenly remembered the pie. "Hold on. I have something for you." I opened the driver's side door, reached across the console, and grabbed the brown box.

The purple bow was a little deflated. I crunched it in my hand to freshen it up. The box was warm from the heat in the car from the sun.

I was pleased. It was the perfect serving temperature.

I beamed with pride as I gave it to him.

He smiled, eyebrows raised, surprised. "Thank you. What is it?"

"It's a pie. From the blackberries you gave me. I hope you like it. The crust is my secret recipe."

He grinned. "I'm sure I will."

He put the box down on the roof of my car and pulled me in close. "Today was nice. Thank you for letting me show you around. I liked playing show and tell with you."

His arms were warm and strong around me. I couldn't get over how perfect his height was for me.

He leaned in and gave me another kiss. I liked that I was getting used to them. With every kiss, he made me want him a little more.

His hands supported my back as he pulled me in closer. He gave me one final flourish of a kiss and pulled away.

"I have to go," I said.

I could see a glint of disappointment in his eyes as he grabbed the box from the top of the car and leaned against it as I got in the Land Cruiser. I rolled the window down.

"Drive safe. Maybe you could call me when you get there. That'd be nice. Just to make sure you made it."

He made my heart flip. "I'd love to."

I turned on the engine, and he stepped back with his box, watching as I pulled out.

He waved in my back mirror as I drove into the dusk.

He was handsome in his rumpled black tee and jeans. His brown hair was framing his face.

I pulled onto the highway, and he was gone.

I couldn't wait to call him when I got home. What could we possibly talk about? I was excited to find out.

10

I stepped out of the Uber and closed the door. My foot twisted on the curb.

I quickly adjusted my dress, surveying the space around me. I hoped no one noticed. I hated these stupid heels. They always betrayed my balance.

Eric Owen Moss's Waffle Building grew from the ground like an organic metal monstrosity. Its curved beams and glass stretched to the sky like it was trying to reach something but not quite getting there. It was still muscling out of the ground. Its burgundy rust beams were Dr. Seuss-inspired. Teleported from the pages of *The Lorax*.

I walked down the path leading to the entrance. A green light illuminated shattered rock. I could smell the vague fragrance of frankincense.

"Fiona!" Liam smiled at me as he approached. "Good evening."

My breath caught in my throat.

He wore a simple dark suit with a linen shirt unbuttoned at the top, his collarbone peeking out. The olive color of his shirt accentuated his green eyes. His hair was tamed and neat, slicked back from his face.

He studied me a beat. "You look amazing."

I tried not to blush.

"Are you ready?" He smiled. "Trust me. This will change your life."

"I certainly hope so," I said. I was praying to the heavens that this would be my breakthrough.

He held the door open for me, and I walked inside.

Vestrano's lobby was beautiful. A stark white sculpture of a serpent's skeleton levitated in the air. The movement of the lines of the sculpture was seductive and smooth.

Liam pushed the elevator button. "I want you to consider this experience a trip to outer space—a foreign land. Pretend you're going to Io or some moon of Jupiter's. Leave your expectations at the door."

The elevator door opened. We stepped in, and the door closed behind us. The ascending elevator matched my twisted stomach.

His eyes met mine. A soft smile crossed his lips.

The elevator door opened, and a beautiful woman wearing a dark smock greeted us. "Good evening."

He leaned in and whispered something in the woman's ear. She smiled and nodded. "Come this way."

The room was lit from underneath. Wine glasses reflected from the tall ceiling. The windows let in the last oranges of the summer sunset. The room was a glorious sanctum. It took me out of myself as we sat down.

I studied Liam from across the table. The low light complemented his strong jaw. His eyes were braced with excitement.

Servers in dark flowing robes and slippers walked up and down the side stairs from the kitchen. They seemed like monks, delivering strange plates to tables like a ceremony. The whole vibe felt like we were in a temple.

"Tonight, there's no menu. There's just experience. Get ready. You're in for the ride of your life," he said.

A server filled our glasses with wine. "This is a Rombauer Chardonnay. Jordan picked it for you to enjoy tonight. Enjoy."

She left, and Liam studied me quietly and held his glass up. "To clarity."

I clinked his glass, and he held my gaze as I took a sip. The buttery hints in the wine of apple and vanilla teased my palate, preparing me for the journey ahead.

My ear shifted to the odd music in the air.

It was like a tone poem. I could pick up different pitches from different parts of the room. It created a baseline in my brain that anchored me.

"Ultimately, this is a universe that I want Lucien to occupy. I want Lucien to be in its own dimension. I want it to transcend perception."

"Do you always speak in platitudes?"

He smiled provocatively. "Only when I want to make myself clear."

The server set the first dish of the evening in front of us. "Queen Kaluga Caviar and rillette of smoked and fresh wild salmon. Enjoy."

A stem of green bedazzled with what looked to be yellow roe and a delicate blossom of salmon were garnished on the plate with mysterious flowers. Some of the pink and purple blossoms were familiar from my father's garden. The whole thing was presented on a stone tortilla. I was perplexed.

How was I supposed to eat this?

His eyes were bright and excited. "Try it."

I followed his lead and took a bite.

The salty roe popped into my mouth with a salty aftertaste. The silky salmon massaged my tongue as I swallowed. It was whispering something I struggled to hear. Was it longing? Or maybe yearning.

It wasn't food. It was a statement of flavor. A performance art piece.

"What do you think?" He leaned in closer. His broad shoulders were perfectly symmetrical with the table.

"Interesting," I said, struggling for the right words.

He grinned, holding back a laugh. "I'm always suspicious when someone says interesting." He laughed.

I took another deep sip of the wine. The entrée had triggered something in me.

The server broke the moment, whisking our dishes away. Another server put the next plate in front of us. "This is a Poiroux, with slow-cooked leeks with roasted hazelnuts, roasted in a dressing of Dijon mustard, chives, and tarragon."

It was a wheel inside a dark wheel. A flourish of leeks was spotted with dollops of hazelnuts, along with a kiss of mustard. The chives and tarragon delicately accented the showstopper.

The server bowed. "Enjoy." Her robe flourished around her as she left.

"Jordan's vision is intriguing. A ghost of something like El Bulli. But different ... unique ..." Liam's fingers centered the plate as he took it in, studying it. "He drives in with the architecture of the food. The moment of the dish ..."

He plucked the leek from the dark clay bowl with his fork and held it out to me. A seductive smile crossed his lips. "Here."

I took it from his hand, my fingers brushing against his, and took a bite.

The leek tasted salty, and the mustard had a faint honey taste. It captivated my tongue with complex opposites of salty and sweet.

It made my head hum. My senses were waking up to something mysterious.

Liam's eyes focused harder on me, and he leaned forward. The veil of his armor was lifted, and I could see his passion.

"Are you beginning to understand?" he said in low voice. "There's a statement in this. It's visceral yet, at the same time, grounded. I love the touch of mustard underneath the sweetness of the honey. It's almost sensual." He smiled.

I took in the space around me, trying to get my head together. The architecture of the space took my breath away. The glow of the lights. The stretch of the beams. I peeked out to the windows. A beautiful Los Angeles night was emerging.

"I love how a great dish can allude to something more … Punctuate the moment … Elevate the mood …" he said as he took me in. "A great dish can be more seductive than a touch. A thought … Or a kiss …"

Where was he going with this?

A server whisked away our plates, and another set a plate down in front of us. A black one with a beautiful white mystery flower embellished with white asparagus and purple blossoms sat on my plate.

The curves of the stems drew me in. The angles of the elegant, crafted flower seduced my eyes.

It was the most romantic plate I'd ever seen. It made my heart hurt. It held the magic of a Picasso. A Van Gogh.

I was so transported that I hadn't heard what the server said it was.

Liam smiled at me, eager to share the moment. "What are you waiting for?"

I didn't want to break the beautiful spell of the plate. How was it even possible to eat something like this? I gently plucked a petal and took a bite.

It was a mystery of flavors. Asparagus. A nut. Macadamia in the milk? A grain? Squid? The meat was tender. A savory hint of the ocean, bursting and juicy, teased my palate. Delicate and alive in my mouth.

He looked down and straightened his plate. He touched the flower's petals, tracing the edges. "Beautiful, isn't it?" He smiled.

I took another bite. It was a seduction. My head became dizzy as the subtle flavors of the asparagus and some mysterious rice came together, teasing my tongue.

"I don't even know what to say ..." I sipped some wine. It paired beautifully with the delicate and savory aftertaste of the petals.

I studied him from across the table. I could tell he was in the same headspace as me.

A quiet beat of understanding crossed between us.

A server whisked away the empty dishes, and brought the next dish and set it down. "Savory tarte aux fruits. Enjoy."

It was a simple tart. Embellished with sliced dates, it flourished into a blossoming lotus flower. The plate evoked a celebration of something simple. Something special.

I took a bite. A tiny date balanced on my fork.

It was the best date I'd ever had. Simple and sweet. The grainy texture pasted my tongue and massaged my taste buds. I took another sip of my wine and washed everything down.

It was so simple. So delicious.

How could something so simple be so transformative?

Liam's gaze brought me back to earth. I couldn't help but watch his jaw as he chewed. He gazed at me intensely. "I want to convey this artistic excellence," he said. "But with more of a masculine edge. I want to drive into your brain. Take over. Mettle with your subconscious."

"How is everything so far?" Chef Jordan Kamou approached. He was like a yogi in his black chef coat. His calm smile defined quiet wisdom.

"The tarte aux fruits ... It was beautiful. So simple," I said.

Jordon smiled. "I'm pleased that you like it. Picking the dates in Thomas's garden at French Laundry was one of my favorite things to do. I always come back to that feeling when I create."

The moment stopped. I was suspended in space by his words. Clarity.

I understood what he meant. My inspiration came from an organic place. Taste. Feel. Flavor. A place in time. A simple taste of something as simple as a date.

All of it meant something.

Jordan knew it.

The outside world muted as I put the pieces together in my mind. It could be as simple as a date.

I looked at Liam and Jordan talking as my ears clung to the tones of the music.

I caught Jordan's gaze. "Thank you," I whispered.

Chef Jordan nodded to me with a smile and went to another table.

Liam watched me with quiet pleasure. "You see it, don't you? Do you get it now?" His face melted into a fierce smile. It was almost scary. "Now that you get it, you'll do exactly what I want. You'll convey my vision." He held my gaze. "You'll help me get my stars."

A pleased smile settled on his lips.

I took a sip of my wine. Overwhelmed.

Something was coming together in the far reaches of my mind. Or was it escaping me? I was grasping at some sort of eternal truth.

I studied him from across the table.

He was mysterious in the shadowy light. Larger than life. Powerful.

I pushed my thoughts down. All of it was just way too much.

The server brought another dish and set it on the table. "Black truffle risotto with Jamon Iberico broth. It's a creamy Carnarloi rice cooked in a broth of Jamon and Iberico and truffle juice. It's finished with aged Castelmango cheese and brown butter. Enjoy."

I glanced from the beautiful plate to Liam.

He was taking in the plate with a quiet intensity. Studying. Savoring. Exploring. "I told you to trust me. Was I wrong?"

I studied the beautiful plate. I was afraid to taste it. Fearful of what I would find.

Clarity was almost too much.

Was I Icarus? Was I going to get burned?

Could I trust him? Could I trust his vision? The power behind his promise was too hard to comprehend.

I lifted my fork as I took a bite.

The taste and texture of the creamy rice and truffle juice brought me back to the moment. I met his potent stare, and we tasted the magical dish together.

For a moment, we connected on another level. Another dimension.

Was it Io, or was it Jupiter? All I knew was it was some foreign land.

* * *

The patio reminded me of a topiary maze. The sharp edges of the foliage created an intimate, mysterious place. A cool breeze teased my face and cleansed the air.

I took a sip of my Moscato de Asti. The sweet after-dinner wine was a perfect punctuation of the meal.

Liam grinned at me. Saying nothing.

I was trying to decide what his silence meant.

"Watching you was almost better than the meal itself ..." He finally said.

His shadowed outline stood in the dark. There was a static silence between us.

His gaze lingered with mine. "What do you want to do now?"

Another breeze washed across my face.

I needed air.

There were earth, fire, water, and air people.

Maybe Liam was fire.

"What are we doing here, Fiona?" His eyes were lit from within. This situation was more than I could handle. How was I going to get out of this diplomatically? This was a dicey situation, and if I didn't handle it well … well, I didn't even want to think of the consequences.

I took the last sip of my drink. The wine had turned bitter and sharp. I set it down on the table.

"Thank you for tonight. It's been enlightening." I stood up straight, neutralizing the moment.

"I hope you understand what I'm trying to do now. I certainly think this is a game changer …" He straightened his jacket.

"It's been an extraordinary evening, Fiona. I've learned a few things myself …" He broke my gaze and stepped forward to leave.

I shifted, and the heel of my shoe caught on a ridge in the stone trivet. I felt myself falling forward.

These stupid fucking shoes.

He turned and caught me. His arms stabilized my body.

We stood there. His arms around me. Face to face.

I could see the flecks of brown in his green eyes up close. Were they hazel?

His body was firm against mine. His smile lingered on me for a beat.

He leaned in and gave me a brush of a kiss. Almost imperceptible, but there was something.

He pulled away and grinned. Triumphant. "You're delicious."

He turned, breaking the embrace, and walked down the path, through the topiary to the street.

He unstrapped his helmet and slung it on. Straddling the bike, he started the engine.

I watched as he pulled away from the curb without looking back. His ruby taillight disappeared into the night.

I searched for something to bring me back to earth. The topiary surrounding me matched my confusion. All my convictions of clarity were gone.

What the hell had just happened?

* * *

I sat on a beach chair with my feet propped up on a paint can. The hints of dry heat were stirring in the early morning air. It was going to be a hot day.

Luna lay next to me on the sidewalk. It was too early in the morning, even for him.

Kate liked to get started early in the morning when she had a project. Before it got too hot to work.

The Venice Chamber of Commerce had commissioned a mural from her for one of the underpasses by the beach. She was painting her signature flowers and sea. It was an elegant and sensual production that only Kate could pull off.

She stretched with a paintbrush, arcing a grand purple swirl on the cement wall in front of her.

I plucked a can of Diet Coke from the cooler sitting beside me and cracked it open, taking a sip. "Those stupid fucking shoes ... I hate heels. I don't understand how any woman wears them ..."

"What do shoes have to do with anything?" she asked as she filled purple into the arc she'd created.

"I tripped … Then he kissed me … Or didn't kiss me … I'm still trying to figure it out."

"Usually, you pretty much know the score on that one," she laughed.

"Exactly! That's how Liam messes with my head!"

Charlotte stopped painting and turned. "What weird code are you living by? In some situations, a kiss is a friendly handshake."

"You're mocking me. I shouldn't have said anything."

Kate smiled, enjoying this. "It could be like one of those French New Wave movies. You could have a real relationship with Rory and a tortured love affair with Liam. With lots of Vespa rides, crazy sex, and cigarette smoking."

"Liam doesn't have a Vespa. He has a stupid motorcycle."

"Exactly."

I sipped my Coke as I watched her paint. I loved the sticky sound the paint-coated brush made as it met the wall. It was oddly satisfying.

Kate swished her purple brush into a can of turpentine. "You had some wine. A great meal, and you had a moment. I think you're overreacting. Just pretend it never happened."

The heat of the morning sun started to burn on the top of my head.

"Maybe you're right."

Kate stepped back and assessed her work.

"Do you think I should go sage or emerald for the leaves on the gardenias?"

"How should I know? I'm a spectator here." I sipped my Coke. "What's the darker shade?"

"I'll go emerald. Sage will work better with the Birds of Paradise …" She bent down and pried a can of paint open with a screwdriver.

I watched as she dipped her brush in the can and continued painting.

"How did it go with that manager guy at the show?" I asked.

"I don't know. He said I needed a rhythm guitarist. How the hell am I going to find someone to get along with Harvey? He's so resistant to change," she said as she painted.

"What are you going to do?"

"I don't even know. I don't know any good guitarists." She arced the green paintbrush against the wall. It trailed the pretty shade of emerald.

"Rory's taking me to his vineyard in Santa Ynez. He's going to show me his place."

"Wow! This is like a French movie. Your love life has been a wasteland forever, and suddenly, you're torn between two men. Being a pastry chef definitely has its perks."

I glared at her. "I thought you said Liam was a moment."

She laughed. "I was just taking the opportunity to poke at you. I'm sorry." She stuck her brush into the can of green paint and painted the base coat of leaves onto the wall. "Rory seemed nice. He certainly held up in front of the stage. I was impressed."

"He's amazing," I mused. "He's so genuine," I said. "But he has a daughter. And he's torn in so many directions with his busy life. I don't even know how I'd fit into that."

Kate smiled coyly. "If you think about it, he's sort of passed your three-date boredom …"

"What do you mean?" I asked.

"Well. It's always the same. You get excited for the first two dates with someone, and then the third one comes along, and you're bored. You've been that way with everyone I've ever seen you with: Eric, Steve, Jason … It's always the same. So this is something to think about."

I thought to myself for a moment. I hadn't even thought about it, actually.

"Just go with the flow. Love finds a way." She smiled. "If he's showing you his vineyard, it must mean something, don't you think?"

I scratched Luna behind the ears. "It does. But he seems almost too good to be true."

"There you go. Overthinking again. You need to get back into doing your yoga meditation with Charlotte. You're both driving me crazy.

My heart darkened. "What has she said to you?"

Kate kneeled and continued painting. "She's disappointed. You're distracted. It's a mess. You just need to apologize to each other and get on with life."

"I should have never looked at the place with her. I feel bad for leading her on."

Kate arched her paintbrush as far as she could reach. "Was it a good space?"

"It needs a lot of work and maybe a fumigator, but it had everything. She could easily swing it on her own. I don't understand why she wants me to do it with her so badly. It's just another one of her harebrained schemes."

"You're symbiotic. You're both talented and at the top of your game. It makes sense."

I frowned at her, doubtful.

"I'm hardly even close ..."

Kate shook her head. "You go on and on about how Julia's going to give you a reputation. What does it mean to have a reputation? And what is a reputation anyway? It's just a lot of people saying great things about you. If you're not careful, you can hold on so tight to finding acceptance that you lose who you are. You can lose the reason why you started doing this thing in the first place."

"I'm not going to forget. I've worked my whole life for this."

"Well, you're talented. Charlotte's talented. And you have an opportunity to do something great. I'd think about it if I were you."

"That's easy for you to say."

She stepped back from the wall and looked at me. "I've said so much about this. Honestly, I'm getting a headache from it," she said. "You have to ask yourself, what do you want?"

"All I want is to be the best pastry chef in Los Angeles. That's it."

"Then be true to that. Do whatever you think you need to do to fulfill your dream."

She dipped her brush into the green paint and continued painting.

A silence hung between us.

What did I want? Was I doing the right thing? With Charlotte? With Rory? With Liam? With Julia?

A heavy pall washed over me. It was all too confusing.

The morning sun on my head was beginning to cook my brain. I should have worn a hat.

I tried to think of one of my father's quotations or a Yogi Dave mantra to fit the mood. Broken pieces of yamme and raaam popped into my head. My ears trained on the paintbrush, making that familiar sticky sound as Kate dragged it on the wall.

Luna nudged my hand and licked me, giving me a sharp bark.

"What do you want, sweetie?" I asked as I scratched his ears.

He stood up and started wagging his tail. He was ready for a walk. His affection brought me back to the present.

"I'm taking Luna for a walk. I'll be back," I said.

"Don't get mugged. You know the neighborhood." She laughed.

I stood up from the lawn chair too fast. The sudden dizziness brought me back to my senses.

Maybe Kate was right. Maybe I overthought everything.

As Yogi Dave always said, I needed to go with the flow.

Or it was like that quote my father always said: *Don't go with the flow, be the flow …*

Yogi mantras and my father's positive affirmations were getting too jumbled up in my brain, mixing in a soup of confusion.

Luna licked my leg, expectant. I scratched his back.

Did I need flow? Or did I need to stop overthinking everything?

11

"Thank you for the donuts, Ma'am," Grace said from the backseat. She had chocolate smeared on her chin as she took another bite from her Oreo donut."

"You're welcome. You know, you can call me Fiona."

She smiled. "Thank you for the donuts, Fiona."

Rory looked at her from the rearview mirror as he drove. "Grace, wipe your face off. You're a mess."

"Can I have another donut?" she asked sheepishly.

"What do you think I'm going to say?"

"Yes!"

"You know what I'm going to say, Grace. One is enough for right now."

She shrunk back into the backseat popping the last bite of the donut in her mouth and wiping off her face. She grabbed her iPad and started scrolling with her sticky fingers.

"Did you know a shrimp's heart is in its head?

Luna was curled up beside her. She balanced an iPad on top of his head. He didn't seem to mind.

Kings of Leon's "Taper Jean Girl" played in the background.

I glanced over at Rory. He was handsome in his faded blue chambray shirt. His wetsuit was pulled down to his waist like pants.

When Rory picked me up, I wasn't expecting Grace, but it was turning out to be a good surprise. She was hilarious. I never realized that five-year-old humor could be so fun.

Rory's Suburban was littered with his tools of the trade. Shovels, buckets, and mysterious implements packed the car. The faint metallic smell of soil lingered in the air.

"Did you know that slugs have four noses?" he shot back.

"I told you that one. That doesn't count."

Rory smiled as he glanced in the rearview mirror.

"I bet you didn't know that elephants are the only animals that can't jump?" She smiled proudly, like she'd outdone him.

He grinned. "Did you know that kangaroos can't fart?"

"Dad! That's gross." She giggled uncontrollably. Luna licked her on the face.

"I still can't believe you're taking me surfing. You're full of surprises," I said.

"I like keeping you on your toes." He grinned.

He turned left onto a narrow side road on PCH.

A beautiful, deserted beach emerged from the trees. He parked and turned the engine off. "You wore your swimsuit like I asked, right?"

"Of course," I said.

He gave me an excited grin. "This is going to be fun. I promise."

I opened the door and hopped out. The moist ocean air on my face was refreshing and I breathed in deeply.

Thin clouds covered the afternoon sun, so it wasn't too hot. It was a beautiful day.

Grace scrambled out the Suburban's passenger door, and Luna hopped out behind her, wagging his tail. He sniffed around, homing in on a pile of kelp. He jumped back like something bit his nose.

Rory opened the back doors to the Suburban and passed Grace and me wet suits. "Put these on."

"I don't know if I emphasized it, but I've never done this before."

He shook his head. "Come on. You said you could swim. You grew up in L.A., and you've never surfed?"

"I'm a city girl. Give me a break."

He laughed. "You don't have to do this if you don't want to."

"Are you kidding? This is gonna be great." My stomach felt otherwise.

I'd hated the beach growing up. Sand would stick to my skin because my dad put too much oily sunscreen on. Plus, no matter how much my dad covered me with hats and creams, I still burned.

I shucked my shorts and pulled the suit on. The legs were tight and awkward. It was like pulling on a pair of tight, stretchy jeans. I tried to zip the back up, but it was impossible. He laughed, watching me.

"Grace, come here." He pulled out a tube of sunscreen.

She cringed. "Ugh. Dad don't put too much on. It's gross." Her face scrunched up as he slathered her neck and face. I completely understood the way she felt.

He finished, threw the tube of sunscreen at me, and handed her boogie board to her. "Don't go too far out. Stay close to the beach."

"You always say that." She smiled sweetly.

"And you never listen." He gave her a stern glare.

"I'll be okay." She gave him a naughty smile and ran towards the shore in the distance. Luna followed behind.

He grabbed me by the waist and pulled me behind the truck.

He gave me a stolen, sweet kiss.

My heart opened, and all my cares floated away as his lips met mine.

He reached behind me and zipped me up. "You're ready, right?" The tightness of the suit made me feel like a Martian.

"Yes …? No …?"

"Don't worry. The waves are gentle today. It'll be fine." He gave me an excited smile and turned, pulling a surfboard out of the truck.

I stood there, buzzed from the kiss.

He handed me the board. "Trust me. This looks harder than it really is."

"Easy for you to say. How long have you done this?"

He grabbed the other board and shut the doors. "I practically lived here when I was a teenager."

I rolled my eyes. "Great. You're a seal."

He laughed. "Not quite. Come on."

I grabbed the board, followed him down to the ridge of the waves, and looked at the water lapping on the shore.

He was right. The waves were small. It didn't seem as scary as I'd imagined it.

I took a step. Right foot first into the water.

"It's so cold!"

"Keep going. You'll get used to it."

I stepped further into the water. The water on the suit was impervious to the cold. It felt kind of nice. I stepped further in, where the water hit my waist.

He looked back at me, excited. "This is the worst part. Trust me."

A shock of salty water splashed on my face, waking me up. I held onto the board for support.

"Hop on the board. Paddle into the waves. When a wave comes at you, duck your head and hold the board. Swimming past the break will take just a moment, and then it'll be calm."

He was so gorgeous at this moment. His wetsuit accentuated his torso. His hair was slicked back. The ocean water wet his face, made him crisp and alive.

I'd follow him anywhere.

I pulled myself onto our board, belly first, and started paddling. My wimpy arms were no help. I was helpless and weak. Why didn't I work out more?

A wave broke and crashed in front of me, slapping me right in the face.

I forgot to put my head down, and the water went up my nose and into my eyes. It burned into my sinuses. I felt the warmth of tears as my eyes watered.

Rory grabbed the front of my board and effortlessly tugged it forward with one arm in the water. I could feel his strength in the torque of the board as he pulled it through the break.

I made it past the waves somehow.

He was right. It was calm. Cumulus clouds hung on the horizon, and the beach was a short distance away.

I swung my legs around the board, straddled it, and pushed myself up. The board was slippery, and it was hard to hold onto.

The waves were hypnotic as they lapped underneath me. The sun glinted on the water, the horizon ahead. It was so quiet that you could hear the deep silence hanging in the air.

"Hang on." He smiled. He pulled my board around to face the shore. Our boards bumped as the waves bobbed us up and down.

Grace was closer than I thought she'd be.

She was running into the waves and jumping on her boogie board. Luna bit at the water.

"I like to come out here and think. It's a good place to get away from it all."

"I can see why."

My face hurt from smiling so hard. I couldn't help it. The cold water that had slapped my face made me hum from inside.

He grinned back. He understood. "The set's coming in right now. It's going to be small. You'll be able to manage it."

"I can barely manage this."

"Let me give you some pointers. Paddle into the wave. Push your body and pull up. It's exactly like popping up into a lunge from a plank in yoga. Just adjust your feet so they point to the side." He smiled at me. "Don't worry. You'll do great."

The yoga reference settled my nerves.

The waves started getting a little bigger. We were bobbing with more force. "Lay down. Get into a push-up position. Hold onto the sides."

I followed his lead and laid on the board. I glanced over at him. He was a little boy in a man's body. Playful and excited.

"Now, when your wave comes in, you'll know. It'll be instinctive. Paddle into it. Let it grab onto your board. When you feel it hook in, push yourself up and balance." He saw the look on my face. "Don't worry. You got this."

He looked over his shoulder. "I see your wave. Start paddling."

I paddled forward with my pathetic arms. I inched forward, the rhythm of the water carrying me along.

The water suddenly started pulling backward. The water lifted me. I glanced behind me, and all I could see was a wall of water.

I swung forward and paddled for my life. The board sucked and pulled into the wave.

My brain kicked in by some miracle. I pushed myself into position, bent my knees, lifted myself up, and let go.

Holy shit, I was riding the wave.

It was all moving way too fast. The water beneath the board foamed and crashed forward, creating a vortex under the board.

Euphoria and adrenaline kicked in as I hurled towards the shore.

The board became unsteady. It rocked back and forth, responding to my panic. The wave overtook the board, and I crashed into the water.

The wave's strength pulled me into the cold water and pushed my body into a ball. The force pulled me forward. It was like being in a washing machine, churning in the water. I couldn't fight the momentum as it spit me out on the shore.

Another wave broke behind me, and the water crashed over my head. The cold water trickled into the neck of my wetsuit and pushed me forward, right in front of Grace.

Luna started sniffing at me. He licked the ocean water off my face. Grace jumped around me. Delighted. "That was fun, right?"

I sat there. The force of the water humbled me.

Rory waved to me as he rode a wave to shore. His moves were graceful and strong as he glided.

I thought for a moment.

Hell yes. That'd been fun.

I felt like a kid as I stood up and grabbed the board.

I wanted to feel like that again.

* * *

I tugged the top of the wetsuit off, so I just had the pants on. The cool air felt good on my skin. The sand was warm and moist under my feet, supporting my arches. It was almost like a firm foot massage.

I'd gone out four more times, which was more than enough for me. I was pummeled. I was tired. But this type of tiredness was better than any meditation or massage.

I felt satisfied.

I watched Rory in the distance.

He was graceful as he balanced on his board, almost an extension of his body. He was one with the sea as he caught a wave and rode it in.

It was hypnotic to watch.

Grace dug a hole in the sand. Toys were strewn across the beach. Luna sat, watching her. His ears perked forward in curiosity. Purple and green shovels were sticking up around half-formed piles of sand. She was in her own world as she ran back and forth with a bucket between the water and a tall monolith. She threw the water on the structure and sprinted back to the waves.

She had a plan.

She threw another bucket of water onto the sand hill and glanced my way. "Can you help me?

I was honored that she'd invited me to join her. I sat down, and she pushed a shovel into my hands and pointed to the side of the hill.

I paused. I didn't know where to start.

"What are you making?"

She frowned at me like I was missing the obvious. "A castle, silly. Make the tunnel so it meets mine."

She started digging a deep hole at the bottom of the hill. The wet sand supported the structure. I was impressed by the architecture. I got on all fours and started digging too. I started deep on the side of the pile and dug down. The sand was so wet that it stuck to my skin. The deeper I dug, the more the cold sand got under my fingernails.

Our hands finally met in the middle. Her fingers were fat and soft. She lit up as they touched. "Good. Now pat the sides. Make it strong."

She started patting and smoothing the sides of the tunnel, making it bigger. I followed her lead.

"Look inside. Do you see me?"

I crouched down and looked through the hole. Her smiling face stared back at me, and she started to laugh. "Good job. Let's make a road. So people can drive." She dug a trail around the pile of sand with her tiny hands, carefully making the little road smooth. She crawled and scooted backward, making her way around the mound.

I followed her lead, and our road worked its way all around. She studied it, proudly. "This is good."

She grabbed a bucket and threw a Hot Wheels collection onto the sand.

They were worn and faded. They'd seen a lot of action. She started lining them up on the road. "It's a traffic jam. Quick. Get them through the tunnel." She swung around to the other side of the castle and pushed a car through.

I shoved my arm in, grabbed the car, and drove it back to the road. "Coming through!" I slid it around on the road, knocking the other cars out of the way. I passed it back to her. "Come on. They have to get home. His wife's having a baby!"

I laughed at the lunacy. I passed the car back faster. She grabbed it and plowed it through the unshaped sand to another hill. "Hurry. She's gonna pop!" She took it out of my hands with force, crawled on all fours, and raced with the car, breaking away and scooting further down the beach towards the waves. She made loud car noises, off in her imagination.

Luna watched her go, his tail swishing in the sand, limp and exhausted.

Rory strode to shore like Poseidon himself. Strong and tall. His wet hair was framing his face. His surfboard was his shield.

He sat the board down on the sand and, sat on top of it, and smiled at me. "Would you like a seat? It's much better than where you're sitting."

"Thank you." I brushed the sand off my body and sat down next to him. He opened a water bottle and poured it on my hands, rinsing me off. It was good to get rid of the residue granules on my hands.

"What'd you think? You're a natural out there."

"I don't know. I fell off more than I landed it." I couldn't hold back a happy laugh. "To tell you the truth, it was amazing."

"Maybe I can take you here again sometime." His peaceful gaze met mine.

"I'd like that."

He tucked my hair behind my ear. "You were right about the sun. You got a little sunburned."

"I told you. I turn into a lobster. I was hoping things would be different this time."

He reached around and grabbed the big picnic basket behind us. "Are you hungry?" He opened it and handed me a sandwich. "Do you like peanut butter and jelly?"

I was starving. The ocean water had left me famished.

He handed me a sandwich. "Obviously, my mom made the jam. It's straight-up strawberry made from the Mara des bois. Sometimes, I don't want her to mess around. I just want her to make the good stuff."

I unwrapped the sandwich and took a bite. "This might be the best peanut butter and jelly sandwich I've ever had." The homemade sourdough bread was chewy, and the crust was light and crunchy. Chunky peanut butter, the only acceptable kind, was spread generously on the bread. The strawberry jam was heaven.

There was nothing like strawberry jam made from the perfect part of the season. I chewed it slowly, enjoying the moment.

Grace saw us eating and ran up. "I want one!"

"Where are your manners, Grace?"

She stood up a little straighter. "Can I have a sandwich, please?"

He opened a bottle of water. "Here. Let's wash your hands." He poured the water over her hands, washing the sand off. He pulled a sandwich out of the basket and handed it to her with a bottle of apple juice.

"I want you to sit down and eat it. And remember to throw your stuff away."

She nodded her head and unwrapped the sandwich. Luna perked up. He knew where he could find a free meal. She broke off a piece of her sandwich and handed it to him.

I was impressed by her. When I thought of five-year-olds, I thought of those bratty kids in the grocery store grabbing Fruit Loops, begging their moms with their whiny voices. Or out-of-control maniacs playing in the park.

Kids made me nervous. But Grace was different. "She's very well-behaved."

"I keep her busy. But then again, she's always been calm. She gets it from her mother." He took a bite of his sandwich. "My mom has a lot to do with it, too. They're inseparable."

An imperceptible crease wrinkled the top of his brow. Like a bad thought had caught him.

He changed the subject. "Grace's mom is coming to the vineyard to pick her up for summer break. I hope you don't mind."

"Why would I mind?" The thought of meeting his ex made me nervous.

"Don't worry. You don't have to meet her if you don't want to, but she's okay. I promise."

"How do you do it? You seem so well-adjusted about everything. Are you friends?"

"I don't know if we're friends. I feel like you can be with someone and love them, but you have to let them grow at the end of the day. And if that means they grow out of your life, so be it." A dark light reflected in his eyes.

He stared out at the water. "Alex and I had some great times together. And we fought for what we had. But when it was over, it was over. I couldn't imagine tainting what we had because of ego." He twisted a twig in his hands. "I'll always love her. But I don't love her, if you know what I mean. One thing can destroy it all. That part of our relationship is done."

We watched Grace playing in the distance. "We still have Grace. And that's pretty special." He threw the twig out into the sand. It fell on top of one of Grace's piles.

He looked at me and smiled. "I don't want to talk about that. I want to talk about this." He touched my hand. He interlaced his fingers with mine.

I scooted closer to him.

He unlocked my hand and put his arm around me. He drew my face into his and kissed me.

My heart hung in the air. I could taste the salt from the ocean still on his lips.

He tasted amazing.

He pulled away as Luna ran up. The force of his tail sent sand into the air. Grace followed behind. "I'm bored. Can we go now?"

"Pick your toys up and rinse them off in the ocean first."

He grabbed my hand and pulled me up. "I guess it's time to leave."

He picked up a shovel and threw it in a bucket. I grabbed a beach towel and shook the sand out. I pulled in the corners to fold it. "This was nice. Thank you for bringing me here."

He grinned, vulnerable. "Thank you for coming. I can't wait to show you my place."

I couldn't wait to see it. What could his vineyard be like if he was such a nurturing person, so connected to his life?

*　*　*

A patchwork of farms and vineyards passed by as we drove. Grace and Luna were asleep in the back seat. Her face was like an angelic cherub, with her brown curls framing her face. A fine layer of sand still stuck to her ankles. I could see the granules caked on her feet through her Crocs.

Rory held my hand as he drove with one arm extended to the top of the steering wheel. I studied his profile. He needed a haircut, but his tan skin and square jaw came together perfectly.

A large brick and iron gate greeted us as we drove up to the entrance of his place. "Bella Ange" was incised into the metal arch. White roses and grapevines crawled up the sides and intertwined with rock and metal. It was beautiful.

"Here we are." Excitement crossed his face as we parked in front of a large, craftsman-style house. A set of large barns and industrial buildings stood in the distance. The vineyard stretched for acres across the landscape as far as the eye could see.

He shut the engine off and reached around the back seat. "Grace, we have to wake up. Your mom's coming soon. You have to get ready."

She stirred awake and perked up, a bright glint in her eye. "We're here already?"

She hopped out of the truck with Luna, and we made our way up the steps onto the porch. The porch had a swinging bench, and posies were planted in wine barrel planters.

Luna circled three times, laying on a rug by the door, and we stepped inside.

A massive, river-stone fireplace stood in the center of a large living room. The kitchen beyond was open, connected to the living space, creating an expansive area for entertaining. Light illuminated from tall windows. Relaxed furniture filled the room. He closed the front door behind us. "Grace, go take a shower. Hurry. Your mom's going to be here in twenty minutes."

"We're late, Dad." She put her hand on her hip and stared at him.

He gave her a stern look. "Then what are you waiting for?"

"I'm going to tell Mom on you." She bounded up the stairs.

He shook his head. "She's always trying to get me in trouble." He made his way to the kitchen, and I sat on a stool in front of the kitchen island.

I was blown away by the kitchen. White peekaboo cabinets and granite countertops, a huge refrigerator, a double oven, a six-burner industrial Viking stove, and a floor-to-ceiling wine refrigerator. There was lots of room to work. It was dreamy.

He opened the wine refrigerator and grabbed two glasses and a bottle of wine. "Would you like a glass?"

"I'd love one."

He opened the bottle. His forearms flexed as he turned the corkscrew and poured me a glass. "Do you like Pinot?"

"I love Pinot Grigio. Thank you." I took a sip from the cold wine glass. It was refreshing and light going down.

"Do you know why it's called Pinot Grigio?"

"I don't know that much about wine, honestly. I just like to drink it."

"That's okay. He gave me a secretive smile. "I'll have fun teaching you." He leaned in on the counter. "What does this taste like?"

I took a moment to taste it. "It vaguely tastes like pears. Very crisp."

He gazed at me. "See? That's what it's about. Tasting. Enjoying." He swirled the wine in his glass, studying it. "Pinot and Grigio are two varietals of grapes used." He took a sip. He kept his gaze fixed on mine. "Now, you know about Pinot. How easy was that?"

He set his glass down on the counter and leaned in. I met him halfway across the counter, and we kissed. I could taste the wine on his lips and a hint of the ocean as he went to my head.

"Hello? Anyone home?" A voice called from the cracked front door. We broke away from the kiss, acting like it didn't happen. He tried not to laugh under his smile.

He made his way to the living room. "Alex." He kissed her quickly on the cheek.

She was beautiful in a cool kind of way. Her wavy auburn hair was pulled back in a barrette, and her black turtleneck accentuated her long neck. She was tall and graceful.

An almost imperceptible frown crossed her face as she extended her hand. "Alex Martin. Nice to meet you."

How she said the last name felt like a brag as she sized me up.

"I'm Fiona." I stared her in the eye, relaxed but in control. I tried to stand tall.

"Grace is getting ready upstairs. I'll go get her. It'll just be a minute." He went upstairs. Leaving us alone.

We stood there for an awkward moment in the silence. Each of us trying to be relaxed.

"Don't hurt him," she said, quietly.

I almost didn't hear what she said.

She gave me a stern, protective stare. "He's special. Don't lead him on. He's better than that."

I studied her a beat. Her warning made me like her. I could understand where she was coming from.

"Don't worry. I'll be careful."

Her gaze softened. Rory and Grace bounded down the stairs. Rory had her suitcase in his hand.

"Mom!" Grace raced to her mom, and they embraced.

"She has enough clothes for a month in here, I think. Her shampoo and toothbrush are in a Ziploc in the bottom, and I packed her three pairs of shoes." He reflexed as he handed Alex the suitcase. "She's ready for anything."

"I appreciate it. How's Delia doing?"

Rory tried not to look at me. I could tell there was something under the surface. "She's doing good. Better. We're hoping for the best."

"Let me know if I can do anything." She looked away from him, almost embarrassed. I sensed the tension between them. "We have to go. The flight leaves in three hours. I hope we can make it through security."

Rory glanced at his watch. "You'll be fine." He leaned down to Grace and gave her a big bear hug. "I love you."

"I love you, too, Daddy."

Alex grabbed her by the hand, and we made our way outside.

Rory watched in the driveway as Alex put the suitcase in the back seat, and they climbed into the car. Grace waved as they pulled out of the driveway. He blew her a kiss, and they were gone.

We stood there for a moment in silence.

"Let's go. I'll show you around." He took a deep breath. I could tell he was trying to shrug off something dark. He took a deep breath, and a new smile crossed his face. "I can't wait to show you around."

We walked across the yard to the mess of industrial buildings and barns.

"I'm about to show you my favorite place."

We stood in front of an epic barn. The siding was grey from weathering the sun and the elements. He smiled, proudly, as he pulled the tall barn doors open.

"Some men have a man cave. I've got a wine cave." He motioned for me to walk in.

The inside of the barn was huge. It was dimly lit and set to a perfectly cool temperature. A musty and cold smell hung in the air. Barrels were racked along the walls from floor to ceiling in several rows.

It was a vast space that was dense and dark.

"This is where we age the wine. The wine can stay in the barrels for weeks to months. To give the wine an oak aroma and create tannins. Then it's settled and clarified before we bottle it."

The silence was heavy in the dim light. It made the space between us more intimate. "Would you like to try some?"

"I'd love to."

He went to a cupboard and pulled out some wine glasses and a bottle of Pellegrino. He set them on the sturdy hardwood table in the middle of the room.

He grabbed a bottle of wine from underneath the table, poured two glasses of water, and set everything on the table in front of me.

His smile was seductive. Warm. Mingled with the dense room, he made my head spin.

"Now, just to warn you. You have to taste around the flavors. I have two different wines, one from the beginning of the aging and one from later on. I want to see if you can tell the difference." He set them down.

"The important thing to remember is to taste beyond the harsh flavors. Search for the hints of fruit and sweetness." He handed me a glass of white wine from the barrel. I took a sip.

He watched me, a naughty glint in his eyes.

I choked. It was too tart. Too acidic.

He started to laugh, grabbed a spittoon, and held it out. "Spit it out."

I spit it into the spittoon and set the glass down. "That was disgusting."

"Well, that's a young one." He handed me another glass. "Try this." He poured me another glass of white wine from another bottle. "This is the same wine. Aged for two years."

I took a sip. It was delicious. Sweet and floral. I took another sip.

"What do you think?" He gazed into my eyes.

"Amazing."

"I know, right?" His blue eyes searched mine.

"Is there anything you can't make?"

"I can't make a pie. Like the one you made from my blackberries. It was probably the best I've ever tasted."

His finger traced my jaw as his eyes met mine. He kissed me. The air was even denser as he met my gaze. I loved the way his body loomed in the shadows. Strong and tall. In control.

"I love that you're here."

He pulled my waist into his and leaned down, kissing me again. His soft lips tasted mine.

He guided me to the wall of barrels as we kissed each other. He leaned my back against them. His kisses were more intense. Something deeper than I had felt from him before.

I loved his body pushing against mine—the weight of it against my back. I found footing against the rack behind me.

His lips and hands drifted to my neck. His hands explored my body.

I pulled his shirt from his jeans and found his waist. My fingers traveled everywhere as I kissed him back. I loved the way his skin felt.

It made my brain scramble. My fingers were having trouble keeping up with my brain.

I couldn't think anymore.

I just wanted him.

* * *

I opened my eyes to the bright light. The late afternoon sun was shining through the window. The bed was fluffy, white, and inviting, and the colorful sheets felt good on my naked body. Rory slept next to me.

My head was clear from a perfect nap. I was rested, grounded, and clear.

I studied at him as he slept. His face was innocent. Boyish. The golden sun made him glow. I couldn't help but gaze at him.

He stirred. "Don't you know it's rude to stare?"

"I can't help it. You shouldn't make me."

I laid my head down, facing him. Our heads were close on a pillow. He moved his hand to my face and pulled me in for another kiss. Our energy connected on a vulnerable and sweet level.

I slid closer to him. Tiny granules of sand still stuck to his feet. Evidence of our time at the beach on our bodies. The warm sting of too much sun on my skin.

Between surfing, the wine, and our interlude, it had to be the best my body had felt in my entire life. How could I possibly feel any better?

The only way to make it better was a shower.

I could only imagine being in the water with him. Sudsing him up in hot water, his slick skin under the soap. Rinsing the sand and the filmy layer of salt off. I couldn't wait for the next part. "This has been the perfect day. One of my best, I think."

"Mine, too. You're really something."

He traced his fingers from my head down my shoulders and arms, taking me in. "You have all these little marks on your arms. What are those?"

The ghosts of burns from the oven grazed my arms. "I burned myself all the time at first when I started baking. Before I figured out how to position my arms when I put things in the oven. Even now, I occasionally nick myself. The burns seem innocent initially, but they blossom into a dark mark and become a faint line on my skin when they heal."

He nodded as he grazed his fingers over my skin. "I see."

"I consider them my kitchen tattoos. Some people have tattoos of flowers or skulls. I have kisses from the oven."

He smiled and started from the top of my arm, kissing each mark. "Was that a hint?"

I laughed. "Maybe."

He turned my arm, so the soft part faced up and continued kissing me.

"You love what you do. I like that about you. You seem passionate."

"Being in the kitchen makes me happy."

He propped his head on his arm and looked at me. "That's important."

I sat up. Enough to rest my head on the backboard. "At the end of it all, I just love to make things."

"You have to feel like your days are spent on things that are nurturing for the soul. I get it from my wine." He touched my chin. "Or growing the perfect blackberries for the best pie I've ever had." He smiled at me.

"Thank you." I laughed. "That's not even the best thing I make."

He smiled. "I can't even imagine something better. You must have superpowers."

"Well, I was thinking of someone special when I made it. That makes all the difference in the world."

Our eyes lingered together for a minute. "Between surfing, growing things, and your family, you have the whole package. You have a good life."

"I do. But there's a couple of missing pieces."

I let the sentence sit there. The sound of it thrilled me. Could I be his missing piece?

I didn't want to think about how much I wanted it.

He smiled at me. "Come on. Let's get cleaned up." He grabbed me by the hand, and I slid out of bed.

His body was fit and tight from surfing. He had almost a yogi stature. Strong from his work and his play. He was gorgeous.

He grabbed me by the hand and led me to the bathroom.

My breath caught in my throat—the bathroom.

A wall of frosted glass let the sunlight in. The large shower with spouts that pointed everywhere took a whole corner of the space.

But the huge lion-clawed bathtub was the real showcase of the room. He bent down, turned it on, and poured bubble bath into the water. "Would you like a nice bath? I like to marinate after I surf. It's the perfect end to the day."

I reached up and kissed him, pulling his body close. "I'd love to marinate with you."

"I'll be right back." He grabbed his robe and left.

I stepped into the tub. The water was instantly cleansing as it sloshed against my feet. It was the perfect temperature. Not too hot and not too cold. I sat down and let the bubbles cover my body.

"Here, take this." He handed me a chilled glass of wine. The glass was sweaty from condensation. I took a sip. It was the period at the end of the sentence.

It made the moment perfect.

He let his robe drop on the floor and climbed in. He turned the water off and faced me. The water teased the ridge of the tub, a tiny wave going over the edge. The bubbles framed his upper body.

He sipped his wine and smiled at me. "I think this is the best part."

"I'd have to agree with you. I feel pretty good right now."

I let my legs slide against his. His relaxed muscles under the water pressed into me. The slipperiness I'd imagined before was even better than I'd expected.

He watched me. "What are you thinking right now?"

"Your tub is perfection. I don't think I'm ever going to get out."

He laughed as he put his wine glass down, grabbed a shampoo bottle, and squeezed some into his hand. "Turn around."

I slipped my body around and nestled myself between his legs. My back touched his chest.

He took a cup from the side of the tub and guided his hands around my head as he got my hair wet. He was careful not to get water on my face. He took the shampoo and started to scrub my hair. I fell into a trance as he scrubbed my head. "There's a lot of sand in your hair. You took a beating out there."

"It was a good beating. I'd do it again. You may have changed this city girl into a beach bum."

"That'd be a good thing, right?"

"I wouldn't mind."

He took the cup and rinsed the soap out of my hair, cupping his hands around my face so water wouldn't get in my eyes.

I was touched by how gentle he was.

He took some soap and started to lather my back. His fingers slowly rubbed into my muscles and teased my ribs. The last lingering hints of stress floated away.

I was officially complete.

He took the cup and poured the water over my shoulders, letting the rivulets of water wash the soap from my body. He kissed my shoulders.

"Turn around."

I turned around and let my body extend over his. I stretched from the top to the bottom of my body in an electric, slippery move.

"Where do we go from here?" He kissed me as his arms slipped against my body.

I grabbed the edges of the tub as I kissed him. I wanted to find out. I just wanted to let my heart go free and find out everything.

12

"**O**MG, chef, it's delicious." Rose closed her eyes as she savored.

"What is it?"

"Sabayon. It's egg yolks, sugar, wine, and cream folded together. The peaches are roasted with a dash of cinnamon and cardamom. Do you think it will hold up in a demonstration?"

"It would stand up anywhere, chef. This is one of the best things I've ever tasted. It's even better than the apricot brûlée, which was my favorite." She smiled as she took another bite.

I couldn't read Camille as she tasted. A vague pause crossed her face. "It's okay ..."

She turned and returned to swirling white chocolate on the tiny entremets she'd made for the benefit at the Griffith Observatory.

That familiar uneasiness returned.

I made the final flourish of peaches on the Sabayon on another plate for my presentation to Liam and Julia.

Julia had wanted dramatic and straightforward. This was about as simple as I could get. I'd used the Chardonnay and the

Bonita peaches Rory had given me. The peaches were sweet and delicious and tasted like the divine orchard air.

How was I going to deal with Liam? Was he going to say anything about our night at Vestrano?

Maybe Kate was right. I just had to pretend it never happened.

I just wanted to get back to the art of pastry. I wanted to stretch my wings with the epiphany I'd experienced at Vestrano. To put Jordan's secret into practice. I wanted to convey the magic of a Chardonnay. The magic of a cream.

The magic of a peach.

"Fiona, I want to talk to you about *The Taste*." Liam cruised into the bakery.

Rose darted to the worktable behind me. She picked up a whisk, struggling to look busy.

Liam saw the Sabayon on the table. "What's this?"

I held my breath.

He stood tall, facing me. His familiar stature filled the space. The hint of the other night evaporated away. He was the familiar formidable opponent.

His eyes met mine a beat, and he looked away, studying the Sabayon. He gazed at it for a thoughtful moment.

"What's this all about?" he asked.

"It's for *The Taste*. It's a Sabayon. Julia wanted simple and elegant, and I think this fits the bill. It's something classic that anyone can make."

He took one of the tasting spoons on the table and took a bite. He paused as he tasted it. The ghost of a wicked smile crossed his lips.

"Roasted peaches? Sweet Chardonnay?" He frowned. "It's the sort of thing that you'd find desperate lovers sharing after a meal of rice and fish on a bad date."

He turned to me, pulled a rolled-up batch of papers out of his back pocket, and shoved them at me. "Make this."

I unrolled the recipes and balked. "Blood Orange Mousse with Ras el Hanout and Taza ninety-five percent? Don't you think this a bit extreme?"

"No. It's challenging. If you want to conquer *The Taste*, you'll do it." He gave me a commanding stare and then turned and left

The ghost of his toxic energy permeated the space around me. Cloying? Sentimental? Desperate lovers sharing after a meal of rice and fish on a bad date …?

Fury coursed through my brain. He'd outplayed me once again.

I studied the recipes a beat. I set them on the table. They were too heavy for my hands.

Ras el Hanout? Taza ninety-five percent?

It was offensive. It was harsh. It was the sort of dessert a bully would make. How was I going to make this even palatable?

My heart hurt with a wave of dread.

Was this what I was going to be known for at *The Taste*? An abrasive dessert that assaulted your senses?

I leaned against the table. Disappointment and heartbreak hit me.

Had Jonathan Agnew and Maggie Hughes made their own desserts? Or were they commanded by their chefs to make something that betrayed their vision?

All my musings of celebrity floated away.

I wasn't going to be seen as important. I wasn't going to be an instant flash on the foodie scene. I was going to be some stooge for Liam's stupid vision.

"The entremets are done. What should I do next, chef?" A hint of satisfaction crossed Camille's face. She'd seen the whole confrontation.

"Start on the Armagnac caramel," I said. "Let it cool down on a sheet tray. We need it as soon as possible for the Kouign-amann."

"Yes, chef." She smirked as she turned.

I glanced at Rose as she peeled apples. She gave me a sheepish smile and went back to her work.

I took a deep breath.

This was a disaster.

Who was going to enjoy this? Who was going to be transported by this?

The only thing this dessert was going to do was confuse people. Shock their senses.

Would they be disappointed? What did this dessert even convey?

I picked up a spoon and took a bite of the Sabayon. Rory's Chardonnay had melded seamlessly with the sweetness of the delicate cream. The roasted peaches transported me back to the orchard where Rory had kissed me.

I didn't care what Liam thought. My Sabayon came from my heart. My soul. And he couldn't take that away from me.

In this time and space, I'd created something beautiful. I'd celebrated the ingredients and celebrated where they came from.

But I had to do what Liam asked. Maybe I would have to listen to him if I wanted to make my mark. Maybe I was wrong somehow.

If I wanted to play in the big leagues, I'd have to do what Liam wanted. Maybe Jonathan Agnew and Maggie Hughes had gone through the same thing. They'd made names for themselves with this opportunity. If I wanted to be successful, I'd have to follow Liam's lead.

But where was he leading me?

* * *

I walked through the farmers' market. The hot Santa Ana wind coming off the water was intense, laced with the smell of the ocean.

"Fiona!" I looked up. Delia walked through the crowd, balancing a drink holder filled with coffee. Her floppy hat, garden clogs, and red overalls made her stand out in the crowd. She hugged me.

"I haven't seen you since the celebration. How are you?" I asked.

"I've been dealing with some annoying stuff, but I'm good." We walked through the market, weaving through the crowd. "How did you like Rory's place? I heard that he showed you around."

"It was amazing. I wasn't expecting it to be such a huge operation." A gust of wind blew in my face. It woke me up a little more.

"I know. I'm so proud of him. He's done so much." She smiled. "I think Grace liked you, too. She said you were fun when I talked to her on the phone last night."

"That means a lot."

"It certainly does." She smiled. "Listen. I've been playing around with an oven-roasted apple chutney. I'm trying to decide whether to dress it up with some apricots. Maybe you could try it and tell me what you think."

I could see Rory in the distance. He was wearing his usual uniform of white tee and jeans. My body instinctively remembered the way he felt against me. The way we were skin-to-skin in the tub. Symbiotic. One to one. I couldn't help but smile.

The wind picked up again. It caught the top of Delia's hat and it blew off. I caught it just in time as it flew in the air.

She stood there. Her head was naked, juggling the coffee in her hands. A bright scarf was tied around her head. You could tell she was bald underneath it.

She didn't have any hair.

Her eyes went wide. Like she'd been caught.

My heart dropped in my chest. I placed her hat back on her head. "Delia. What's going on?"

She looked at me, embarrassed. "Oh, it's nothing. I had surgery about a month ago, and I'm just doing a round of chemo."

"Are you okay?"

"I'll be fine, honey. They say my chances are through the roof. It's just a little hiccup."

I felt like I'd been kicked in the gut. I grabbed the coffee from her.

"Delia. I don't even know what to say."

"There's nothing to say, sweetie. I'm doing fine. Being in the fresh air around my people has made me feel so much better. It's so good to see everyone."

She saw someone in the crowd. "Listen. Go enjoy yourself with Rory. He's excited to see you. He's been like a puppy dog all morning waiting for you."

She walked away towards a hip guy with a trimmed beard and flamboyant tattoos. He was head chef at Jane. I watched her as she gave him a generous grandma hug.

It terrified me to see her in a mortal light.

I made it through the crowd to the booth. With every step, anger welled up in me. I set the coffee down on the table.

Rory's eyes caught mine, and he smiled. "I have all of your stuff already picked out. The rest will be delivered later today. I'll go over it with you before you leave." He gave me an excited smile. "Let's go for a walk."

"Why didn't you tell me about your mom? We spent all that time together. You could have said something, but you didn't."

His smile faded. He grabbed a coffee and handed me one. "This one has lots of cream and sugar."

I nodded, distracted. Trying to control my anger. I grabbed the cup out of his hands. "Thanks."

He took one for his own and grabbed my hand. "Let's go."

We pushed through the market and walked down the city block towards the ocean.

We paused at the stoplight, waiting for the light to change.

He turned to me. "Listen. I was going to tell you. But the right opportunity never presented itself."

The light changed, and we walked across the street towards Palisades Park.

Tall palm trees and oversized succulents lined the dirt paths. Runners darted past us as we passed the green Camera Obscura house.

We walked in tandem down the trail. "How is she? I mean, how is she doing?"

He took a deep breath. "We don't know yet. She had a mastectomy. And she's been doing chemo. We're trying to get her on a clinical trial." He took a deep breath. "She shouldn't even be here today, but she insisted."

"How's Grace handling it?"

"For her sake, we're trying to keep it quiet. I don't want her to freak out. My mom means everything to her."

He stopped at a cannon that was at the end of the path. The pier stretched beyond.

He turned and thought a beat. "I'm sorry I didn't tell you. I feel horrible about it," he said.

"I'm sorry you're going through all of this. I love your mom. She's a bright spot in the universe."

He smiled. "Yes. She is."

A hot blast of wind hit my body, waking me up.

"I gave you some Mary Jane peaches that are just about perfect. Keep them out of the cold, or they'll get mushy. And I gave you some English pears. We're starting to shift into fall."

I studied him. He was vulnerable. Scared. There was fear in his eyes.

"Don't do this. Don't change the subject, and do this thing where you're all stoic, like it's no big deal," I said.

He looked at me like he was trying to decide if it was okay to be vulnerable.

"My mom has always been the driving force of my life. She built Fleurcein on her own. Acre by acre. My dad died, and she stepped up and did it by herself. She's always guided my life." He took a sip of his coffee. "She's intertwined with my creativity. Everything I grow and make it to her standard. She's not only my mother. She's my muse."

We walked toward the park's edge and stood at the cliff's perimeter. The cement fence protected us from going over the side to the PCH below.

He stared out at the water, thinking.

"What's weird is how matter of fact it is. Her cancer hit us out of the blue. No dramatic fanfare, not like you see in the movies. It's just a fact of life, and life moves forward. I still have to tend to life and everything in it. She still makes jam. Life just doesn't stop."

I didn't know what to say. I put my arm around him, trying to be reassuring.

He gazed out at the ocean. "I've never had someone close to me get this sick, so I don't know what I'm doing. I'm just fumbling through it, hoping to make the right decisions for her. I don't want to fail her."

"I can't imagine what you are going through. My mother died when I was two, so my father is all I have ... I don't know what I'd do if I were in your situation."

I could see the pain on his face.

"It's good that you're keeping it matter of fact. To face it like a drama, making life stop would make it an insurmountable challenge," I said. I hoped it was the right thing to say.

I took a sip of my coffee. It tasted gross. The sugar and cream were separated. A film of fat stuck to the top of my mouth. I tossed it in the trash.

"She's got a great attitude about it, and that's everything. That's a sure sign that things are going in the right direction," he said. "Attitude is everything."

He smiled at me, but his angst lingered behind his eyes.

"Delia's lucky to have such an amazing son," I said. I slid my arm around his waist, pulling him close.

He settled into my embrace. "I'm so lucky that I met you when I did. You've been such a light spot for me in all this darkness. I appreciate you. Thank you."

"I'm glad I could be here for you. I love the time that we've spent together."

He gave me a thankful smile. "We should get back. I don't want to be away for too long," he said.

We turned and walked in quiet peace as we made it to the crosswalk. He pushed the button to cross the street. I loved the brightness of his eyes.

"I care about you, Fiona." He smiled. "You are quite something."

"I care about you, too. I'm here for you. Believe that."

He gave me a vulnerable, sweet smile. "I might even be just a little bit in love with you …"

My heart stopped as he said it. It was the first time anyone said anything like this to me. A wave of emotion washed over me. It was too much to hold in.

"I … I … I think I love you, too."

The words came out before I could stop them. It was scary territory. Uncharted land.

He stood closer to me, pulling me in. His hand felt so good in mine. It was like home. He felt like home. He felt like true north.

I couldn't stop gazing into his eyes. They were vibrant and clear.

"Come on, people. Get out of the way!" A homeless lady with a wagon stood behind us. Her dirty gingham dress and back-turned baseball hat betrayed her insanity. She pushed through and pulled her wagon between us as she crossed the street.

Rory laughed. The moment was broken. "Let's go." He grabbed my hand, and we crossed the street back to the market. We walked through the packed stalls of produce.

I was alive. I was clear. My heart was buoyant and free. The sky was bluer than I'd ever seen it. His hand in mine made me smile from the inside out. A euphoria that I'd never experienced before washed over me.

"Come here." He pulled me behind a white van with tall, stacked crates of kale and radishes. He put his arms around me and kissed me.

It was soft. Reassuring. Heartfelt. His arms around me were electric.

"I can't get everything that happened out of my mind ..."

I smiled. "I know what you mean."

The earthy tones of the vegetables and my attraction took over my senses as he leaned in and kissed me again. This time, hinting at something more.

My mind flashed back to the vineyard ... The wine sanctum ... The tub ...

I couldn't wait to be with him like that again.

* * *

I hopped out of Lucien's delivery truck. The metallic vapor of burnt oil was the only thing I could smell. Riding shotgun hadn't been such a good idea after all.

I couldn't believe I was standing in the backstage lot at Paramount Studios. It was a carnival atmosphere as tents and food trucks finished setting up for *The Taste*.

The main kitchen stage was slick. It looked like something straight off Food Network. Monitors hung from the sides, and large stage lights shone from above.

My stomach dropped at the thought that I'd be up there.

"I hope you're ready. This could be your night." Liam rolled my plastic-wrapped cart of prep and tiny serving-sized desserts for the promo to me. He shoved it into my hands, and I jumped to catch it.

"Of course," I said, trying to be confident.

I grabbed the cart, rolled it to the stage, and tore off the plastic. Stagehands darted around me, making last-minute adjustments. The scene was a hive of activity.

I gazed at the tiny desserts on the rack prepped for the tasting. On the surface, they were beautiful.

Austere. Clean. Elegant.

The tiny servings of mousse were piped into diamond-shaped plastic serving cups. The chocolate mousse was a rich shade of creamy brown. I'd adorned the top with a dollop of whipped cream and a flourish of raspberries.

I smiled to myself. I'd misbehaved. I'd ditched Liam's Taza ninety-five percent for Guanaja seventy percent. I'd used the tiniest amount of Ras au Hanout as a mild flourish of flavor as opposed to a full-frontal attack on the senses. Hopefully, the whipped cream would help the audience forget the taste altogether.

It was a forward-thinking dessert.

Audacious and severe.

Liam's vision fully realized. Well, almost.

Was this what it took to make it? Could it really be that easy? Maybe I could just skate through and finally have Julia validate me. I was so close. So close to the finish line. Could I ultimately prove myself worthy? Was this dessert worthy?

I had my doubts.

My phone buzzed in my pocket. *Good luck tonight*, Rory texted me. *I know you're going to do great.*

I wish you were here, I texted back.

I wish I was there too. He emoji'd two hearts and a kiss.

He had to meet an investor in Santa Ynez, so he couldn't make it.

I put my phone in my pocket and glanced at Liam, sharpening his expensive Santoku knife. He was loose and comfortable as his blade slid against the steel. The scraping of the knife on the steel made my molars grind.

A beautiful King Salmon, adorned with herbs and delicate greens, was laid out on the table in full display.

Was he going to chop its head and tail off and stab it in the heart with his Santoku for show? The only thing missing from the scene was the bottle of Reposado.

That certainly would be a way to set the tone of the new Lucien.

Liam's new sous chef worked by his side as they set their station up. He was a transplant from Juniper in New York.

So far, Humphry had avoided me in the kitchen. He walked around with a chip on his shoulder, an extension of Liam's rudeness. They had a secret second hand with each other that was hard to miss as they completed each other's movements. They danced well together.

He was a shark, just like Liam.

It made me miss Sammy.

"How are we doing, my chefs?" Julia kissed me on the cheek as she surveyed the stage. "I'm mingling with my good friend, Margo, from *Food and Wine*. We were sampling some of George Sarce's tapas. They're absolutely brilliant. They remind me of this small cafe I'd visit when I lived in Troyes …" She gave me a sharp look. "I wanted to check on everything. Are you ready?"

"Yes. I have it under control."

"Good. Just be articulate. Speak up and exaggerate your hands."

She squeezed my arm. "Make it good. Remember, this is our chance to show everyone we're new and fresh. That we're a real contender." She waved to someone in the distance, smiling her most brilliant smile. "A lot is riding on you. Prove to me that you can do it, Fiona."

I watched her as she left.

She made me even more nervous.

The sun was in the final stages of setting. I watched the mingling crowd. People were starting to arrive and stand in front of the stage.

It was almost showtime. Panic bloomed in the back of my brain.

I slipped off the staging area and stood by the truck behind the stage. I leaned against it for ballast.

Was I going to be able to do this? Would my fingers remember how to work in the spotlight? Would I even be able to speak?

My brain reached for a salve. My chakras needed adjusting quickly. I needed one of my father's quotations. I struggled to find something. *Do or die …? Success is the sum of small parts …?* Nothing came to mind.

I closed my eyes and whispered rhammm to myself. I needed to get my Manipura engaged. I needed power. I needed strength. I needed the energy of the universe right now to shine. I needed the power of a pâte à bombe.

"Are you okay?"

I turned. Liam approached in the dark. His white coat was the only thing that illuminated in the shadows.

I bristled. "I'm fine."

He crossed his arms and leaned against the truck. "You don't look so good."

His white chef's coat was perfectly pressed, and the sleeves were rolled up to show his beautiful tattoo of the siren in the flames.

She stared back at me. Was she taunting me or giving me encouragement?

I looked away. I didn't want to go there.

"I tasted the mousse ..."

He stood silent for a beat. The hush made me squirm. "... And?"

His grin grew. "You didn't use the Taza like I asked."

"It didn't work. It was too bitter and clashed with the Ras al Hanout," I said. Instead of feeling guilty, a sense of triumph washed over me.

"Maybe you didn't try hard enough," he said as his gaze intensified.

"Maybe your recipe was too aggressive," I said. "It's almost like you don't care about the person you're serving. You just want to mess with their head."

He adjusted his body against the truck, lit a cigarette, and took a drag. "You're charming." He laughed. "It's almost like you have artistic integrity."

He smiled, amused. "It's been a long time since anyone's challenged me. I give you points for having the balls ..."

His stature was illuminated in the faint light from the stage in the distance. His dark attractiveness stirred something in me. It made my head spin. "All you have to do is take my lead, and your future's set. You don't have to prove anything."

He grinned at me. Powerful. Seductive. I tried to ignore it.

"I don't know what you're trying to say. I did what you wanted. I just made it better."

He grinned, taking one last drag of his cigarette and putting it out. He was enjoying this. "Better for who, Fiona?"

He stepped closer to me in the shadows. His curly hair framed his handsome face. Even his green eyes had a way of catching the light somehow, like a Cheshire cat. He was gorgeous in the night.

He leaned in closer, and his eyes locked with mine. He was messing with the magnet in my head.

I broke his gaze and saw a familiar shadow over his shoulder. "Fiona!"

Liam stepped back, and the moment was done.

"I've been looking for you!" My dad pulled me into a big bear hug. I was so happy to see him.

"I can't believe how big the stage is. This is your big night," he smiled, proudly.

He turned to Liam, impressed.

"I'd like to introduce you to Chef Liam Auclair. He's Head Chef at Lucien."

My father extended his hand, giving Liam a warm handshake. "It's good to meet you. What are you making tonight?"

Liam smiled tightly. I could tell he wanted to get out of there. "You wouldn't understand."

My mind blew with rage. Who was he to talk to my father like that. "My father is a walking food encyclopedia. I'm sure he'd understand what you mean."

Liam gave a thin smile and turned abruptly. "We have five minutes, Fiona." He strode his way back to the kitchen, getting out of there.

I watched him go, the anger in my gut churning even more.

My dad turned to me. "You're being featured tonight as a real and bona fide pastry chef in Los Angeles. Seriously Fiona. This is huge." He put his arm around me, proud. "I know you have to go. Be relaxed. Be yourself. You'll be great."

I smiled at him. "Thanks, Dad. Wish me luck."

"Luck is what happens when preparation meets opportunity. Remember that, and you'll do fine." He kissed me on the cheek.

"Thanks, Dad." I smiled. A hint of reassurance washed over me.

"Just do your best. I know you will."

I took a deep breath and turned, heading to the kitchen.

This was it. Was I ready? My stomach was in knots.

This could be my shot. This could really define me as a chef. I could really make a name for myself.

Better chefs than me had paved the way for this moment. I could become Head Pastry Chef at Lucein if I pulled it off. I could sense it.

I glanced at the stage. Liam was laughing with one of the producers. He was larger than life and ready to go.

What the hell had just happened between us before my dad showed up? Why did he always mess with my head and make me reel out of my element?

I had to pull my shit together.

Julia saw me and motioned to her watch. She waved me over.

I looked at the crowd. I took a step, right foot forward.

"Here we go," I whispered to myself.

It was now or never.

13

It had been surreal.

Liam had braised the salmon and flipped his skillets of vegetables like a pro. He described ingredients and techniques with passion. Knowledge and energy fired off him as he finished his plates for the crowd.

They sat in rapt attention. His familiar magic had rubbed off on them. His passion had translated to the crowd. He had been a rockstar.

And then it was my turn.

It had all gone too quickly. A bizarre space in time where everything sped up and slowed down at the same time.

I guided the audience through each step of the mousse. I held my head high and accentuated my hands. I even had them laughing for a time or two. I received enthusiastic applause.

It had been thrilling, like jumping out of an airplane.

"What are your influences? What makes you tick?" One of the most prominent bloggers on the L.A. food scene, Simon Crenshaw, stood before me. He was talking over himself and acting like I was something special. I scrambled for something to say.

"I'm inspired by everyone, from Elisabeth Pruitt to Jessica Preaplato and Margerita Manzke. They've been important influences on me."

"You've certainly made an impression on me. You're brilliant." He grabbed his phone from his pocket. "Can I get a picture with you?"

I stood next to him and smiled as he took the picture. He vigorously shook my hand. "I can't wait to see what else you do." He gave me an excited smile as he disappeared into the crowd.

I stood, overwhelmed for a moment.

I watched as Liam spoke with the food critic from *Food and Wine*, whom Julia had been chatting up earlier. With her tortoiseshell glasses, she looked like a sophisticated librarian.

She was lit up, twisting a strand of her hair as they talked, an awkward flirter. She was obviously enamored with him.

Candice Jacobson approached Liam. She wore a revealing floral top and tight jeans with killer Prada boots. She was gorgeous as she stood beside him, squeezing him in for a photo. It was hard to believe a top worldwide food blogger was throwing herself at him. I watched him enjoy the spell she was trying to wield on him.

"Fiona?" A tall and lanky man gently touched me on the arm and smiled. "I'm Calvin Norton. I run Desperado."

I'd heard of Desperado. And Calvin was supposed to be one to watch. He'd been head chef at Mantra and had a lot of awards, including a James Beard. His new place was supposed to be something special. I extended my hand. "Hi. I'm Fiona."

"Your demo was fantastic."

"Thank you," I said, my cheeks flushing.

He glanced over his shoulder. "I don't want to appear too forward, but I've had my eye on you for a while, and I'm looking for someone to head my pastry kitchen. If you're ever unhappy with Liam ..." He gave me his card. "I think you'd be a good fit for my place. Think about it."

He smiled at me as he turned and disappeared into the crowd. I studied the card for a moment. Wow.

"Fiona!" Julia called from across the stage. She pounced at me, excitedly. "You were fantastic!" Julia gave me an enthusiastic air kiss on the cheek and a hug. "How do you feel?"

"It felt good. But I'm glad it's over, honestly," I said.

"Julia, congratulations." A woman approached from behind. Julia lit up.

My stomach dropped to the ground as my brain processed who she was.

"Fiona, I'd like you to meet Marci Strand. She's the Food editor at the *L.A. Times*."

She extended her hand. "It's nice to meet you."

I couldn't believe I was finally meeting her. My hero. In the flesh.

"Your dessert was powerful. The contrast between the flavors of the Ras el Hanout and the whipped cream was just ... How do I say this? ... Conflicting. Passionate and romantic at the same time. Well done."

I blushed. "Thank you."

"You're doing a lot of new and interesting things at Lucien. It's been impressive."

Liam approached from behind. He brushed against me as he extended his hand, almost pushing me out of the way. "Marci. It's good to see you."

She lit up, like she was meeting a food god.

"I want to get a picture of you both. We're going to feature you tomorrow." She waved her photographer over. "You're a great representation of what's happening in L.A. You're both fresh. Interesting."

The photographer pushed Liam and me together. I braced myself as our shoulders touched, and he put his arm around me. Something about it caught me off guard.

He gave me a victorious grin. His eyes were shining. Triumphant. I turned to the camera. I gave my most winning smile as the flash went off. He quickly let go of my waist.

Marci looked at Liam. "Let's discuss your move from New York. I had the opportunity to see you at Juniper. What you're doing now is completely different. I want to talk to you about your vision."

She pulled him aside, and they drifted off to the side of the stage as she started interviewing him, out of earshot.

Julia studied at me a beat. Her hard eyes assessing me. The pause in the moment made me brace.

Julia broke into a bright smile. "Fiona, I'd like to give you the job. You've more than earned it. I'd like to make you the head pastry chef at Lucein.

Here it was. My shining moment. The moment I'd been waiting for my whole life. My dream finally realized.

My body tingled from head to toe. Was I going to throw up? I tried to hold back the tears in my eyes.

"Thank you, Julia. I don't know what to say," I said. I felt numb. Overwhelmed.

"Congratulations. You've passed the test. I'm quite impressed that you hung in there and made Lucien look so impressive. I'm quite pleased."

She gave me her most winning smile. It was the ultimate approval. What I'd been waiting for my whole life. And here it was. The moment of truth.

"Now, our next menu has to be perfect. Now, there's a target on our back. The Michelin inspectors will be scrutinizing us. This is when it counts. This is your shot to kill it."

The purse on her lips returned. "Welcome to the big leagues, darling."

I watched her disappear into the throng.

"Fiona!" My father pushed through the crowd and put his arms around me in a tight embrace. "You did great! I'm so proud of you!"

"Dad. I did it. Julia made me Head Pastry Chef at Lucien."

He gave me a huge bear hug. "Congratulations, sweetie. I knew you could do it. You made all of your dreams come true! I'm so proud of you!"

My heart surged at his approval. It was the ultimate reward.

He broke from the embrace and turned.

A hippish and plump woman stood behind him. It was Astrid, the mysterious woman he'd been talking about for so long.

"Fiona, I'd like you to meet Astrid," he smiled, proudly.

She grinned at me. "It's nice to meet you. Your father has told me so much about you. You must feel pretty great right now with everything."

I smiled, proudly. "I'm still trying to process."

I turned to my dad, almost forgetting. "Dad. There's something else. I met Marci Strand. I really met her. She's writing something about me for tomorrow's food section."

My dad's face melted into a look of pride. "I knew you would. It was only a matter of time."

Ultimate pride washed over me. Triumph in making my dreams a reality was almost more than I could handle.

"I can't believe it! You really made it happen."

He smiled. "I'm going to let you enjoy the fruits of your success. I'm taking Astrid to that Osso Bucco place I've been reading about." He turned. "I'm going to convince Astrid here that meat is a good thing."

"I'll probably just order a salad." She laughed.

He squeezed my arm. "You did good, kid."

He waved as he disappeared into the crowd.

"There you are!" Kate and Charlotte parted the crowd. Their hands were juggling a handful of different food containers and paper plates.

I smiled proudly. "Girls, I'd like to introduce you to the new Head Pastry Chef at Lucien. *And* Marcy Strand's featuring me in the Saturday food section of the *L.A. Times*!"

"OMG, Fiona! I can't believe it!" Charlotte screamed as she tackled me with a hug and jumped up and down. "You did it! You really did it!"

Her excitement melted into a humble smile. "Look. I'm sorry about before. I can see I was wrong about everything."

"Thank you, Charlotte," I said. I was happy that our argument was finally over.

"Who knew you could carry a crowd? I was so impressed!" Kate set down her buffet of Thai spring rolls, churros, and what looked like verde enchilada.

"Seriously, Fiona ... Liam Auclair. Just, OMG ..." Charlotte picked up one of the paper plates and started eating the churro.

Kate smiled. "The post-show buzz ... It's the best part, isn't it?"

"I didn't create a mosh pit like you do. I just entertained a bunch of food geeks. There's a difference."

"Take this." Charlotte handed me her churro, and I took a bite. It was just what I needed. It was crisp and hot. Whoever had made the pâte a choux made it perfectly—sweet and delicate. I took another bite. It was the best thing I'd ever eaten.

I gazed in the distance as Liam mingled with a small crowd. Kate leveled me with a grin. "Spit it out. What's bugging you?"

"It's nothing. Never mind." I turned back to them.

"Well, you have to try some of this stuff." Charlotte was digging into her Thai wrap. "I've eaten so many things. I have that weird feeling you get from a Vegas buffet when you eat waffles with Chinese food."

She wiped her hands off with a napkin and tossed her plate in the trashcan sitting by the table. "I think I saw a wine cart somewhere. Can I get you ladies a glass?"

"I'd love one." I needed it.

"Make that two." Kate smiled.

"I'll be back." Charlotte turned and disappeared into the crowd.

Kate caught me studying Liam from across the crowd. "Yeah, just look at the way he's entertaining those ladies. I don't think they care how he sears a steak." Kate grinned.

He turned and caught Kate and me checking him out. He nodded and smiled. Kate gave him a flirtatious wave back.

I quickly turned. "Crap."

Kate smiled at me. "What? He seems nice."

"Kate. Don't even go there."

She pursed her lips in thought. "Yeah. I guess you're right. It's kind of disappointing that you can't go with the flow on this one. He's sort of a bragging right."

"That's playing a dangerous game and you know it, Kate."

She forked a bite of an enchilada. The green sauce ran down her chin. "You were interviewed by the *L.A. Times*? That's huge, Fiona. It's everything you ever dreamed of."

A warm wave of pride washed over me. "I can't believe Marci said my mousse was passionate. Romantic. What did she mean by 'conflicted'?"

"Sounds like foodie speak to me. Why can't you enjoy the food without all the adjectives?" She held her fork out to me. "You should try this. It's fucking amazing." She held out a fork to me.

Charlotte approached, juggling three glasses of wine. "I grabbed one glass of each. A Chardonnay, a rosé, and a Pinot. Choose your poison," she said.

I grabbed the rosé and took a sip. The cold, delicious taste felt somehow triumphant.

My insides were blossoming with satisfaction. I was head pastry chef. I was going to be featured in the *L.A. Times* food section tomorrow. I'd be vouched for.

It was everything I'd dreamed of.

"Let's cruise past Arco's booth. I want to try their meatballs. I've heard they're insane," Charlotte said as she nibbled on a small flatbread bruschetta. She smiled and licked her fingers as she took the last bite.

"And we have to try the tomato-burrata oreganata at Miriska's booth. I've heard it's out of this world." She licked her fingers again. "This is really gross. Are there any more napkins? Did you get some more?"

"No, I was too busy eating the mini barbacoa dumplings ..." Kate said as she nibbled on a tart.

I took another sip of wine as I watched Liam from across the crowd. He was so cocky as he spoke to another food critic.

His ego was on full display.

My mind flashed to the dark look he'd given me by the truck, back to the strange exchange that had taken place. The conflict in my heart returned.

I took a deep breath, willing it away.

I had better things to think about.

I was Head Pastry Chef at Lucien, after all. I made it. I passed the test. And even better, I was going to be validated by Marci Strand.

It couldn't get any better than this.

* * *

The bounty of *The Taste* was on full display. The white tents and shiny strung lights above created a magical, romantic space.

There were so many kinds of food. It was a landscape of different cultures.

Mediterranean mixed with Mexican. Middle Eastern mingled with classical French and Italian. Japanese, Thai, and Chinese thrown in for good measure.

This festival was a representation of my backyard. I'd grown up with all these foods at my fingertips.

It was part of my molecular makeup.

It was everything I loved about L.A. The melting pot of flavors. The clash of cultures. I was caught up in the smells in the air. The aroma of grilled meat. The sweet scent of fried dough. I was in heaven.

Charlotte nudged me out of my reverie. "What are you going to eat?"

We stood in front of La Mirage's pastry booth. I'd read about Chef Maher Nakhal's Syrian pastry before.

Reading about it was one thing. Seeing it up close was another—lacy filo dough creations and exotic versions of brioche.

It was beautiful.

A man was using some sort of long mallet-shaped thing, slamming it into a large container. It looked like a lot of work.

Chef Maher was spooning out some sort of stretchy concoction to someone.

"I'll be back," I said.

Kate nodded and yawned. "We're just going to be digesting here. Go for it."

She seemed a bit green.

I approached the booth, intrigued. "What is that? I pointed to the silky, white, and stretchy concoction.

"We're making booza. It's Syrian ice cream. The recipe has been around for about 500 years. It's one of the first ice creams in history. It's extraordinary. Try it."

He gave me a proud nod as he handed me a cup.

I took the spoon and dipped it in, grabbing a small bite. It stretched like melted mozzarella cheese. I twisted my spoon to catch it, but caught it in my mouth.

I could taste the faint flavor of rose water and pistachio. It didn't melt right away. It hung on my tongue.

It was magical.

"Fiona." I turned around. Liam was standing behind me. He had some kind of meat skewer in his hand—a beer in the other.

He gave me a winning, calculated smile. "You did great tonight. Julia told me the news." He smiled, pleased with himself. "You couldn't have done it without me."

"Thank you," I said. I tried not to take offense.

"It feels pretty good, doesn't it?" He smiled, triumphantly.

"What does?"

"The success. You've finally tasted it. It's pretty great, right?"

I thought for a moment. "I'm still trying to process all of it. It's pretty overwhelming."

"Well, this is it, Fiona. You can never go back now." He smiled. "Consider this the first day of the rest of your life."

He held my gaze. The glow of the lights illuminated his face. There was a glint in his eye. He made my stomach twist.

"What did you get?" he asked.

"Booza. It's 500-year-old ice cream."

"I hope you don't mean it's 500 years old," he chuckled.

I laughed. "I hope not."

He smiled, curious. "Can I try it?"

"Of course."

He juggled his beer and skewer into his left hand, grabbed my spoon, and took a spoonful. It kept stretching and stretching as he tried to take it. "Oh, weird." He laughed at the awkwardness as he took the bite. "This is interesting."

"Is that good or bad?"

He shrugged and tipped the skewer of meat to me. "You want to try this? It's lamb, Adobo."

I plucked a piece of meat off the skewer and took a bite. The savory, garlicky taste, mingled with the sharp grilled flavor, made my tongue explode. It was delicious.

"It's not the best I've had. They could have marinated the meat more, and it's a bit overpowered with Adobo."

He let the comment hang there while he looked at me.

"We have to go, sweetie." Charlotte and Kate crashed the moment. Kate gave me a brisk hug. "Have fun."

Kate squeezed me, whispering in my ear. "I'll see you at home. I won't wait up."

And just like that, in a whirlwind, they were off.

"Are those your friends?" Liam watched them leave, confused.

I rolled my eyes. "I thought they were."

His eyes met with mine. I tried to ignore the intensity of his gaze.

He frowned at the skewer and tossed it in a trashcan. "Let's go see Benito Taco. It's the best. It's two-star Michelin."

He extended his hand, gesturing me forward.

As we walked through the crowd, people nodded and smiled. It was so good to be recognized.

"I'm beginning to see what you meant by no center," Liam said as he navigated the crowd. He nodded effortlessly to a passerby, who recognized him.

"What do you mean?" I asked.

"When you said L.A. has no center. I get it now. It's a free-for-all. I like the idea of plucking the best of every culture and applying it to the present. It's another way of thinking. It's inspiring."

"I didn't mean it didn't have a center in a literal sense. I meant the melding of culture was the center. You can't just cherry-pick things. It doesn't work that way."

"Then how's it supposed to work?" he asked.

"There's a certain spirit that culture occupies in L.A. You have to understand it to knit the elements together. It's a vibe. Not an absolute."

He frowned. "Great cuisine doesn't come from vibes. Great food comes from discipline. Order. Definition. Otherwise, it's just an afterthought."

He smiled as the Benito Taco booth came into view. "Stay here. I'll be back."

He gave a hearty handshake to the chef. There was a warm exchange between them.

There was something in the way he carried himself. He knew he was larger than life. In this moment, his energy radiated even more. It was blinding.

He returned with two paper boats of tacos.

"Try this. It's the real deal." He handed me the taco like he was giving me a present.

The purple corn shell was filled with some sort of baconish meat and Mexican cheese. The savory smell wafting from it was appetizing.

He met my gaze. "What are you waiting for? Try it." He smiled.

I took a bite of my taco and focused on the flavors in my mouth. The purple corn shell had a unique sweetness that regular corn lacked. The savory bacon and cheese were a perfect balance of flavor and taste.

It was deliberate. Calculated. It was the perfect twist of tang and texture.

"What do you think?" He asked.

"It's delicious."

I smiled to myself. Bobo's on Flower Street downtown was better.

I watched Liam as he took another bite of the taco. He rolled his eyes and chewed like he was eating something holy. "This is unforgettable."

I could see his ambition cloud his palate.

I wanted to laugh. I felt triumphant for some reason. Like I'd won this round.

He finished the taco and tossed the plate in a trashcan. His deep gaze pinned me in place. I squirmed. I tried to ignore the force of his energy. It was all too much.

"Liam, my man!" James Frye grabbed Liam from the throng with a bro-hug. His blond hair was slicked back, and he looked buff in his tight black tee. He was the quintessential winner. "You killed it."

His actress girlfriend trailed behind with a quesadilla in her hand. She somehow made it look elegant, shaking her beautiful blonde mane in indifference.

"Thanks, man. When's your presentation?"

"Tomorrow night. I'm after Alex. I'm sure he's going to make some version of Beef Wellington again." He shook his head. "I have no idea why he was invited."

He turned to me. "Your dessert was great. It was challenging and different. It's inspired me to try some new things. Well done."

"Thank you." I beamed inside.

The actress turned to me and extended her hand. "I don't believe we've met. I'm Margo."

I grabbed her and shook it. "Fiona. It's nice to meet you."

She smiled. "I liked your dessert. It was perfect. The best thing I've had here so far," She gave me a kind smile. Maybe I had her wrong.

"Listen. We're meeting Alex and Jay at the tequila-tasting bar down the way. Why don't you join us. We can celebrate."

"Sure. That sounds great. I want to talk to Alex about his purveyor. I'm thinking of using someone else."

What!? My breath caught in my throat.

Was he thinking of ditching Delia and Rory? How could he? The rug was ripped from underneath me.

"Come on, Fiona. Why don't you join us? It'd be good to have you come," Liam said. He gave me a hypnotic smile. "I can introduce you to Alex and Jay. Alex is chef at Haywire. Jay runs Marsimo. They'd be good for you to know."

I paused for a beat. I was invited to hang out with the best of the best. It was more than I could take. I surged with an inner pride.

"Sure. I'd love to."

"Then let's go!" Liam and James turned and made their way through the crowd. Margo and I followed behind. It was hard to keep up.

"So, where are you from?" Margo asked. I was amazed that she could walk so fast in her impossibly tall high heels.

"I'm from L.A. I grew up here."

"Wow. That's cool. I'm from Minnesota. So sometimes, it's still a little overwhelming for me. I mean, I still can't figure out where my house is half the time." She laughed.

"I still get lost. Don't worry." I smiled. "I don't think you ever get a handle on it. Thank God for Google Maps."

"Well, that makes me feel better," she smiled. "I'm going to remember that the next time I'm lost."

A retro tequila company sponsored the tequila bar. It was a startup like so many others that popped up here and there. A raucous crowd was mingling and drinking. I could see so many recognizable chefs in the crowd: Anthony Smith, Sally Adams, Alex Shannon. Liam gave Alex a generous hug, turned, and looked for me in the crowd. "Fiona! Get over here. I want you to meet Alex."

Alex smiled with a wry look in his eye as he sat at the bar. His rumpled flannel and slouchy jeans betrayed how unimpressed he was by everything around him.

Alex sized me up and shook my hand. "Hi Fiona. How does it feel to have survived?"

"I'm honestly glad it's over."

"I felt the same way. Honestly this shit is so boring. I'd rather be working. Thursday is a shitshow at the restaurant. I shouldn't even be here." He smiled.

Liam shoved a shot of tequila in my hand. "Here! A toast! A toast to your success."

Alex raised his beer.

Liam gave me a high-wattage smile and downed his tequila. He slammed it on the bar and motioned to the bartender for another round.

"What are you waiting for Fiona?" Liam smiled. The ghost of the smile I saw at Vestrano. Teasing. Seductive. Tempting me.

I turned to James and Margo. They smiled as they raised their shot glasses to mine. "Cheers!" James exclaimed, and we all downed our drinks.

The alcohol burned as it made its way to my stomach. I could feel it instantly go into my head.

"Damn. That's good. I love the charcoal undertones," James mused as he took another shot glass from Liam. "I think I need to try that again." He smiled slyly and downed the other shot.

Margo giggled. "I love tequila. It really wakes me up. I've heard it's good for your pores." She laughed as she drank the second shot.

"Come on, Fiona. Drink up!" Liam exclaimed.

I looked at the second shot for a beat. A surge of excitement surged through me.

I did deserve to celebrate. Becoming pastry chef. Marci Strand. Making my dreams come true. And what better way to celebrate than to be here? Among the who's who of the L.A. restaurant scene. I made it. I finally made it, and I was accepted.

I drank the second shot, and Liam smiled at me with a vaguely seductive grin. I felt my head begin to spin even harder. A giddy surge of energy coursed through me, and I felt supernatural pride.

Liam was right. Once you felt this way, there was no going back.

It really was the first day of the rest of my life.

* * *

I opened my eyes and looked at the clock on his nightstand.

It was seven-thirty a.m.

My head was pounding from a supernatural headache. I still felt drunk behind the fog of my headache.

I turned over and gazed out the large window. It was raining outside. A view of the 101 Freeway was the full view from the window. Traffic was sparse. The sound of cars was like the ocean outside. Passing headlights illuminated the room.

Liam was lying beside me. His back was turned, and he was tangled up in the sheets.

Nooooo ... coursed through my mind. I couldn't do the math.

How did I get here? And where was I? Panic surged through me. What the hell had I done?

My eyes focused on the space around me.

His apartment was small.

It was a studio, old-fashioned and charming. A French marble fireplace occupied a wall. Heavy furniture and dusty books filled the room, stacked on tables and against the wall.

Honestly, he needed a bigger apartment to hold all the books. He had way too many.

His kitchen was organized. Sharp knives were hanging on the wall. Pots hung from a rack on the ceiling. Fresh herbs sat on the counter in little terra-cotta pots. I could see basil, rosemary, and chervil blooming and healthy.

I sat up and got out of bed. I grabbed my underwear and T-shirt and pulled them on.

My head hurt. I had to get out.

But his books caught my eye. His inner sanctum was laid bare. I grabbed one of his books that sat on top of a stack.

It was a cookbook.

I focused a little more.

All the books were cookbooks. Every facet of savory was covered. Indian, French, Italian, and Asian. Everything. His collection outweighed mine by one-hundred percent.

I picked up one and fingered through it. It was an advanced tome in French. Old-fashioned sketches of various dishes and an indecipherable language filled the pages.

He stirred, turning over. "Don't leave."

He sat up. His hair was rumpled from sleep. His chest was bare. I tried not to think of what had happened.

I set the book down. "I have to go. I'll call an Uber."

He smiled at me. "Stay. I'll make you breakfast."

He stood up, wrapped in the sheet. He was like a Greek statue.

He walked toward me and wrapped his arms around my waist. He wrapped the sheet around me, leaned in, and kissed me. His lips lingered on my neck.

I pushed away from him. I couldn't go there again. His eyes met mine, and he smiled.

"Sit down. I'm making you coffee, and you can't say no."

He guided me to a kitchen stool sitting up against the bar. I sat down, fighting my instinct to leave.

He dropped the sheet. I glanced at his muscular butt as he grabbed a pair of flannel pants from a pile of clothes on the floor and pulled them on.

"You like lots of sugar, right?" He pulled a coffee press from a cupboard, set the teapot to boil, and grabbed some coffee beans. He poured some into a grinder and turned it on. It smelled heavy and delicious.

I took a deep breath. His muscles flexed as he worked. The waist of his pants sat just right on his hips.

He turned around. "Let's look at the food section. Let's see if Marci came through."

He grabbed his laptop and sat it on the kitchen bar. He opened it, clicking on something, and sure enough.

There we were.

We were on the front page of the *L.A. Times* Saturday food section.

My brain reeled.

It couldn't be real.

I blinked and looked again.

Sure enough. There we were. Our picture was large. It took up the whole screen.

"How does it feel to be famous?"

My eyes froze on the picture. I blushed.

The photographer had caught a ghost or an apparition of something. He'd caught the chemistry between Liam and me and how we smiled, looking at each other.

I was unsettled by the candor captured in the moment.

I gazed outside to settle myself. The cars whizzed past the window. The rain made the air dark.

"Listen to this," Liam read. "Lucien is rearranging thought. Rearranging taste. Creating an abstraction of thought that Los Angeles has been waiting for. Chef Liam Auclair is creating a pocket of truth in the new food movement. If there were a revolution, Liam would be leading the charge. Lucien's three stars are imminent."

A powerful smile crossed his lips. He was enjoying the spoils of war.

His ambition showed in his eyes.

He stood silent, scanning the rest of the article. He was sucked into his own moment of greatness.

I sat impatiently. Waiting. Greedy for my part.

Liam glanced up at me, laughing. "Oh yeah. Let's see what she said about you." He read a bit more. "Here we go …" He cleared his throat. "Fiona McConnell, a Los Angeles native, is a new voice on the scene. Her sexy and vibrant interpretation of pastry is the perfect seduction after a challenging meal. Her provocative desserts leave you wanting more. She's a chef to watch."

I sat there for a minute, trying to process what Marci wrote.

I was a chef to watch.

He leaned in and gave me a lingering, seductive kiss. "You're basically sex on a plate."

There was a surge in my center. My ego being massaged.

He reached into the fridge and grabbed a carton of heavy cream, crème fraiche, and some eggs. He set them on the counter in front of me, as he looked at me, amused—a flicker of understanding in his eyes. "I'm going to make you the best omelet you ever had. But first: coffee."

He pressed down on the plunger of the coffee press, pulled a cup from another cupboard, and poured. He grabbed sugar from a tiny bowl on the counter, sprinkled a generous amount in the cup, and stirred it.

His movements were precise as he worked. He set the cup down in front of me and watched as I took a sip.

"It's perfect. Thank you."

"I know."

He grabbed a metal bowl from a cupboard, opened the egg carton, and started cracking eggs into the bowl, one-handed. He expertly pinched his fingers to release the contents from the shell, moving on to the next one.

His body moved like an interpretative dancer.

I let the silence fill the moment. There was nothing to say.

He was mesmerizing as he poured cream into the bowl of eggs and whisked everything together. His tattoos flexed as he poured the contents into the omelet pan and grabbed a rubber spatula.

"Honestly, Fiona, this is our chance. This is the white-hot opportunity you get before you come in for the kill."

With an elegant flourish, he flipped the omelet. It landed perfectly as he set the pan back on the stove. He swung to the refrigerator, grabbed some fontina cheese, and pinched some chervil from his little terra-cotta garden.

He grabbed a knife from the wall and quickly chopped the chervil into a chiffonade.

"I bet you can't do this?" He smiled, naughty.

"Do what?"

"This." He flipped the knife into his other hand and started to mince the chervil with his other hand. It was weird—the exact precise movements, but like a mirror.

"You can chop with both hands?" I was beyond impressed.

He shrugged as if it was nothing. "It's one of the first things I taught myself."

His expert hands sprinkled the chervil on the cheese and folded it over. He slid it on a plate, topped it with a tiny dash of crème fraiche and a slight flush of parsley.

He set it in front of me and handed me a fork. "What are you waiting for?"

I took a bite. Let it linger in my mouth for a moment.

He was right.

It was the best omelet I'd ever had.

The eggs were light and creamy. The fontina cheese was tangy and soft, and the chervil gave it a hint of freshness that was the perfect complement between the eggs and the cheese.

It was magic in its simplicity.

I chewed slowly, savoring it.

He grabbed the fork from my hand, and his fingers brushed up against mine. I couldn't look away as he took a bite from my fork, chewing slowly.

He took another forkful and held it to my lips for me to eat. I held his gaze as I took it.

His eyes shifted to another shade of green as his body leaned close to me against the counter.

My wires were getting crossed. The smooth skin of his shoulders. The perfect bridge of his nose. I was getting mixed up again. My head spun from the vague drunkness I still felt.

He took a sip of my coffee and handed me the cup. I couldn't let go of his gaze as I drank. Even the way he made coffee was magical.

He walked around the counter, took the cup from my hands, and set it on the counter.

He took me in his arms and kissed me. His fingers were touching all the electric points of my body. I realized I didn't have any pants on.

"I can't do this. I really have to go."

I grabbed my pants and shrugged them on quickly. I couldn't tell if they were inside out.

"Really Fiona, don't go. We have so much to talk about.

I grabbed my bag from the chair by the door. I had to get out of there fast. I had to leave.

"I can't. I'm sorry."

I pushed past him and reached for the doorhandle. I swung the door open and let it slam behind me before he could say anything else.

This was a huge mistake.

14

I double-stepped to the elevator and pushed the button. The door opened, and I jumped in, and pushed the button for the lobby.

My stomach lurched as the elevator descended. I thought about what had happened last night.

I'd given in.

The elevator door opened. I pushed my right foot forward as I walked through the lobby and made my way outside. I pulled my phone out, ordered an Uber, and quickly pocketed it.

The rain was coming down in a consistent sheet.

I stood there waiting and getting wet.

What was I going to do about this?

This was a frigging mess.

The Uber pulled up, and I jumped in. I glanced behind my shoulder one more time as the car pulled away from the crime scene.

How could I look Rory in the eye after this?

He'd know.

I should've had discipline. I shouldn't have given in to the moment like I had. My ego had gotten the best of me.

I hated myself.

I watched outside as the cars whisked past in the rain. I could hear the static wash of the water on the road. The sound fit with the turmoil in my heart.

How could I face Rory after what I'd done?

He'd know, and he'd hate me. I was such an idiot. I was a weed in his beautiful vineyard.

My phone vibrated in my pocket. I pulled it out and looked at the screen.

It was Rory.

A wave of panic washed over me. Had I sent something out into the universe? A guilty signal?

Why was he calling me right now?

My palms sprung into a cold sweat as I answered my phone. "Hello?"

There was a clipped fear in his voice. "Can you come to Santa Monica? I'm at Saint John's. On the way to the market this morning, something happened to my mom."

I shuddered, my heart sinking. "What's wrong?"

"They're doing tests on her right now." He paused, deliberating. "I was hoping you could be with me if you can. I would understand if you couldn't. It'd be nice to have you here with me, though."

The Uber pulled up to my apartment. I grabbed my bag and hopped out.

I needed to wash my deception off.

"I'll be there in twenty minutes. Let me get myself together, and I'll be there as soon as I can."

"Thank you, Fiona. This means more to me than you'll ever know." He hung up, and I stood on the sidewalk, letting the rain drench me. I was frozen in guilt.

I felt even worse now.

Shame filled my heart. How could I face him after this?

* * *

Rory leaned against the waiting room wall, lost in thought. Anxious people scattered the room, sitting in uncomfortable chairs.

Scattered pages of the *L.A. Times* and worn magazines were mixed up with used coloring books and broken crayons. A television was on mute. Judge Judy waved her arms around and stared through her reading glasses at some poor soul.

Rory glanced up, seeing me. "You came," he said.

I gave him a big hug. Even now, his hug was comforting. Warm.

"It's good to see you." He smiled. "Let's get a seat." He pulled two chairs together, and we sat down.

He was strong and in control, but I could see the fear lingering in his eyes.

"What happened?"

"She collapsed at the market. I told her that she should stop going, but she insisted."

I gazed at him, helpless. I wanted to say something right, but the words weren't coming.

"We thought things were going well." He thought for a moment. "She's so stubborn. Honestly, she's worse than Grace on a bad day."

He gazed toward the cluttered table, shaking his head. "She thinks she can power through anything and conquer it. That's the way she's been my whole life." He sighed. "This is too big for her. I just wish she'd face it and do what she needs to do."

I took his hand. It was cold and clammy.

A weird look crossed his face. "Is that you?"

"What do you mean?"

He stood up and grabbed one of the rumpled-up newspaper pages off the table.

It was the *L.A. Times* Saturday food section.

I was smiling back at me.

Liam was smiling back at me.

Rory was looking at me, confused.

My stomach dropped to the floor. I felt cornered. Naked. Like I'd been caught.

The picture of Liam and me was embarrassing. Flagrant in its pride. Naked in our conceit. I wished I could bury it back under the pile of papers on the table.

"This is from last night? Wow, Fiona. This is amazing. Congratulations."

I cringed. "Please. Put it down. It's nothing, really."

"Fiona. It's definitely something." He scanned the paper, reading through it.

He found my part. He smiled as he read it out loud: "*Fiona McConnell, a Los Angeles native, is a new voice on the scene. Her sexy and vibrant interpretation of pastry is the perfect seduction after a challenging meal. Her provocative desserts leave you wanting more. She's a chef to watch.*"

He set it down and smiled. "This is huge for you."

I took the paper from his hands, rolled it up, and crumpled it aside. "It's stupid. It's a distraction from what's going on right now. I don't even want to think about it."

"Well, you should be proud. You deserve it."

Did I? Did I deserve the attention?

I certainly didn't deserve to be sitting here. To be his confidant. His support.

I was a fraud.

He smiled at me, thinking. "I remember the first time someone wrote about me. It was for *Wine Spectator*. It was for a 2010 Shiraz, one of my first presses. I'd just opened the vineyard for tastings, and one of the magazine writers rolled through my place on a tasting. He interviewed me on the spot, and the next thing I knew, I was thrust into the whole wine world and taken seriously. I got my medal from San Francisco based on that. It catapulted my career. My business. My vineyard. It gave me a solid reputation to build on."

He smiled. "This could be that for you, Fiona. This could help you. It certainly puts you on the map."

My stomach was a mess. Everything about it was rotten. "It seems silly right now. It's just an article. It doesn't mean anything."

He took my hand. "No, Fiona. It means a lot."

A doctor strolled into the room. A chart in his hands. "Mr. Martin?"

Rory stood up and pulled my hand.

The doctor reviewed her chart. "I'm concerned about your mother. Her bloodwork came back highly abnormal. She had high inflammatory markers, a high monocyte count, anemia, and a low lymphocyte count. Is she in chemo right now?"

"Yes. We're trying to get her on a clinical trial."

The doctor nodded. "We'll need to do some more tests. In the meantime, would you like to see her?"

"Yes. Please."

The doctor glanced at me. "Only next of kin can go back. You'll have to wait here."

I could see the panic in his eyes. "She's my wife."

The doctor studied me for a moment and nodded. "Okay. You can see her for a minute. Be quick. She's in queue for a CT scan."

Rory pulled me behind him.

My head echoed the words he'd said: *She's my wife …*

He just called me his wife.

I almost stumbled as I followed him through the doors back to the curtained spaces in the treatment area.

A crazy scream pierced the air from behind a closed curtain. "I'm getting out of here! You can't stop me, motherfuckers!"

Two nurses and a security guard jumped into action and quickly made their way to the situation.

I glanced through the crack of another passing curtain. A boy in a baseball uniform was holding his arm. His face was pinched from pain, and he looked too exhausted to cry anymore. His mother cradled his head in her hands, waiting. Nervous and worried.

Another bed held an older man. He was hooked up to an assortment of machines. He had tubes and wires hanging from all parts of his body. His tiny wife was holding his hand. She was terrified and trying not to cry.

I could see other patients through their curtains. Hear the tears and dull conversations between doctors and nurses.

I looked away, not wanting to see the scary things that could happen: heart attacks, broken bones, insanity.

It was all too real.

This was the baseline of life. This is what happened when life got real.

I felt stupid for the drama I was creating for myself.

The doctor pulled back a curtain and led us in. Delia was in bed. Her hospital gown made her seem small and diminished.

Her coveralls and hat had given her superpowers somehow.

Now I saw a frail old woman. I could see the fear in her eyes.

"Fiona! What are you doing here?" I grabbed her hand.

Rory smiled at her. I could tell he was trying to be strong. "I thought you might want someone to lighten the mood."

"Well, this is nonsense." She squeezed my hand. "I just want to go home."

"Mom, they have to finish testing you. Please relax and do what the doctors tell you." He sighed. "I need you to take this seriously."

Delia took a deep breath and steeled herself up. She straightened her shoulders in resolution. "I am."

"Thank you, Mom. I love you, and I want you to hang around a while."

A doctor poked his head in. "Can I speak with you a moment, Mr. Martin?"

Rory nodded. "I'll be right back."

Delia smiled at me. "Thank you for being here today. For Rory. For me. It means a lot."

Even now, her bright light showed through.

"I forgot to tell you" I tried the roasted apple butter. Don't worry about adding more cinnamon. It was perfect," I said.

"Thank you, honey. I thought it turned out pretty good. It's the first apples of the season, so I sort of jumped the gun making it, but I couldn't wait."

She smiled. "I'm so glad you and Rory have hit it off. He's going through so much right now. I'm sorry for being a part of that. But I'm thankful that you've found each other."

I was numb. My heart couldn't take anymore.

All I could do was squeeze her hand.

Rory and a technician pushed through the curtain. The technician rolled a wheelchair into the partition. "Ms. Martin, we're ready for you."

Delia looked at Rory, searching for strength.

He nodded and smiled. "It's going to be fine. Just pray."

The technician disconnected her IV and helped her sit down in the chair.

Rory gave her a brave face. "I love you, Mom."

"I love you, too." Her eyes were uncertain.

We watched as she rolled down the hallway and rounded a corner. She disappeared into the chaos of the ER.

I grabbed Rory's hand.

"Let's go. We'll wait outside." I pulled him to the waiting room.

We walked together. Hand in hand back through the ER.

She's my wife …

He had called me his wife. It kept running on repeat in my head.

He had actually called me his wife.

I glanced up at him.

A distant yearning sparked in me.

I knew he was trying to get me through the door. But imagine really getting through it? Imagine being on the other side?

With an amazing person like him.

How could I have been so wrong? How could I have even toyed with the dark side?

I had to step away from the cliff.

Could this scenario still even be a possibility? Could I put my mistake behind me?

He was the whole package. And he had called on me in a time of need.

She's my wife …

I knew what I had to do. It was time for me to get my shit together. What had happened would never happen again.

* * *

I drove down the rainy freeway. The rumble of thunder murmured in the distance. Did that counting-off game work on thunder or lightning?

I focused on the traffic in front of me. My head was a mixed-up mess.

I had to sever this thing with Liam right now. It couldn't wait. I needed to get it off my chest. Discard the bad situation once and for all.

I saw his motorcycle parked in the rain. It represented everything about him.

Black. Shiny. Sexy. Fast.

I thought of riding fast down the freeway on the bike with him. How it had ignited all of the adrenaline in my body. It had heightened all my senses. It had made things smell better. Feel better. Sound better.

Rory made me was like that without the pomp and circumstance. Rory made things smell better. Sound better. Feel better.

The motorcycle was a cheat.

Rory didn't need some stupid motorcycle.

I couldn't believe I'd bought into the whole Liam thing. It seemed so cheesy now that I was seeing clearly.

His tattoos. His bike. His knives. His larger-than-life chef persona.

What had I done?

I took a deep breath. *Do or Die.* I was going to end this stupid thing once and for all.

I stepped around the bush and steeled myself up, looking at the front door.

Then I saw her.

A beautiful woman walked down the sidewalk and turned toward Liam's building.

It was Candice Jacobson.

She was tall and gorgeous. Under her black umbrella, she was stunning in a sleek raincoat, back seam stockings, and the sexiest pumps I'd ever seen. Her hair was pulled back and matched her perfect berry-tinted lipstick.

I stepped behind a bush.

She pushed in a code at the box at the front door and waited. She folded her umbrella in one elegant sweep.

Liam opened the door and took her in his arms, giving her a deep kiss. He slipped his hand around her waist and led her inside.

I watched the door close, standing in the silence of the rain. The drops pelted my naked face.

What the fuck?

How could he? How could he be such a dog!?

A slow rage boiled from the bottom of my stomach. A fury blasted through me that I'd never known before.

I was outplayed. Paralyzed. I couldn't move.

"Excuse me." I was startled out of my moment. An old man with a fluffy white dog stood behind me on the sidewalk. His umbrella's reach filled the space around us.

"Sorry." I stepped aside to let him pass. My foot landed in the gutter, getting my foot drenched.

The cold of the water woke me up.

I needed to do something. Anything. I had to get out of there.

15

"Fiona, it's official. You've officially blown your life up with an atomic bomb."

Charlotte shoved a pile of my cookbooks aside and sat at the table.

"So what are you going to do?" Kate asked. She fiddled with a box of beads sitting on the table. A rumpled copy of the *L.A. Times* food section sat on the chair beside me. Liam and I smiled back at me. I shoved it away.

"About what part, exactly? It's all an awful mess," I groaned.

"It's just a matter of compartmentalizing in your head," Charlotte said. "Yogi Dave says it best: Imagine each problem like a train car in a station. You're standing on the platform. You can choose which train to ride."

My heart hurt. "I should have known the score when he slayed that poor fish ..."

Kate and Charlotte looked at me, confused.

I sighed. A heavy weight hung on me. "I basically did to Rory what Liam did to me. So where do I stand with that? I'm just as evil as him."

There was a thoughtful silence.

Kate frowned. "You're right." She mulled the thought for a moment. "Your motivation is different, though. For you, it was a mistake—a hiccup. Liam knew what he was doing. He was just a jerk."

She set the box of beads to the side for later. "Right or wrong, it happened. You can't control that. What you can control is how you react from now on."

Tears welled up in my eyes. I pushed them back. "This is the biggest mistake I've ever made. Rory's the whole package. He could be the one."

Charlotte shifted in her chair. She picked up an errant cookbook, studied it, and put it back down. "What if you just forgot about it? Why does he have to know? Chalk it up to a bad night and move on?"

"When I was at the hospital, he called me his wife."

"What!?" Charlotte's eyes widened. "He didn't."

"He was trying to get me back to see his mother. It just sort of happened."

Charlotte took a deep breath, excited. "Forget this Liam business. Take it as a sign."

Kate leaned forward. "If some guy, even in jest, called me his wife, that's something."

Charlotte smiled; a dreamy look traced her face. "Think about it, Fiona, you could be the queen of his whole empire. His farm, his vineyard. You could marry, bake rustic bread in a barn, and become one with the land." She smiled, "It would be perfect. Wine. Cheese. Bread. It's the pairing that goes back to ancient civilization. It's so romantic ..."

Kate rolled her eyes. "How many cookbooks have you been reading? This smells of foodie porn—foodie fairy tales. You both read too many cookbooks. You need to get real."

Charlotte shook her head. "I still can't believe he called you his wife. That's epic."

"That's why this situation is so awful. He was so vulnerable, and I stabbed him in the heart. And then there's Liam. I should be happy that he slept with Candice Jacobson. It's a clean break. But I can't help my feelings. I'm so angry. It's nauseating. How could he do something like that?"

Charlotte choked on her breath. "He slept with Candice Jacobson!? What the hell!?"

Kate rolled her eyes. "He's a dog. Walk away. That's all you can do."

"But how do I face the whole thing tomorrow? It's so complicated."

"Fiona, think about it. You have power now. You were featured in the *L.A. Times* as a chef to watch. When you walk into that kitchen tomorrow, you're important. Your work means something. You're making a mark with Julia. So why should this petty shit with Liam even matter?" Charlotte said.

Kate picked up the newspaper from the chair and held it up. "Fiona, it's really simple." She pointed to the picture of me and Liam on the front page. "This is you. This is Liam. Are you really going to let this guy destroy your dreams?"

I studied his face. His sheer cockiness and bravado shined through the photo. There was a certain calculatedness to his smile. It was practiced. Too bright. His eyes were cold. They weren't smiling back.

It made me shudder.

All of the rage and anger came running back at me. How he'd made me feel small. Unimportant. Lost. How he thought he could show me something at Vestrano that I'd had all along. I remembered how he'd stabbed my strawberry mousse that first day. He'd had no respect for what I was trying to say.

My defeated energy turned into something else.

Rage.

I had my own voice. I was sexy. I was romantic. I was provocative.

Marci Strand said so.

"You know, Charlotte, you're right. I am on a train platform. I have two choices. I can choose to be a pawn or I can stand up." I grabbed the *L.A. Times* from Kate's hands, balled it up, and cast it aside. "All of this drama is done. The only thing I care about is … well, I should say, the only *two* things I care about are Rory and being the best pastry chef in Los Angeles. I'm not going to let Liam get in the way of that. I'm not going to let him destroy me. I'm going to show him who he's dealing with."

"How are you going to do that? Get better knives? Bake a cake?" Charlotte gaped at me, confused.

"Julia said the next menu has to be stellar. Perfect. There's a target on Lucien's head. Michelin could show up at any moment. Well, I'm going to show Liam what a real dessert is. He can't confine me with his stupid, angry flavor profiles. I'm not going to use his stupid Ras el Hanout or his disgusting bitter chocolate. This time, I'm going to show him what real dessert is all about."

I grabbed *Pierre Herme Pastries* off the stack of cookbooks on the table. The stunning raspberry tart on the cover stared back at me. I held it up and pointed to the cover. "This. This is real dessert. This is what it's all about. I'm going to make something better than this. I'm going to spread my wings and show Julia that I really am a chef to watch. Liam's stupid 'vision' doesn't matter. What matters is the muse."

Kate looked at me, confused. "Muse …?"

"You know, the taste of a warm strawberry in the afternoon sun. A peach plucked off a tree in the dense, humid air. The apricot undertones of a fine Riesling. Tasting the love that went into every sip. That's the muse. That's what I'm going to celebrate. I'm not going to bully a palate into submission."

I stood up. "You're right, Charlotte. I'm going to chalk this whole thing up to just a bad night. A weak moment. I'm going to forget the whole thing happened. I'm giving it all to Rory. I'm stepping onto the right train car."

"Good. Show that cretin Liam who you really are," Charlotte said. "I still can't believe he slept with Candice Jacobson …"

Kate glared at her. "You can do it, Fiona. Just be careful. He might be a formidable opponent."

"He's a fraud. A charlatan. He doesn't even know what a good taco is."

Kate frowned, confused. "Okay …?"

I took a deep breath, my anger melting into resolve. "I'm going to live up to possibly being in Rory's life for good. I'm going to live up to being a chef to watch. Nothing can stop me."

Determination washed over me. I was going to make the best dessert menu that anyone had ever tasted. And I had my muse.

Rory.

Everything on my menu would be a dedication of love to him. His strawberries. His peaches. His wine.

I had the perfect Riesling gelée with strawberry conserve in mind. Things were already coming to me.

The only atomic bomb going off in my life was my inspiration.

I was going to fight Liam.

And I was going to win.

* * *

"Grab some more plates, Rose. We're going to need them," I said.

"How are we going to survive, chef? I've never seen it this busy?" Terror showed in Rose's gaze.

"Trust me. Follow my lead, and you'll be fine. Grab the plates."

"Yes, chef." She disappeared into the crush of white coats milling like electrons in the mayhem of the kitchen.

I turned and studied the action in the galley. It was a hot mess. And Liam was somehow keeping the chaos together.

How could he live with himself?

I watched him direct the ugly dinner service. His familiar bravado commanded everything as he took charge of the army of white coats. Tickets spewed out of the machine, and the cooks on the line struggled to keep up.

Grass-fed filet mignon and fresh Ahi sizzled on the grill station. The cook at the garde station was overwhelmed with plates for the third course. I saw him swish some kind of ruby reduction as he worked his way through precisely dressing each plate.

There was an intensity as cooks swirled sauces, stacked potatoes, and arranged the various meats and vegetables on each plate with tweezers, tongs, and an exact eye for detail. The pressure was excruciating. The galley was a chaotic dance floor, and Liam led the charge with his oversized ego.

The mix of angry indifference in my brain blanked out the noise. All I could see was the pandemonium.

I didn't want to think about his stupid omelet. I didn't want to think about Candice. I didn't want to think about any of it.

I had more important things to consider.

His silence only strengthened my resolve. Eventually, he'd have to deal with me, and when he did, I was going to be ready for him.

My menu was ravishing.

I had a sample of each course laid out. A reference point for Rose to recreate.

My semifreddo was laced with strawberry sorbet with a blackberry reduction. The flag of burnt sugar stood proudly, along with strawberry blossoms. The fresh strawberries popped on the plate, celebrating the negative space. Their sheen stole the show.

I was inspired by the strawberry fields that Rory had shown me. The swirls of apricot butter reduction echoed the attraction I'd felt in my heart.

I hoped I'd captured the sweetness of the berry. The way the strawberry had burst into my mouth when he'd fed it to me on that day—when everything had been uncomplicated.

I flourished the plate with delicate strawberries and chrysanthemum blossoms. The flowers I'd seen everywhere on that first day. Bright and clean. They exemplified the simplicity of new love.

My pear cheesecake was even better. The cinnamon sous vied pears flourished on top like a rose, adorned with a Riesling and apricot reduction.

The arc of caramel reflected the sensuality of his touch on my body when he'd kissed me. How electric I'd felt.

The brush of nappage accentuated the pears' delicate champagne hue. The same way his soft kiss felt on my lips.

I embellished it with a cage of spun sugar. It sparkled in the light. It represented the way my heart felt when I was around him: shiny, bright, and safe.

I used my tweezers to lay a single candied rose petal to complement the fragile nature of the dish.

The last course was chocolate. I'd made a rich flourless torte with Valrhona Abinao eighty-five percent. The dark chocolate was more intense than the typical seventy percent. It reflected the passion I'd had when we'd connected in the cellar. How deep my brain had settled. It also represented the rich soil that he grew everything.

Substantial. Bountiful.

I'd flourished it with glazed cherries. The cherries were dark and rich red. Sensual. Carnal power.

They represented potential.

I'd finished it off with a Sonora almond-infused vanilla ice cream. The ice cream was sweet and simple. Just like him.

"Michelin's here!" A fraught server burst into the kitchen. "Maxwell Davis is sitting at table ten."

Everything stopped.

Liam's face flashed with a fierce frown. "What do you mean?"

"He's sitting at table ten. He just ordered a bunch of stuff."

"Let me see the ticket." Liam grabbed the server's notebook from his hand and studied the order. He ripped the page out. His face traced desperation. "Quick. Fuck the other orders. Get this out. NOW."

He cruised through the list. "I need a smoked trout roe, kumamoto oysters, kampachi crudo, duck pâté en croûte." He studied the list. "Marco, start the proteins. Angelo, get the agnolotti and the casarecce going."

If the service was fierce before, it doubled in its intensity. The white coats jumped into action.

Rose approached with the plates. She glanced at the galley. "What's going on?"

"Michelin's here. Quick. We need to plate everything as if our life depended on it."

Terror bloomed in her eyes. "What do you mean, Michelin's here?"

"I mean, we have to move. Let's get our desserts ready." I grabbed the plates from her hands and shoved them above our station. I grabbed three off the top and set them reverently on the board.

I paused for a beat.

Michelin.

Michelin would be judging my desserts. A wave of terror bloomed in my heart.

I glanced at the galley. The plates for the inspector were being carted out. I was amazed by how fast the crew had pulled it together.

The crew huddled by the window to watch. Liam peered over his shoulder and joined them. I followed behind.

Maxwell was sitting at the best table in the house. He wore a tailored dark suit, and his reading glasses were perched critically on his nose. He had his pen and paper at the ready as the plates were scattered in front of him.

He took a bite of the first dish. He paused, considering it a beat. Then he took another bite. He gazed over his reading glasses as he studied the other dishes on the table.

His face was unreadable.

"What do you think he's thinking?" Leo asked.

"Maybe he's thinking about the fine juxtaposition of warmth and umami between the sage and fontina in the agnolotti."

"You idiot. He's not eating that. He's eating the kampachi crudo." Another cook chimed in.

"Enough!" Liam stormed. "Get going on the next courses. I don't want him waiting around. We don't have time for this."

The cooks got back into position and continued the frenetic pace of service. Humphry, the sous chef, barked orders for the next round of plates.

Liam turned to me. "What are you serving?" he asked. A stern look washed over his face.

There was an animal-like fire in his eyes.

This was his time. His whole career hinged on this one moment. From changing his name in his unremarkable small town in Nevada to his brilliant ascension through the ranks of fine dining.

It all came down to now.

Julia burst into the kitchen and looked around, eyes wide and terrified. "Maxwell Davis is here! Tell me we gave him the Uccelli Scappati." She was terrified. All the poise and elegance she'd always exuded was gone. She was a freaked-out mess. "I need to make sure the sommelier gave him the Fonodi Flaccianello della Pieve." She gave Liam a desperate stare. "It's the best for this evening, don't you think?"

"Go with the Dominus. I think it's a better pairing overall," he said. "Serve it to him and see if he'll tell you anything."

She turned in a flourish, and she was gone. He leveled me with a look. "Show me what you have. Now. I can't believe you didn't run your menu past me. What the hell were you thinking?"

He pushed Rose aside and stood close to me at the pastry station. His siren emerging from the flames tattoo stared back at me from his flexing forcep. Was he looking for her dangerous fire right now? I gave her a closer glance and recoiled. She was vaguely like Candice. Her eyes stared at me. Daring me.

"I think you'll find it says something," I said.

"It better say something. If there ever was a moment when your food needed to say something, it's now," he sneered. "Show me. We have to move."

He glanced at the demo plates on top of the station. "This is what you have? These are ridiculous." He grabbed a spoon and tasted the strawberry semifreddo. A strange frown crossed his face. He took the spoon and stabbed it into the pear tart. He tasted it and frowned.

"What is this?" He took one last taste of the torte and threw the spoon down. "No. Not this. This isn't my vision. Have you learned nothing from me? Get back."

He grabbed a plate from a stack and frantically started constructing his own dessert with the various accouterments on the station. He positioned the torte on the plate and used the various strawberries, sauces, and reductions. He picked up one of the chrysanthemum blossoms and studied it. "This is ridiculous." He tossed it over his shoulder, placed the torte on the plate, and fashioned the sugar-spun cage with a scoop of the Sonora almond ice cream. He stepped back. "That's passable." He glared at me. "That's at least something I'd try and say with the garbage you've given me."

I looked at the plate. It was pristine. Sharp. The plating was harsh. The negative space was cold. Calculated. Perfect. It was the plate of a sociopath.

"No. You're wrong." I elbowed him out of the way, quickly fashioned my strawberry semifreddo on the plate, and adorned it with strawberries and the blackberry reduction. I placed the spun sugar on top of it and the strawberry blossoms on the plate.

"What are you doing?" he boomed. "What the hell are you thinking?"

"He's ready for the dessert!" Julia cried.

"Give me what you have."

Liam startled and turned, surprised.

I shoved him out of the way and handed Julia the semifreddo. "Here you go." I gave her the plate. She whisked it out of my hands and left.

Liam glared at me. "What have you done?"

I stood tall and took a deep breath. "I know about Candice. I know what you did."

His face twisted in confusion. Then it melted into rage. "I don't know what you mean."

"No, Liam. I think you do."

We stood there, facing each other. He locked into my eyes and stared me down.

Julia burst back into the kitchen. "Quick. Liam. Fiona. He wants to meet you both."

Liam frowned. "He wants to meet us both? Right now?"

"Yes! Come on!" She waved.

Liam glared. "You're finished." He turned and followed Julia out of the kitchen.

My breath hitched in my throat. The inspector wanted to meet me? What did he want?

Julia burst back into the kitchen. "Fiona! Please. Come on."

Right foot first, I stepped behind her and made my way to the dining room.

The wise old eucalyptus stood tall in the dining room, twinkling with tea lights. My eyes adjusted to the opulence of the dimly-lit room. Well-dressed patrons paused from their reverie and stared at me as I passed.

I approached table ten. Liam stood tall beside the inspector. A wolfish smile seized his face.

"I hope you've enjoyed what we have to offer," Liam cooed. "The culture and vitality of Los Angeles has inspired me. I've made the spirit of the city my own."

The Michelin inspector removed his glasses, closed his notebook, and pinched the top of his nose, studying us. A pause hovered in the air as he gathered his thoughts.

I stared at the table littered with wine glasses and plates like tarot cards. This was the moment of judgment. There was no going back.

He cleared his throat, wiped his mouth with a linen napkin, and placed it on the table.

"The kumamoto oysters were exquisite. I especially enjoyed the agnolotti and the casarecce. The Uccelli Scappati was an exceptional revelation.

Liam stood straighter, almost falling over himself. "Thank you."

He cleared his throat. "The real revelation of this meal is the dessert. Chef Fiona. There's something breathtaking about the torte. It's one of the best desserts I've ever tasted. I can sense your passion. There's love to be found in your dish. It's magnificent. I've been transported. I'm speechless." He gave me a warm smile. "Well done." He nodded. "You should be proud."

A huge smile washed over Julia's face. "Fiona is our new pastry chef. She's really come into her own under my watchful eye," she said.

"Something like this talent doesn't come from tutelage. It comes from somewhere else. You can't teach this sort of genius. It comes from the heart." He glanced at Liam. "You can't pretend. You either have it or you don't."

An uncontrollable smile washed over my face. A pang of pride surged through me. I gave Liam a triumphant grin. He looked away. A confusion washed over his face as he continued. "Would you like to perhaps taste the Baccalâ mantecato? Or maybe you'd like to try the Canederli? They've been inspired by my passions. I'm sure you'll be pleased."

The inspector took a sip of wine and smiled, content. "No. I do believe I'm finished here." He stood to leave. "You'll be informed of my decision soon."

He turned to me as he grabbed his notebook and shook my hand. "Well done, chef. You should be proud."

Liam's smile faltered as the inspector made his way through the restaurant. Julia followed behind, showing him out. I could see her gushing over him as they made their way through the dining room.

Liam stood there, baffled. The patrons looked on, intrigued, as they ate and made merry.

He turned to me, seething. "You've really done it."

Then he stormed back into the kitchen.

The cooks gathered around the door, trying to see what was happening.

They scattered as he pushed his way through.

"Get back to service! What are you all doing? Get back to work!" he fumed. The cooks quickly went back to their stations and continued service. No one looked at him. They were too afraid.

He stood in the kitchen in shock. A feverish sheen glinted on his face. He ran his hands through his hair, frantic. "Who is he to say you can't learn craft? What does he know?"

He glowered at me. "I've spent my whole career waiting for this moment. Who is he to say you have it or you don't? I have it. I've worked my whole life to have it."

He stormed to the worktable and studied the tapestry of work, seething. "He doesn't know what he's talking about."

He paced in a lost daze. "How could he not see?"

Julia burst into the kitchen. "How do you think it went?" she asked. Anticipation crossed her face. "I think that went well, don't you think?"

He glared at her. "You know what I think? I think we lost it. We're not getting our stars. I didn't hear him say he was transported. I just heard him say it was exceptional." Hot anger crossed his face as he stared at me. "How dare you upstage me. You're an amateur at best. It was an accident."

Julia glanced at me, confused. "But he loved the dessert. What a beautiful thing to end on, Fiona. You should be so proud of yourself. I've never received such praise from any food critic. Let alone Michelin."

"And that's the problem. She upstaged me. It's not supposed to be about the dessert. It's supposed to be about the show. Not the final act."

The cooks looked on. Frozen. The frenzy of the service paused. The only sound was the ticket machine spewing orders in the corner. All eyes were on Liam.

He grabbed his Santoku knife from the table and regarded it a beat. "I'm finished. This whole thing is finished." I could see the rage and frustration boil to the surface as he stood there. Taut.

He swung the Santoku knife and stabbed the wood table with all his might. The blade stood tall, like a flagpole in the middle of all the half-dressed plates.

The whole crew recoiled. Confused.

"I'm done." He turned and stormed out of the kitchen.

"Liam, wait." Julia chased after him.

"What happened?" Rose looked at me, confused.

I shrugged. "The Michelin inspector liked my dessert. Chef didn't take it very well."

Rose smiled. "Congratulations, chef. That's awesome!"

The crew turned and returned to service. Humphry stepped in and took over. The tickets started spitting out of the machine for dessert orders. I hung them above the station. "Come on. Let's get going." I grabbed some plates and got to work. Rose stood next to me, following my lead.

Michelin liked my dish best. He'd felt my passion. My love. He understood exactly what I was trying to say.

It was better than confronting Liam for his transgression. I smiled, triumphant.

A wave of pride washed over me. Was this what winning was like? Is this what it felt like to create something magical?

I began to plate the strawberry semifreddo. I flourished it with delicate strawberries and strawberry blossoms.

This was my shining moment. And Rory had inspired me.

A wave of love for him washed over me as I finished the plate with the blackberry reduction.

My love for him had been a part of the whole endeavor. If I hadn't felt his touch, kisses, or attention, maybe none of this would have happened. Maybe I wouldn't have found my voice.

I'd created a transformative experience because of him.

I smiled. I couldn't wait to see him tonight.

I couldn't wait to share everything.

I didn't need Liam and his stupid vision to show me the way. I was already there.

* * *

The night was dark, and the street was deserted, but I didn't care. The forcefield of euphoria kept me safe as I walked down the sidewalk to my apartment.

How could anyone mug me now in my moment of victory? I was superhuman. Excited and proud, I could lift a car off a small child.

I grabbed my keys out of my bag and went to my door. I could smell the rancid odor of the restaurant on my clothes. After a long day, the ghost of grilled meat and burnt chicken stock always radiated off me. Sometimes, I struggled to get the smell out when I washed my clothes. The funky hint of restaurant never fully washed out when I did laundry.

I had to get a shower before Rory came over. I couldn't wait to tell him everything.

My dessert had impressed the inspector more than Liam's food. I couldn't help the fine feeling of superiority.

"There's something breathtaking about the semifreddo. It's one of the best desserts I've ever tasted. I can sense your passion. There's love to be found in your dish. It's magnificent. I've been transported. I'm speechless..."

I couldn't get his words out of my head. The movie kept playing out in my head. It was almost unbelievable. Like it never really happened.

"Something like this talent doesn't come from tutelage. It comes from somewhere else. You can't teach this sort of genius. It comes from the heart ... You can't pretend. You either have it or you don't ..."

I smiled to myself, satisfied.

The inspector had called Liam out. He'd seen Liam for the fraud he was. I almost felt bad for him. Almost. I couldn't help but gloat. All his stupid pontificating meant nothing at the end of the day. He got what he deserved.

I rounded the corner to my apartment, and I stopped midstep.

Liam's motorcycle was parked in front of my building, and he was sitting on the steps. He still had his whites on. They glowed in the darkness. A cigarette hung from his lips. I could tell he'd been there a while.

What the hell? Why was he sitting there? What did he want from me now? Was he going to berate me some more? Did he have more insults to wield at me?

Anger bloomed from my chest. He'd have to say a lot to ruin my mood. I walked toward the doorstep, right foot first.

"Fiona!" He put his cigarette out as he stood up. A strange smile animated his face. I couldn't read him.

"I've figured it out. I was all wrong about everything," he said.

"What are you doing here?" I tried to make my way past him on the steps.

"Don't go. At least hear what I have to say. A seductive smile crossed his lips. "I've thought about it and the inspector was right. I had it wrong all along."

"What do you mean?"

"I didn't see it before. I was caught up in the whole drama of trying to impress that I didn't listen to my instincts. I didn't see you for who you really were. I should have recognized your genius. I should have been inspired by you, but I was too closed minded to see it."

I stood there, shocked.

"Listen. I have it all planned out. We can do this together. I have amazing things planned that I haven't even told you about. Together, we can pick up the pieces and still earn our three stars. I can draw from your inspiration. You can show me your vision. I can learn. I can take what you have to say and be taught by it. Together, we can win. Together, we can be a force. I want you to show me."

"Isn't it a little late for that?" I said.

"It's never too late. Don't you want to be the best pastry chef in Los Angeles?" He gave me a desperate smile. "I'll put aside all of the things I've said before. I was clearly wrong about you and want to make it right."

"What about Candice?"

"What about her. Things happen. Forget about it. It doesn't matter. All that matters is us. Together, we can be a force. Nothing can stop us."

He put his arm around my waist and pulled me in for a kiss. "Look inside of yourself. You know you want what you want." He whispered.

He leaned in and kissed me. His familiar lips touched mine.

A flash of anger hit my brain.

I pushed him back. "No. You can't do this to me. This thing we had. It's done. I'm not doing this with you. It's over."

He stepped back, and his eyes recalibrated. He stood straighter and straightened his whites.

I turned.

Rory was standing on the sidewalk. He stood frozen with a bouquet of flowers, and one of his fancy bags with a bottle of wine peeking out was in his hands. Betrayal burned on his face.

"Rory, wait. This isn't what it looks like." I scrambled for something to say. I pushed Liam back. "Let me explain."

Liam smiled, amused.

Rory turned and walked away, quickly disappearing into the night. He tossed the bouquet of flowers into a trashcan on his way.

I stood there, frozen. What was I going to do?

"Aren't you going to go after him?" Liam smiled, satisfied. "Or are you planning on staying here?"

I pushed him away and followed Rory.

My heart beat uncontrollably in my chest as panic surged through my body. My steps weren't fast enough to keep up with my adrenaline.

I made it to the corner and looked both ways.

He was gone. Horror washed over my body.

What had I done?

I turned back to my apartment.

Liam got on his motorcycle, slid his helmet on, and fired up the engine.

He gave me a sinister smile as he pulled away.

I watched as his taillights disappeared into the night.

It had all happened too fast. The kiss. The proclamations. The betrayal.

Suddenly, all of the pride disappeared like whiplash. My triumphant feelings of accomplishment meant nothing.

It felt stupid.

What had I done?

I'd ruined everything.

I'd lost Rory.

I turned and made my way back to my apartment. Maybe I could call him. Text him. What would I say? I had to think of something quick.

He was everything to me, and I'd just ruined it.

Could I make it right? Could I fix this?

16

"**F**iona, this is terrible." Charlotte pinched her noodles into the air with her chopsticks, dipped them into the gravy-like broth, and settled the ends into her oval spoon. She took a huge slurp.

I stared at my noodles. I couldn't eat.

I sat in the worn, red booth. The vinyl was sticky and cold on my legs. I was cold to the core.

I should have been comforted. Mianteo was a part of my heritage. Marci Strand proclaimed it the best Japanese noodle in the world when I was a little girl, so my father made the pilgrimage.

Life was never the same.

I even remembered the day.

I was four years old and didn't know how to use chopsticks. My dad fed me the noodles one by one like I was a baby bird.

The noodles usually comforted me. With its savory, salty taste, the slow stewed heavy umami broth usually made me whole again.

"So, what are you going to do?" Kate let her cube of salmon balance on her chopsticks. She always got the Ikura Don. I could never understand why.

"About what part, exactly? It's all a fucking mess."

Kate leaned in, talking low. "You're better than this. You don't have to do this to yourself."

I took a deep breath, picking at a noodle. "None of this 'chef to watch' or Michelin shit even means anything anymore. It all seems so trivial now. All of it. All I want is to fix things with Rory. I just want to get him back."

Kate fished her last piece of rice from her bowl and took a bite. Set her chopsticks down.

"At what point do you call the game, Fiona? At what point do you say you're good enough? At what point do you decide that you've won? You don't have to go through hell to prove you're worthy. We already think you're the best."

The server cleared the table, nodded to me, and left my noodles in front of me. Charlotte grabbed my bowl, set it in front of her, and dove in.

"This is the biggest mistake I've ever made. He really could have been the one."

Charlotte wiped her noodle juice off her chin with a thin paper napkin and let her elbows rest on the table. "What if you went to him? Explained everything?

"Impossible. I'm too chickenshit. I'm too embarrassed. I don't even know what I'd say. 'Sorry, I slept with someone else. I like you better, I promise.'"

Kate rolled her eyes. "You're a human being. You made a mistake. Maybe he can forgive you? You had an honest moment of weakness. Shit happens."

"Yeah, but I can't even look at him. I'm too ashamed. I hurt him. He doesn't deserve that."

Charlotte took a deep breath. "You have to face it. You can't leave it like this. Think about what you could have had."

"He opened himself up to me. He was so vulnerable, and I stabbed him in the heart."

"You said yourself that he had a great relationship with his ex. Maybe it's a sign?"

"Yeah, but she wasn't a Jezebel. I'm sure if she had an affair with someone else, it'd probably be a lot different."

"Fiona. Stop. You always do this."

"Do what?"

Kate studied me, exasperated. "You get so caught up in your fucking head with 'what ifs' and speculation. Your imagination goes into overdrive, and you paint yourself in a corner. You get caught up in the drama in your head and create more drama. It's a snowball."

Charlotte nodded. "Yeah, I have to admit, it's a little crazy."

"Charlotte. Don't judge. You're just as bad. You both get into it and create whole worlds together. Complete with action scenes. Is this what happens to you when you grow up in Movieland? Because this whole narrative could be a blockbuster."

"Shut up. We're stretching the situation out. Weighing all of our options."

"No. You're creating an impossible situation in your head."

She looked at both of us intensely. "I'm going to boil it down for you. You got sucked into some asshole's narrative. You gave in. You fucked up. If you really love Rory, you have to go apologize. That's it. That's all you need to do. Everything else is speculation and dead air space."

My stomach tensed.

Why was she always so blunt? It made it even worse.

"But what about my job?" I asked.

"You're going to have to make some hard choices. If you love Rory, maybe Lucien isn't a part of your future. Maybe it comes down to that. Are you willing to choose between them?"

I thought for a moment—both of them staring at me.

"I don't know if I have the courage to face him. What am I supposed to say?"

Kate frowned. "Say that you love him, and the past is the past. It was a mistake."

"That's easy for you to say. You didn't see his face. You didn't see the way he looked at me. There's no way he's taking me back. It's over."

"You don't know that until you talk to him. I mean, really, what does he know? Liam was on your doorstep. He kissed you, sure, but Rory doesn't know the context. For all intents and purposes, he was trying to lure you in. Maybe it would make a difference if you explained it like that."

"But that's a lie. I can't lie to him anymore. It cheapens everything. If I lied to him again, it'd poison our relationship. I'd always know in the back of my mind that I'd been untrue. I'd always feel guilty. You can't build a relationship on that. A relationship that hinges on that is doomed."

"Well, it's doomed anyway."

Charlotte pushed the bowl of noodles back and wiped her mouth. "Just go to him. Apologize. The rest will play out, and you'll know where you stand. You have to at least take a chance. At this point, what do you have to lose?"

I thought for a moment. "I've already lost it. I don't see how we could go back to the way it was before. The innocence is gone. He'll always see me as the woman who cheated on him. The whole situation is tainted."

Kate took a deep breath. "Just go to him. Apologize. The rest will fall into place. I promise. If you don't face it, you'll always wonder. That's the only thing you can do."

"I don't know if I have the courage. I'm so scared. I don't think I can handle it if he says no. I can't imagine him saying the words 'it's over' to me."

"Well, if you don't go to him, you'll never know," Kate said.

I sat there for a moment, deliberating.

Kate cupped her hands in mine. "Just do it. I promise whatever happens is better than asking yourself what if. If you see him, at least you'll know where you stand."

The thought of Rory saying goodbye to me was more than I could bear.

My friends stared at me with empathy in their eyes.

"I'll try. I'll go to the farm and see what happens. God only knows how I'll feel if it turns out how I think it will."

"But think about if you're wrong. Think about how much better it'll be. Then this will all seem like a silly drama. It'll be your first fight. Then you'll know your relationship is real. If a relationship can withstand a small storm like this, then anything is possible.

I sat for a beat. What if they were right? What if I could make this thing right?

The thought of Rory taking me back sparked a longing in me that felt ridiculous.

"Trust us on this. It's the only way," Kate said.

I wanted to trust them. I wanted to believe in what they had to say.

Optimism is a legitimate response to failure ... My father's quotation rang in my head.

What if I could make things right? What if I faced him and made everything okay again?

I had to at least try.

It was the only thing I could do.

* * *

A line of pink bloomed to life on the ocean horizon. Early morning surfers looked like seals in the surf. There was hardly any traffic on PCH as I drove to Rory's farm.

My hands were cold and bony on the steering wheel. I was metallic from the stress.

I'd laid in bed all night, mulling my options. Would he even have me back? What was I going to say?

Luna was in the backseat, sniffing through the crack in the window I'd left for him. He was biting at the wind as it blew through the glass. His tail was wagging. He knew where we were going.

At least someone was happy.

I pulled into Fleurcein's driveway and got out of the car. A fog was socked into the valley. Golden god light illuminated the early morning air.

I looked at my watch. It was seven—a decent early morning hour. At least, I was hoping it was.

I let Luna out, and he sniffed the ground.

I walked to the house, gazing at the strawberry fields. The orchards. The vineyards. Workers dotted the distance, making their way to their working day.

"Fiona! What are you doing here?" Delia came down the steps of her porch. She was tending to the flowers that were overtaking everything.

She had her green overalls and sunhat on, even at this early hour.

A pink scarf peeked out from beneath her hat. Her garden clogs were blossoming with red tulips.

She set the basket of dead leaves down and gave me a big hug and a kiss on the cheek. "It's so good to see you."

"It's not too early, is it?"

"Not at all. Rory's just taking Grace to school. He'll be back in a bit. Come in. I'll get you some coffee."

A knot of stress bloomed in my stomach.

Luna curled up in front of her door. His eyes watched as I followed Delia into her home.

It was the first time I'd seen the inside.

I instantly loved it. It was country casual, with doilies protecting every surface. Her antique furniture gave the room character.

An oak piano stood in the corner—the wood bench worn with use. Black and white pictures mingled with colored photos, reflecting a deep family history.

"Let me put the water on. Would you like some coffee?"

"I'd love some."

Her kitchen was old-fashioned. Her yellow gingham wallpaper was kitschy. All her kitchen stuff had chickens on it. Chicken flour and sugar canisters. Chicken butter plate. Chicken salt and pepper shakers. Chicken clock. Chicken tablecloth on the old farm-style dining room table.

Delia really loved chickens.

"What brings you here?" she asked.

"I wanted to see how you were doing."

She put the chicken kettle on to boil. My eyes fell on the kitchen windowsill.

Too many prescription bottles littered the shelf.

She poured me a cup of coffee. "Rory won't let me go to the market anymore. He says it's too dangerous."

"I'm sorry. I know how you loved that." I watched her. Her movements were faintly fragile. I could tell her will was making her strong. "How are you doing?"

She smiled. "I'm trying to do what Rory tells me. It's hard to let go."

I glanced out the window at her farm. "Well, you're used to running an empire. How could you not want to boss everyone around?"

"That's true. But I don't know what to do with myself. I don't think I can make any more marmalade. I'm done. "Here, grab your coffee. Let's go outside."

We took a seat on her porch. It was so peaceful. The flowers grew from planters and baskets. A view of the vast landscape stretched beyond. I sat in a comfortable wicker chair.

Under different circumstances, it would have been perfect. Now I was counting the moments to Judgment Day. I braced myself in my seat.

She thought for a moment and leaned in.

"What's going on? I love that you came to visit, but honestly, why are you here?"

I sat for a moment, gathering my courage. My stupid actions could have collateral damage.

"I hate to admit it to you, but I did something to hurt him. I don't know if he'll forgive me."

I held my breath.

"I shouldn't even be here. I've betrayed him on such a deep level. I made a huge mistake, and I don't know how to make it better."

Delia looked at me and took a sip of her tea. She deliberated a moment.

"Another man?"

"How did you know?"

"What else could it be? I can see the panic on your face."

"I'm sorry. I'm embarrassed. Ashamed. I would understand if you asked me to leave."

She thought for a moment. "You want to hear a story?"

I frowned, slightly taken aback. "Sure."

"When I was in my twenties, I was reckless. I was newly married, and my husband had a cattle ranch in Washington. Ellensburg, to be exact. Our ranch was next to one of the biggest ranches in the United States." She smiled, remembering. "Aron Muller was the head rancher. One of the largest landowners in Washington, which is saying a lot." She took a sip of her tea. "Andrew, my husband was busy all of the time. Which in hindsight, I understand. He was trying to make his way, and life is hard if you're doing it right." She thought for a moment. "On the other hand, I was bored with the cows and couldn't find my niche. It was before I knew I could grow stuff. I was bored. I drove around in my blue convertible Karmann Ghia down country roads. I had all of this energy and no place to put it."

She shook her head. "It's really true that idle hands are the devil's work." She picked at the dead leaves off the marigolds blooming in a pot next to her. She piled the carcasses onto the saucer of her cup.

"Anyway, it's the same old boring story. Good-looking, older rancher, restless young girl. Trouble started." She shook her head. "I was a toy. A game to him. He was older and just as bored as I was. He'd established his empire and was restless. In any event, you can imagine what happened. I'm embarrassed, honestly, at the cliché of it all." She set her cup down, gazing out towards the strawberry fields. "In a small town like Ellensburg, people talk. My husband found out. And I was outed." She shook her head.

"What happened?"

"I left. I was too much of a coward to face him. My embarrassment got the best of me. I packed my car and drove to California. So, in a way, I'm here because of a simple mistake." She leaned in, close.

"Every day, I ask myself, what if? What if I'd stayed? What if I'd faced my mistake? He was the love of my life."

She made a prayer motion to the sky.

"Forgive me, George."

She reached across and grabbed my hand.

"I'm upset that you've hurt my son. But I respect that you came to face your mistakes. It's more than I could ever manage."

She took a deep breath.

"I hope Rory can forgive you. I'll never know if Andrew would have forgiven me. And I've had a lot of time to think about things. Now that I'm facing all of this. I walked away from true love, but on the other hand, I created this. I made a life with George, and I have my kids. But at the end of the day, I'll never know what could have been."

She stared me in the eye. She was trying to make her point.

"Your mistakes define you. You may make mistakes. We're all human. The test is how you face them. Do you run away? Or do you swallow your ego and face them? It's one of my greatest regrets that I didn't face Andrew. I never found out."

Rory's Suburban wound its way down the road. The dust trailed behind and clouded the air behind it. I could hear the gravel crunching under the tires.

My heart dropped as he parked.

Luna poked his head up. His tail started thumping on the wood.

Delia stood up. She squeezed my hand and let it go. "At least you're here. Keep that in mind. You're already doing the right thing."

She opened the door and made her way inside. I stood there, alone on the porch.

Rory got out of the truck, deep in his own thoughts. He stopped when he saw me.

I could tell I'd surprised him.

I saw the deliberation in his eyes. He was trying to decide if he would get back in the truck and leave.

I took a deep breath and walked down the steps. I felt like a cowering dog.

"What are you doing here?" He looked at me, cold. His eyes reflected none of the warmth that I was used to. I was out to sea, sensing his iciness.

"I need to talk to you. Explain this."

"There's nothing to say."

I took a deep breath.

"If I could take it back, I would. It was a mistake."

His body was braced. His usual casual self was gone.

"How long has this been going on?"

"It was an accident. A one-time thing."

He regarded me as he put his hand against the truck. I could see his handprint slipping from underneath his hand in the dust. "It doesn't matter anyway. Maybe I don't want to know."

"If I could take it back, I would. It's the worst mistake I've ever made." I wanted to step forward and put my arms around him. I wanted to make him feel better.

He studied me. His face was sad. "Look, Fiona. I like you. I really do. But I can't make this work. I have more going on in my life right now than is even remotely manageable with running two places and raising Grace and my mother. It's already too much. I can't expend the energy on collateral drama. I just don't have the time or the energy."

"I understand that. But if you'd let me have another chance. I can make this right. I can do the right thing."

"It's already too late. It's not possible to be vulnerable to you after this. I can't work like that. My wife did the same thing, and I just can't go there."

Luna trotted to us and sat down. He looked up at Rory and wagged his tail.

We stood there in silence for a moment. I didn't know what to say. The right thing wasn't coming to me.

"I think it's time that you go. I've got a lot of stuff to do. Let's get this over with."

The sting at the top of my nose twinged where the tears started. I sniffed to hold them back.

"I'm really sorry."

He opened the back door of the Suburban and reached inside, searching for something, turning his back to me. I could tell it was over. There was nothing left to say.

I turned and made my way to my car. Luna followed behind me, and I opened the back door of my car. Let him in and shut it.

The sound of the door closing was final, like a period at the end of a sentence.

I opened my door, got in, and peered through the windshield.

The morning fog was burning away to a glorious day.

I'd given up all of this. All of this beauty. All of this sanctuary.

I'd sacrificed my place in Rory's world for a moment of weakness.

I'd fallen from the sky. Like I was just another mortal on Earth. Like I'd been banished from heaven.

I started the engine slowly, backed up, and crept to the road.

I couldn't believe it was over.

* * *

I sat outside of Lucien in my car, deliberating.

I could see contractors going in and out of the back door like worker ants. They were starting whatever project Julia and Liam had up their sleeve.

The drive back from Fleurcein had made me late. I'd had to drop Luna back home, pushing me over the edge.

I wished I could take Luna to work. He'd make everything better. At least he would like me.

I didn't know how to step through the back door and put my coat on.

How the hell was I going to face all this?

How could I face the day after everything that had happened?

I took a deep breath. I had to jump in.

I opened my door. I stepped out right foot first and slammed the door behind me.

"Excuse me, chef." One of the construction workers danced out of my way as I walked through the narrow hallway.

I glanced around. This was bigger than a little project around the restaurant.

The air was heavy with activity. A thin layer of dust covered everything. It was out of character. Usually, everything was shiny and spotless.

I made my way down the hall to the kitchen, pushed the door open, and glanced around.

The prep cooks quickly averted their gaze when they saw me.

I braced myself. Uneasy.

The Hobart, ice cream machine, and sheeter were pushed against the wall. My wood table was tipped on its side. Why was the equipment out here?

What the hell was going on?

I stopped as I rounded the corner.

Holy Fuck.

The bakery was being destroyed.

Workers were pulling out the sheetrock. A jackhammer was hammering in the corner for some ungodly reason.

And the worst. A forklift was pulling the beautiful Italian oven from the wall. The back door was open, ready for it to leave to some unknown place.

I couldn't breathe.

My world was being destroyed.

I charged through the kitchen. "Where's chef?" I snapped at the prep cooks. They all flinched.

"Where is he?"

Leo pointed with his knife to the savory walk-in.

I pushed through the metal door. Liam was alone, sorting meat on a rack.

He glanced up. "Good morning, Fiona. You're late." His green eyes were dark and glinting with humor.

"What the hell is going on?"

"I decided to make some changes."

"That's obvious," I fumed.

He chucked a round of wrapped filet mignon in the lowest bin and stood up.

"We're extending the kitchen to the bakery. The restaurant is going to be open for everyone to see. I want people to see the beauty that goes into their experience."

His platitudes were beyond obnoxious.

"Why didn't you tell me about this? You fucking knew what you were doing. You knew! And you didn't bother to tell me."

A sinister grin crossed his face. He was enjoying this. His hands braced the racks on both sides—an aggressive stance.

"There's something else. Giana is my pastry chef from New York. She's going to be joining our team. She's in the office. I'd like you to meet her."

The look on his face said everything. He was a monster picking the wings off butterflies.

I stood there stunned.

"She's in tune with what I want. I think she'll be an excellent mentor to you. She can show you how I want everything to be."

"And what is that exactly. Murder? How can you possibly stab someone in the heart with a pot of crème."

He glared at me.

"You don't get it. I can't make my stars with you."

It was a slap in the face. His smile was a death blow. "It doesn't matter. It's done."

Familiar rage coursed through my veins. He bulled past me. He was finished.

The door slammed behind him.

I stood there, cold and alone. Staring at a bin of parsley. I kicked it. The thud was unsatisfying.

He had outplayed me. I was a fool.

How could I walk out there? Face everyone. I was utterly humiliated. I was that salmon that had been slayed on the table.

My tail chopped off. My head disconnected from my body.

And to think, after everything that I'd done here. Everything I'd put my heart and soul into.

I'd bled on the table. I'd grown fangs. I'd given it my all.

I'd been featured in the *L.A. Times*, for God's sake. Michelin had praised me. I had credibility.

I was better than this.

I took a deep breath and straightened my shoulders. I stood tall. My right foot first as I walked out the door. I had to find Julia.

I charged through the kitchen, headed down the hall to the office, and pushed through the door.

I felt like I was going to barf. I hated the defensiveness that braced me. I hated being behind the eight-ball.

Gianna was tall. Her blonde hair was so blonde that it was almost white. It was tied up in a severe knot at the top of her head. Her chef's coat was pressed and stiff. I could tell she used more starch than me. It gave her a military look.

A single tattoo decorated the inside of her forearm. It was an old-fashioned French doodle of a whisk. I recognized it but couldn't remember which cookbook it came from.

She extended her hand, sizing me up. "It's nice to meet you, Fiona." Her heavy French accent accentuated her iciness.

I couldn't even speak.

I took her hand. She squeezed tight with her delicate, bony, cold hand. The pressure was so intense it almost hurt. She was trying to dominate the situation.

It only pissed me off.

Julia looked at all of us, clearing her throat. "I'm so happy we have our whole new team here. This is going to be brilliant." She stared at me, eyes uneasy.

She stepped up to the conference table and grabbed one of the rolled-up plans. "I'm excited about what we have planned for pastry. Come, let's see what I mean."

She unrolled the scroll and braced herself, sheepishly.

I glanced at the plans.

There it was.

Liam's grand kitchen. The bakery was gone. Pastry was now situated in a small corner. A dark space next to where the oven had been.

Liam had won.

The restaurant was his. He'd officially taken over everything.

I could see Gianna already doing the math.

Our eyes locked, staring each other down.

There was only room for one.

A condescending grin crossed Camilla's face.

I was just another chef caught in the crossfire. She'd outlasted me. Her alliance had shifted. She knew the game.

Rose looked at me, confused. She was scared.

Julia's familiar purse of her lips crossed her face.

The tension in the room was overwhelming.

I took a deep breath and stepped back. Right foot first.

Gianna grinned at me. The balance of power had shifted. She turned to the girls. "Let us go look at the kitchen. Let's plan."

Camilla and Rose followed her out the door.

Rose glanced over her shoulder at me. Guilt betrayed on her face as she disappeared around the corner.

Julia was braced.

"I was going to say something, but Liam wanted to tell you on his own. I thought he told you yesterday. I thought you both had worked it out."

She put her hand on my arm. "I'm sorry. This is cruel, I know."

She stood there. Her black Hedley & Bennett apron was pressed and perfect. Her flawless bun pulled back. She really did look like a foodie version of Audrey Hepburn.

She was my hero. I'd looked up to her and given her everything I had.

And it wasn't enough.

"Julia, thank you for everything."

She took her hands in mine. A quiet understanding passed between us. She gave me a sad smile. "I know you're going to do amazing things, Fiona. Don't give up."

I broke from her and turned to leave.

Anger and sadness surged through my brain. I had to get out of there.

I pushed the door open. The fan blew on me, and I walked through the threshold. It would be the last time I'd be standing here.

Did Angela feel like this when she was fired?

The hot air of the morning hit my face as I walked outside. The door slammed behind me. It was a sad punctuation mark to the moment.

The rotten smell from the dumpster wafted towards me. It smelled like cardboard and robust blue cheese. I associated the scent with the satisfaction of hard work.

Now it smelled disgusting.

This was it. It was over.

I would never stand here again. Never rush to the back door, my head full of the tasks needed for the day. I'd never have the pride of slipping my Lucien chef coat on and feeling like I'd made it. Like I'd secured a position of prestige. Like I was really somebody.

I was ashamed of how easily my illusions had been ripped from me—embarrassed that I'd bought into the dream.

I took a deep breath. I grabbed my keys out of my bag, made my way towards my car, and unlocked the door.

My rage and anger melted into sorrow.

I sat in front of the steering wheel, paralyzed. The silence of the car pinging in my ears.

This was the worst day of my entire fucking life.

17

I knocked on my dad's kitchen door and waited. The familiar gash on the door and the old, decaying rubber mat on the ground made me feel anchored and safe.

The smoke shop next door was still there. A stale stench of marijuana still lingered in the air, even though it was closed.

My father's catering truck was parked in the front. He'd finally had enough money to upgrade to a nicer model. This one was larger and had a V8 engine.

"Fiona! What are you doing here?" my dad said as he opened the door. A bright smile illuminated his face. He still had bedhead from the night before, and his apron was splattered with some sort of ragù. He was in the middle of a busy day.

He took one look at me and frowned. "What's wrong?"

I couldn't even speak. I couldn't find any words to say how screwed up everything was.

He took me in his arms and hugged me as he ushered me in. The bell hanging from the door jingled as the door shut behind me.

His familiar golden Lucky Cat stood on the shelf, waving to me with his happy face. I wished I could be that happy, with the aura of luck.

I was a world away from having any luck at all.

The kitchen was in full swing, and his crew was preparing for the day. Hotel pans filled with sauce and salads littered the table, along with sheet trays filled with roasted pheasants and salmon.

It was going to be a busy day for him.

"How about making the biscuits for the party? We're a little behind this morning."

"I'd love to."

I grabbed a faded denim apron off the worn hook on the wall and tied it around my waist.

Steely Dan's "Deacon Blues" played from the tiny pill speaker on the counter.

I opened the walk-in to get some eggs and butter. He still needed to fix the door to the tiny walk-in. The special hook and rope you had to jiggle to open the door were still jerry-rigged.

I put the cream, butter, and eggs on the tiny workspace in the corner and grabbed a bowl.

"You saved me. Angelo partied all night and called in sick. I just need the recipe times one, and I think we'll be okay."

I grabbed a cheese grater and started shredding the butter.

My dad worked, fabricating the pheasants on the table. "What happened?"

I took a deep breath. To say it would make it real. "Liam destroyed my kitchen. My career is finished."

I turned around and grabbed the edge of the table to steady myself.

I started to cry.

My dad rounded the table and pulled me into his arms. He let me cry, not saying anything.

He grabbed a kitchen towel and handed it to me. I covered my face and let everything go. It was a reflex that I couldn't stop. Everything that had happened welled up and took me over.

I blew my nose and composed myself.

"Everything I put my heart into is gone. I had my big chance, and I lost it."

My dad gazed at me with a tender look in his eyes. "Fiona. You'll be fine. I promise."

I wiped my face, washed my hands in the sink, and dried them off. "Liam Auclair burned me down. He destroyed my reputation."

My dad chuckled. "I saw Marci's review in the *L.A. Times*. I don't think it's going to be that easy to destroy your reputation. You barely have one."

I met his gaze, trying not to be offended. "I lost my chance because of Liam. I had an opportunity to be great—to really do something. Marci Strand even wrote about me. And he killed it."

I took a deep breath, trying to get myself together.

He took the towel from me and put it in the dirty towel bin. "What happened?"

"He destroyed my beautiful kitchen. He lied about everything. He was a monster. His ambition to win three Michelin stars was too much. His desire to win destroyed me."

I cringed. I realized I was babbling.

I turned and set the bowl on a scale and started mising the flour from a bin underneath the table.

My dad finished fabricating the last pheasant and started to set them up into a hotel pan for transport.

"Fiona. Don't you think you're being a little dramatic?" He thought for a moment. "Usually, as a pastry chef, you must reflect the chef's voice. That's just the way it works."

My anger flared. "There's no way I'm going to make something to complement how offensive he was. I couldn't do it. It goes against everything I'm about."

"Then you have your answer."

"What do you mean?"

"You were polar opposites—two negative magnets. You pushed up against each other, and the electrons wouldn't mesh. It happens."

I stood there, trying to sort out his metaphor.

I poured the cream into the flour and started mixing it with my hands. It was a sticky mess.

We let the moment of silence hang there. It was comfortable, in only the way two people who have worked together for long hours can do.

"This might be the best thing that ever happened to you."

"What do you mean?"

"He pushed you into a corner, and you pushed back. He gave you a reason to fight for what you wanted to say. And by doing that, he helped you define yourself." He smiled. "You survived a trial by fire."

He put the lid on the hotel pan and started sectioning the salmon into serving sizes. "I have a question for you. I know you've always dreamed of making it, but in your heart, why did you do it?"

"I thought I had a chance to do something great. I mean, Julia has two Michelin stars. She's won James Beard awards. She's written cookbooks. She's one of the most important and famous chefs in L.A. I always dreamed of Marci Strand's attention. You know why I did it. It's a silly question."

I poured all the biscuit dough on the table and started shaping it with my hands like a sandcastle. It made me think of Grace and me, playing in the sand with her Hot Wheels at the beach.

A pang of sorrow washed over me. I pushed it back. I brought myself back to the conversation.

"I mean, look at all the pastry chefs she's vouched for and made famous. She even made Aaron Carmichael famous. He wouldn't have his empire if it weren't for Julia. It was my shot to make my dreams a reality."

He thought for a moment as he sectioned the salmon. "Maybe part of the problem is my fault. Maybe I shouldn't have made Marci Strand so important. It's not everything, you know."

He finished cutting the salmon and started to set them inside another container.

"There's something in you. I knew you had it back when you peeled carrots as a little girl." He thought for a moment. "You recognize the language. That's why you picked everything up so quickly. You can make things that elevate the craft. You can make anything that I make ten times better."

He put the lid on the container and hefted it on top of the hotel pan filled with pheasant. "You took that gift, and Julia gave you the opportunity to fly to the sun. But maybe you were like Icarus."

"What do you mean?" I shaped the biscuit dough into a compact square.

"What are you doing it for?" He made his way to me and leaned against the table. "Are you doing it for the love of the work? Or are you doing it for another reason?"

He leaned against the counter next to me as I floured the biscuit dough and started to roll it out with a rolling pin.

"If you're doing it for prestige, then that's something. The articles and reviews from Marci Strand matter more than any-thing. I mean, you can buy into that. And your work will reflect that."

He wiped the corner of the station with his fingers, brushing the flour off with his hands. "If you're doing it from your soul because you have something to say, that's something else alto-gether. Who cares what Marci Strand thinks?"

He paused, thinking. "What's that famous movie, the one where the guy says, 'Build it, and they will come …'?"

It was on the tip of my tongue. *"League of Their Own?"* I knew that wasn't right.

"Anyway. If you're doing it for the right reasons, people will come. That part is easy. The accolades will come, but that's not what you should be doing it for. It should be an afterthought."

"I don't understand ..."

"Maybe you were in the wrong place at the wrong time. Lucien isn't the only restaurant in town, you know."

"Yeah, but the chance to be with Julia was epic. I don't know if I'll ever have that opportunity again."

He thought for a moment. "What if you don't need Julia? What if you could do it another way? For the right reasons."

I shook my head. "I don't even know what that means."

"You're in a beautiful place. You're not at a dead end. You're at a crossroads. Follow your gut. Your instincts will tell you. They've taken you this far, you know."

"Dad, not everything is a positive quotation. This is a little more complicated than that."

He laughed. "No, it's not. But there is still some truth in them. Positivity can take you far. It's kept me going for all these years, you know ..."

He put his arm around me, giving me another hug. "You don't need a review in the *L.A. Times* food section for me to be proud of you. I'm already proud of you. Follow your heart, and the rest will follow."

He went back to his work, preparing for the party.

I stood there with sticky dough on my hands. Confusion and heartbreak washed over me.

What was I doing it for? Did I even know?

* * *

I sat in the dining room with a sweaty glass of ice water in front of me. The rivulets of water soaked the cocktail napkin beneath it.

I''d circled Calvin's card on my counter for two weeks. Two weeks of mourning. I'd walked around the apartment in a daze. Sleeping until noon and hiding out. I wanted to be left alone—my brain on overdrive in a cycle of self-pity and depression. There was only so long someone could listen to Amy Winehouse on constant repeat.

I couldn't endure it anymore. I needed to do something.

I had to get back out there. I had to face it.

Desperado was everything you'd expect a modern haute place to be. High ceilings. Lush leather chairs and starched white tablecloths underneath a forest of glassware. Pink Los Angeles light showed through the tall windows.

I recognized the artist whose paintings hung on the walls. Kate had taken me to one of his shows in the Arts District last year. His work was sharp and intuitive at the same time. Echoes of Basquiat and Haring mingled with a strange instinct.

It made me smile that Calvin supported an underground artist.

I could feel Calvin's energy in the space. It was inviting and comfortable—none of the heavy pretense of Lucien. The air was fresh.

"Fiona! I'm so glad you came!" Calvin was Ichabod Crane reincarnated. His lanky body was graceful as he weaved through the dining room. His chef's coat was unbuttoned at the top and looked like he'd been in a fight with something dark.

He held his hands out to greet me. I made a move to stand up.

He shook my hand. "No, sit, please."

He pulled a leather chair out and sat down across from me. "I'm so glad you called me. I was hoping I'd hear from you. I heard what happened at Lucien. How are you holding up?"

I lied. "I've been doing great. It's given me time to rearrange my goals. It's given me clarity."

"Well, I'm glad you thought of me." He leaned in. "I liked the way you reinvented Julia's stale menu. Before you arrived, Julia's dessert selection was insanely old-fashioned. Dull and French. Too classical. I liked how you twisted the convention. You gave it a certain femininity that was refreshing."

He leaned forward, excited. "That sort of invention is what I'm looking for now. I feel like my dessert menu isn't hitting the marks." He rolled his eyes. "It's nothing special. I need it to stand up to the rest of my menu. I need someone with your talent to interpret the spirit of Desperado."

He thought for a moment as I sipped my water.

"My vision comes from Spanish and Middle Eastern influences, but I don't limit myself. It's just a jumping-off point." He poised his hands in a prayer position on the table, thoughtfully. "Our tasting menu consists of eight to ten courses per night. I tell a story with my food. Engage my guests on a journey. I want to challenge. Push up against boundaries. I want to turn things on their head. I want to make you think."

He was another astronaut flying to the stars.

A server in all black with a long white apron placed four tiny plates in front of me and left.

"This is what I have right now. Taste it and tell me what you think."

The first plate was some sort of custard. The cannel of pastry cream was flourished with burnished strawberries—a strange purple glaze. Burnt sugar flagged the plate. It was weird.

I picked off the nasturtium blossoms and took a bite.

The frozen cream lacked lemon and had too much cardamom. I couldn't even figure out what the purple sauce was all about. "What is this supposed to be?"

"An interpretation of strawberry Fromage Blanc," he said.

"Interesting." I studied the next dessert. A flourish of glazed cherries adorned a tiny square of cake. The cake was layered. Slivered almonds peeked from the sides in some kind of whipped cream and caramel. It was pretty. "What's this?"

"An amaretto opera cake. It's one of our most popular."

I took a bite. The amaretto was overpowering, and the cherries were too sweet. The almonds tasted raw. They hadn't been toasted.

I put my fork down. I was done. "Who's doing your pastry now?"

"Stephanie Page. She came from Asiago. I'm beginning to get the feeling like she oversold her experience."

"Can I be frank here?" I asked, clasping my hands together.

"Of course. That's why you're here."

"The technique is spot on. Well, in most ways. But there's no understanding of flavor. Everything is all over the place."

"I know. That's what's so frustrating. There's no connection. No vocabulary."

"How married are you to traditional desserts?"

"I'm not married at all. In fact, I'd like to explore more regional, more native desserts. I'd like to reinterpret things like Tarta de Santiago, or leche frita. That's the tip of the iceberg. There are so many things to say." He shook his head, excited. "Mandazi and Gelatiana de Mosaico from a new perspective? I tried with Stephanie, but she just doesn't get it. Not to use puns, but I get half-baked, elementary things from her."

"How much freedom would I have? I mean real freedom. Would you trust me to be creative? To come from my own place?"

He studied me for a minute. "Obviously, you would have to stay within my boundaries. But within that, the sky is the limit."

He adjusted himself in his chair. I could sense his impatient energy.

I mulled over the situation. I was so unsure. "Can I see your kitchen?"

He smiled. "Of course. What was I thinking? Follow me."

I tried not to stumble as he quickly returned to the kitchen. I studied the room … I liked the vibe of the dining room.

It was growing on me.

He pushed the kitchen door open and held it for me. I took everything in.

It was a beautiful kitchen. Everything was shiny and new. Open, with lots of table space for working.

The familiar smell of prep punched me in the face. His crew was working quietly. Their chef's coats were pressed and perfect. They were clean. Studious. You could easily confuse the energy with the space of an operating room.

No one had tattoos. Or any that I could see. They were all clean-cut and in control as they quietly wielded their knives, cutting the produce for service, trussing chickens for roasting, and filleting fish for the evening. Deep in concentration, a cook stood by the stove as he lorded over several saucepans of mystery sauces.

They didn't look up as I passed.

He guided me to a corner of the kitchen and smiled. "This is my pastry area. When I was planning my kitchen, I wanted to make sure I had all the right tools."

It was an amazing space. Large tables. A brand-new Hobart. A combo deck and steam oven.

Brand new cake pans and various molds and rings were precisely organized on a rack. The lowboys were polished to a shiny finish. Clean and waiting.

"Let me show you the walk-in." He guided me to a corner and opened the door to the walk-in. I peeked through the door.

It was a dream.

The shelves were neat and tight, with all the ingredients for the trade. Butter, dairy, and a clean array of fruits of the season.

There was lots of space for containers of product. "Is this just for pastry?"

"I like to keep pastry separate. I don't want the pastry cream to smell like onions."

I closed the door.

It was perfect.

"You'll have someone to help you. The pastry cook is out sick today. She's dependable, though. She's a student at the cooking school in Culver City."

I took a deep breath. Thinking.

The austere space was everything a chef could want.

"When would you want me to start?"

"Immediately. Yesterday. Tomorrow if you could."

I thought of my schedule and my pattern of sleeping till noon and staring at Julia Child on my iPad. It was an unsatisfying pattern of events. I needed to get my shit together.

A part of me still dragged my feet. A part of me was scared to start again.

Could I try to be good and not step on any toes? I could tell Calvin was friendly. It'd be a good place to be.

"I'll start next Wednesday. That way, I can start getting a menu together. We can work it out before the weekend."

He lit up. Relieved. "I'm so glad." He patted me on the back. "It's going to be great. I promise."

I scrutinized the space around me. I could do this. I could rise to the occasion. I could work for another chef.

Only I'd do it right this time.

* * *

"Here's to a new you!" Kate smiled.

"Here, here!" Charlotte chimed in as they clinked their plastic cups of Modelo, amped.

We were seeing Amy and the Sniffers. Our favorite front girl, Amy Taylor, was a short blonde firebrand. She fronted a crazy bunch of Australians who played crunchy punk pub rock.

An amateur metal punk band was opening. They sounded like a wall of noise.

The frontman, looking oddly like Iggy Pop, was giving it his all as he jumped off the drum kit and bounced into the guitarist, writhing on the floor. The bassist's riffs were all over the place. What they lacked in musicianship, they made up for with insane energy.

The audience was filing in, making a wall around the stage. I could tell it was going to be a crazy night.

I tried to match Kate and Charlotte's vibe as I lifted my beer to create a triple link.

Kate gave me a distracted grin. She was taken in by the excitement in the ballroom. The Teragram was one of our favorite places to see shows. "Come on, Fiona. It's time. You have a new job and a new road in life. You've shrugged off all the fuckery. It's time to be free and happy."

I sipped my beer. It was cold, and the faint taste of barley was comforting. The only thing missing was lime.

"Come on! Let's get to the front." Kate shouted. She bumped into Charlotte. A warm-up for the night to come.

I tried to keep up with them. The further we pushed through the crowd, the more compact the people were. We found our place in front, right in the center, between the monitors—the perfect place to experience the show.

The background music started playing, and the crowd cheered. Amy and the Sniffers emerged from backstage and picked up their instruments. Amy pranced across the stage and waved to the crowd, grabbing the mic. "Is everybody ready to have some fun!?" she screamed.

Her bleached blonde mullet, simple cropped tee, and infectious smile promised naughty debauchery.

The band looked at each other and ripped into the first chords of "Monsoon Rock."

The hair on the back of my neck raised. The crushing volume instantly numbed my body.

A light switch flipped on: One moment, a calm crowd. The next moment, a crazy free-for-all all. The bodies behind me crushed me against the stage.

Amy bounced in front of us onstage as she started singing: "It's a Thursday Morning ..."

The crowd rocked me back and forth. I glanced at Kate and Charlotte. They were lost in the moment, amped and screaming along.

A chunky guy dressed in disintegrated jeans, an Idles shirt, and a dog collar made his way to the top of the stage. He leaped into the crowd—the first surfer of the night.

I cringed. Was he breaking the 180-degree rule?

The crowd didn't care. They lobbed him with outstretched hands, and he disappeared.

The floodgates opened. Hands and fingernails grabbed from behind as people slammed in front of me and hefted themselves to the stage. Fearless fans danced on the edge of the stage and hopped off, having faith that the crowd would catch them.

Amy didn't care. She just worked her way around them as she detonated onstage. She ripped into "70 Street Munchies," my favorite song. It was a symphony of chaos.

Amy held her microphone out to Kate and Charlotte. They screamed into the microphone:"And I'm wearing my flare pants, my lipstick and all that, and I'm wearing my favorite sweater ...!"

Leave it to them to be the white-hot center of crazy.

A Doc Marten cruised past my face. I ducked just in time.

My bad feelings came back to me in a crush. My body lunged into a panic attack.

Claustrophobia washed over me. I was small. Alone. Vulnerable and unprotected. I lost my grip on the stage and was carried from the crowd's momentum to the edge of the mosh pit.

Bodies bounced like electrons against each other. The danger of the energy washed over me.

Another foot sailed past my head. I could see the Converse label on the back of the shoe as it disappeared in the distance.

It was out of control.

A heavy longing for Rory overtook me. I thought of how his body had braced itself against mine at Kate's show, how his strength electrified me. How happy and carefree I'd been with him.

How safe I'd felt.

A full beer splashed into my face, waking me up. It was cold and sticky and coated my skin. The collar of my shirt was soaked.

I wiped my eyes to see. I couldn't figure out who the offender was. There were too many people. I glanced at the stage. Amy was holding a large pillow over her head.

What the hell was she going to do?

She jumped up and down and ripped the pillow open, flinging it over her head. Feathers went everywhere in the sky.

It was like snow as the feathers drifted in the air.

The crowd went even crazier. Tighter. More anxious.

I pushed up against a shiny, muscular guy with no hair—just a shiny bald head. A few feathers stuck to the top of his scalp.

Another Doc Marten sailed in front of me, and I wasn't fast enough this time. It slammed straight into my face.

The last thing I saw was the burgundy toe as it crashed into my nose.

Then black.

I hovered on pause in the dark.

Nothingness took over me for a beat.

I opened my eyes.

Kate and Charlotte stood over me. The crowd was dissipating.

It was time to go home.

I glanced across the empty floor. A large chunk of somebody's hair and a broken pair of glasses littered the floor. Feathers were everywhere. Sticky dried beer and feathers covered my body.

"You're a mess. Are you okay?" Charlotte held my hand, concerned.

"Thank God you woke up. Do we need to take you to the hospital?" Kate looked scared.

I thought for a moment and did a body scan. The only thing I felt was the bruise slowly forming on my brow and a raging headache. After a long hot shower, I'd be fine. "I'm okay. I just want to get out of here."

Kate laughed, relieved. "You look like a mess. What the hell happened to you? Why didn't you stay with us?"

I stood up and tried to brush myself off. The stems of the feathers stuck inside the fabric of my shirt. It was ruined. "It was a little crazy. I got carried away."

Charlotte laughed. I could tell the adrenaline of the show had tapped her out. She had a happy glow. "That was the most insane show ever. No offense, Kate, but she's nuts!"

Kate shook her head, amazed. "I know. She's the best. She's my hero."

"Let's get out of here." Kate put her arm around me. Charlotte graced my other side. I was flanked by friendship.

We made our way to the front doors and walked outside. The cold breeze made my headache feel better. I was glad to get out of there.

"Let's go get pancakes. I want syrup and sausage!" Charlotte was hyped and ready to move on to the next thing.

I just wanted the night to be over.

My phone vibrated in my pocket. I pulled it out.

One voicemail. From Rory.

My heart stopped. Had he felt my physic energy? Had he heard me? I scrambled to listen to the message.

"I'm sorry to call you so late …"

There was a long pause. "… I just wanted you to know that my mom died …"

I stood there. I'd been hit by a Mac truck.

There was another silence. I could tell he was wrestling with what else to say. "That's it. I wanted you to know. I'll send details for everything later."

He hung up. Abrupt.

I stood there. The cold air sucked at my body's warmth. I was frigid. Brittle.

Delia was dead.

18

The expanse of the cemetery felt heavy. Old-fashioned, weather-worn stone tombstones mingled with modern granite headstones, which would eventually become artifacts.

A dark hum in my head overcame my brain as I struggled to make sense of the gravity of the circle of life.

The heels of my shoes sunk in the grass. I had to balance on my toes to avoid getting stuck in a divot.

My shoes had been a bad choice. I should have considered the circumstances and worn something better. I'd plucked my only black dress from my closet and ended up with these shoes. I'd been too sad to worry about what the hell I was wearing.

I took in the room around me. It was an epic crowd.

The who's who of the L.A. restaurant scene mixed in front of me. Marcus Sanders mingled with Sandy Anton. Jacob Pinot and Jamie Fielding were in conversation together.

The army of workers Delia had employed mingled in their own crowd off to the side. I could hear the quiet chatter of Spanish as they packed tightly together.

Fleurcin's neighboring farmers had come out, too. They stood in another crowd. I could only imagine them talking about life cycles, watering patterns, or whatever farmers talked about.

Delia's reach was laid bare. She was the backbone of so many restaurants. Her bounty was the foundation for so much of what Los Angeles had to say about food.

I thought of her overalls. Her big straw hat. Her tulip clogs. She was a special force in the world.

My gaze shifted to the white chairs set up for the service. Delia's coffin stood at the front.

My heart hurt.

I gazed up at the canopy of trees. I could see the first leaf of fall in the tall tulip trees. They were always the first to change color when the season shifted.

I sniffed the air, searching for the first crisp scent of fall. I came up short. All I could smell was the overpowering aroma of fresh-cut grass.

A small crowd parted, and I saw Rory standing with Grace and Alex in the front. His face was neutral as he spoke to a well-wisher in the line of people waiting to give him their condolences.

Grace stared blankly into space, holding her mother's hand. I could see that her face was pink and swollen from too much crying. She seemed so small. She was too young to have to deal with something like this.

Alex caught my eye from across the crowd.

She glared, icily. A moment of judgment passed between us before she looked away. My stomach cinched up inside. I was an intruder. I didn't belong.

I found a chair in the back and sat down. I needed to hide.

The duo of guitarists from the farm celebration started playing in the front. A beautiful rendition of Pachelbel's Canon. The crowd shifted and sat down around me.

I glanced to the front as the service started.

I could see Rory through the sea of heads in front of me. His profile in plain view. I wanted him to turn and see me.

But what would I say? What could my look convey? Pathetic want? Sorry smile? I kicked myself for being so selfish.

My brain went on autopilot as people spoke about Delia. They echoed my sentiment of how special she was. How she had affected them. How she had changed their lives.

A striking, tall, older man emerged from the last row. He was still handsome, almost regal in his old age, as he stood at the podium and cleared his throat.

I knew who he was.

"I met Delia at a barn dance in Valentine, Nebraska. The first time I saw her, she was dancing with another boy. She was the prettiest girl in the room. I remember the boy being too short for her. I could tell she was bossy. She took charge. I decided then and there that she would be mine." He paused, keeping himself together. "I lived in North Dakota, and I'd drive for over an hour, over the state line, each way to see her on Saturdays."

He chuckled. Remembering. "Delia was a wild one. Even now, I remember her shimmying down the oak tree next to her upstairs window. We'd drive too fast down country roads. Chase through the wheat fields as we talked about everything. We were reckless. The faster I'd drive in my rusty Hudson Hornet, the louder she'd laugh."

He paused. "I loved her laugh. I loved the way she embraced life. Took it and made it her own. She was the only one who ever made me feel like that: Carefree. Alive. Young."

He darkened.

"If I could do it again, I wouldn't blame her. I would have chased after her. The biggest mistake of my life was not chasing her here to California. I was an idiot. A fool."

He clenched his jaw. "I'll always love her. Always."

He held his head high as he left the podium and walked across the cemetery. I watched as he disappeared over the hill. He wasn't staying for more.

I sat there. Trying to hold the tears back.

Delia had lived such a profound life. Full of nooks. Unexpected turns. She had embraced life to its full potential, from being a silly girl at a barn dance to her farm becoming a foundation for so many people.

She'd held her head high in the face of mistakes. Open-minded and willing to embrace what life had to offer. I remembered how she said she didn't even know how to grow anything before she moved to California. What kind of person was that?

She was an anomaly. An inspiration.

I watched as Rory as he made his way to the podium. His face was sad and numb. His brow was cinched. Even now, he was strong.

I felt his emotion as he spoke. "Thank you for everything you've said about my mother. You've left me with so little to say. You've said it yourselves." He paused. "I'm lucky to have called Delia my mother. She was my rock. My mentor. Even if it's possible to say this about your parent, she was my friend. She gave me a starting point and a foundation to follow my dreams with confidence and bravery."

He smiled to himself. "When I think of her, I will always see her strength. Her grace."

I could hear the collective mourning in the crowd. The loss expressed in the sounds around me.

He stepped back from the podium, and the minister took over. Everyone stood up as he gathered everyone in prayer.

I let the invocation wash over me. The guitarists struck up a version of *Clair de lune*. The rich tone of the guitars highlighted the somber notes of the piece.

People got up and mingled. Dispersed. The service was over.

I watched Rory from across the crowd. He was alone. His back was turned.

Now was my chance.

I was deaf and dumb inside as I approached him. What could I say? Was there anything I had to offer?

I stood there a beat in his space, in his presence. I felt a ghost of the connection that we'd shared before.

"Hi."

He turned around, eyes widening in surprise.

"Hi."

I stalled. I didn't know what to say. Loss and guilt washed over me. "I'm sorry. About all this. Your mother was so important to me. I will miss her."

"Thank you for coming. And thank you for your kind words."

I could feel the distance. The disconnection. He didn't give anything away. He was simply polite. Cordial.

"I'll see you around, Fiona." He walked away, disappearing into the mingling crowd.

Now I really wanted to cry.

I watched from afar as he approached Alex and Grace. He picked her up and kissed her head. She wrapped her arms around him and snuggled in.

I felt their loss. Delia was their rock. A foundation for their family. And she was gone.

Her powerful ghost would always hover over them. Guiding them. Keeping them together. Her ghost would be with me as well. I'd always remember her as a totem. A person to aspire to.

Always in her overalls and her funny sun hat and clogs. She'd always hold a special place in my heart.

And for that, I was grateful.

* * *

"Breathe. Ask yourself: do you have the patience to wait until your water is clear and your mud settles …?"

Yogi Dave was in a supercharged mood. The class was packed, and the room was hot. I'd enjoyed exerting myself. I'd spent the toxic mess in my body. I was clean. Purified. It was good to feel the hum of movement.

I sat there with my legs crossed and my hands in a prayer position at my chest. A rivulet of sweat dripped down my back.

I closed my eyes and joined my peers in meditation.

My brain was a mess of electricity. I couldn't focus on the mantra.

The silence hung in the room. The only thing I could hear was everyone's breathing.

Desperado was turning out to be a dream. In the short time I'd been there, I'd cinched the menu into shape. The first item I'd come up with was an interpretation of a Melktert. It was basically a custard pie. I'd twisted the recipe and used korintje cinnamon to finish. I'd used it the right way. I'd flourished the plate with spun sugar, caramel sauce, and creamy lemon sherbet and finished it off with candied rose petals. It was complex and delicious.

I'd also tweaked his opera cake. I'd switched out the flat chocolate they'd been using with a Valrhona Oriado sixty-percent. I didn't want the intensity of darker chocolate to interfere with the whipped cream's delicate nature and the almond flavor. I'd infused the cherries with a Madeira and cooked them down until they were glazed and rich. I'd paired it with a banana caramel ice cream and garnished it with a cherry reduction.

The banana with the complex cake was surprising. It complemented the almond and cleansed the palate from the cake's richness. The final flourish had been a tiny bouquet of nasturtium and pea flowers. It was delicate and beautiful.

And the damn almonds were toasted.

Gina, my new pastry cook, was tiny and efficient. She was Vietnamese. Not only was she going to school for pastry, but she was also in the process of becoming a citizen. She was quiet and precise. Every move perfect and disciplined.

Service was always more intense than at Lucien, but Gina wasn't rattled. She was methodical, and we worked as a synchronized team.

I was impressed by her. She was driven to perfection.

But it made me miss Rose and how hard she'd tried to do everything. How awkward she was. I loved being able to teach her new things.

The kitchen was quiet. No music, none of the nonsense and chaos of Lucien. Cooks didn't gossip and plot at their stations. Sous chefs didn't yell and broadcast direction.

They were quiet. Efficient. You could sit down in the middle of the prep table and meditate if you had to. I'm sure the cooks would keep going. Quietly chopping their carrots and potatoes.

The dishwasher was another cooking student. He kept the pit clean and organized. There was none of the chaos of random silverware and disorganized dishes with pots and pans. Everything was scrubbed and stacked in its proper place.

Calvin was kind and open-minded. So far, he'd liked what I'd come up with. There had been no friction, no clashing of ideas. He'd been calm and thoughtful when I gave him what I'd made.

Desperado was a clan of professionals at the top of their craft.

Everyone knew they were the best. It was just taken for granted. And it felt good to be accepted.

Something inside of me was still unsettled. Something was missing.

It was still hard to believe that my life had blown up.

I'd lost Rory.

Liam had burned me down.

Delia had died. I was still reeling from the intensity of it all.

I had so many questions, even still.

After the funeral, I'd let any hope of reconciliation with Rory go. The finality of Delia's death had put a close to the whole situation. It was over.

It was time for me to center myself. Gather my energy. Let my water and mud mix—or not.

What did Yogi Dave say?

"Fiona, come on." Charlotte nudged me gently. I opened my eyes and looked around. Everyone was exiting the room. I was the only one still sitting on the mat.

"Are you okay?"

I shook my head. "I'm fine. I guess I lost my head."

She smirked. "Let's go get some coffee."

I stood up and grabbed my mat, and the blood rushed to my head. I got up too fast. Why did I always do that?

"Namaste," Yogi Dave called after us. He gave us a friendly wave.

We walked down the sidewalk. I took a deep breath. Another morning, another beautiful day. The marine layer was heavy and damp as it hung in the chilly air. The only thing I could see was the haloes of streetlights lit in the distance.

"That damn shawarma truck is going to steal my spot again. He keeps outplaying me. I don't even know what to do."

"It'll be fine, Charlotte. You just need to find another place. There are millions in the city. I'm sure you can find one."

My head felt even—a flatline silence. I tried to conjure up something—anything. I wasn't stressed, or angry, or happy.

I was numb. Dead air space.

"I'm going to get you your shit coffee. Have a seat." She disappeared into the coffee shop.

I sat at the wrought iron chair and studied the colorful Mexican tiles' tapestry on the table. I could see the repetition of the pattern throughout.

I took a deep breath. I turned and surveyed myself in the storefront glass.

I was like a stranger.

I felt nothing.

Was this what being Zen was like?

I tried to conjure up happiness. Nothing. A sense of anger. Nothing. Something.

I was just bored.

I couldn't even conjure up an unsettled feeling from the boredom.

Charlotte handed me my coffee. "You're very reflective this morning. What's going on?"

"I don't know. I guess I'm just happy that everything is finally looking up. I'm so glad that things ended up the way they did. I'm feeling really good about Calvin. It's the perfect situation. He's so nice. Did I tell you how nice he was?"

"You've mentioned this about a million times. Believe me. I'm convinced." She rolled her eyes, taking a sip of her coffee. I knew she'd gotten a quad shot. There were Red Eyes and Black Eyes. I don't even know what eye you'd call her drink.

Maybe the Third Eye.

My coffee was delicious. She'd put the perfect amount of sugar in it, and it hit all the right taste buds. The espresso almost tasted like chocolate.

We walked down the sidewalk. I was soaking in the caffeine. Feeling nothing was a luxury.

I gazed forward. My eyes were focusing on something.

It caught my eye.

A sign in the window. Frankie's place.

The space was still for rent.

I saw Charlotte see it. She averted her eyes. Her step quickened, trying to skate past. Not see the evidence of one of her harebrained ideas.

She was too embarrassed.

I broke from her step. She walked forward ahead of me, fleeing.

I stood there and studied the sign.

"For Rent."

It stirred something. Was it longing? Hope? Something I couldn't understand?

I peered into the window. I could see the small dining room. Dusty and empty. The brick walls blank and waiting for someone to adorn them.

I could see the kitchen, remembering the small work area. The worn tables. The beat-up stove. The ancient oven.

I'm sure the walk-in had to be jerry-rigged somehow to open it right.

In my mind, I could see the dining room full of people sitting at tables illuminated by votive candles. Enjoying the ambiance.

I could see the busy kitchen turning out steaming plates of food. I could almost smell the aroma of Charlotte's cooking coming through the doors. Or the smell of my fresh-baked bread.

It could be the perfect place for someone to pick up a croissant and a galette for breakfast. Or a loaf of rustic baguette for dinner.

I stepped back, meeting my gaze in the window.

It was suddenly so clear to me. A wave of certainty washed over me.

"Come on, Fiona, I have to get out of here. I'm already late." Charlotte stood back, her expression grumpy.

"Charlotte ..."

A smile crept across my face. A twang of excitement sparked in my heart.

She frowned. "What?"

"What if we met Frankie again? Just to look at it."

"What do you mean?"

I took a deep breath. I knew the minute I put it out there, it'd be over. I knew that Charlotte would be off to the races.

"What do you say? Maybe we could give it a go. But only if you still want to."

Charlotte's eyes widened and then her face melted into a smile.

Our eyes locked in an epiphany.

I took a deep breath and stepped right foot first. "What if we made Looking Glass real?"

Charlotte leaped at me and tackled me with a hug. "Are you serious? I mean, for real. Are you really saying this?"

Her coffee spilled all over my jacket and on the sidewalk.

I glanced at the puddle on the ground. Was this what muddy water looked like? Is this what Yogi Dave was talking about?

Charlotte wiped me off. "I'll call Frankie right now. Let's do it. Let's give it a go!"

She jumped up and down on the sidewalk, like she'd just won the lottery as she pulled her phone out and called Frankie.

I stood there.

I was giddy. I wanted to laugh. I wanted to cry.

I'd been so wrong about everything. About looking for Liam's approval. For expecting Calvin to validate me.

No one was going to make my dreams come true.

My father's quotations came to mind.:'*Do or die ... Don't trade your authenticity for approval ...*

Charlotte and I could do it on our own. I didn't need validation from others. I just needed the balls to do it.

* * *

The dead carcass of a cockroach was upended on its back. Its tiny legs spayed out in the air.

The fumigator had come by three times to spray. After each visit, I'd sweep up the crusty brown carcasses, but they kept returning. At least each wave was a little smaller. Hopefully, he was the last.

I grabbed a paper towel, wiped his dead body off the floor, and threw him in the trash.

I glanced around. Boxes filled with dishes were littered among pots and pans that we still had to put away. A large stockpot was filled with dirty towels used to scrub the kitchen clean. It was overflowing with filthy rags.

The kitchen had all the equipment, but everything was a total mess. The last tenants had never cleaned anything.

It was a total disaster.

The grease traps were full. The lowboys had ungodly sticky residue from whatever they stored. It seemed like some industrial-grade goo—it smelled like dill pickles.

The dish pit had more dried food and mystery mess than I'd ever seen in my whole life.

I'd scrubbed the corners of the floor with a knobby brush that'd seen better days. Thank God I'd gotten the ten-pack from the supplier.

It felt good to scrub.

My kitchen.

It was weird to think of it as mine. And that Looking Glass would be real. I'd borrowed money from my father, and we'd gotten a bank loan. It was just like Charlotte said. The hardest part was saying yes.

"We got the last permit cinched up, Fiona," Charlotte said. Her faded chef's pants and T-shirt were stained from scrubbing the dry storage. "We just have to pass the health department inspection, and then we can open next Thursday!"

"Thursday? Really?" It was all coming at me too fast. "Are you sure?"

She beamed. "It's coming together, just like we planned!"

"I don't know what I'm more afraid of: the inspection or opening night."

"Our dry goods order is coming tomorrow, so soon we'll be well on our way! We can start doing prep as soon as the kitchen is clean!"

"Easy for you to say. Have you seen the dry storage?"

I laughed. "I've scrubbed the damn thing all week. Believe me, I know."

"Well, let's just get through so we can start prepping. It's going to be great!" she called as she turned and returned to the work at hand.

I couldn't wait to get cooking.

Charlotte and I had our whole menu plotted out. We wanted the menu to reflect our favorite food. A reflection of our love. A contribution to the conversation.

We'd cinched it all together in the tiny prep kitchen she used for her truck. She'd sold her truck to the falafel guy she'd battled so many times before. He was branching out and was going to turn it into another pita truck. Now Charlotte didn't have to worry about parking spaces.

Our new cooks, Gio and Larry, were sweet and worked hard. Gio was scrubbing the walk-in, and Larry was fixing the dishwasher. I loved working with them. They were generous with their energy and incredibly protective of us.

Charlotte and I had our own tight ship and were ready to take on the world.

We'd found an old deck oven from a restaurant surplus warehouse when we realized the Blodgett didn't work. It fit perfectly next to the geriatric oven. The deck was well worn, and a dark patina coated the bottom.

I could only imagine what sort of things were baked in it. Pizza? Baguette? Who knew? Whoever owned it before had taken excellent care of it. I already decided it was my prized possession. I couldn't wait to turn it on and go to work.

Charlotte and I had it all planned out.

I'd get to do my take on pastry. Charlotte would cover the savory aspect with new twists on breakfast and lunch.

Then nighttime was a time to let our personality shine.

The point was relaxed romance. Charlotte had so many ideas, and my desserts were the perfect punctuation mark on our shared vision.

My vision.

I was like Willy Wonka. There was so much to explore. It was scary as hell to think that I could actually do it. Charlotte and I had crafted a beautiful menu inspired by our backyard—one that reflected the charm of Los Angeles. Mexican, Thai, Indian, Italian, Middle Eastern, all flourished with a French twist. It was tied up in our language that we'd perfect along the way. We came from a place of truth—our truth. Our love of food punctuated the menu.

"Fiona, where are you?" my father called from around the corner. "There you are! Have you found the dead body in the walk-in yet?"

"Dad!" I hugged him. His aftershave made me realize how dirty I was. I was a stinky mess.

I laughed. "I wouldn't be surprised. We're still trying to clean the damn thing. I can't tell you how dirty this place is."

He laughed as he pulled away from me. "You smell like someone who owns their own kitchen."

"Thanks, Dad."

He smiled as he surveyed the space. "I remember when I got our prep kitchen. It took six months to even figure out what color the floor was."

"What are you doing here?" I asked, happy to see him.

"I was in the neighborhood, so I thought I'd stop by."

He handed a present to me from underneath his arm. "Here. Open this."

It was heavy and sloppily wrapped in newspaper. The tape was falling off of the edges.

I took the present from him. "Let's go sit down. I need a break."

I led him back to the dining room. The tables and chairs were set up, and boxes of glasses and silverware filled the tables. I could already imagine the white tablecloths, glassware, and candles on the tables. I couldn't wait to set everything up.

Kate had painted a mural on the brick wall. An elegant white lotus flower with a fierce angel emerging from its center. The pale-yellow wisps of flame surrounding her reminded me of a pâte à bombe. It fortified me. It made me strong.

It was provocative—a powerful piece. The angles and lines were graceful. Pretty. It was one of her best.

When I asked her what it was, she said it was a phoenix rising from the ashes.

A soul reborn.

"Hi Charlie," Kate beamed at my dad as she dusted liquor bottles, placed them on the shelves, and put the bar together.

"I see they've put you to work! Are you the new bartender?" He laughed.

"I don't know if Fiona wants me to make drinks. I might be a little too generous with the vodka." She laughed.

"Well, that's a good sign of someone who knows what they're doing!" He laughed.

I pulled a chair out for my dad and set the present on the table. "Here, Dad, have a seat." He sat down, taking everything in.

"What do you think?" I asked.

He grinned. "It's everything I ever dreamed of when I opened my own place. I'm so proud of you, kid."

"I can't believe it's real. It's really happening," I said.

"Well, you're living the dream. It's hard to beat a man who doesn't give up. And you didn't give up, Fiona. You did it, do or die."

We'll see. Next Thursday is opening night. Do or die, we're opening."

"It'll be great. Whatever happens, you'll do fine. You've already taken the hardest step."

He leaned in, excited. "Come on, open it!"

"What is it?" I asked.

"Open it and find out." He smiled.

I tore it open, and the gold Lucky Cat stared back at me. Kitschy and beautiful.

The one he had waving on his kitchen shelf.

"Dad, you shouldn't have." I sat it in front of me. It smiled at me, smug with a coy grin.

He glanced around, smiling. "I want you to know that I'm proud of you. For all of this. I'm proud of you for making your dreams a reality."

I tried to ignore the tears springing from the back of my eyes. "Thanks, Dad."

"It's always good to have a little luck watching over you, not that you need it, of course, but every little bit counts."

"I know exactly where it goes." Kate approached the table and grabbed it. "I have the perfect place."

She cleared a space for the cat on the counter and plugged it in. The cat's gold paw started waving.

"Now, I know you're going to be a success." Kate laughed. "Good vibes all around."

My father pulled a folded newspaper from his back pocket and handed it to me. "Did you see this?"

"See what?"

I unfolded it. A picture of a young and handsome chef and Julia brandished the front page of the *L.A. Times* food section.

"Liam's not with Julia anymore ..." My father smirked. "I guess she didn't get her stars ..."

"What!?" I sat there, dumb, as I scanned the article quickly.

"Listen to this" I read. "Alistair Graham and restauranteur Julia Stone are a new force on the L.A. food scene. With Alstair's interpretation of French new-wave cuisine, Julia is well on her way to earning her three stars. "I'm proud and excited to have Alistair in the Lucien family. His leadership will steer our ship in an unstoppable direction. He's the most intuitive and brilliant chef I've ever encountered, and I'm excited to see where he will take us ..."

I sat there for a moment, dumbfounded. "Wow ..."

"See, Fiona! You got out just in time. It's almost like everything was supposed to happen. Everything happens for a reason, you know, and who knows, maybe Marci Strand will write about you. It'll be for the right reasons this time."

"Dad, honestly, I don't care if Marci Strand comes. I just want to make good food that people love to eat. If she happens to come, that's fine. But I don't need her validation." I smiled at him. "I've already been validated by the most important person in the world."

He smiled, proud. "You got it right. New challenges are coming for you. Just remember, it's hard to beat a man who never gives up."

I glanced at Kate's mural on the wall. The determined phoenix rising from the calla lilies. The vibrant yellow tones spoke to me.

Was I a pâte à bombe?

Hope, excitement, and terror welled up in me. I was facing the unknown. I was facing my dreams. I was doing everything that I ever wanted to do.

I gazed across the table, my dad smiling at me with his proud grin.

I'd really done it. I'd worked hard. I'd stayed positive. I'd made it happen.

19

"It's perfect." Charlotte put her arm around me, her eyes glistening.

We stood in front of the kitchen watching everyone.

A large crowd mingled in our beautiful dining room. It was just like I'd imagined it would be.

White tablecloths. Votive candles. Garden lights were strung along the ceiling, creating a warm glow. Colorful paintings from Tom Yang, a Silver Lake artist, hung the brick walls.

Chill music mix punctuated the background. Kate had put it together, selecting a variety of local musicians.

We'd found a couple of servers who knew what they were doing. Gabe was an actor, and Jenny was a student at Northridge.

Gio and Larry were in the kitchen, serving small plates. They were chatting, relaxed and happy.

Kate approached and grabbed three Pinot Grigios from a tray as Jenny passed.

"You guys did it. You really did it." She held her glass high. "To taking on the world. To being brave and doing it on your own."

We clinked our glasses and took a sip. The moment was so much better than a toast.

"You both are so punk rock. No one can take this away from you. This is yours."

Charlotte and I smiled at each other. Here it was, laid bare. There was no hiding. We'd exposed our souls. We'd been honest, given it our best.

Kate saw someone across the crowd and waved, animated. "I'll be back. I see Manny. He just left that band Placebo Chamber. I think the bassist used to be in Panko."

Charlotte rolled her eyes. "That band sucked. They were only together for three months."

"Let's get it straight. The frontman sucked. He was weird. I think he was a librarian." Kate finished her glass. Set it on the counter behind us. "Manny's a rhythm guitarist. He's just what I need. Wish me luck." She was gone.

I glanced at Charlotte. There was a giddy bond between us. This was beyond anything I'd experienced before. I could see that Charlotte felt it too. "We did it." A proud smile crossed her face.

I beamed inside.

I understood those mountain climbers who had stuck their flags at the top of Everest. I never expected to feel the sheer pride of something.

I was in a dream.

"Girl, this place is killing it." Sammy broke our revelry. He pulled me into a bear hug.

"Sammy! I'm so glad you came!"

Charlotte smiled. "I'll see if the guys need help."

Sammy took everything in, impressed. "I couldn't miss this for the world. Hell, I'm still putting my barbecue concept together. But you went to the dark side. Good job."

I squeezed his arm. "How have you been? What have you been up to?"

"I settled down at Monroe in Beverly Hills. It's actually better for me. The bureaucracy drives me crazy, but the food is great and the crew listens."

"I'm so happy for you," I said.

"I'm happy for me, too, girl. Lucien was toxic. I only realized that when I got out." He fist-bumped me. "Here's to getting out."

I bumped his fist and smiled.

"Holy shit, honey." Sammy clocked the room. "Do you realize Marci Strand is here?"

"What?"

"For real. She's talking to someone. Eating your apple filo rose thingies, which were delicious, by the way."

I looked across the room, and sure enough, there she was. Marci Strand.

Talking to my dad.

They were deep in conversation, pointing at my dad's plate. They were waving their hands in only the way two people who speak the same language do.

I broke out in a cold sweat.

Sammy saw Gabe pass by in the distance with plates of Charlotte's spring rolls. "Excuse me, sweetie. I gotta try me some of that." He squeezed my arm.

"Don't worry about Marci. Your food is amazing." He chased down the tray. I shook my head and smiled as I surveyed the room.

It felt good to see everyone eat what Charlotte and I had created. Warmth blossomed in my heart. This was a creation made for the right reasons.

My gaze stopped as it surveyed the room. My eyes froze. My breath caught in my throat.

What the hell?

My blood ran cold. Instant rage hit me.

Liam.

His eyes moved quickly, taking everything in. Judgmental, sipping his drink.

He met my eyes.

A wry smile crossed his face as he headed over. His steps were predatory. "Congratulations, Fiona." He kissed me on the cheek.

I pulled back. "What are you doing here?"

He was drunk. His hair was slightly rumpled, and his green eyes were cloudy and wild. He smiled deviously. Almost wicked. "I wanted to see what you did. I wanted to see everything. Your vision. Your romance."

He finished the last of his drink. A dark look flashed in his eyes. "I wanted to see your fuck me food."

He staggered a bit. His tall frame stabilized.

Rage coursed through my body. I studied the room, looking for a good way to get rid of him.

I didn't want to make a scene.

I grabbed him by his motorcycle jacket and pulled him through the kitchen.

He stumbled behind me, dragging his feet.

"Nice kitchen. It's very quaint. How the fuck do you work in such a small space?"

I opened the back door for him. He stood between going in and going out.

"You have to leave. Now. I don't want you here."

He stood on the threshold, blocking it. The fan tousled his hair. It made him seem more ominous.

I pushed him out, and the door slammed behind us. We were alone in the dark.

"You should thank me. If I hadn't done what I did for you, you wouldn't be here now."

"You can't take credit for this. This is mine."

"Yeah, but Marci wouldn't be here if it wasn't for me." He smirked like he had something over me. "She only knows who you are because I gave that to you."

"You didn't give anything to me. And anyway, why does that even matter? Why do you care?"

"I think you have to give me some credit. I gave you your voice. I gave you some exposure. You are who you are because of me."

His green eyes burned. It mingled with my rage.

"You can't be serious. You really think this is all because of you?"

"Of course it is. Why wouldn't it be? You want to be like me."

All the rage I had came rushing through me: How he had bullied me. How he had made me second-guess myself. How he had seduced me into thinking I needed him. He'd discounted me and made me feel small.

"There is no way in hell I'd ever want to be like you. You're a fake. A fraud. All you've ever wanted are your stupid Michelin stars." I stepped, right foot first, to face him. "Fuck your stupid stars."

He was impervious. It made me madder. I straightened my shoulders and stared him down.

"That night at Vestrano, I should have seen you for the fraud that you are. You didn't understand. You should have taken a few notes, Liam. You'll never understand anything. You'll always be lost at sea trying to find it. Hell, you don't even know what a good taco is."

I stared him down a beat. Triumphant.

"And your stupid fish? You're the one who has no head or tail. You'll never swim upstream. Never. You're just a disconnected mess."

He glared at me, enraged.

"Leave. Now." The words left a stern silence in the night. His toxic mess made my head burn.

He glared at me and gave a mock salute.

"Good luck, Fiona. You're gonna need it." He turned and walked into the night, disappearing into the dark.

Why had I even seen anything in him?

I took a deep breath, opened the backdoor, and made my way back inside. The door slammed behind me.

I stood there for a moment, collecting myself. Why had I bought into that whole Michelin business? Why did I think I needed him?

Was selling my soul worth the baggage?

Liam and Julia were the product of selling your soul to the devil. I never wanted to go there. I never wanted to be like that.

I was doing it for the right reason. Inspired by my beautiful city.

All of it.

Sushi made by Japanese grandmas in Japan Town, tortellini made from first-generation Italians in Montebello. Cobbetts and exotic spareribs at Bahooka ... Curtido and pupusas ... moles and tamales from strip mall dives... Loup de Mer "en ecailles" from Melisse.

This was where my love came from. This was where I was inspired. It was in my own backyard.

Who cared if Los Angeles didn't have a Michelin three-star restaurant? We had so much more.

My city shared a love of food that you couldn't deny.

I turned and straightened my jacket. I made my way back to the dining room.

"Fiona, come here! Guess who's here!" My father grabbed me by the arm, excited. Marci was smiling behind him.

Charlotte stood there, dumbstruck.

My father stuttered over himself, giddy. "It's Marci Strand!"

Marci extended her hand with a warm smile and kind eyes.

I shook her hand. "Thank you for coming. It's nice to have you here."

"You've done well with yourself since the last time we met." She smiled at Charlotte.

I could tell Charlotte was trying to find her Zen-space. She pushed in close to me.

Marci waved her photographer over. "I want to feature you Saturday. Your menu is so eclectic, yet it comes together in such a romantic way. It captures the spirit of the city." She smiled. "Congratulations, girls. I think you might be a hit."

Her photographer pulled us in front of the kitchen. I put my arm around Charlotte as the photographer snapped the picture.

Charlotte laughed. "I think I had my eyes closed."

I laughed with her. "I think mine were closed, too."

The photographer was annoyed. He lined us up for another picture. "Okay, ladies, on the count of three, let's do it."

Charlotte and I gave our best smiles. We held our heads high.

"One, two, three. Say 'Looking Glass,'" Charlotte stammered.

We grinned wide. Our voices locked in harmony. "Looking Glass!"

The flash popped.

Charlotte and I lingered in a stare. A beam of pride between us. The world came into focus around me.

I took in the moment a beat as I gazed around me. A beam of pride flashed in my heart.

Charlotte and I were authentic. We hadn't traded our authenticity for approval.

We'd done it from our hearts.

* * *

I unlocked the back door and made my way inside. I grabbed my dark denim apron from the hook. It was nice not to wear a chef's coat. I liked wearing a simple T-shirt. It was definitely more comfortable.

I walked through the kitchen. Gio's cousin and Larry's brother were working on getting everything ready for the day.

Spanish rock filled the background as they chopped and sautéed vegetables. They were fabricating and roasting the meat for the evening.

The smell of bacon wafted from the oven. I inhaled, taking in the beautiful fragrance.

My place was a machine.

And it was mine.

I walked to the pastry area in the back and checked my racks of bread and croissants. Everything was proofed and ready.

The croissants were delicate and poofed like balloons. They were going to be perfect today.

Rose would walk in any minute, and we'd get through the bake-off. I'd get her started, and it was off to the market.

I grabbed some egg wash and trays of croissants. I brushed them quickly, shoved them into the oven, and set the timer. I grabbed a bunch of bananas, a mixing bowl, and a scale and started scaling sugar and butter. I popped it on the mixer and added the bananas, mixing it on low.

I had my own variation of banana muffins.

I liked to mix the bananas in with the butter, sugar, and baking soda first. It made the crumb dense and moist. It also gave the muffin top the right amount of crunch on the edges.

I added the baking soda and the flour and mixed it into a pale batter. I grabbed a yellow scoop.

It was my recipe, just like everything else.

"Good morning!" Rose stashed her backpack into her cubby, grabbed her apron, and washed her hands.

"Here. Take this over. I'm going to the market." I handed her the scoop.

I took off my apron, hung it on the hook, grabbed the list and my car keys, and pushed the back door open. The air was moist, and the sun was coming up—my favorite time of the day. I'd get to the market just as all the vendors had everything set up. I'd get the best.

I started the Landcruiser and headed out.

The tables at the market were mounded with greens, squash, and rich and ripe produce. I passed the flower vendor and took in the smell of winter jasmine.

I couldn't be here without searching for Rory.

I wanted to see him through the crowd.

Like one of those stupid movies where the heroine reunites with the man she loves, and they run through the crowd and embrace.

All past mistakes forgiven.

French New Wave movies didn't end like that. They always ended with the heroine staring off into space, off some balcony. Alone. Heartbroken. Paying for her mistakes.

And Rory was never around. He'd disappeared like an apparition. He was a ghost. I almost wondered if all of it had really happened.

The memory of Delia was everywhere. I always expected her to jump out of the crowd. Wearing her bright overalls, with her beaming smile, coming at me with her jam.

I felt her absence.

I needed coffee—black with a shit ton of sugar. I headed to Coffee Bean, cutting through the early morning crowd.

And there he was. I saw him.

He was putting together an order for Antonio, the chef at Saxon. I had heard about his place. It was a take on Indian somehow. It sounded interesting—a place I wanted to try.

I watched as Rory patted Antonio's back and gave him a handshake goodbye. He turned to the table, completing the paperwork for the order.

I watched him from afar. All my longing for him came rushing back.

I remembered the first time I'd seen him.

The cool breeze that washed across my face.

The way the air evaporated into a hum. How I'd been transported into another dimension where time and space didn't matter.

His faded flannel shirt complemented his broad shoulders and neck. His dark jeans and work boots made him rugged. My mind drifted to our time together.

I thought of everything that had happened between us.

He had been the one.

I took a deep breath. I stepped toward the table with my right foot forward. "Good morning, Rory."

He didn't look up.

"Good morning, Fiona."

"How have you been?" I asked.

He gave me a thin smile. "I'm fine. How are you?"

"Well, I opened my own place with Charlotte. So far, it's been really good. We're staying busy, so that's a good sign."

"I saw you both in the *L.A. Times*. Congratulations." He was still unreadable.

It was driving me crazy.

"Listen. I need you to hook me up with some pears and apples. Maybe some persimmons. My other vendor sucks. The apples are mushy, and the pears are always bruised. And don't even get me started on the squash."

He stood there a beat.

The silence was agonizing.

He moved to pick up a bronze pear off the table. He grabbed his pocketknife from his back pocket and cut a slice. "This is our Duchesse. Try it."

I put the slice in my mouth. It was juicy and sweet. Mild. It was the best pear I'd ever had. I looked at him. I had forgotten how wonderful his gaze was.

"I'll take some."

He smiled. Imperceptible.

"How about apples? I'll need a lot of those. I'm doing pies and clafoutis."

He reached into another crate and pulled out a perfectly rounded red apple. It was dark and burgundy. It could have been the apple the witch tempted Snow White with.

He cut a slice and gave it to me. "This one is a great cooking apple. It's a variation of a Gala. It's tart and hearty. It keeps its structure when you cook it. I think you'll approve."

He watched me as I tried it.

The combination of sweet and tart made my taste buds spring to life. I could imagine how good it would be to pair it with a bit of cinnamon and all-spice.

"I think I showed you that one at the farm." He put his knife away.

We stood there for a moment, letting the silence hang between us.

He picked up a square of cheese with a toothpick off the table and gave it to me. "Try this."

His cheese was the perfect complement to the sweetness of the fruit. My tastebuds were going crazy.

"I've really missed you. You have to know that, at least," I said. Quiet. Just for him to hear.

I took a deep breath.

It took everything for me to say it. But I had to. I had to take the chance. "Could we try again? Fresh? From the start?"

He studied me. I still couldn't read him. It was driving me crazy.

"Let me get your order together. I'll help you to your car." He moved away from me, cherry-picked boxes from the different stacks in the back, and filled his dolly.

I watched him. I tried to make my mind think different thoughts.

Anticipation raged through my body.

"I'll put together an order for you. A mix of everything we have for you to try. I'll have the rest delivered to your place."

He rolled the dolly up next to me.

"Where are you parked?" he asked.

I could smell his aftershave. He smelled nice. Familiar. It made me want him even more.

"I'm right around the corner." I pointed the way.

We walked in silence—what I'd asked stagnated in the air. I was too raw even to think.

We made it to my car. I popped the back open, and he loaded the apples and pears inside. He finished and pushed the door shut.

We faced each other. He met my eyes.

"Fiona. I've missed you too. More than you can imagine." He took a deep breath. His eyes met mine.

I saw the deliberation in his eyes. He was pushing boundaries and doing the math.

This was torture.

"We're having a winter festival at the farm this weekend. Why don't you stop by? I can show you some new things I've planted, and you can try that new batch of wine you tasted in Santa Ynez. Maybe we can arrange a deal for your place."

The air shifted.

"I'd love to." My heart skipped a beat.

He leaned in and gave me a brush of a kiss on the cheek. He gazed at me in the eyes for a long moment. "It'll be fun. I can't wait."

He pulled his dolly towards the sidewalk. "I have to get back. I'll see you Saturday."

Hope sprang into my heart.

Was he going to give me a second chance?

I got in the car and shut the door, not taking my eyes off him as he walked down the sidewalk. I loved the way he moved. His shoulders. His back. I loved his kind heart. I loved everything about him. My brain was scrambled with possibilities.

He smiled and waved to me as he turned the corner. I waved back, and he was gone.

I sat there.

I thought about everything.

Everything happened for a reason in the universe. Maybe it was all supposed to happen. For me to be sitting at this moment.

Not holding onto the past. Not pushing the future.

Just here.

Well, maybe pushing the future just a bit.

I was seeing Rory on Saturday. And that's all that mattered.

About the Author

MICHELLE CHRISTENSEN is the author of *La Pâte à Bombe*. After working in the film and music industry for ten years, she became a stay-at-home mom. When it was time to return to work, she followed her dreams of becoming a pastry chef. She earned her degree in patisserie and baking from Le Cordon Bleu in Pasadena, California. She's worked at The Fairmont Miramar Hotel in Santa Monica and some of the best restaurants and bakeries in Los Angeles.

Michelle lives with her husband and three children in Santa Monica. When she's not running, or looking for the next best recipe, she's a roadie for her kids' band.

La Pâte à Bombe is her first novel.

Acknowledgments

First, I'd like to thank my husband, Ronnie. You always support me in my crazy endeavors. I also want to thank my children, Cameron, Tyler, and Riley. You are my light and inspiration.

Thank you to my wonderful parents, Lois and Lundy Adkins. Your attention and devotion to your craft really inspires me.

Thank you, Ron and Linda Christensen. Without you, nothing in my life would be possible. You truly bless me.

I also want to thank Vicki DeArmon and the team at Sibylline for making my author's dreams come true. Writing a book is something that I've always wanted to do, and you made it happen for me.

Finally, I want to thank all the cooks and chefs I've worked with. I've learned so many things from you and have many precious memories of being with you all in the kitchen. I've enjoyed every moment with you.

Study Guide Questions

1. What were the most memorable moments or scenes in the book and why did they stand out to you?

2. Did you trust the characters?

3. What was the main message or theme of the book and how did it impact you?

4. How did the author effectively build tension and suspense throughout the story?

5. If you could change one aspect of the plot, what would it be and how would it alter the story?

6. Which character did you relate to the most?

7. Which character's actions or decisions had the biggest impact on the plot, and how did it change the story?

8. Did you like or dislike the characters and why? Did it influence how much you enjoyed the book?

9. What might have happened to the characters after the book ended.

Sibylline Press is proud to publish the brilliant work of women authors over 50. We are a woman-owned publishing company and, like our authors, represent women of a certain age.